BITE MARKS

BITE MARKS

A Vampire Testament

TERENCE TAYLOR

St. Martin's Griffin ✖ New York

This is a work of fiction. All of the characters, organizations, and events portrayed in this novel are either products of the author's imagination or are used fictitiously.

BITE MARKS. Copyright © 2009 by Terence Taylor. All rights reserved. Printed in the United States of America. For information, address St. Martin's Press, 175 Fifth Avenue, New York, N.Y. 10010.

www.stmartins.com

Library of Congress Cataloging-in-Publication Data

Taylor, Terence, 1954–
    Bite marks : a vampire testament / Terence Taylor. — 1st ed.
        p. cm.
    ISBN 978-0-312-38525-5
    1. Vampires—Fiction.   I. Title.
    PS3620.A978B58 2009
    813'.6—dc22

                                                2009012526

First Edition: October 2009

10 9 8 7 6 5 4 3 2 1

For the women who made me the writer I am today; my seventh grade English teacher, Jewel Finley, who planted the seed; my mother, Hazel, who sheltered it; and most of all, my grandmother, Gladys, who nurtured and shaped its growth. I love you all and always will.

I

SUNSET

New York City
Wednesday, 24 December 1986

DO YOU BELIEVE IN VAMPIRES?
Book researchers seek true stories of encounters with psychic or supernatural vampires.
Don't send proof until requested. Mail your
story to POB 1408 Brooklyn, NY 11217.

— *Village Voice* Bulletin Board
December 1986

CHAPTER 1

10:26 P.M.
Times Square, 24 December 1986

Snow falls on the just and the unjust alike, Momma used to say. Young and old, rich or poor, the open sky treats us all the same. Nina hoped God felt the same way, that He was every bit as open-minded as his heavens when He looked down on Times Square. That in his eyes a hooker deserved the same happiness as a housewife and had the same right as any mother to spend the holiday at home with her baby.

Christopher was only five months old and always sick with one thing or another. He had a problem the doctors called—congenial? Congenital? They all said he wouldn't live this long but he was still here to spite them, and she'd keep him alive one way or another, damn them.

She stood on Eighth Avenue above Forty-second Street, across from XXXtasy Video Center and the Cameo theater, "3 Super Hot Adult Hits." She'd been there most of the night between tricks; huddled against the wind in a short rabbit-fur jacket, tube top, hot pants, and platform shoes. Her work clothes.

Brown bangs blew around moist gray eyes that followed a chubby man who passed and kept walking until he was half a block away. He turned and walked back. Nina watched him search the street. No one nearby but sight-seers, winos, hookers, and drug dealers—none of them could be cops, right? She nodded encouragement, watched him try to decide if she was a decoy.

"Hey, baby," she said, as he rushed past again.

Nina knew he wanted her. At seventeen, she was the youngest, prettiest white girl out here tonight and a real one to boot. All he had to do was make up his mind. It was too cold and too late for this shit. When he came back she stepped in front of him.

"Look, it's Christmas Eve. Time to go home and celebrate."

The guy looked down, embarrassed. "Yeah. Sure."

"Got a car?"

"No," he lied. "I hoped . . ."

He mumbled into the wind.

"What?"

The man raised his face, red as Nina's cherry-colored lips.

"I want to tuck you in. Be your daddy, not just . . ."

She rolled her eyes. "Jesus. That's extra, okay? There's a place down the block." Nina turned and walked down the icy sidewalk. The man didn't follow. She looked back and saw someone who didn't want witnesses.

"Anywhere else we can go?"

She tossed her head to one side, laughed.

"Your place or mine?"

"Yours, maybe?"

She spun away, headed down the street.

"Wait! I'll give you one fifty! Two!"

She stopped. *God, this is stupid*, she thought, *real stupid*. If it weren't Christmas Eve, if the rent weren't due, if baby weren't sick . . . "Four. Twenty minutes," she said.

"Half hour for two fifty? That's all I've got." He paused, sighed. "Three. I'll leave right after."

You've got that right. In her head she located the Bowie knife she kept hidden under the mattress for protection, bought on sale almost a year ago at the army surplus down the street.

"Let me see it."

He pulled out a wad of new bills, fresh from a cash machine, counted them out, then tucked them back in his coat. She nodded. They started toward her place.

"Asshole," said Nina. "Show some girls a roll like that, they'd take you out, here on the street."

The john smiled at her, cheeks flushed with more than the cold. He hurried to keep up with her.

"You're not like that," he said. "It's my job to know people."

"Oh, shit. You're not a priest, are you? Or a shrink?"

He laughed. It was a nice sound. Maybe this wouldn't be all bad. Maybe this was God's way of getting her home early for his kid's birthday.

Maybe He did care.

By the time they got upstairs, Nina and her john joked like old friends. She opened the door to her apartment. Inside a nine-year-old girl watched MTV while finishing off a Twinkie and a joint.

"Yo, Carmen. He okay?"

The child nodded, sleepy, and held out her hand. Nina slapped a handful of bills into it.

"Here you go. *Gracias mucho.*"

Carmen scampered out with a grin, whispered back season's greetings in Spanish as she giggled, and pulled the door shut behind her. The man stood by, out of place, while Nina locked the door, turned off the TV, and went to check on her baby. Christopher was still asleep, his thumb in his mouth. Nina smoothed the blanket and tucked it in. The heat wouldn't be up again tonight and he was still getting over his cold. She caught sight of their reflection in the cracked mirror over the bureau. She looked worn and pale next to her radiant boy.

"That the bed?" the man asked softly behind her.

"Don't worry. Clock starts when I say it does." Nina held out her hand. "Money first."

He pulled it out slow, like he still didn't trust her. She counted the bills and slipped them under the mattress in the baby's crib. Nina adjusted his blanket again and walked to her bed as she pulled off her jacket. She lifted an old *Village Voice* newspaper off the blanket, glanced again at the ad she'd circled in pink neon marker on the back page.

"DO YOU BELIEVE IN VAMPIRES?"

The apartment was cold, but that didn't explain the chill she felt or the goose bumps on her skin. She looked at the rest of the words, memorized from rereading, unable to believe they could be real. That anyone could ever believe her.

Nina tossed the paper on the floor. It was too late to save herself, but not Christopher. She'd answered the ad weeks ago, sent her diary home for safekeeping in case Adam found out she was going to tell what he'd done, what he was. If she could sell her story, maybe she could get enough money to save her son. But that money was months away, at best.

Nina unfastened the gold filigree crucifix hanging on a chain around her neck, a gift from her mother and another bleak reminder of the holiday. She dropped it on the night table and turned to look up at her john like the innocent little girl he wanted.

"I'm so sleepy, Daddy. Can you tuck me in?"

The man stepped closer, reached out and gently grazed her cheek with a fingertip. He moaned as he lifted Nina, carried her to the bed, and laid her down on the worn electric blanket. It hummed beneath them as he opened her skirt, her bra, slipped them off her freckled pink skin.

She looked away as he pulled off his jacket and shirt, climbed onto the bed, and kissed her softly, groaned. His rough, hairy chest scratched her bare nipples. His breath came in short, sharp gasps as he stroked her breasts, her ribs, her ass. . . .

Then, without a sound, someone else was there.

"Naughty Nina . . ."

A shadow fell across the john's face as he rolled away and saw an expensively dressed red-haired young man beside the bed.

"Hard at work, I see."

Nina sat up, stammered.

"Adam . . ."

He raised an eyebrow, cold.

"I hear you've a tale to tell." Adam looked at her with large, beautiful eyes, one gray, one blue. "A tale to sell."

"Please, don't . . ."

"Don't what?" he said. "Live up to my word? I told you what would happen if you ever told anyone."

"I didn't!"

The john reached toward his jacket.

"Look, buddy, whatever you want, it's yours."

He held out his wallet to no response. Adam ignored him as he dropped his black overcoat on an empty chair. He sat beside Nina, slipped an arm around her. She flinched.

The john slid to the edge of the bed and reached for his clothes. "Let me leave you two . . ."

"Don't interrupt."

Adam gripped him by the soft skin of his chest, gathered furred flesh in his fist like a rumpled shirtfront, and lifted him from the bed.

"Please," grunted the john. "Just lemme . . ."

He stared into Adam's eyes. They were cold, dead. Adam gave the skin of the john's chest a painful twist. He screamed.

"What do you want? Anything . . ."

"Anything?" Adam relaxed his grip, as if he'd waited for just that. He pulled the john closer, kissed him lightly on the forehead as if in blessing, then whispered into his ear.

"Drop dead."

He slammed his head into the wall, hard.

The man's eyes popped as his breath was forced out; an arm whipped out and smashed the lamp by the bed. His body slid down the wall, blood and brain trailing down the wallpaper behind him.

"Jesus!" Nina shrieked. "Oh, my God, help me!"

"I am your God, Nina," answered Adam.

She rolled over as he bent down. Her hand whipped under the bed and came up knife blade first. Chrome flashed, slashed deep into his side, near the heart. Nina rammed it up and twisted, released a thick, clear fluid that seeped through his Armani jacket.

Adam plucked the blade out, his full lips twisted into a poor imitation of a smile. He flipped the knife far behind him to stick in a wall, then ran his tongue along her ear, her cheek, down her neck, sending shivers up her inner thighs.

"Oh, please," she gasped, "please," not sure if she begged for release or for rape. She tried to push him away as he pulled her closer, willed her to desire him. It was so easy for Adam to get what he wanted from her, from anyone. As afraid as she was of what he'd do next, part of her wanted him more than life itself. Her vision dimmed, swam out of focus as Adam's lips brushed her ear, soft as moth wings.

"You see?" he whispered. "When people find out, the killing starts, and doesn't stop until the breach is sealed and our secret's safe again." The room whirled around them. Nina's head was light, felt like she was floating up and out of her body. "You've made such a mess of things, Nina. Wouldn't death be better than this hell?"

When her vision cleared, they were on a massive red-eyed black stallion, wet with blood and sweat. Adam held Nina tight as they galloped through smoke, flew through fire to leap into the air, over a cliff to razor-sharp rocks below. . . .

"Wouldn't the grave be quieter?" soothed Adam.

Nina lay facedown on a wooden platform before an angry crowd, hands tied behind her, as a guillotine blade fell. Her head rolled into the basket below. She stared up from the bottom, still seeing. As the executioner leaned down, she glimpsed familiar eyes through slits in his hood, one gray, one blue. He lifted her head and turned it to face her body as it twitched to death below her. . . .

"End the pain," Adam breathed, stood on a city street, extended a hand, and looked at her with Japanese eyes, one gray, one blue. Light bloomed behind them as he smiled. The sky turned white, then to black ash as she watched his fingers and face flare up and fade away. His body burned to a shadow on a shattered wall as atoms devoured the city around them.

Nina screamed in fear and desire, watched her clothes melt and blow away on radioactive wind along with her skin, surrendered to the pain and pleasure Adam forced on her. She wrapped her legs around him, dead john beside her forgotten, as she died a hundred deaths. She burned with lust and the fires of the Inquisition, drowned in an icy lake as their passion drenched the sheets and mattress like night sweats.

"Release yourself to eternal rest . . ." Adam whispered. "Let go of your life."

"Yes," she said and gave in, any thought for her child or future forgotten, anything to stop this torment of death after death, without end. Anything to please him.

Nina threw back her head, spread her legs, and welcomed Adam as he bit deep and drank her blood for the first time. Razor-sharp teeth sliced open her tender throat as he took her mind and body with her consent. There was time for one last thought as savage snarls above her grew louder—that this death wouldn't be enough for her master, not nearly enough.

Her agony was just beginning.

CHAPTER 2

10:54 P.M.
Hell's Kitchen, 24 December 1986

Adam Caine stumbled to his feet.

Fresh blood pulsed through his veins, brought color to his cheeks, heat and fullness to his muscles. He was alive! For this moment, full and brimming with Nina's blood, he felt mortal, looked mortal, but was still so much more. He ran his fingertips along her lifeless body, savored the vivid colors and enhanced sounds of the blood rush. Even the limp rag beside him had renewed beauty. He kissed the traitorous little bitch's cheek.

"Time to wake up, Nina," Adam murmured as he rose and arranged her on the bed, legs straight, arms extended along her sides. He walked to the foot of the bed and wiggled one of her toes.

"I said wake up."

Nina's body jerked once, twice, three times. Her head rose, then fell back to the pillow. Her eyes opened slowly, large and liquid. She looked up and saw her ceiling, familiar cracks and plaster patches she'd known well before her death, and shrieked long and loud as she remembered that death. Windows shattered, showered the street with broken glass. Angry shouts rose as passersby complained to one another and the innocent sky.

Nina sat up, stared around the room.

"My God," she stammered. "What did you do?"

Adam scowled back, still drunk on her blood.

"When I bite you, you're infected. I can kill you and bring you back any-time after that." He reached out, ran a fingertip down her throat in a crooked line. "You're one of us now." He licked the outer edge of her ear.

She recoiled.

"Did you have to . . ." She felt her neck, touched smooth skin where mo-ments ago there had been a gaping wound.

"No." He kissed the spot, lingered too long. "Just more fun that way." He massaged her breast.

"Why?" She closed her eyes as he brushed his lips across cool nipples, ran the tip of his tongue over marble white flesh.

"To teach you a lesson."

Nina didn't like the sound of that. Before she could stop herself, her eyes roamed the room, settled on Christopher's crib. Nina flinched, despite her-self, and looked away too late. Adam sat back, grinned as if he could hear her thinking. He laughed.

"You know I can't read minds. Feelings, moods, perhaps." He stood. "But I still know what's going through your little head." He stroked her cheek, leaned down and kissed her.

Christopher started to cry. Adam pulled away from Nina, his face dead, expressionless. He grabbed her by the wrists and dragged Nina from the bed to the floor. She struggled as he pulled her across the room, kicked over a chair and a TV tray with the remains of Carmen's dinner.

He hauled her to the crib. Christopher was awake, flushed and feverish again, hungry and angry. Adam hoisted Nina over the side of the crib, pinned her arms to her sides, and hissed into her ear.

"He's your baby. You're mine." He chuckled, a sound like dead leaves crushed underfoot. "Babies need food, Nina. Hungry yet?" Nina struggled in his grip as she realized what he wanted.

"God! No!" She cursed him as he pushed her closer to the crib. Christo-pher cried for his mother, reached out pudgy fingers as she struggled to get away. Her baby's face turned red as he wailed. Nina wept, watched him blur as hot tears took away her sight, left her with only the sweet scent of fresh blood, inches away. . . .

"Can you smell it?" Adam pressed her closer. "Your first taste of the Big Apple. Just take a bite."

Nina sobbed, felt her baby's life drain into her starved system as it automatically began to feed. The infant kicked his legs and screamed again for its mother.

"Bite!"

"No!" Nina pushed against Adam as he forced her down again to her son's eager arms.

"Let's make it easier," said Adam, reaching out a razor-sharp thumbnail to slice open the child's throat and expose virgin blood to the air.

As if in slow motion, Nina saw blue blood spout from a ruptured vein and burn red as oxygen hit it, smelled the rich scent. She plunged like a shark in a feeding frenzy, mother's instincts forgotten as she dropped her head into the baby's bed and tore the cut open.

Then there was nothing but the sound of her heart as it beat, beat, beat, tiny as a toy, a sound that faded as she pulled life from the ragged body in her hands; drank deep and realized it wasn't her heart she heard, her fear she felt, but that of her first victim, her firstborn. She dropped the broken doll that had been her son, fell to the floor, and wept tears red with his stolen blood. Adam left her there for a moment, then dropped to the floor by her side.

He began to rub her shoulders, her neck. Still dazed from blood fever, Nina resisted at first, then gave in, rolled back and opened her legs, let his hand fall between her thighs. Her skin felt more than ever before, but there was none of the passion of the past at his touch.

She let go of guilt, of pain, of fear. Adam slipped his fingers inside her, explored. Lost in new sensations, Nina relaxed, then twisted away as he began to hurt her. His fingers dug deeper as she tried to pull them out. The pain didn't stop, no matter how hard she struggled.

There was no way to stop him. He was stronger, had her pinned down, worked his way inside as his fingers dug through her gut on a slow path to her heart. She was sure the bastard was going for her only weak spot, in the worst way possible.

The pain was worse than any she could imagine. Death was her only release from this torture and she knew death was impossible until he reached her heart and tore it out, knew he would keep her alive for every second of misery.

"How can you live with what you've done?" he moaned into her ear. "Wouldn't death be better?"

He'd release her only after he'd drained the last drop of misery from her shattered body. Nina couldn't expect mercy and she wouldn't give him the satisfaction of begging for death again. She had to distract him long enough to fight her way free, hide until she could heal. As bad as the damage was, she was sure she could recover.

If she fed again.

"Say it."

She thought of her baby, Christopher, how he'd died because of a mother corrupted by a monster that destroyed them both. Not yet . . . almost, but not quite yet.

"Wouldn't death be better? Say it," he crooned in her ear, "say it," again and again, as his claws found new places to wound, flesh still whole to shred. "Say it and it's yours."

Through her pain Nina flashed on one clear fact: the same vampire blood that infected her had also infected Christopher when she bit him. She could call him back to life, just as Adam revived her. Dazed with pain and nearly unconscious, Nina choked out a word.

"Christopher . . ."

"Shut up!" Adam snarled. He rammed his fist into her faster, deeper, as she called up the last of her strength.

"Christopher . . ."

The word hung in the air like a spell, filled the tiny room like the sound of a gong. If Adam told the truth, she'd have help, no matter how little. All she needed was a second to break free, to save them both.

"Christopher! Wake up!"

"No!" Adam screamed in fury. Hands busy, he tore at her throat with his teeth. She let out one last scream before he cut her off, a banshee shriek that woke the neighbors, brought shouts from the hall and fists on the door.

Adam's fingers found their goal, squeezed and ripped her broken heart free as Nina died for the second time that night. He ignored the danger of discovery as he shook his arm free and staggered to his feet, stared stupidly at the heart in his gory hand. His mouth hung open, red spittle rolled down his lower lip as he gazed at the raw muscle through the fevered haze of his blood frenzy. Adam raised the heart to his lips, bit in and sucked, drained the last drops of blood as he buried his teeth in the meat. A mother's heart, so tender, so sweet . . .

The hall was quiet now, but there was a rustle from the crib. Adam spun and tossed Nina's heart aside. He scanned the room with eyes that saw more than most, but didn't see a dead baby. His buzz died as his brain snapped back to attention.

It was up.

That was the only explanation. Even though Nina was new, she'd called the damn thing up. The blood high had dulled his common sense. He should never have explained anything.

Adam turned on the rest of the lights and searched the room. It had to be here somewhere. Nothing. He cursed under his breath. Nina had turned it into a vampire, but he still couldn't sense the damned thing, much less track it down. It seemed impossible until he caught a sudden movement from the window. A curtain blew out through broken glass. Adam ran and looked down in time to see the child crawl off the fire escape.

He heard police sirens. There was time to follow it or cover up his crime, not both. He went back into the room and grabbed his overcoat. A glint of gold caught his eye as he headed back for the window, a small golden crucifix on the table next to the bed. Adam slipped it into his pocket and followed the baby out the window.

The street was filled with wandering tourists, hookers, drug dealers. Adam lingered out of sight on the fire escape and scented the wind for any sign of the damned thing.

There was none.

Adam summoned his chauffeur with a thought and waited for his limousine to arrive. He was still so high from the blood that he could barely conceal himself from the police officers who rushed past the fire escape and poured into the building to see his handiwork. Usually he would have sent them on their way with the illusion that everything was fine, and had his slaves purge the apartment. Adam was in no shape to control the scene tonight. Once he was safe at home, he could decide how to conceal his crime and find the baby, make sure it was destroyed.

The murder scene upstairs could be explained away, but unleashing an uncontrolled baby vampire on the streets of New York wouldn't stay secret for long. He had to find it fast. Revelation, revealing vampire existence to humans, was the only crime that carried the ultimate penalty—eternal entombment, imprisoned alive and starving, forever. The last thing he wanted was a hearing before the Triumvirate of the Veil, the sole enforcers of vampire law.

Not again.

CHAPTER 3

There were many tales, with minor variations, of why the Romans had built the Temple of Dendur honoring Isis on the banks of the Nile in 22 B.C. Perenelle de Marivaux's favorite was that the emperor Augustus had it built as a political gesture, to appease the wrath of the Kandake Amanirenas, elected leader of the Nubians he'd invaded. Having lost an eye when the Romans tried to kidnap her, and a son in battle, peace was probably a hard sell. After years spent negotiating a truce, Augustus seemed willing to do anything to make her happy, even swallow his pride to honor her gods with a gift.

Perenelle had her own history with the temple.

In 1870, Perenelle and her husband, Nicolas, both already more than five hundred years old, had accompanied a private expedition down the Nile, led by an adventurous British woman and her longtime female companion on their way to an excavation. The woman later wrote a bestselling book about the river journey, but left out any mention of their uninvited guests. Perenelle had been careful to wipe the women's minds of all memory of her and her husband before they parted.

She'd seen the temple for the first time on that trip, in its original setting, and fallen in love. They got their first glimpse of it just after sunset, joined their hosts in time to watch the valley behind it fall into shadow, as if eclipsed. Perenelle had wrapped herself in several cloaks before leaving their covered wooden boat to filter out even the weakest rays of the setting sun. Her husband was no vampire, but she was. As the stars came out, so did she. Mortals and immortals all sat in admiration on a stone plaza before the temple, a miniature in comparison with those seen already.

In true European fashion, instead of being awed into silent homage, they'd sipped cognac and cocktails and commented on the cunning details of the carved artwork, the grace of the building's overall lines, how well it fit into the rough cliff and desert foliage behind it. Carved in relief on an outer wall, Caesar Augustus in Egyptian pharaoh's garb honored the goddess Isis, her husband Osiris, and son Horus, along with two local gods, Pedesi and Pihor, children of a local Nubian chief who had been deified after drowning in the Nile.

Perenelle's party drank and talked for hours into the night about the true meaning of the place. Before dawn, it was decided that despite its irrefutable beauty, the Temple of Dendur was a political ploy meant to curry many favors: placate the Kandake, ingratiate the Roman emperor to the Nubians, and pay off a local politician by telling everyone that his drowned sons, probably only clumsy swimmers, were now full-fledged gods with a home of their own.

Everybody won.

The ruin, reconstructed in its own wing of the Metropolitan Museum of Art, seemed the perfect place for Perenelle to hold an assembly of the hundred members of the high council of the vampire Bloodlines of New York. After all, this event was a political ploy of her own, an elegant soiree in a timeless setting, used to maintain the peace. She'd avoided hosting any of the council's quarterly meetings for almost fifty years, but when it finally caught up to her, she'd decided to make the best of it. If she had to do it, she'd show them all how it was done.

The rock arch of the front pylon and the larger pillars of the entrance to the temple's inner chambers behind it were backed by a high granite wall where the cliff face had been, with a wide reflecting pool in front to represent the Nile. It always amused Perenelle to see the ancient sandstone illuminated by modern electric lights, no matter how discreet and low, instead of Egyptian moonlight. She liked to slip in here to think after the museum closed, to float happier times to the surface of a centuries-old sea of painful memories.

When its original location was to be flooded in 1963 because of the Aswan Dam, it had taken very little effort on Perenelle's part to influence the right people to make sure the temple ended up here, at the Metropolitan. Though it was self-serving, it had been the right thing to do. The sight of it safely reassembled in the custom-built crystal case of the Sackler Wing always reassured her that a good end could justify almost any means.

The leadership of New York's vampires glided around the expansive space, elegant in their individual perfection. Lights near the floor faded to night at the top of smooth rock walls that soared over the temple to support a transparent paneled ceiling. Perenelle knew that the glass of the roof and windows were designed to simulate the way sunlight played on the temple in Egypt, but she'd never seen it during the day, in either location. The thought gave her a momentary pang that she thought she'd abandoned centuries ago: a burning desire to see the sun, to walk in daylight. . . . Perenelle shook off the mood.

She had to attend to her guests.

The wall of windows on Central Park was guarded by a team of vampire enforcers outside who protected the council and edited the memories of anyone who saw anything they shouldn't have. At the end of the night they'd do the same with the museum staff. Once they cleaned up all the evidence, it would be as if nothing had ever happened here.

A string quartet positioned in a semicircle in front of the temple played classical songs of the season. Perenelle had instructed them to stay more secular than religious, despite her Catholic history. She'd limited herself to votive candles that filled the room.

Enthralled young men and women were available for light feeding, offered bare wrists and forearms to guests and cleaned their own wounds with antiseptic wipes after each bite. Human waiters and waitresses served pure alcohol that vampire metabolisms could burn off. Vampires couldn't get drunk, but their enhanced senses enjoyed the scent and flavors of aged spirits far more than any human could.

Perenelle took a cognac from a passing tray, a rare vintage older than many vampires in the room, and moved among her guests. She greeted some, introduced others; played the perfect hostess until the evening officially started.

She could tell that more than one top New York designer had been mesmerized into dropping their usual work to create a gown here, a suit there. Most Old Bloods were in the same classic styles they'd embraced decades ago. New Bloods, vampires under a century old, showed off the latest designs, but seemed more interested in how much they could spend than in how good they looked.

Perenelle preferred to stay firmly in the middle, was dressed in a contemporary black haute couture gown flown in from a Paris house along with the designer for a final fitting. It reflected her fourteenth-century French origins in a subtle way, with soft velvety fabric and embroidered gilt detail.

Her hair was long and dark, shoulders bare. Perenelle's body was petite, more sensuous and sleek than she'd ever been in life. That was the power she enjoyed most, to be able to reshape her body on a whim, to alter her appearance to meet her needs. She'd almost forgotten what her age was when she died. Among her own kind she wore a face of youth, that of an attractive woman in her late twenties. For her work at home, she disguised herself as a senior citizen, a mask of maturity that had fooled her West Village neighbors for decades, as she appeared to grow old with them.

A rumor spread through the room that the Triumvirate of the Veil would make an appearance. They were the anonymous heads of the secret society that had organized the hundred Bloodlines of New York and brought them peace almost fifty years ago. Perenelle knew for sure, but the air of whispered excitement the uncertainty caused, especially in the New Bloods, pleased her.

She saw Dr. Burke coming toward her and tried not to let him see her wince. Townsend Burke was the current Superior for the East Village Bloodline. Since 1937, all Bloodlines in New York sent elected representatives called Superiors from each territory to settle disputes, vote on new leaders, and resolve any other matters, peaceably.

Perenelle was Superior of the West Village and had been for the last fifty years. She had only five vampire neighbors, and was the only one who expressed any interest in the post. New Bloods seemed to regard serving on the council in the same way humans viewed jury duty. Old Bloods like Perenelle knew how much power the council held over all their lives and that of the city.

Perenelle smiled, cool, as Burke approached, knew what he wanted to talk about. They had a long and difficult history. Her late husband, Nicolas, had consulted Burke in London in the 1840s about treating Perenelle with the new science of transfusion, used to help hemophiliacs.

Together they'd examined microscopic organisms in her blood unlike any he'd ever seen. Once he understood the implications, Burke became so obsessed that he begged her to turn him into a vampire, so he'd have lifetimes to study it and find a cure. After Perenelle refused, he used an earlier sample of her blood to infect himself without her permission. The consequences of that action haunted them to this day, and were about to be raised again tonight.

"Perenelle. A lovely evening," said Burke. He stopped at her side, bowed stiffly. "Is everything ready?"

He looked at a large, rusted metal box lying on a wheeled platform under a tarpaulin between the pylon and the temple entrance.

"Of course. You're sure you still want to do this?"

"Claire is my responsibility, always was. She's suffered too long already. I should have . . ." He stopped, overcome.

Perenelle reached a hand out to his as the lights flashed to alert them to the beginning of the night's duties. "We know better than most, the past is past. All that matters is what we do next." He smiled sadly, squeezed her hand, and walked away. Perenelle went to the podium under a pool of light in front of the pylon, smiled at her guests as they left conversations and assembled around her.

"Good evening, brothers and sisters, elected Superiors of the Bloodlines of the five boroughs. I welcome you all, in the name of the Veil," said Perenelle.

"We are one, with the Veil," they all replied.

The night's business began and moved quickly. Ordinary affairs held no interest for anyone tonight. Everyone's attention was on the elephant in the room, the rusted seven-foot-long antique safe that lay under the dirty tarp behind Perenelle. Even if they wouldn't admit it, no one could think of anything else.

They were all waiting for the main event.

CHAPTER 4

3:00 A.M.
Upper East Side, 25 December 1986

It was finally time.

The last speaker left the microphone and Perenelle stepped up. Everyone went silent, even those who'd talked through the meeting. The mood in the Temple of Dendur was somber, more serious now that the moment they'd waited for had arrived.

"Next year we approach a very special day for us all, the fiftieth anniversary of the founding of the Veil."

There was enthusiastic applause.

"You all know what it's brought to our lives. Security. Peace. Justice. Our world is safer, better, because of the Veil. In the last twenty years, similar organizations have risen around the world. We have representatives with us tonight. *Le Cauchemar* in New Orleans, *The Agency* in Los Angeles, *Shroud* in London, *Red* in Moscow . . ." As she said each name, their emissaries nodded or raised glasses to acknowledge their presence.

"At a time when humans had risen from their superstitious stupor enough to potentially exterminate us, these organizations kept our secret safe and secure. It's no exaggeration to say that none of them would exist if not for the example of our own Veil. Please join me in welcoming its representatives, the current Triumvirate of the Veil." She stepped aside as the lights faded to darkness. A few guests gasped. There was no applause, only anticipation of what was to come.

Everyone waited, the temple lit only by faint moonlight from outside. A red glow appeared from nowhere in front of the pylon, and rose in brightness to reveal three figures. The Triumvirate stood in front of the arch in silence, as if in judgment.

This decade the Triumvirate was two women and a man. Always anonymous, their hands and features were blurred like hummingbird wings, as if in constant motion. It was understood that the real members of the Triumvirate were elsewhere in the room. These disguised images were only avatars, psychically projected manifestations that spoke for their true identities. But an appearance meant they'd been among them all night long, like disguised royalty. The figures spoke, three voices in perfect unison.

"Next year we celebrate the fiftieth anniversary of the founding of the Veil. Those who were there in 1937 remember why." Heads nodded. Even if they hadn't been, everyone had heard the story by now. *"Tonight, a request has been made that one of the first vampires imprisoned by the Veil be freed."*

A low buzz of conversation ran around the room as workers in black coveralls wheeled the massive metal box forward. The Triumvirate moved back as it passed through the high arch of the front pylon, flanked it on three sides in a triangle.

The workers pushed it to the broad plaza in front of the temple and stopped, pulled off the tarpaulin to reveal a vintage floor safe that looked like it had been buried for decades. Chipped layers of concrete still encrusted the sides, as if it had recently cut out of cement with jackhammers.

"Nearly fifty years ago, Claire St. Claire conspired with the vampire Tom O'Bedlam to commit crimes that would have put humans at war with vampires. Because he could no longer control his actions, he was sentenced to eternal entombment. He will never be seen again."

Even Perenelle shuddered at the words.

The ultimate punishment for total Revelation—to provide absolute proof of the existence of vampires to humans, a breach in the veil of secrecy that protected them—was worse than death, if the scale of the breach warranted it. Eternal entombment. To be sealed up, buried alive and hungry forever. Execution would end your punishment, but entombment prolonged it. Not to feed, forever, unable to die . . . that was the worst torment a vampire could face.

"Dr. Townsend Burke has petitioned for Claire St. Claire to receive an early reprieve. Instead of waiting until next year's anniversary, her fifty-year

sentence would end tonight. Dr. Burke is reminded that Claire is a fledgling New Blood less than one hundred years old. Though she was created by Tom O'Bedlam, you will act as her sponsor, and, as current rules stand, would share any punishment imposed on her in the future."

Burke nodded.

The amendment was passed in 1965, after Adam was banished from New York for his excesses. Perenelle convinced the council members to exile him for twenty years instead of entombing him, but they blamed her for not keeping Adam in line. If the amendment had been in place before, she would have been exiled with him. Infection was her last bond to Adam Caine. Until he was over a hundred, he was her responsibility. Her child.

The thought made her ill.

"All in favor?" The Triumvirate faced out to the assembly. Hands rose, or casually gestured assent as if at an auction. It was an easy majority. *"Opposed?"*

There was token opposition, but not enough to prevent Claire St. Claire's early release. Burke turned back to the Triumvirate as they nodded assent.

"So be it. Take care, Dr. Burke. Be sure she does not fall back into her old ways, or you will both pay the price. . . ."

The red light faded as the Triumvirate of the Veil vanished and the house lights rose back to normal. Two masked workers stepped in with blowtorches and began to cut through spot welds along the edge of the door that kept the safe sealed.

When they finished the last one, a worker referred to a series of numbers cut into the door of the safe and spun the dial of the combination lock. Tumblers clicked into place, still working after a half century underground. He turned the handle and lifted the door up with a rusty creak, like the lid of an ancient iron coffin.

A cloud of light, dry dust rose into the air.

Dr. Burke stepped forward to look inside. What he saw seemed to pain him. He frowned, signaled to two medical assistants in sterile white coveralls. They wheeled in an aluminum gurney, carefully lifted the frail, mummified body of a small female out of the safe, and placed it on the padded surface.

A delicately designed iron mask covered her lower face. Her forearms were bound together by long custom-made iron clamps that held them tight against her chest, hands curled under her chin. Similar clamps kept her shins locked together.

Dr. Burke pulled the cap from a needle on an IV line attached to a hanging bag of whole blood. He slipped it into her jugular and the plastic pouch drained almost instantly. Burke replaced it with another, and another, until the flow slowed to a normal drip.

He worked hinged pins on the front of the leg clamps and they fell open. Dr. Burke handed them to one of the assistants, opened the arm clamps in the same way, and handed them off. He laid Claire's limp arms out by her sides.

The catch on the faceplate stuck, took a moment to extract. When it came off, the shape of the mask was still imprinted into her dehydrated lower face. Burke stroked dry hair away from her forehead and laid a small pillow under her head.

His undead audience stirred uneasily as they watched. None of them knew what to expect. The idea of a half century of forced isolation was inconceivable. Many of them had seen her imprisoned, and no one else had risked it since then. She was the first to be freed. There was no way to predict how she would react once revived.

They all jumped when the body snapped upright.

Claire looked around, her eyes wide open, full of blood. Her mouth moved, as if trying to speak, but nothing came out. Her head rolled back, and the last sound anyone expected to hear escaped her cracked lips.

A giggle.

Then another, and another, that built to a titter, until the tittering burst into a shrill cackle that rose to high-pitched laughter, echoed off the hard walls of the museum.

The assembly stood frozen.

They'd all considered rage, tears, hysteria, but this was far worse. The crowd pulled back out of her range as Claire stared around wildly, her thin, dry lips still curled in a hideous grin as she laughed.

Burke stepped forward and soothed her, whispered something into an ear that calmed Claire down. Now that she'd been fed, you could see the dark-haired Eurasian teenager she'd once been. Still desiccated, her face and flesh had started to fill out, and her skin gained color from the blood. Burke lay her back down and nodded to his assistants. They moved in to wheel her out.

Perenelle gave a signal. The quartet began to play again as Burke left with his charge. He would have his work cut out for him with that one. Adam had always been unruly, but Claire . . . no matter how guilty Burke felt for the girl's plight, she was a dangerous responsibility to take on.

Perenelle was sure he was making a mistake, but it wasn't his first, or his worst. His worst had ended in Claire's fifty-year confinement, and the birth of the Veil.

A birth announced by the wreck of the *Hindenburg* . . .

II

TWILIGHT

Frankfurt-am-Main, Germany
Monday, 3 May 1937

With a host of furious fancies
Whereof I am commander,
With a burning spear and a horse of air,
To the wilderness I wander.
By a knight of ghostes and shadowes
I summon'd am to tourney
Ten leagues beyond the wild world's end.
Methinks it is no journey.

"Tom O'Bedlam's Song,"
author anonymous,
(circa 1615)

CHAPTER 5

5:47 P.M.
Frankfurt-am-Main, 3 May 1937

Transatlantic air travel was Perenelle's latest luxury.

Zeppelins were one of her favorite innovations of the modern age. Airplanes annoyed her. To sensitive vampire ears, the constant droning of their engines was painful. On ships she always felt confined for too long, with no means of escape. Gliding across the Atlantic in less than three days, sleeping in her cabin during the day and gazing down at the vast starlit ocean at night, was magical.

A few years in Tibet had renewed her spirit and relieved decades of inner turmoil in America after her husband's death. Despite painful memories of losing Nicolas in a Himalayan avalanche at the close of the eighteenth century, she'd reconnected with old friends and made new ones. Perenelle wanted her return home to be as swift and soothing as possible. She'd booked last-minute passage back to America on *der luftschiff Hindenburg*. A Hotel Frankfurterhof concierge had told her about a false bomb threat that reduced ticket sales before it was dismissed, so tickets were easily available.

The zeppelin had already made seventeen trips to the Americas in the last year, and she looked forward to hers. She made arrangements for a private cabin onboard and used her power over mortal minds to bypass customs and check-in at the hotel. Perenelle waited in the lobby with her fellow passengers for their transportation to the *flughaven*, some distance across the river, near a little town called Mitteldick.

Promptly at six, with German precision, buses came to take them to the *Hindenburg*. Perenelle boarded with the other passengers. She enjoyed playing human on the road, when it wasn't inconvenient. They arrived at the air dock in a little over an hour; drove through a pine grove to approach a building that filled the horizon under a cloudy night sky. Huge doors slid apart as they approached, opened to reveal a massive space filled with bright electric lights that illuminated the airborne behemoth that would carry them across the Atlantic.

They left the buses to enter a side door that took them onto the broad, cold floor of the hangar. The ribbed belly of the zeppelin loomed over them, a solid shadow, silent. It always seemed impossible to Perenelle that something so immense could float as light as a cloud.

Young pages in uniform led them up a gangway to enter the belly of the beast. They entered an onboard lobby filled with flowers and good wishes, but the other passengers ignored them and raced to the promenade, leaned out tall slanted windows angled toward the ground to wave at friends left behind.

Perenelle slid past them all to go to her cabin.

The idea of manned flight hadn't been even a dream in her day, an idle thought that only reminded her that her beloved Nicolas wasn't here to enjoy this marvel. He would have spent the trip exploring it, unlocking its secrets. It wasn't until she closed the door to her room that she felt something else. . . .

The unmistakable presence of other vampires.

Perenelle stayed in her small cabin until well after takeoff, while she considered what this could mean. There were two ways for a vampire to travel in the modern age: pay your fare and blend in, or stow away and use your powers to keep anyone from knowing you're there. It was obvious now that the bomb threat had been a trick to keep the airship as empty as possible so that an unseen assembly of vampires could make the trip free of charge, feeding on the passengers and staff during the voyage.

Outside, trained ground crew took hold of drag ropes and a movable mast to haul the great ship out into the open air. Perenelle heard the airship's four diesel engines start up in the distance with a soft purr. The crew released the ropes and Perenelle could sense the airship rise into the sky, even if her human fellow passengers couldn't.

Whatever was afoot, they were on their way.

CHAPTER 6

It was six hours since takeoff.

The airship had sailed across the continent and over the ocean so smoothly that no one onboard felt a thing. There was no turning back now. Perenelle hadn't left her cabin yet, knew she'd have to seek out the other vampires aboard, but dreaded it. Whatever their reason for being here, their methods made it clear they were up to no good.

There was a soft knock at her door.

She'd half expected it. If she could sense them, they could sense her. It wouldn't take long for them to decide to confront her. Perenelle braced for the worst, and opened the door, ready to defend herself.

Outside was a petite girl in her teens, pretty, in a black men's suit, white shirt, and tie, very Marlene Dietrich. She looked Eurasian, perhaps Japanese and German, short straight hair in a 1920s flapper bob, bangs cut just above black-lined green eyes. She smiled, dazzling white teeth flashing against the pale porcelain-perfect skin only vampires have.

"Hello. Hope I'm not intruding." The upper-deck room wasn't large enough for her to enter easily. She stayed in the hall, peered inside like a sightseer and registered everything in a glance, looked back to Perenelle. "You've been invited to meet my master."

"I'm honored. May I know his name?"

The girl held a hand to her mouth and giggled.

"He'll tell you. My name is Claire. Claire St. Claire."

Perenelle stepped out and locked the door behind her.

She followed the girl down the hall, quite sure her room would be searched while she was out. It didn't matter. Perenelle packed little that would tell them anything. With the power to control human minds, she just held out a hand and they saw whatever they needed to let her pass. Her only personal possession was a small daguerreotype portrait of her late husband, and she carried that in a locket around her neck.

They walked down the narrow hallway and turned into the observation lounge on the starboard side of the same deck as their rooms. It was long, surprisingly roomy with a high ceiling, a minimalist design of creamy surfaces edged with aluminum trim. On one side was the promenade along a slanted window the length of the wall that overlooked the sea below, with facing leather banquettes underneath. A wide ledge under the window was illustrated with a relief map of their route.

On the other side of the room, past a low divider, was a lounge area with lightweight chairs and low tables, a smaller reading and writing room located beyond the lounge. There were a few human occupants, chatting, reading, or enjoying the view, but most of the room was filled with vampires, thirteen in all. They masked their presence from the humans, who went about their business as if no one else were there.

Perenelle smiled as she joined them, made herself invisible to the humans as well when she entered. She sat on one of the banquettes under the window. Claire sat across from her, crossed slender legs that ended in stiletto heels.

"*Bonsoir, mes amis,*" said Perenelle. "To whom do we owe the pleasure?" She looked around the room and immediately recognized a face, one she had hoped never to see again. She hid her shock behind a smile.

"A pleasure, indeed, madame." It was a British voice, circa the 1800s from the accent. A tall, thin vampire with a toothy grin stood and bowed low. He had close-cropped white hair and wore a pinstriped bloodred suit, black shirt, and tie. Perenelle raised an eyebrow. His hair was black the last time she'd seen him, like his robes. "Call me Tom O'Bedlam. These noble kinfolk are my disciples."

Perenelle nodded. "And your purpose for this trip? Business or pleasure?"

They all laughed, but it was like the sound of glaciers cracking. "Oh, business, madame, but isn't our kind of business always a pleasure, love?"

Perenelle laughed with them, but felt like an infant abandoned on a frozen plain, at the center of a pack of hungry wolves closing in for the kill.

O'Bedlam's disciples looked newly made for the journey. They were all in modern dress, young, blond, and Nordic, the cream of the crop of the rebuilt German republic. Evidently so perfect that the earthly power their new führer offered wasn't enough. One of the vampires poured another round of drinks and handed Perenelle a snifter of cognac.

"What business would that be?" she asked.

Tom perched on the edge of Claire's banquette.

"I like to think of it as mergers and acquisitions. Sort of a hostile takeover." Again, icy laughter from the room, insincere but enthusiastic, the way big-salaried office workers laugh at a boss's bad jokes.

"Of what?"

"We'll take Manhattan." He stood. "The Bronx, and Staten Island, too. I've been in Europe for years now, and watched the rise of the new Deutsches Reich. They've been an inspiration. In fact, they've inspired me to pursue my own little dream of paradise."

Tom turned to the bank of dark windows, gazed out at the reflected moonlight on the waves below. "Millions of people, enough prey for a lifetime. Our lifetimes. Can you imagine if New York City was ours? No opposition, no investigations, no consequence? It could be an Eden, filled with fun and profit."

"How does one take over a city?" asked Perenelle, keeping her smile in place with difficulty.

"That's the Nazi inspiration. You don't. You take the head." He circled Claire's delicate throat from behind with his hands. "My disciples all have their parts to play. Once we land, they'll seek out and enthrall key members of city government and law enforcement.

"With them under our control, we'll run everything. The best part . . ." he squeezed, and the girl tossed her head to one side, crossed her eyes, and stuck out her tongue in exaggerated Noh theater style, "no one will even know it's happened!"

"Aren't you clever."

"Yes." Tom released Claire's throat and the girl sat up, stared without blinking, like a reptile. Tom smiled back at Perenelle. "Yes, I am. Are you clever, too, dear lady? Clever enough to join our little troupe?"

She looked deep into his eyes as she had the first time she'd seen him, long ago, on midnight at St. Paul's Cathedral. The bottomless emptiness she'd seen in his eyes then was still there, a lunacy that defied all description or definition. He was a monster molded in a madhouse, fired in blood. To defy him to his face was certain death.

"*Mais oui, monsieur.* You are too generous. I'm fortunate to have fallen into such company."

He acted satisfied with her answer, and proceeded to brief them on the final details of the plan. Perenelle was given the name and address of a minor official who ran the coroner's office; the others confirmed their targets and proceeded to celebrate by feeding on the passengers seated unaware among them, careful not to kill them yet.

Perenelle joined in, put on a good show, but her mind spun back to the past and memories of London in 1891, to the first time she'd met Tom O'Bedlam.

The damp.

It was what Perenelle always remembered most about London. Not the fog, but the effect of the fog, how everything in the city seem mildewed to her acute senses. Perhaps it was only her French roots that held the English and their climate in such contempt, but she'd looked forward to moving on as soon as possible.

Sadly, that was not to be the case.

While Perenelle and Nicolas passed through London on what would be their last trip to Tibet, Dr. Townsend Burke had stopped them to beg for their help, despite their past history. He'd created a vampire in 1888 who was out of control, and threatened to expose the existence of vampires to humans.

"This could be the end of us all," he had said, words that had cut through her heart. Perenelle had finally come to terms with her new life, one that depended on staying undetected. She'd had five centuries with her husband, and wanted five more. In time they'd find a way for her to join him during the day.

The vampire called himself "Tom O'Bedlam," after the street beggars who feigned madness for money. No one knew his real name; even he had erased it from his fractured memory after he killed off his family line, to the last member.

Tom was an inmate of London's Bethlehem Hospital for over thirty years, the infamous "Bedlam," his stay paid for by a well-to-do and highly puritanical family. When he was fourteen they'd found him raped by a male servant, fired the man, and blamed the boy, locked their son away to hide their shame. Tom was sane when he was committed, but decades of violent physical and sexual abuse at the hands of the hospital staff had driven him completely mad.

Burke was drawn to Bedlam after he stole Perenelle's blood to become a vampire. Actual madmen made him feel saner, as he adjusted to living with his new state. The hospital admitted visitors on certain days, and charged admission to see the inmates perform. Burke watched Tom act out his tragic story in a Punch and Judy puppet show, many times, and in his own dementia wondered if a curse that drove a sane man mad might restore sanity to a madman.

Burke returned one night and infected Tom, then killed and brought him back with disastrous results. Madder than ever, Tom freed himself from Bedlam, attacked his horrified family, and drew out their torture for days before he killed them, much to Burke's dismay. Tom burned their country house to cover up his crime, and then bought a home in Whitechapel with their money.

He began to kill local prostitutes for fun. When there was a public outcry, he turned the deaths into increasingly gruesome *tableaux mort* to terrify a populace that once had gawked at his mad antics for entertainment. Over the years, the more attention his murders received, the more daring Tom became, and dubbed himself "Jack the Ripper." He taunted the police for years, wrote to the newspapers, and planted false clues. Burke and others warned him that he went too far, that the authorities would discover his secret and come down on them all.

But nothing stopped him.

Tom created more vampires, building an army to enslave mankind. The others realized how mad he was and that if he attacked the city, the humans would rise and destroy them all. Many vampires had already died trying to stop O'Bedlam. Perenelle and Nicolas helped Burke unite the survivors, and used Nicolas's scientific and alchemical knowledge to create weapons to use against him, including a primitive flamethrower.

Their final showdown was on Christmas Eve, midnight Mass at St. Paul's Cathedral. Tom made his entrance to a full house, in black ceremonial robes on a sedan chair borne by altar boys in red. Perenelle had been afraid that Tom was going to kill them. The truth was far worse. He'd already turned his acolytes into vampires.

When he reached the altar, Tom slit a wrist and filled a golden chalice with his own blood. He offered it to mesmerized congregants who drank willingly. His altar boys did the same, filled their goblets with their blood and held them out as dazed parishioners lined up at the railing to be infected. Before Tom could kill them all and bring them back to life as his army, the vampires of London attacked.

The battle was long, bloody, and fierce.

Tom's nest was purged in the battle, with sword, crossbow, ax, and fire. Human survivors were sent home with harmless holiday memories of the night.

For the next week the cathedral was sealed and secretly rebuilt, a cover story created to explain the deaths. Vampires erased all memory of the fire and the repair in everyone involved. Newspaper and other records of the time were revised, and to this day no one remembered the great fire of 1891 in St. Paul's Cathedral. Tom was condemned to death by a popular vote of London's vampires, but when they had him cornered, he vanished like Houdini and escaped.

She never saw him again. Until now.

Perenelle maintained her self-control by sheer will.

Tom's new plan was only a refined, scaled-down version of his original scheme for power and glory. He either didn't remember her, not surprising under the circumstances, or pretended not to; whichever it was, he had to be stopped at all costs before they landed and his agents scattered to their missions.

While the others were distracted with the passengers, she pretended to follow a crew member outside to feed, but instead followed him down to the bridge. She found and mesmerized the radioman, and had him send a simple telegram to Burke onshore for her in secret after she left: "*Burke. Our old friend Tom is back, on the* Hindenburg *with company—a baker's dozen. We land Thursday. Do see if you can round up a welcoming party. Love, Perenelle.*"

All she could do now was wait for landfall.

CHAPTER 7

7:13 P.M.
Lakehurst, 6 May 1937

They were flying into New Jersey between two storms.

Their landing time had been delayed until after sunset. Perenelle thought she saw Tom's hand at work, until she heard that their course had changed much earlier, while the vampires were still asleep. She remembered that in her exploration of the airship she'd seen a chart of the North Atlantic on a table in front of the Captain, marked with the positions of every ship at sea.

The chart showed weather conditions on both sides of the Atlantic, possible changes in between, and was kept up-to-date by radio reports from land and all the ships. The Captain routinely changed course as often as necessary, to avoid inclement weather. Evidently, they'd been avoiding severe electrical storms all day.

She watched rain clouds from the observation deck. They churned below like a thundering stampede of airborne buffalo. She'd gotten no answer from Burke, could only hope he'd be waiting with reinforcements when the zeppelin arrived. They drifted down into a clearing between storm fronts. The coast came into view as the zeppelin sank below the cloud cover.

"Home sweet home," said a small female voice behind her.

Perenelle turned to see Claire St. Claire and Tom O'Bedlam in the doorway. She was alone with them. The other passengers were in their rooms, preparing to disembark. Tom grinned and stepped forward, a dark cloak folded over one forearm.

"America already. The land of opportunity." He walked to the window and looked out. The view was dark, but the shore was still visible through the mist. "When I think of the time wasted getting here in the past."

"Usually worth the trip." She backed away from the window. Tom O'Bedlam wasn't above hurling her out if he suspected she plotted against him. "Do you have anyone meeting you? I'll need a ride to Manhattan."

"Please, Madame de Marivaux. No more illusions. No more lies. You know very well who'll be waiting for us, love." Tom lifted a slip of paper from his pocket, flipped it open. "Dear Dr. Burke. How nice of him to take time to make a house call. He has quite the little reunion planned."

Tom crumpled the telegram and tossed it at her feet.

"Sorry to spoil your fun," she said.

"There's always more to be had." He chuckled. "Never put all your eggs in one basket, eh?"

"We can help you, Tom. If you surrender, we can . . ."

"What? Get me a doctor? Sod off. I've had my share of help from your medical authorities, thank you. Between Bedlam and Burke, doctors made me the man I am today."

"You mean madman."

"What you call mad, I call visionary. I see the world put in proper balance, vampires raised to our proper place as rulers, not scurrying in the dark like vermin.

"I said no more illusions, but there's time for one more." Tom opened the cape draped over his arm and shook it out. Claire stood in front of him and he held the long cloak in front of her like a curtain, raised it above her head until she was out of sight.

There was a change in the sound of the engines as they turned to bring them in for a landing. Perenelle looked out the window. The ground was already beneath them, and she knew the airport was near. She'd have reinforcements soon. All she had to do was keep him busy.

"I understand what you've been through. . . ."

"You? You understand nothing. You pray for order, when the stars worship chaos. Things fall apart, not together."

He whipped the cape away with a flourish to reveal that Claire had vanished. Perenelle looked around. There was no way the girl could have gotten past her. Claire must have gone out the window. Perenelle thought she was distracting Tom, when he was really distracting her.

An explosion at its tail rocked the airship. Perenelle saw flickering yellow light outside the window, and smelled smoke. It had to be Claire. She'd sabotaged the *Hindenburg,* just as they were about to land. Tom had obviously opted to destroy his European allies in a fiery crash to provide misdirection while he escaped, regardless of the cost to other lives, vampire or human. She'd seriously underestimated how mad, how brutally selfish he was.

When Perenelle turned back to the door, O'Bedlam was gone, of course, off to rejoin his nimble magician's assistant. She followed them down the stairs. Fire was one of the few sure ways to kill a vampire. As she ran, Perenelle wondered just how fast a cloth balloon filled with hydrogen would burn, no matter how large.

Cries of alarm elsewhere on the deck turned to screams of fear as the crew and passengers understood what had happened. Panicked passengers rushed to any exit they could find. Several had already tried the leap to the ground, but the zeppelin was still too high for them to survive. Perenelle made it to the lower deck and decided to try a window like the others, instead of the boarding stairs. They were still winched up, and there was no time to lower them before the crash.

She climbed onto the wide ledge under the observatory windows, with what passengers remained. They watched the ground rise, faster, faster, felt the heat behind them increase as flames burned closer. Perenelle judged her moment and leaped, hit the ground and rolled, saw others follow behind.

Her vampire reflexes had her up and running before the humans could get to their feet. She sensed other vampires around her, stopped and stared through the smoke long enough to see Burke's associates chase down O'Bedlam's surviving allies, stake them out or decapitate them with axes. Others posed as rescue workers to pull human survivors aside and erase their memories of vampire activity, or to finish off the bitten.

It was a scene from the heart of Hell. The air was filled with the smell of burned flesh as survivors and witnesses wailed and dashed in all directions, tried to make sense of the fiery pandemonium. The scene was lit almost as bright as day, events obscured only by the acrid fog of dark smoke that blanketed the airfield, punctuated by random bursts of flame as the collapsed inferno consumed the last of its fuel.

The crash was over in minutes.

"Perenelle!"

She heard the doctor's voice, and spotted Burke at the edge of the airfield. Vampires retreated as human rescue crews filled the area, put out the fires, and assisted survivors. The gargantuan vessel that had been Perenelle's home for the last three days lay in ruins on the ground, burned cloth and the crumpled metal ribs of the shell all that remained. Perenelle rushed to Burke's side, and they walked away unseen from the still-burning wreckage.

"You said thirteen in all?" he asked.

"Yes," said Perenelle.

"Then we got all but him and one other."

"Claire St. Claire, his consort. If we lose them we've lost everything." She sighed. The madman was a master of escape. "It won't take him long to regroup. He must be found."

"What then?"

She stared up at him, heard the larger question in Burke's voice. Not what do we do with Tom, but what of the future? What stops the next Tom, or the one after that, from unleashing who knows what havoc on the world? She'd pondered that since her first encounter with the madman, and still had no answer.

"You make sure no one in Lakehurst remembers anything," said Perenelle. "I have a way to catch Tom and Claire."

She just had to call in an old favor, one long overdue.

CHAPTER 8

9:26 P.M.
New York City, 6 May 1937

A three-foot-wide round metal grate at the south end of Sheep Meadow in Central Park was almost concealed by bushes. It was maintained, regularly replaced and kept clear, by parks department workers, even though none of them knew where it led. Invisible to human eyes, Perenelle approached it, lifted the grate, and climbed down a steel ladder into the shaft below.

Down the ladder was a short tunnel to an iron door that opened into an enormous, antiquated subway station, erased from every plan after its construction and wiped from the memory of any who had known it existed. It was Sheep Meadow Station, according to the mosaic signs on the tiled walls and enameled metal plaques on ornate ceramic pillars.

There were decorative scenes of the park above, and a raised wooden chair in the center for the stationmaster, currently empty, like the station. An ornately carved marble well stood before it, older than anything else. A tile mural on the wall behind showed a great white Worm rising from the well to claim a victim that dangled upside-down overhead.

It was an underground art nouveau palace, illuminated by a multitude of gas lamps on walls and pillars and overhead that flickered like candles. There was peeled paint, cracked and fallen tiles, and scattered building debris covered in dust, as if work hadn't quite been finished when the station's future occupants fell on the crew and devoured them. Tarnish and grime only gave a dull patina to the faded finery.

This was a sanctuary for the Autochthones, the lost tribe of the B'alam, holy shamans to the ancient Olmecs of Mexico. They were vampire warrior-priests, thousands of years old, created by blood sacrifices to jaguar spirits in 950 B.C. to enforce the empire's rule. In time, the B'alam grew too hungry, too savage, and fed on the nation they were made to protect.

In five hundred years they brought down the empire, and migrated north. Over centuries they'd worked their way up into what became upstate New York, where Rahman-al-Hazra'ad ibn Aziz, the Moorish vampire who in-fected Perenelle, found them.

At more than a thousand years old, he was the oldest vampire Perenelle had ever met. Rahman had left the Old World to find the Autochthones after he failed to find any answer to his curse in Africa, China, or Europe, in sci-ence or in alchemy. He'd lived with them for almost two hundred years, and uncovered their past in an attempt to learn their secrets.

When work on subway tunnels under New York began at the dawn of the twentieth century, Rahman decided to take advantage of an opportunity to leave the caves, and enthralled anyone necessary to give the Autochthones an urban headquarters. The young subway system with a growing city above proved an effective base of operations. As the system expanded, the Autochthones fed freely and moved unseen throughout the entire city. They saw or heard everything that went on and reported back to Rahman. In time, he became the best-informed vampire in New York, the one to go to for answers.

And he owed Perenelle.

She stood in the dimly lit station for several minutes without feeling the pres-ence of anyone or anything else, except rats. Perenelle had been to Sheep Meadow Station many times before. There were always at least a hundred Autochthones hidden here at any moment, to watch over anyone who en-tered their domain. Rahman had explained to her that the Autochthones had a different origin, like mutant strains of the same virus, and that was why other vampires couldn't sense them. After he found them, Rahman drank their blood to share their power. It was disturbing to know she was being watched without being able to tell for sure.

"It's been a long time," said Rahman.

Perenelle turned to see him seated in his great chair, high above her, the one that had been empty only seconds earlier. He'd learned his lessons from the Autochthones well. As she looked around she saw them slip out of hiding or fade into view as they stopped blocking her ability to see them. She shuddered, understood why her kind was frightening to ordinary people.

"Rahman," she said. "A long time. With good reason."

He looked the same as he had when she'd seen him last, tall, lean, in long dark layered robes suitable for a sorcerer or high priest. Long thin twists of black hair hung to his waist behind him, framed mahogany features and large golden eyes.

Rahman stood out like a storm cloud in a blue sky beside the subterranean creatures that filled the station around him. The Autochthones were hairless and thin, with blank ivory eyes and albino skin dry as parchment, dressed like homeless winos, in rags, or naked. They sat still and silent as dolls as they stared, unblinking. Rahman frowned and stepped down from his chair to Perenelle's side.

"I hope you didn't come here to rehash our history. I know I've wronged you, Perenelle. You know I'll do anything to make it up to you."

She thought of the unholy experiments that drove them apart, and the Book of Abraham that made them possible, her late husband's grand grimoire of alchemy. With its secrets, the three of them had deciphered and distilled the long-sought elixir of life that made Nicolas immortal, or would have if a mountain hadn't fallen on him. But the price of that success had been too great to continue.

"All I ask is your help. There's been an incident . . ."

He nodded. "Tom O'Bedlam. The *Hindenburg* crash."

She was astonished that he already knew, but also encouraged. She'd come to the right place. "You do not disappoint me. I need to capture him and his associate, so they can pay for their crimes."

"Done." He signaled, and a dozen Autochthones slid away into the tunnels.

"I need something more. This disaster threatens us all with exposure. If the humans discover that we're real and a danger to them, they'll fight back. The power they brought to bear in freeing Europe during the Great War will be turned on our kind. We would be exterminated."

"The possibility of political sabotage will make the *Hindenburg* probe even more rigorous. I agree there's cause for concern," said Rahman.

"We need to do more than stop Tom O'Bedlam. We have to prevent any more. We need laws that make us accountable, and a way to enforce them, to keep vampires from committing the kind of excesses that led to . . ."

Perenelle wanted to say to her own creation, remembering that monstrous night, but she stopped short of that. She needed Rahman, and couldn't afford to antagonize him by bringing up the most painful moment of their past. Rahman got her point, anyway, thought it over.

He nodded.

"I'm at your disposal. Ask what you want of me."

CHAPTER 9

3:31 A.M.
New York City, 7 May 1937

A silent call went out through the city.

Every vampire in New York felt the summons from Rahman to come to Sheep Meadow Station. Without words, they assembled in less than an hour to fill the ornamental underground chamber where Rahman housed the Autochthones.

Perenelle stood by Rahman, who was seated on his throne. They watched as their fellows crowded in, sat or stood on the subway platform or spread out across the tracks. In a human gathering of this size they'd all be chattering like chimps by now, demanding to know why they were here, pestering one another for details. The vampires filed in, silent, with precision. Each took his or her place with equal dignity and waited for the meeting to begin, knew that all would be explained in time.

From all five boroughs they came, the thousands of immortals that lived on the blood and life of the city of New York, as varied as the millions they fed on. Perenelle was surprised by the turnout, but pleased. They'd all heard about the *Hindenburg* crash, evidently understood the importance of this meeting, and hadn't ignored the urgency of the summoning. She held up a hand and called them to order.

"By now you all know what happened in Lakehurst, New Jersey, barely yesterday." There was a rumble of agreement through the station. "The actions of the mad vampire Tom O'Bedlam put us all at risk of discovery. We live in a new world, ladies and gentlemen. Humans are no longer the superstitious peasants some of you are used to. They believe in their science now, as much as in their God. He can't harm us . . . but their science can!"

There was a stir in the crowd, and one vampire leaped to his feet, a young-looking man in stylish apparel surrounded by obvious colleagues. "This is your obsession, Perenelle," he shouted. "For years you've fretted about *livestock* rising up to defeat us! They're prey! Nothing more!" He sat, as friends around him patted his back, nodded, and spoke up in agreement.

Perenelle glared at him. He was the head of the New York Hunt Club.

These were the fools who still organized monthly safaris in Central Park, picked off muggers and whores they thought no one would miss. "Does no one remember St. Paul's?" she said. "I know some of you were there. Tom O'Bedlam nearly exposed us to the entire city of London. It took the combined efforts of every vampire there to cover up his crime, weeks of work. This one can't be hidden.

"Investigators are on the site with every tool available to modern man, and if they look closely enough, the trail leads to our door. If they keep asking questions, they'll break the memory blocks we put in the survivors. People will remember we were there, and they will come for us."

"Then kill the witnesses before they remember!"

This started off another round of shouted arguments, as Perenelle's supporters pointed out the insanity of using mass murder to cover up a mass murder. The opposition called them cowards for worrying about mere mortals. Pained, Perenelle looked to Rahman for support. He smiled, understood the impossibility of getting them all to agree, without a dramatic gesture.

The gaslights flared, brightened the room like noon before it plunged into darkness. The sudden change silenced everyone. It unnerved them, even though their vision was sharp enough to see in the dark. A ball of red light appeared from nowhere, floated through the station, and settled in front of Rahman's great chair. It expanded, brightened, then faded to reveal three figures, two men and a woman in 1930s evening dress.

By some strange means their faces were blurred, fluttered in and out of sight so quickly no one could identify them. The red light kept them in sight, but had no visible source. It was as if they emitted the light themselves. When they spoke, it was in unison. Their voices echoed through the station.

"We've heard enough. We are the Triumvirate of the Veil."

"The who?" shouted the boy who'd started the fight.

"The Veil is a society of vampires, formed when Tom O'Bedlam tried to conquer London. We've worked silently since then to prevent further breaches in the veil of secrecy that protects us."

"You sure cocked up last night," the boy said with a sneer. His compatriots joined him in laughter. "You don't seem to be able to handle this guy at all!"

"On the contrary. We are here to offer him to you."

Massive double doors at the back of the station platform swung open. Autochthones pushed a wheeled cart out of the shadows and into the red-lit chamber, as loud gasps spread through the room. Two figures were chained to large wooden chairs on the wagon, Tom O'Bedlam and Claire St. Claire. Their shins were locked together by iron braces, forearms bound in an upright position, hands curled into fists under their chins.

Sculpted cast-iron masks ornamented with art nouveau thorns exposed their upper faces so that they could observe the proceedings, but kept their jaws clamped shut to prevent any biting or outcry. The cart stopped at the edge of the platform, and the Triumvirate surrounded it in a triangle, faced the assembly.

"This stops here. Madness that will take us all down." They gestured to one another. *"What you see before you are psychic projections to conceal our true identities from harm. We are here among you, have only come out of the shadows because tonight is bigger than this creature. Tonight we decide our future. Do we rise or fall?"*

Perenelle stepped forward as the other vampires looked around for clues to the avatars' real identities.

"The Triumvirate approached me to present their case because I was at St. Paul's, on the *Hindenburg*, and they knew I was sympathetic. Our greatest weapon is secrecy. What humans do not believe in, they have no defense against. All the Triumvirate proposes is that we establish a democratic secret society in New York to make sure that humans stay ignorant.

"You already know and defend your own hunting grounds. Your territories become one hundred official Bloodlines, each in charge of enforcing the veil of secrecy in your own backyard. We form a high council with a representative from each Bloodline voting for all." She held up a scroll. "Sign the accord and we make the judgments; the Triumvirate enforces the law and keeps our secrets. Every ten years, a new Triumvirate is elected from our number—"

She was shouted down before she could finish.

Perenelle threw up her hands. There was more fighting, more shouting, but as the night wore on, the simplicity of the Triumvirate's proposal began to appeal to them. They watched Tom O'Bedlam's eyes burn with mute rage, knew he'd like nothing better than to kill them all slowly and horribly, and they began to agree. Perenelle relaxed as she made it clear one last time.

Their only law was to conceal their existence.

No one would be told how to live or how to kill. Feed as you like, but don't attract attention. If you do, cover it up, close the breach. Destroy all evidence so no human can ever prove anything. It was nothing most of them didn't do anyway, and the ones who didn't would finally be forced to comply. Simplicity itself.

It was the twentieth century. It was time to change.

For the first time in history, the vampires of New York united and signed an accord to establish a form of government, the secret Society of the Veil, and to allow the Triumvirate to act as its arbiters. The Autochthones would enforce the Veil's edicts and report violations.

Some in the assembly complained that they were at risk of becoming as bound by bureaucracy as the humans, but, to Perenelle's amusement, they were voted down. With only a few hours to dawn, that left only one matter unresolved.

What to do with Tom O'Bedlam and Claire St. Claire.

"Death is too easy."

Perenelle looked around the room. There was no one, no matter how long dead, who didn't shiver at those words when the Triumvirate intoned them. Most of their own deaths were in the distant past; the deaths of others were commonplace. A "second death" penalty hadn't been considered, much less that there could be a worse punishment.

No defense was heard. She'd made sure that Tom O'Bedlam was kept muzzled, like a wild animal. The Triumvirate insisted that O'Bedlam had no defense to offer. He was a danger to them all. He hadn't been brought here for judgment; he'd already been condemned by his own actions. They had more than enough witnesses to his crimes in New Jersey and London among those present to prove their case. This was not a human court. Protecting their veil of secrecy justified any means taken.

But his punishment had to be agreed on by all.

"There's only one ultimate penalty the undead could ever fear. Only one we might respect.

"Eternal entombment."

In years to come, Perenelle would wonder why no one had questioned the finality of that. The Triumvirate said it so easily, as if it didn't bear the burden of forever. The idea of sealing up wrongdoers for the term of their punishment was definitely a deterrent. When the idea of being entombed forever arose, it was only in regard to Tom O'Bedlam.

In truth, it was cowardice. No one wanted to face him in fifty or a hundred years, released with that much more rage and crazy under his belt. To erase him from the landscape seemed simplest. So they took a vote. Perenelle counted them and announced the verdict.

It had to be unanimous, and it was.

Tom O'Bedlam was sentenced to eternal entombment, Claire St. Claire to fifty years. Saying it was one thing. Before they disbanded for the night and returned to their newly appointed Bloodlines, they had to see the sentence carried out.

The Autochthones lived up to their duties, built two large wooden crates in no time at all. The means of executing the final sentence had obviously been considered ahead of time; all materials were close at hand. Once the crates were finished, two man-size metal safes were wheeled in and laid on their backs. Tom and Claire were unchained from their chairs and straightened up, limbs and mouths still bound; muffled rage and tearful shrieks leaked from their masks. They were laid out in separate safes; the doors were closed and welded shut.

There was silence.

The combined ages of all the vampires present were in the thousands. They'd experienced all the natural and unnatural horrors of life, seen bad and done worse, but this exceeded any of their nightmares.

The Autochthones ran ropes under the safes, hoisted them up with pulleys, and suspended them in the center of each crate. They began to carry in buckets of wet cement in a brigade, passed them along the line from the back room up the ladders to pour into the wooden molds, for that's what they were.

That was when the weeping began.

Vampires are not noted for their compassion. Perenelle was shocked to see that some of them were actually moved to tears, tinged with the blood of their last victims, even if only at the thought of this thing happening to them. The room stayed otherwise silent as the sentence was carried out, except for the slow sliding sound of concrete being poured into place. Slowly but surely both safes were sealed on all sides, top and bottom, by several feet of cement.

The gathering broke up as the monoliths were left to set and harden. They would be stored in an undisclosed location, known only to the Autochthones and the Triumvirate, until it was time to release Claire. Tom O'Bedlam's location would never be known. The room emptied, everyone somber and silent, as if they left a funeral.

Perenelle watched the room empty, relieved that it was over, while Rahman sent Autochthones out on patrol to make sure no one tried to free the condemned before they could be interred.

Dr. Burke caught Perenelle's eye as he passed, nodded in farewell, but looked like he had his doubts. It didn't matter. However many of them remained uncertain, the majority could still outvote them. They'd needed only one unanimous vote to put O'Bedlam away. No one would risk that again. She finally had their cooperation. The Society of the Veil was officially established, and its word was law. The vampires of New York were united and their secret was safe. Perenelle smiled as she left the station.

A new age had begun.

III

EVENING

New York City
Thursday, 25 December 1986

What manner of man is this, or what manner of creature is it in the semblance of man? . . . I am in fear—in awful fear—and there is no escape for me; I am encompassed about with terrors that I dare not think of . . .

—Jonathan Harker's Journal,
12 May 1897,
Dracula

CHAPTER 10

6:17 A.M.
Times Square, 25 December 1986

Marlowe was celebrating.

Usually he'd have spent the night at some downtown club, rounding up Adam Caine's dinner for the night, but the boss had let him have the holiday off. He'd even given him a cash bonus for ratting out Nina. Marlowe hoped she wouldn't be too pissed when she found out, but he had to stop her from doing something stupid. Working for Adam was the best gig he'd ever had, and he wasn't about to let her blow it for him by blabbing.

Marlowe knew just where to spend his Christmas present.

He strolled into the Peep Palace off Times Square in his metallic blue fifties' sharkskin suit and sunglasses, well-oiled hair buzzed short on top and faded to bare brown skin on the sides. He handed the cashier a twenty-dollar bill for a pocketful of tokens and hurried through a maze of private video booths.

Anonymous shadows ducked in and out of doors on either side. Marlowe's eyes trailed slick video covers posted outside each, a pornocopia of pouting lips, inflated breasts, and overblown cocks. He was holding out for the real thing, and that door lay just up those red-lit stairs. Marlowe bounded up two at a time, entered a free booth, and slapped a brass coin into the slot under the window.

The black shutter slid up and there was his Jill.

She rolled her pelvis to a pounding disco beat that pulsed with the same steady rhythm as her hips, timing so exact that Marlowe couldn't be sure which followed which. He watched her give fans a slow smile as they stared in solemn silence from the darkened booths around her, as if at church. Marlowe slid down his sunglasses to see her better.

Jill was still fresh, lively, and eager. He hated to catch her at the end of a day of faked orgasms, humping the glass for the lunchtime crowd. When he was here early, it was easy to believe she was here for him and him alone.

Father, forgive me, I know not what I do, Marlowe thought with a grin. Except, of course, he knew damn well what he was doing. Blood rushed to his cheeks in shame, even as it filled the monster in his pants. He was only nineteen and still a virgin, but he'd seen enough porn to know what he'd do to her if he dared.

Jill saw Marlowe and winked, rubbed an enormous vibrator along her inner thighs and between her legs. She yelped, feigned passion at the dildo's touch as she did once an hour, six times a day, starting now. Marlowe started a rosary in his head. The penance Father Sullivan would give him if Marlowe ever went back to church.

He figured that if the gospel meant anything, as long as he performed the right rituals and was really sorry before he died, his Act of Contrition would be accepted and he could still be forgiven all his sins. So, after every sin he did penance to stay in a state of grace. This was New York. You could go anytime, and the Church might be right after all.

Between Hail Marys, Marlowe ran through a list of the things that he could never tell Father Sullivan, from his visits to Jill to his work for Adam Caine. All sins, all mortal; except Adam. He laughed and watched Jill moan and lick her lips, kept slamming tokens into her slot to keep her in view. Marlowe licked his lips and jacked off, as close as he could ever, would ever, get to actually touching her. He was too afraid of AIDS for that. It was all that kept him a virgin.

Then the pain hit Marlowe like a sledgehammer to the back of his head, caught him off guard. The boss was calling. Even though Adam hadn't enslaved him with a bite like he had the brain-dead meat boys that watched over him during the day, he didn't need a pager. If Adam wanted him, Marlowe knew. He shoved his cock back into his pants and ran to get up Fifth Avenue before Adam's call ripped the top of his head off.

The sun was almost up by the time Marlowe arrived.

It was after seven. Adam was usually locked in his bedroom vault by now.

His bodyguards were already on duty but Adam was still awake when Marlowe arrived, pacing the front room like a damn panther, pissed, real pissed.

"Yo! Sorry, Mr. Caine, had trouble getting a cab." Marlowe dropped the morning papers onto the table next to the door and shouted excuses from the foyer as he pulled off his black trench coat, leaned in to see how bad things were.

Adam didn't let him finish his excuses. "I have a job for you. A little job, but a very important one."

Marlowe relaxed. Obviously not pissed at him. He grinned, hung his coat in the hall closet and entered the study, snapped his shirt cuffs and adjusted the sleeves of his suit jacket.

"Name it, and it's yours, Mr. C. You know I'm always here when you need me."

"Yes, you are, Marlowe." Adam was at the bar, pouring a cognac. "I must remember that. . . ."

He walked to French doors that opened onto a terrace overlooking Central Park. Seen through Adam's shaded UV-filtered glass, the dawn sky was still night. He looked out at the view, his back to Marlowe.

"There's a baby out there, very small, really. I lost it in Hell's Kitchen. I want you to find it." Adam stood a safe distance from the window, stared at the brightening sky. "Ask around. Use your connections, that's why I keep you around."

Marlowe snorted to himself. How was he supposed to find this kid if Adam couldn't track it?

"Sure thing. No problem." Marlowe played along. It wasn't like he had holiday plans, other than the peep show. "What's the kid look like?"

"You've seen it. Nina's brat."

The tip of Marlowe's tongue sliced across dry lips.

"What about Nina?"

"She won't be needing it."

Poor Nina. He felt a flash of guilt over telling Adam about her planned betrayal after she confided in him, but he'd have found out anyway. Then he'd have found out that Marlowe kept it secret, and that would have been worse for him. Adam had special ways to punish traitors. Marlowe didn't ask what he'd done to Nina.

"Find the baby. And be careful."

One eyebrow rose over Marlowe's sunglasses.

"Why?"

"It's . . . precocious."

"Want me to bring it here?"

"You may not be able to." Adam downed the rest of his cognac, thought. Marlowe could see the idea grow. He always got sharper, nastier, the longer he thought.

Even Marlowe hadn't realized just how nasty.

"Yes, of course! Its head!" Adam whirled around to face Marlowe, his face lit up like the filtered morning sky in full bloom behind him.

"Just bring me its head."

CHAPTER 11

10:17 A.M.
Fort Greene, 25 December 1986

Lori Martin was on the subway, running away from Christmas. Running away from home. Her Wicked Stepmonster had invited her to Long Island for their annual holiday reunion. The only way she could get out of it was to use work as an excuse. Her Stepmonster understood putting money over family.

If her dad were alive, Lori would have been there in a heartbeat. Without him, there was no good reason to go. Her Stepmonster had done her best to erase Lori's mother from the house after she moved in. There was nothing left but the shell to remind Lori of where she'd grown up. Sparing them both a long, painful holiday of "catching up" was probably the best gift Lori could give. Even if the price was spending the day with her ex, instead, so that they could work on the damn vampire book.

The train was stuck in the subway tunnel just before his station in Fort Greene, Brooklyn. At least the lights were on. She wasn't sure what she'd do left alone in the dark, buried underground in a steel coffin. Lori opened her oversized red Danish school bag and dug for something to read while she waited for the train to move, something to fend off claustrophobic fear that danced on the edge of panic.

"ANGEL OF JUSTICE!" blasted a *New York Magazine* headline about a vigilante group called the KnightHawks. Their leader, Angel Rivera, glared from the cover, backed up by a multiethnic group of brooding young thugs, male and female. They all wore matching black berets and T-shirts with the KnightHawks logo, front view of a subway car on a medieval shield, wings spread on either side.

Lori turned up Tracy Chapman on her Walkman and read the cover story, then read about SafeDate, a controversial dating service that tested for AIDS, herpes, and other venereal diseases before giving members monthly "Positive I'm Negative" cards. It made being newly single even more depressing.

The train still wasn't moving. Lori couldn't help but feel it was a sign to turn back, to return to Manhattan and the warm sofa bed at her friend Faith's, where she could spend the day hating her life in peace. Tracy's song slurred and stopped as the battery in Lori's Walkman died. Then the lights went out.

Lori screamed. She felt like an idiot.

But at least she knew what she'd do in the dark.

Steven Johnson woke to the sound of jazz from the bathroom radio, brassy horns muted by running shower water. In the next instant he remembered that Lori was on her way and was hit with sudden panic, like he'd been caught doing something bad. He wasn't sure if it was male reflex or the thought of seeing Lori for the first time since she'd moved out and left him only a neatly typed and signed note to say it was over.

His head hurt from too much to drink at his Christmas loft party the night before. Steven looked at the clock to see how little time was left before Lori arrived. Enough. He dug under the bed for his stash box to relieve at least one pain.

Steven rubbed his eyes clear as he sat upright, opened the old Cuban cigar box, and pulled out half a joint. He lit it, inhaled deeply to clear away the dull throb in his forebrain, and tried to remember who was in the shower. As he narrowed down the list of possibilities, Steven was relieved to see Yuki come out of the bathroom.

She was a hot little photographer from Tokyo, living in New York for a year on an arts grant. She'd cock-teased him mercilessly when he was with Lori, but made it up to him last night, once she was sure he was really back on the market.

Yuki grinned, dropped her wet towel, shook out bright blue shoulder-length hair, and hopped back into the bed. Petite, with a tight hard body, she was even more athletic in bed than she'd been on the dance floor. Steven handed her the joint and scratched his balls.

"I'm out of here," she said, lungs filled with smoke, talked like a cartoon duck to keep it in. "Gotta go work." She exhaled, coughing, as Steven stood and stumbled naked across the cold loft floor to the bathroom.

"Take your time."

What did it matter if she was still here when Lori arrived? It wasn't like she could expect him to stay heartbroken forever, even if a part of him still was. As he crossed the hall to the bathroom, Steven saw the party debris that filled the front of his loft. He should really spend the day cleaning, instead of sparring with Lori while they tried to negotiate a working space to get through the next year together on the book.

The next year . . . He groaned at the thought.

Goddamned book.

CHAPTER 12

Jim Miller reached Hell's Kitchen by late morning.

He'd been on the road for over a year searching for his sister, Nina, and this was where her trail had finally ended, Christmas Day, thanks to Nina herself. If she hadn't mailed her diary home to the Murphys for safekeeping, he'd never have found her apartment in a city the size of New York.

The Murphys were the kindest folks they'd lived with since they were orphaned. After their mom died in the fire, they had no family to take them in. The state put them into foster homes for a few years. It didn't work too well. Most places they stayed, folks were just doing it for the money, spent as little on the kids as they could. Jim was grateful that they had at least kept him and his sister together.

One or two homes were worse, folks worked them too hard or foster parents tried to put the moves on his sister, or him. He usually stopped that with a kick to the nuts, and a threat to call the cops. They usually got moved pretty quick after that.

Jim invented a game at the first foster home they lived in, to calm his sister down. They'd pretend they were there on a sleepover, and that their parents were coming the next day to pick them up. They could have fun all day, eat and play with the other kids, because they were just on a visit. Their folks would be back tomorrow.

It was a stupid game, but it kept his sister happy, sometimes even helped

Jim to forget their loss. It kept going for years after she was too old to really believe it, any more than believing in Santa or the Tooth Fairy. They'd make jokes when things went wrong: "It's only till Mom and Dad get here," or, "Mom and Dad are sure gonna laugh about that when they pick us up!"

Then came the day one of the older boys overheard them and jeered, called them freaks. "Your folks is *dead*! They ain't coming for ya! Ain't goin' nowhere, 'cept to the worms!" Nina was twelve and started crying, but Jim, two years older, took a swing at him and the fight started, rolled through the yard. Then the house mom broke it up.

When the other kids found out what the fight was about, they got pissed. Said if Jim and Nina were so much better than the rest of them, they could go on home to their dead parents.

He took off that night with his sister, hit the road for almost a year before the state caught up to them. It was tough out there, but no tougher than the places they'd lived. Jim wasn't proud of all he'd done on the streets to provide for them, but he'd learned to take care of his sister, how to keep her safe.

Until now.

When they got brought back to Ohio, Sarah Murphy was the one who talked her husband into taking them in as foster kids. Her husband needed help at the farm, she needed the company, and they sure needed her. Her son was off at college and graduating soon, headed to the city then. She had an empty house and an open heart, and the two kids were just enough fill them both.

Sarah was the only one who never believed that Jim went crazy when Nina ran away. He'd taken off to find her soon as they figured it out, but Mr. Murphy reported him as a runaway and the cops brought him back, even if they couldn't find Nina. When he tried to explain that she was in danger, he got too excited and hit a cop.

That's when they gave him the shot, muttered words like *bipolar* and *delusional* to the Murphys, and kept him confined on a locked ward for observation until they could sort him out. The police will find Nina, they told him. They'll do their job and we'll do ours. That meant him.

He wasn't crazy. He was scared.

Jim and his sister had been scared since their mom had died. He was sure her death and his father's were no accident. Someone had killed them, no matter what anyone said about suicide or electrical fires. Crazy as it sounded, there was someone out there who wanted his family dead, and he had to save his sister from him.

It was hard to escape the hospital after he turned eighteen, but not impossible. The state doctors weren't the best, neither was their security. Once he got out, he hotwired a neighbor's old motorcycle and started his own search for his sister.

Jim called Sarah regular after he left, told her only as much as she'd let him, so she didn't have to lie to the cops looking for the bike. He'd been on the road since then, had turned nineteen last week following up a lead, and celebrated alone in Philadelphia, if you could call it a celebration. When Sarah got Nina's letter and diary in the mail, she sent them to him with enough cash to bring her back. It was his only present, but the best one he could have gotten.

He didn't open Nina's diary. She hadn't sent it home to read, but to protect; that's what her letter said. Jim would return it in person and give his sister time to tell him why she left, before he persuaded her to come home.

Jim had no trouble getting inside her building when she didn't answer the downstairs buzzer. He didn't expect the lock to work anyway, after a good look at it, not easy in the lightless hallway of the rundown tenement. Not the kind of place he liked to think of as his sister's home.

He checked her letter again for the apartment number while he climbed the stairs. Jim found it, and a white police department sticker seal across her door: CRIME SCENE — DO NOT ENTER. He stood and stared at it as if the bold black print had no meaning. Crime scene? Was this the right apartment?

A neighbor's door cracked open, kept chained to keep anyone from opening it more.

"What? I'll call the cops you don't get out!" rasped a dry voice. Jim saw one red eye in the crack and a gnarled hand ready to slam the door shut and relock it while the old man called the cops.

"The girl who lives here . . ."

"Dead. Don't you watch the news?"

"I'm her brother! Please, tell me . . ."

"Buy a paper!" The door slammed, locked, and slippers padded away. There was no use calling him back. No matter what Jim could say, all the old man saw was a scruffy teenager in a worn black leather jacket and ripped jeans, causing trouble. Jim tried the knob to Nina's door, threw his weight against it. It was secure. She'd managed to buy good locks at least.

Jim left the building in a daze. The unthinkable had happened. He'd lost his sister, the last member of his family. All dead now, except him. He felt the emptiness inside him like it was physical, like a stab in the gut. Jim found the fire escape, jumped until he caught the lowest rung, and climbed up the iron stairs to her window. It was easy to break in from there, one of those things he'd learned on the road.

While Jim had been searching for Nina, he'd wondered what he would find in her apartment. Neither had had a room of their own since their house burned down, the night their mom died. At the Murphys' they'd shared the son's old room. This was the first chance Nina would have had to decorate the way she wanted, on her own. Now was his last chance to see the woman his sister was becoming, the woman she'd never be now.

There wasn't much here, but it still had Nina's touch. Pictures of fashion models she'd taped to the wall, the brightly colored wall paint. The only furniture was a worn armchair with a side table next to it, a TV tray and small TV on a cheap metal stand, a twin bed and nightstand against the far wall.

That was where she had died. Jim's head swam. The bed and wall behind it were splattered with so much blood it was hard to believe. He looked away, sickened; had been told she was dead, not butchered. Nothing could have prepared him for this sight. Jim covered his eyes, took deep breaths, and tried not to vomit. His sister was dead, and he had to find whoever had done it. He had a job to do. Jim opened his eyes, turned his back on the bed, and went through the rest of the apartment.

It was littered with the debris of a life interrupted, laundry piles, floor dirty, dishes in the sink, all the things she hadn't done before she died. Things she'd probably meant to do later. There were fashion magazines on the table, pages folded to outfits or hairstyles she must have liked, a few sketches of dresses, drawn with care. Jim guessed she'd dreamed of being a designer. She'd never talked to him about anything like that, but maybe she'd confided in Mrs. Murphy. He knew there was a lot he wouldn't know about her after a year apart, things he'd looked forward to learning.

Things he'd never know now.

He found a cheap white plastic bassinet tumbled over on the floor, spattered with dried blood, crushed between the chair and the bed. Jim stupidly wondered what it was doing there, until it hit him. She'd had a baby. In over a year apart, his baby sister had given birth to a child. And now they were both gone.

He fell to his knees beside it, pulled the crib upright and hugged it like it was his dead sister, wept for her and her lost child, sobbed for his dead parents and himself. For a moment he forgot where he was, that he'd broken in and shouldn't make any noise. Jim quieted his sobs, pulled himself away, and went through what the police had left behind. Nina's new mail was piled under the door, mostly junk, bills and catalogs. Jim flipped through it. He had to start somewhere.

There was a postcard from the writers of a book called *BITE!*—a note, *"Definitely want to hear more,"* with a name and phone number. Nina's letter to the Murphys said she wanted to sell her diary. This had to be the buyer.

Jim memorized the number in case he lost the card and stuffed it in his pocket. There was a commotion in the hall. He heard, "noise inside" and "tried to break down my door," and hightailed it out the window.

He needed to find a phone.

CHAPTER 13

10:41 A.M.
Fort Greene, 25 December 1986

The train still wasn't moving.

With her Walkman dead, and only the buzz and clicks of the subway car for company, Lori felt she wasn't alone in the darkness. Like that night in the attic, so long ago . . .

She shook off the feeling as fluorescent lights struggled back on overhead, gray and squirming. Lori breathed deep, gulped for air. The conductor muttered insincere apologies over a distorted intercom. The train lurched forward and stopped. More meaningless static crackled overhead, the only audible words, "Thank you for your patience."

Lori gave it the finger, opened her bag again, and flipped through her *BITE!* file folders, desperate for more distraction. For the thousandth time she read the clipping of the ad she'd placed in the back page bulletin board of the *Village Voice*.

"DO YOU BELIEVE IN VAMPIRES?"

It summoned everyone who did, nuts, every damned one of them. It was Steven's fault. Two years ago at a SoHo party he'd introduced Jason, the owner of his gallery, to Lori's agent, Eloise, a thin woman she'd since exchanged for one who ate. Eloise was there with a publisher friend. Steven hunched over a low Japanese table and rolled weed in Big Bambu paper while the rest of them lounged on enormous pillows around him with cocktails. He lit the huge joint and they all talked, smoked, and drank until someone asked Lori and Steven if they'd ever worked together.

Steven and Lori looked at each other and laughed.

"We're just learning to live together. Work together?" Steven shrugged, with a wink at her.

"Come on, think high-class coffee table books." Jason waved his arms and almost fell off the pillows. "Lori writes the words, you paint the pictures, guaranteed quality project. Do it for the money! Publish the book, sell the paintings!" He was into something he called "packaging," claimed it was the art form of the next decade. "Make it something offbeat and hot. Like haunted houses—hot portraits of New York's ghosts! HAUNTS! *If These Walls Could Talk . . .*'"

The publisher spoke up. "If I was going to publish, I'd want more than one book to get sales up. Maybe a series."

"Is that an offer?"

"What else do you have?"

"What else? We need two more for a three-book deal." Jason looked around for ideas.

"Sexy werewolves."

Eloise blushed after she said it, as if she'd revealed something secret about herself. The publisher grinned as if to confirm it.

"Love it! FANGS! *This Fur IS Murder!*' What else?"

"Wait . . . I see the cover already," Steven said, sketching furiously on a napkin with a felt-tip pen. He finished and held up his dummy of the last book cover.

It was a punked-out nude blonde with a Mohawk and piercings, wrapped in huge bat wings that sprouted from the broad shoulders of a sexy black man behind her, his long ivory fangs in her bare throat. The title leaped out above, with a tag line underneath: "BITE! *Do You Believe in Vampires?*'"

"And that's three!" crowed Jason.

"A trilogy of high-end art books on the supernatural," said the publisher as he pulled a fresh joint from his gold cigarette case. "Love it!"

"Everybody's into all that supernatural crap now," Lori's agent said as she held out her lighter. "They'll sell like crazy with a downtown-art twist!"

"Does it have to be vampires?" Lori almost surprised herself when she spoke up.

"What else?" laughed Jason, almost choking on the joint. "Sexy zombies? Fairies? Everybody loves vampires!"

Lori didn't. She didn't see the mystery and glamour everyone else did, just thinly veiled sadomasochism, fake fangs, and mechanical bats. Lori hated vampire movies, vampire novels, anything vaguely about vampires. She sure as hell didn't want to spend a year researching and writing about the damned things.

But, of course, the publisher had loved it, her agent had loved it, and Steven's gallery had loved it, so Lori had given in. She and Steven were still a couple then, wildly in love. Lori remembered idyllic afternoons spent in his oversized claw-foot tub while they soaked in hot soapy water and steam-filled bubbles, sipped champagne and read Toni Morrison and William Burroughs aloud to each other. Remembered a romantic picnic at Versailles on their first trip to Paris, a surprise weekend birthday party in the Hamptons with friends, the way he'd always known when holding was all she needed.

Then she got pregnant and it all went bad.

Steven kicked the bathroom door shut behind him with a bare heel, aimed into the toilet as well as he could, and let fly as he yawned. He tried to stay casual about seeing Lori for the first time since she'd left. He'd never admit to her or himself how hard he'd taken the breakup or the way she had done it. He was a guy, right? Guys aren't supposed to feel those things, especially black guys, but she'd caught him off guard, hit him low and hard when he least expected it.

He could understand if it had happened after their last fight, but she'd left weeks after. As if she'd brooded over what had happened, replayed it in her head enough times to be sure leaving was the right thing to do. Typical. Lori overthought everything. It took her an hour to make up her mind about appetizers at a restaurant. Why should he expect her to storm out of his life the same day he pissed her off one time too many? Bitch.

Except that she wasn't, not even close, dammit.

She was a smart, sexy woman he'd loved for almost two years, longer than he'd stayed with anyone without fucking it up. Lori was the first woman who'd accepted him despite his mood swings, knew enough to be close when he wanted her and to back off when he needed to be alone. Whether he was celebrating or mourning his latest work, looking for inspiration or comfort, she knew the right thing to do. It was inevitable that he'd find a way to drive her away, even without the excuse of a baby.

When he left the bathroom, Yuki was already dressed. She picked up her shoulder bag and gave him a long, wet kiss.

"That was fun. Call you later."

"Sure."

Steven grabbed a pair of wrinkled sweatpants from the floor to slip on while he walked her downstairs. He stepped into them as Yuki headed for the door, caught up with her in time for one last lip lock before they headed down the stairs. He unlocked the downstairs door to see Lori coming down the snowy sidewalk. Yuki saw her, too, gave him one last smack on the mouth, whispered "Merry Christmas" with a laugh as they parted, and strutted away with a nod to Lori as they passed.

"Hey, Lori. Thanks for the loan," she said with a grin.

"Keep him," said Lori. "He's all yours." She nodded to Steven with a look he couldn't read as she walked inside and upstairs. "I see you're already opening your presents." Steven shook his head and locked the door behind them.

It was going to be a long cold Christmas.

CHAPTER 14

4:46 P.M.
Hell's Kitchen, 25 December 1986

The sun was going down.

Winter was always cold, so damned cold. Especially when you were fucked up on painkillers. 'Manda slipped on melted snow refrozen during the night into sheets of ice, stumbled into a wall as Kirk kept walking. All she wanted to do was lie down, go to sleep, and not wake up again. She stumbled faster down Eighth Avenue to catch up, lost her footing, and fell to the ground. He didn't stop.

"Jeez! Kirk! Kiiirk!"

"Shut the fuck up!"

He spun around, hit her with his voice instead of his hand, which was what she knew he wanted to use. She had a moment to gather what was left of her thoughts and remember why her soul hurt, why she was crying, why she felt scraped raw inside.

Her baby . . .

Kirk had killed her baby, beaten her, punched her out for no reason right there on the Deuce while she was working, until she miscarried and had to go to the emergency room on Christmas. He'd said it was an accident, said he was wasted, said he was sorry, but she knew, she knew.

"Bad for business," he'd said back when she told him she was knocked up. Bad for business. Couldn't be his junkie whore with his baby in her belly. The bastard.

"Come on, I think I'm bleedin' again. Kiirk . . . help me!"

Kirk walked back to get her, grabbed her arm, and yanked. "Get up. Come on. I got a delivery to make, then we go home."

"Oh, God . . . I can't move. I can't walk. . . ."

She started to cry again. Kirk cursed.

"You up or not?"

'Manda moaned, covered her tear-streaked face with her hands. "Leave me alone . . ."

"You know you don't mean that," he said. Kirk stooped down, reached for her. She slapped at his hand. "Watch it, bitch."

She swung again.

"I said watch it," he repeated as she hailed blows on him from nowhere, found strength she'd thought was gone for good. Not enough. Kirk gave her a second, then hit her hard, twice, in the face. She stopped swinging and wailed like a newborn.

"I told you to stop. You don't, I leave you here to freeze. Okay?"

She slapped at him again, more for effect than anything else. He slammed his fist into the Dumpster in the alley behind her.

"No more! I'm walking away! You hear me?" He strode away as she curled into a ball and cried louder. "I don't need this shit! You know where I am!"

Tears came again, with a fresh sting in her gut as the shot the doctor had given her began to wear off. She crawled out of sight in the alley behind the Dumpster, fumbled in her pockets for her penknife and her pills. 'Manda spilled her coat's contents on the ground, pushed through stolen syringes and needles in airtight plastic packs, through crushed remains of cigarettes and sweets. That fucker Kirk, he'd pay for what he did. He'd pay one day, in blood.

She finally found her blade, the little red Swiss army knife she'd stolen years ago from someone's desk when she visited her mom's office on Take Your Daughter to Work Day.

'Manda didn't know then why it appealed to her, why she'd snatched the key-chain trinket from the desk and tucked it in her pocket. Not until later that night, locked in her bedroom after another screaming fight with her mom. She'd sat on the bed, gotten stoned, and played with the knife, angrily opened and closed it until she'd slipped and accidentally stabbed the tip of a finger.

It stung, surprised her with how much and how long the tiny cut hurt, but the unexpected pain also took her mind off the fight and the shithole of her life in the Jersey 'burbs. She watched a small ball of blood well up on her fingertip, so perfect that she could see her reflection in it, a tiny 'Manda who stared enchanted as she expanded like Alice in Wonderland in the shiny scarlet sphere.

The ball grew like a mushroom until big enough to burst and pour a trail of red down to her palm, where she licked the freed blood off. Another grew and another, each rolled down to be licked up, until the cut clotted and scabbed. 'Manda took the little blade and stabbed another finger, opened a fresh wound, continued finger by finger until she fell asleep.

She kept the little blade with her all the time after that, graduated from pricking her fingertips in high school to slicing inch-long lines across her wrists in college, thin enough to be barely noticeable when they healed. Later, she didn't care who saw, or what they thought. By then all that mattered was feeling the pain, smelling the fresh blood as it rose to the surface of her skin before she licked it clean.

Her scarred forearms were a roadmap of her life, a stripe for every bad day she'd had before and since leaving home. She found a spot on her wrist where scar tissue wasn't too thick, where there were still live nerves, and slit the surface, gently scored her skin again and again until it was red and raw, until thick blood oozed into the cold air like honey.

Watching it put 'Manda in a kind of trance. The world faded around her along with the snow, the pain in her belly, and the fight with Kirk. Her wrist was stained red, stung in a crisp delicious way that made her feel in control again, even if only for how long she'd cut.

'Manda heard a baby cry and it made her cry, too, haunted by her loss. She really was fucked up. The cries sounded so real, even though she wasn't doped up enough to be tripping. She stood up and looked around. Something was wrong.

This was no dope dream.

There was a Dumpster beside her in the dark alley. 'Manda opened the lid and looked inside, pushed trash aside. As impossible as it seemed, she saw a pale baby boy shining under the streetlight, as if someone had thrown him out. Like he was just as unwanted and abandoned as she was. 'Manda's tears turned from grief to joy. It was the best Christmas present she could have asked for, to see her child alive, she didn't care how, she didn't care why. It was a real Christmas miracle, no matter how impossible, and she wasn't going to turn it down.

The baby raised its arms, reached for her with a whimper. As she lowered her hand to touch it, blood dripped from her wrist onto the baby's face and the crying stopped. Its tiny eyes locked on hers, seemed to reach out and connect, and suddenly she knew what to do.

'Manda lifted the baby and held it close, felt its tiny body warm as it nuzzled against her. She pulled the baby closer and pressed her wound to its cold white lips. It gripped her wrist with tiny hands and suckled as if starved. 'Manda gasped, started to pull away, but its saliva flowed into her veins like venom and paralyzed her will. Any fear, all thought of retreat vanished. 'Manda smiled, ecstatic, higher than she'd ever been on smack, and rocked the baby, hummed to it.

"Shhh . . . Momma's here, baby. Everything's all right now." She soothed it with a lullaby, sung low and tender in the early evening chill of the alley. 'Manda wrapped her coat around it, hurried to the subway to get Baby home safe and sound.

Where it could feed in peace.

CHAPTER 15

4:57 P.M.
Fort Greene, 25 December 1986

Lori's eyes drifted to Steven all day, despite herself.

He was still the same lean golden brown guy she'd screwed in the storage room of his downtown gallery, the night they met at his first solo show. Thin dreadlocks hung over his face, obscured just enough to be provocative. Each time he licked his soft full lips she remembered what they felt like against hers, what his tongue had tasted like when they kissed. Her body remembered, even if she wouldn't let herself. She pulled her eyes away when he looked up, caught him stealing peeks at her when he thought she wasn't looking, like a clumsy tango of darting glances and secret stares.

They'd stayed professional all day and talked only about work, for all the good it did them. They read responses to their ad, sorted letters into stacks of rejects and follow-ups, and tried to find a focus, a reason for the book.

What was it about? What story were they telling? So far, all they knew was that it was about vampires. The longer it took to find a real theme to give them direction, the more frustrated they felt. They both knew the longer it took to come up with the big idea, the longer it would take to complete and the longer they'd have to deal with each other.

More days like this, months of strained silences and polite talk, as if they'd just been introduced. Not even that. People who've just met ask questions, make jokes, and relax the more time they spend together. This would just get colder and colder, until the distance between them made work impossible. Collaboration was nothing if not communication.

Steven stretched and threw aside the letter in his hand.

"Okay. That's it," he groaned. "Enough work." It was as if he'd been thinking the same thing. He climbed to his feet, changed the music from a bootleg cassette of Prince's *Black Album* to a remastered CD of Phil Spector's Christmas covers.

Lori yawned. "That's right, it's still Christmas Day, isn't it?" The sun was already setting. It would be over soon.

Steven lit a joint, took a deep hit, and held it up.

"No, thanks," said Lori. Steven raised an eyebrow. "I quit smoking, remember, when I found out . . ." She couldn't finish the sentence.

"Oh, right. Sorry, I wasn't sure." He looked a little embarrassed, changed the subject. "Look, no big, but before we . . ." He waved his hands between them, as if to make up for not having the words to describe their breakup. "I shopped early. It seemed stupid to return your present just because we . . ."

"I get it. Just because you got me something, doesn't mean you expect anything, blah, blah, blah . . ."

Steven went to the closet and dug out a large flat parcel, about three by four feet. When he came back he saw Lori pull a small wrapped gift from her Danish school bag, with a sly smile on her face.

"I shop early, too," she said. He handed her his package with a grin and took her gift.

"What is it?" she asked, puzzled, as she tried to rip packing tape off two sheets of cardboard.

"Just open it."

She gave him a look from under the long bangs of her short blond hair, an expression that had always made him wild with desire. It said, "I know all about you." It said, "I want you anyway, dammit."

Steven tore the paper from his present while Lori struggled with hers. The wrapping came away to reveal a battered early edition of Bram Stoker's *Dracula*. Inside was a card: "Saw this and thought of you. Lori." *Nice*, he thought, *appropriate, yet insulting*. She hadn't lost her touch.

"Hope you like it," she said. "I wasn't sure what to get you, but when I saw that at the Gotham Book Mart, it seemed . . ."

Steven looked up to see her stare in disbelief at her present. He grinned. "Like it?"

It was two full-size pages of original art for a *Tales of Terror* comic book, matted and framed to show the title stamp with publication dates and hand-written correction notes scribbled in nonreproducing blue pencil in the margins outside the inked panels. Lori stared.

On the left was the title page, a lurid black-and-white drawing of a flaming corpse in a wedding dress pointing an accusing finger at her groom. Over it rose the words *"Burnin' Love,"* and in a box below the artist's name was *"Writer—Lori Martin."* She gasped, in pleasure and disbelief. Writing horror comics had been just another freelance gig to pay the rent, but Steven knew it was a dream come true for her inner child. He was beside himself. He'd finally left her speechless.

"I considered perfume. . . ."

"Steven!" She swung at him, missed as he ducked. "How . . ."

He laughed.

"I called Meg at Mystic Comics, told her you wanted the title pages of the first comic you did for them, but were afraid to ask. She offered me the whole thing if the artist didn't want it. I had those two framed; the rest of the art's in here . . ."

Steven kept babbling once he'd started, unable to stop himself. The gift had been a great idea when they were together, but it felt too personal now. He didn't know how she'd react.

"I grabbed one of those cardboard portfolios, but she suggested a zippered presentation book . . ."

Lori grabbed him and pulled him closer, kissed him hard on the lips to silence him.

"Dammit! You make it so hard, sometimes," she whispered as she pulled him into a hug. They held each other for a long time as Ronnie Spector's throaty wail swelled over the stereo's speakers as the Ronettes burst into "Sleigh Ride."

"You realize that's it," he mumbled into her neck, "You'll never get a present this good from me again. Even if we'd stayed together."

"Cheap perfume and cotton panties, the rest of my life."

"Yup."

"I'll live. . . . Goddammit, Steven. I wish things were different."

"Yeah. Me too," he said, and pulled away. "Can we talk about this yet?"

"Steven . . ." Lori looked down, her eyes teary.

"You're not having the baby," he said. It wasn't a question. They hadn't seen each other in months. She obviously wasn't pregnant. He just wanted to know why. That was a lie. He just wanted to know it wasn't his fault.

"No," she said after a long, pained pause. "I'm not."

Steven saw her reaction and wanted to apologize, take it back, but knew it was too late. Before he could say anything, the phone trilled. The sharp sound broke whatever connection had opened between them.

"Answer it," said Lori, wiping her eyes, glad for an interruption. "Please."

Steven started to protest, but grabbed the phone instead.

"Yeah?"

He listened for a few moments. His face fell.

"Hang on . . ."

He covered the mouthpiece with the palm of his hand. "One of our reply postcards, Nina Miller. It's her brother."

Steven had to take a deep breath before he could finish. As soon as he did, Lori was sorry she'd been grateful for the call.

"He says she's been murdered."

CHAPTER 16

6:32 P.M.
Upper East Side, 25 December 1986

Marlowe had roamed Times Square all day, shaking down his contacts, asked the right questions of all the right people. But fuck, man, trying to find Adam's damned baby in a city this big was like trying to find a real virgin in this neighborhood, other than himself. Marlowe entered Adam's Fifth Avenue penthouse with his key, as usual, and dropped the morning papers on the side table.

He'd already laid out a story in his head.

"Evenin', Mr. Caine, sir. Don't have the kid yet, but got a lead or two, darn good ones . . ."

Adam was in a chair by the fireplace in the study, a snifter in his hand. He didn't look up.

"I see."

"It's hard, man. You'd think a little white baby on the loose in Hell's Kitchen would be easier to find, but I'll keep looking."

Adam didn't reply, or look up.

"Mr. Caine?"

"I'm not sure you fully understand the urgency, Marlowe. Perhaps you need incentive. . . ."

Marlowe didn't like the sound of that.

"Look, boss, I'm doing the best I can. Maybe we need to . . ." He stopped talking. Adam was nowhere to be seen. His Ray-Bans weren't that dark. Marlowe slid them down his nose. He was right. They weren't. The lights were out.

A voice rose from the shadows.

"You've been a bad boy, Marlowe."

Uh-oh.

"A bad, bad boy, from what I hear."

There was a slap. Wet leather against bare skin.

Oh, God, no.

Marlowe nearly shit his pants. Not him.

"A bad, bad, bad boy. And we know what happens to bad, bad, bad boys, don't we?"

Adam's voice slurred, slid down into the gravelly growl of the man who'd raised Marlowe, the man who had run the group home they sent him to when his crackhead mom finally managed to snuff herself. Allan Griswold was his name, called "Grislyweird" once, by a paperboy who got his teeth smashed in one night by an unseen assailant.

"Coincidence," Griswold said when the police questioned him, chewed his cigar and laughed. Did anyone really believe he'd take a kid's insult that seriously?

The children in the home spoke of him in whispers and only when they knew he wasn't in range. Most homes, the kids had gag nicknames for their keepers. No one dared it with this one. He'd made that clear. There was only one name they called him, other than Sir. One name, as they cowered under the covers and tried to block out screams that drifted up from the basement in the dead of night; too quiet for neighbors to hear, too loud to hide from inside. One name whispered only at night . . .

The Spanking Man.

It was his only nickname and it stuck because he liked it, the ring of authority it lent him. The way it gave his penalties an official air. Marlowe heard the sound again, a wet leather razor strop slapped against bare flesh. Heard the cough-riddled laugh that used to rock him to sleep at night as he wondered when it would be his turn again, and could he please, God, pretty please, die before then . . .

"A bad, bad, bad, bad, bad boy . . ."

He knew what that meant. God knew he'd heard it often enough growing up. Every "bad" meant another dozen stripes. The Spanking Man was mad, all right, and when it was personal, it was always worse, much worse.

When he got this mad he'd take them down to the basement, so the neighbors wouldn't hear. He'd strip down and put on a big black rubber apron so he wouldn't leave any bloodstained clothes for the authorities to admit in court as evidence if he was ever caught. He'd lock himself and his naked victim in the white-tiled laundry room, easy to scrub clean when he was done.

Then he'd wet the strop and go to work.

His job, he called it.

"I've got a hell of a job, keeping these nigger bastards in line," he'd tell the neighbors, when asked about an occasional welt or broken bone he couldn't conceal. "Products of incest, most of 'em. You don't know what they're like!"

Marlowe tried not to think of the Spanking Man, tried not to give Adam more fuel for his punishment. He put Jill out of his mind, afraid that the thing Adam created could somehow read his thoughts and twist his fantasy of her into a nightmare vision that would turn him off sex forever. *Please, let me keep her at least,* Marlowe prayed, *even if he flays every last inch of skin from my skinny black butt, please let me keep my Jill. . . .*

Then Griswold stepped from the shadows, pale white and naked except for his rubber apron, dead and decayed, but walking, swung his wet leather strop with a grin. The first strike hit and all thought for Jill left Marlowe's head to leave plenty of room for the pain.

CHAPTER 17

After he sent Marlowe home chastised, Adam sat in his study, twirled a delicate gold crucifix under the halogen light next to his armchair. The agonized golden Christ glistened as it had the night he'd brought it home from Nina's apartment, snatched from her table on his way out the door, the night he was flung into this mess.

Adam had grabbed it without thinking for his trophy collection. Now it was a grim reminder of an evening he'd rather forget. This thing with Nina and the baby was too damn complicated. It wasn't just that Revelation threatened discovery by humans and death, or worse punishment from the Veil. No.

It was that Nina had won.

In the end, he got her to kill her child, but not betray it. When she called it back to give them both hope for escape, she did what none of his subjects had done in over twenty years.

She made Adam wonder if he was wrong.

Could love be stronger than death, self-sacrifice stronger than self-preservation? Jesus glittered as he twirled under the light, as if laughing at him. It was the problem with not enthralling the subjects of his art projects, so he could savor their conflicted emotions as they descended into desperation. They could still surprise you.

If he infected them with a bite, they'd worship him and sacrifice themselves gladly. He always waited until the last minute, when they begged him to feed, to end their pain, even if they knew he'd inflicted it. Perenelle, the one who'd infected him, would say Nina had given him what he secretly wanted all along: someone to prove him wrong.

Perenelle de Marivaux . . .

He looked at a small oil painting on the far wall, almost out of sight behind a screen. It was the last one he'd painted of her, back when he was still mortal, still able. She looked back with a slight smile, beautiful, serene, and seductive, like a fallen Raphaelite angel. That was how he'd seen her then. Despite his feelings about her now, he could never bring himself to dispose of the portrait, no matter how it pained him. It was his masterpiece, as he was hers.

If Marlowe couldn't track down the baby, she was his last and only hope. Again. Adam was almost tempted to accept the Veil's consequences rather than ask her for help. To admit his mistake to Perenelle would be agony. He could already see the smug look on her flawless face as she made him squirm before she granted any aid. There was always a price for her favors. This would be the highest yet.

Adam hated Perenelle for his sterile existence as only the undead can hate, hatred that could last lifetimes. She had created Adam Caine. He was still human when he met her; young master Frederic Hartwell, merely a boy, innocent and unsullied. She'd found him in a moment of weakness and raised him like the son she couldn't have. As much as he despised his dependence on her, she still owed him a debt for bringing him into her world.

In the end, like it or not, Adam knew he'd run to Perenelle to save himself. He didn't know what else to do. Something had to be done or he would face eternal entombment. That was all he was sure of, that and one other thing. . . .

Even that would be easier than facing Perenelle.

CHAPTER 18

11:36 A.M.
Palm Beach, 30 March 1912

Hartwell House in Palm Beach, Florida, was a white two-story mansion in the Classical Revival style. Tall Grecian pillars along its stately front framed a long walk to the grand entrance. An open inner courtyard gave the house a Spanish flavor. Frederic's mother, Olivia, had filled the lushly decorated rooms with appropriate antiques, marble, murals, and Tiffany windows. It reflected his father Nathaniel Hartwell's station in the world, as did his wife and family.

Olivia Hartwell was raised in the old school.

She knew her place and everyone else's and made sure they did, too. Her husband's job was building his rail and real estate empire. Olivia's job was running his household, which included raising their son as she saw fit, to inherit his father's mantle. No one understood Frederic the way she did, or made him feel as safe and protected.

He ran along a beach, the wide white stretch of sand behind their old home. Frederic played a last game of fetch on the shore with a spotted black-and-white spaniel he'd found at the beginning of the season. He'd asked to keep it while they were there, and his father said no.

"Don't be absurd. You can't have pets at home, and you can't leave it here to breed more bastards. Place is littered with abandoned pets as it is. Taking care of it when you can't keep it is only a waste of time and food."

But his mother interceded.

"Frederic understands that he can't keep it. He just wants to play with it. For now. When we're ready to go home, he'll take care of it," she said, and made him promise his father that he would at the end of the season. He did so gladly, and ran to the beach with his new friend to play.

It was time to go back north before he knew it, after a happy winter spent frolicking with his dog in the Florida sun instead of the frosty Northeast. Negro servants, always immaculately dressed in crisp white linen, packed their things and closed up the house. Frederic heard his father bellow down the empty halls.

"We're almost ready to go! What's being done about that damned dog?" He found Frederic's mother and told her to make sure the matter was handled properly. Olivia made assurances, took Frederic aside, and sent him to the beach to look for his dog.

It was where it always was, waiting for him with a stick in its mouth, spotted tail wagging. Frederic finished his goodbyes and hugged his dog to his chest one last time. His mother came down to join him on the beach.

"Are you done saying goodbye?" she asked him.

Frederic nodded, eyes filled with tears.

"Good boy. Now take care of it. We have to leave."

Frederic looked up at his mother, not sure what she meant. She frowned back at him as dark clouds gathered on her perfect brow. "The dog. You can't bring it home and you can't leave it here. Just take care of it, as you promised your father you would at the beginning of the season."

"What do you mean?" He clutched her skirt with one hand. The other held his dog fast.

"What do I mean?" His mother mocked his voice and pulled away, looked at him the same way she looked at beggars on the streets, or servants. "What do you think I mean? Just take care of it."

He looked at the dog in his arms, then back to her.

"Don't be thick, Frederic. You can't keep it and you can't leave it here to breed more mongrel bastards. What's left?"

He stared up at her and the light dawned, as he understood what she wanted him to do. What he had to do.

"I can't! I can't do that!"

"You can't?" She stared at him as at trash left uncollected, the way she'd stared at a maid just before she slapped her face and fired her for incompetence. "You can't. Then stay here with your bastard pet. You're no son of mine."

She spun around in the sand and walked away.

"Mother! Mother!" little Frederic shouted against the sound of the crashing waves, but it was no use. His mother still walked away, as if she couldn't hear him over the ocean or didn't care to hear him. "Come back! Look! I'm doing it!"

Frederic screamed for her as he dragged his dog into the water, into the waves until he was up to his thighs. He plunged its head under the water. "Come back, Mother! I'm doing it! I'm doing it!" He screamed to be heard over the surf, wept as his puppy struggled in his hands, clawed at his forearms. It bit his hand, hard and deep. Frederic's anguished scream for his mother turned to one of pain as the dog's fangs tore at his tender flesh, broke the skin.

Why? Why did it bite him?

Salt water filled the wound with fresh pain as Frederic cried in confusion. He'd thought his dog loved him the way he loved it. He'd treated it well all winter, better than it deserved, better than it could have expected when he'd found it. Frederic fed it, brushed it and petted it, played with it and loved it, and now it tore into his flesh like an angry shark.

Scared and furious, Frederic squeezed tiny hands tight around the dog's neck, pushed it down into the water, choked it and held it down until the beast went limp. He released the dog. Through his tears he watched blood from his gored hand darken the seawater as his pet floated to the surface.

He grabbed it by the scruff of the neck, pulled it to shore, and stumbled toward his mother with his trophy. She'd returned to the beach in silence, crouched down to embrace him after he dropped the dead dog at her feet.

"It bit me, Mother. It bit me," he said, and fell into fresh tears. His mother took his wounded hand.

"Bad dog. Bad, bad dog. And after all you did for it, the vicious little ingrate. Here. Give me your hand. This will make it better." She lifted his bloody palm to her lips, and kissed it, long and tender.

He could see her lips stained with his blood when she finally pulled her mouth away, as if her lingering kiss had been more of a taste. She smiled sweetly and licked her ruby lips clean as she lifted the low hem of her long skirt to reveal a delicate ankle covered by high-buttoned shoes. Olivia tore off a strip of her petticoat and wrapped it around his hand like a bandage.

"My sweet darling. This will stop the blood. We'll fix you up properly at the house before we leave."

"Can we go home now, Mother? I want to go home."

"Of course we can, my beautiful boy. Come to me." She gave him a long, loving hug and stood. "One last thing." She looked at the dead dog. It lay in the sand, tongue out. Frederic sighed, picked up the carcass in both arms, and carried it up to the house by his mother's side to dispose of in the trash.

"I took care of it, Mother. Didn't I?"

"You certainly did, precious. Just as I knew you would. Mother's brave little man. *Mon petit soldat . . .* "

They walked side by side, back up the beach to go home.

CHAPTER 19

7:16 P.M.
Lower East Side, 25 December 1986

It was finally night.

'Manda sat in a frayed armchair salvaged from the street, wrapped in blankets away from shattered windows, inside an empty apartment in the condemned Lower East Side squat she called home. She held Baby close as it woke, and rocked it in her arms.

'Manda had smuggled it in through the back, hidden inside her oversized Salvation Army coat. Kirk didn't waste good help on guard here; usually Trick or Treat and she could walk an elephant past either one of the twins. She'd brought Baby here, far from the others, to the room where she'd stayed since the night she fought with Kirk after she told him she was pregnant.

She'd worshipped him once, after she ran screaming from her mother like a fugitive from justice. He got her high, taught her what sex could be, opened her head and body to a new world before he got bored, started to use her to wipe his ass.

Now Baby was her world.

'Manda held it closer, felt its body warm and fill with life as it nursed from the tiny slit she'd cut in her nipple, smelled the sweet aroma of mother's milk, mixed with the rich smell of fresh flowing blood. 'Manda sighed, unafraid, pulled the baby closer, and wrapped the blanket around it. She rocked it, cooed.

"Momma's here. It's okay." She soothed it with a song, sung low and tender in the chill dark of the abandoned building. Nina tried to put Baby down so she could go pee. It twisted her mind, just a little. She winced, stroked it. "Everything's all right, everything's fine."

It released control, and 'Manda put it down, pulled the blanket up around her precious bundle of joy. Hiding Baby here was stupid, even 'Manda knew that, but what else could she do? It wanted food and a home, and this was the best way to give it both. She didn't know how she knew that. It was like it could just slip inside her head and make her see what it wanted, like the way it made her nick her nipple with her knife so it could feed properly, cradled against her breast. All she had to do was keep it away from Kirk, until Kirk didn't matter. And what if he did find out? She wasn't worried.

Baby would tell her what to do.

"'Manda?" A big shadow filled the ruined doorway behind her like a curtain. 'Manda threw the blanket in place over Baby, covered it, and turned to see Glenda's bulky body fill the doorway. "I been worried, honey. Where you been all day?"

'Manda met her at the door and led her away from Baby.

"Sick," she said, and couldn't think of anything else. Baby would know what she should say, if it were close enough to put ideas in her head. 'Manda wasn't good at lying, could barely remember the truth half the time. "I hurt. Real bad . . ."

"S'okay, honey. I understand."

The big black woman took her in her arms, tenderly stroked 'Manda's hair as she folded her in arms that held her too close for friendship. "I'll always take care of you. You know that. . . ."

"Yeah, sure. I know that." *That's good. Just agree with her. Easy.* Was that her idea or Baby's?

"Got somethin' fer ya . . ." Glenda pulled away with a smile and slipped a packet of dope from her jeans pocket. 'Manda dug through her coat pockets for works she'd copped from the clinic.

They cooked the stuff and shot it together as they had a thousand times, still shared a needle despite warnings of AIDS on the news. Mingling their blood made them family, a bond closer than sex, more permanent than marriage. Everyone but Kirk, who always used his own works, shared nothing with anyone.

The high meant nothing to 'Manda anymore. She faked it, made all the right moves, but knew she was hooked on something stronger now, something she'd taste again only if she did her job right.

"Oh, 'Manda." Glenda swooned; her eyes rolled up as she slipped against the wall, sighed. "Oh, baby . . ."

"Lemme show you somethin'," whispered 'Manda. She took Glenda by the hand, pulled her to her feet, unsteady.

"What is it, baby? What you wan' . . ."

Glenda's words slurred as she stumbled across the room. What was wrong with this lil' white girl? Where was she taking her? Her mouth tried to ask, but failed.

"Just a little farther . . ." 'Manda was just ahead of her. Glenda could barely see her in the dark. A pale hand beckoned Glenda forward. "This way. Just a little more." 'Manda lifted a bundled blanket from the floor of the closet, held it out, and pulled up a flap to reveal a baby wrapped inside.

Even high, Glenda gasped.

It was so small, so pale, at first Glenda was afraid it was dead, that 'Manda had been hiding a baby corpse up here to comfort herself. Its eyes were wide open, though, and the infant stared at Glenda like no baby she'd ever seen, so quiet, so peaceful, like it knew something she didn't. It was prettier than any baby she'd ever seen, and the more she looked into its eyes, the prettier it was, the more she wanted to hold it close and take care of it.

Without thinking she held out her arms, and 'Manda stepped forward. Even in the streetlight the baby was white as marble and just as cold, too, when 'Manda put it in Glenda's hands. "Where'd you get this, sugar?" asked Glenda.

"It's mine," said 'Manda.

Glenda shook her head, confused and sleepy, so sleepy. The longer she held the baby, the sleepier she felt.

"Can't be, baby. Kirk beat yours out of you. Who'd you steal this from?"

'Manda frowned at her. "It's mine."

"Your baby's dead, sugar. I'm sorry, but it's true."

'Manda ignored Glenda, thrust the infant against her.

"Not like that. Hold it closer . . ."

Glenda tried to get a better look at it. There was something wrong with this baby, and it wasn't only the dope that made her think so. It was too cold, for one thing, too damn cold for a baby, and she didn't like having this cold thing pressed against her. 'Manda unbuttoned Glenda's shirt to put the infant inside against her breast, as if to warm it.

The baby pawed at her skin, dry lips felt for her nipple. Glenda had to laugh. The damn thing was trying to suckle and there was no point to that with her. She saw a flash from the corner of her eye, saw 'Manda's hand holding a small penknife.

"Hey," she started to protest.

"Shhh . . ." 'Manda laid an alabaster hand on Glenda's arm. Fingers like steel held Glenda still as the blade pierced her breast. Blood oozed to the surface, glowed in moonlight that fell through the bare window frame.

"Hey . . ."

Glenda tried to speak again, but the baby sucked at the cut. She felt the cold rush of a new high as its saliva entered her bloodstream, and all concern for safety slipped away in the raw childlike wonder of being enthralled to Baby.

CHAPTER 20

Lori hated fanatics.

She went out of her way to avoid Jehovah's Witnesses and Seventh Day Adventists on street corners, Hari Krishna at airports, Scientologists in L.A. She didn't want anyone without a life of their own telling her how to live hers. There was something pathetic about people who had to pay psychics or TV evangelists to find out what to do next, when what they usually heard was give more cash. It didn't matter if they paid twenty-five bucks to a prayer circle in the Midwest or a hundred bucks to channel a dead guru in the West Village.

It was all bullshit, yet here she was, headed downtown on Christmas to pay some faker a hundred bucks because Faith believed she was real and had convinced Lori that the experience could be used for *BITE!* It was easier to go along than to argue with her, so instead of being curled up in a nice warm apartment with a quart of Häagen-Dazs and a good book, she was in a cold taxi, trying to evade Faith's questions about her day with Steven.

"Did you tell him what happened to the baby?" asked Faith.

Lori frowned. Leave it to Faith. She'd finally gotten to what she really wanted to know.

"We started to talk about it, but got interrupted. I can't, anyway, not yet."

"He has to know sooner or later."

Lori sighed. "Then it's later."

"But he must think you had an abortion. If you tell him the truth . . ."

"What truth? That I lost the baby before I could decide if I wanted it or not? I can't deal with him right now. Not after the way he reacted when I told him I was pregnant."

It was at a friend's party. She'd just found out that afternoon. Steven was drinking and she wasn't. When he asked why, she was forced to tell him instead of waiting for the right moment. He freaked out, practically begged her to have an abortion, in front of their friends. It was their worst fight, maybe the worst night of her life.

Lori and Faith rode in silence until Faith changed the subject. "Oh, shit!" said Faith. "Before I forget, Duane's back in the hospital, with pneumonia."

"Damn!" Lori kicked herself mentally. "I've been meaning to call him." Her friend Duane had developed full-blown AIDS. Every time he was hospitalized, it dragged Lori through the pain of her mother's last year of life. AIDS or cancer, it was all the same thing, a slow fade she couldn't stop, a disaster she was forced to watch frame by frame, knowing the full nightmare of what comes next, like Zapruder's film of JFK's assassination.

She was not in the best mood for the evening ahead.

The cab pulled up in front of a large brownstone in the West Village. Faith leaned forward to pay the driver, while Lori climbed out for a better look. She reflexively reached for a cigarette she didn't have, then banished the thought.

The building seemed ordinary enough, weathered but well maintained, Gothic, built of stone with stained-glass windows. Faith stumbled up behind her, shoved things back in her purse and guided them up the stairs to a carved wooden door. Woodland animals frolicked across it, performed a pagan dance under a full moon.

"Lions and tigers and bears, oh my!" whispered Lori. *We're off to see the Wizard.* She was getting the giggles.

"Shhh! Do me a favor," said Faith. "Can you please, just for tonight, accept everything you see and hear? Just for tonight. You can rip it to shreds tomorrow. . . ."

Before Lori could retort, the door swung open.

An elderly woman with long white hair greeted them. It was hard to tell her exact age, but she was exquisite, the kind of old woman Lori hoped to be one day, slender and stylish in a way that made Jackie O. look gauche. She wore an ivory floor-length silk dress with an embroidered shawl thrown around her shoulders. Her smile was radiant as she waved them in.

"Faith! So good to see you! You've brought someone new to the circle?" She spoke with a touch of a French accent, turned to Lori as she led them inside.

"Yes," said Faith. "This is my friend Lori; she's writing a book about vampires. I thought Rahman might be able to help her." The old woman closed the door behind them. "Lori, I'd like you to meet an extraordinary woman and trance channeler, my spiritual guide, someone who's changed my life since I met her . . ."

The old woman laughed and bowed slightly.

". . . Perenelle de Marivaux!"

"I have the means within my grasp . . ."

Lori barely suppressed laughter. She was seated on a tatami mat in a circle of successful downtown artists, Wall Street wonders, and ex-hippies who'd sold out in the early eighties and wanted to buy back their spiritual salvation. The room was dimly lit by gentle spotlights mounted in the ceiling and candles in the center of the circle. Silver stars on the dark blue walls twinkled with reflected glory.

"I have the means within my grasp . . ."

They chanted in unison, with the practiced ease of a mindless cult. Lori joined in, but couldn't help repeating in harmony or subtle rounds, like they were singing around a campfire. Faith shot her a dirty look, but she was the only one who noticed.

Perenelle's head dropped as a moan rose from her thin lips. The others waited expectantly in the soft blue semidarkness, just a little afraid now that the moment they'd waited for was actually here. Lori didn't know what to expect next. She felt her head swim, as if something in the incense had intoxicated her, as if they'd all been inhaling opium without knowing it.

When Perenelle's face lifted, it was changed. Even Lori was caught off guard by the difference: her expression, even the shape of her face, seemed harder, more masculine. Her gray eyes were now a deep gold, dark, as if not all light that fell into them could escape.

"As salaam alaikum!"

Her voice was low, rougher. Though Lori was far from convinced that anything supernatural was happening, she was caught up in the moment. However she did it, Perenelle put on quite a show. Briefed before the session, the others responded appropriately after a shocked pause.

"Alaikum as salaam . . ."

Most of the members of the circle had been here before. Lori knew how affected she was as a skeptic—she could only imagine how the regulars felt. They all believed that the thousand-year-old spirit of a Moorish warrior sage inhabited Perenelle's body to communicate secrets of the ages, and it sure looked like she delivered the goods. Big time.

"You have questions."

There was a nervous shuffle as they looked around to see who had the courage to start. Lori spoke up without thinking, tossed out the question she'd been dealing with for weeks.

"Do you believe in vampires?"

Perenelle, or rather Rahman-al-Hazra'ad ibn Aziz, her channeled sage, turned gold eyes on Lori as if she were the only one in the room. Lori swallowed, gulped like a kid in the principal's office. For a moment she saw cold fury in his eyes, murderous rage, even a little fear. Then thin lips curled upward in a smile, as one hand waved aside a cloud of incense smoke, dismissive.

"My belief in anything is insufficient to make it so or not. Hence irrelevant. One might as well ask if you believe in me."

The laughter that followed cleared tension from the room, as if a frightening stranger had stepped out of shadows to be revealed as a beloved uncle. The thousand-year-old warrior in Perenelle's body led the conversation, and questions flowed. Guests asked about their careers, love, and lives, concerns more worldly than spiritual, but these were the same people who chanted for promotions and houses in the Hamptons. For them, spirituality was just a way to network with the dead or divine, someone with real clout.

Lori felt a somber mood settle on the room. Conversation slowed and stopped. Members of the circle looked at one another, confused, as if unsure of the script. Rahman's eyes rolled up.

"There is one who wishes to speak. . . ."

Perenelle's head rolled back as she arched to the floor. A low, sustained moan squeezed from her throat as she writhed, twisted upward to face them again.

It wasn't Rahman or Perenelle they saw now. The face was deathly pale, eyes wide and blank, dry skin so tight there seemed to be nothing between it and the bone beneath. When the lips opened, the teeth were yellowed, sharp, the tongue black. Lori didn't know how it was possible, but the effect was terrifying, more so when the skeletal face swung around the room to face her.

"You . . ."

A hand rose, pointed a bony forefinger at Lori, as the arm reached out to her, closer than possible. She wanted to run.

"*Beware . . .*"

The word was hissed, serpentine. The lights went out and the window shutters flew open, pounded against the walls outside as Perenelle's possessed body was lifted to its feet as if by wires, rose from the floor toward the ceiling. Wind whipped around the room, extinguished candles, and tore at their hair and clothes.

The monster floated in midair, seen in flashes of light from the windows as shutters crashed open and shut. Blank red eyes glowed in semidarkness. Perenelle fell to the floor and the shutters snapped shut one last time. The room was left black and quiet.

Someone fumbled a lighter from a coat pocket, relit candles. Lori helped pass them around to relight the rest of the room. Faith went to Perenelle's side, lifted her head, and looked into her eyes, back to their usual gray, her face the one they knew.

"Perenelle . . . can you hear me?" Faith spoke softly, like she'd dealt with this before.

"We had an intrusion," said Perenelle. "I remember nothing, but I can feel it. . . ."

Lori wandered away while they spoke in whispers, wondered if all Perenelle's get-togethers ended in pyrotechnics. She stretched and wished even more for the cigarette she'd craved on the way in. The old woman squeezed Faith's hand as they finished talking, stood with help from her and a cute broker.

"Please. You must all go. I must purify the space. You . . ."

She turned to Lori as the others headed for the door, wagged a finger at her like Maria Ouspenskaya chastising Lon Chaney Jr. in *The Wolfman.*

"There's danger if you continue down the path you're on. Grave danger."

"Yeah. I got that."

Lori didn't feel nearly as flip as she acted, was more shaken than she wanted to admit, but her defenses were always first to recover. The old woman scowled at her like an angry parent as she followed them out.

"Do not take my warning lightly. Tread carefully, if at all." As Perenelle led them out, a redhaired young man pushed his way past them to get in before she closed the door. Lori walked to the street and looked for a cab as Perenelle locked the door behind them.

Faith frowned at Lori like a doctor about to give a patient bad news. "She's worried about you. She says your research is more dangerous than you know." Faith stayed on the top step, arms folded tightly. Lori knew Faith took this more seriously than she did, but she'd never seen her take it this seriously. She looked shaken.

"Yeah, well, danger's my middle name," said Lori, waved her arm. A cab clicked on its Off Duty sign as it slid past them.

"Stop joking," said Faith. "I've never seen Perenelle scared before and she was scared tonight. Whether you want to believe it or not, something happened. I think you should listen."

Lori glared as a cab slowed and stopped. In times like this she wondered how their friendship had survived Faith's unreasoning love of occult bullshit. Faith walked down, stared into Lori's eyes as she opened the car door.

"Please, listen, Lori."

"I will. Over drinks." Faith protested as Lori pushed her into the cab and gave the driver the address of a crosstown bar. "It's the only way I can get stupid enough to believe in any of this." Even that wouldn't be stupid enough.

There wasn't enough liquor in New York.

CHAPTER 21

10:37 P.M.
West Village, 25 December 1986

As Perenelle started to close the door behind her guests, Adam pushed it open again. It was no surprise. She'd felt him before she saw him, as they all could with their own kind.

He brushed past her.

"I have to talk to you," he said, in a voice that told her that once again he'd created a crisis he couldn't undo alone. Her bad seed had come home to be saved, as always. He'd made an obligatory check-in to inform her of his new identity, after twenty years in exile for his last scandal. She hadn't seen him again until now. Perenelle sighed and led him downstairs to her personal quarters, never suspected just how deep he'd dug his hole this time.

Perenelle was silent when Adam finished his tale of Nina's death and revival, of the cruel game he'd played with her, stunned that even he could have been so careless as to let the undead child escape. She didn't bother to restore her true face as she usually did after human guests were gone. Perenelle glared at him like a judgmental grandmother with the mask of age she wore for her clients.

"I should expose you to the Veil immediately," she said when she'd recovered enough to speak. "Except it would mean my own doom as well."

Perenelle wanted to dash his brains out on the floor, tear him limb from limb for what he would bring down on them if they couldn't locate the child, all because of his ego, his stupid games!

"I blame myself," she said.

Adam groaned, pounded fists to his head. "Dear God in heaven, not the I-never-should-have-made-you speech again! Spare me that!"

"More. I should have killed you that night on the beach."

"But you didn't. We don't have time for this! I need help, more than ever. This isn't another scandal or body I can't hide. This could be the end of us all."

Perenelle remembered the last time she'd heard that, when Townsend Burke asked for help to stop Tom O'Bedlam in London. Adam wasn't so different from either of them. In a daring gesture, he took her hand, but she didn't pull it away.

He was still her only child, the one she could never have in life. The laws of the Veil bound her fate to Adam's, and she hated him for bringing them to the edge of entombment. But, despite his failures, deep inside she still felt like the only mother Adam had left. And he knew it.

"It would be the end of you," she said. "That's all you care about. If I did nothing, the Veil would seal the breach and you with it. Unfortunately, they'll seal me up, too."

"Unless we close the breach; then they won't have a reason to, will they? We can do it before anyone finds out. Before it spreads." He kissed her hand softly, catlike. "We'll be heroes."

At that, Perenelle laughed out loud, so hard that the windowpanes rattled. He was worse than a scoundrel. There was no word for him. The rage within her knew no bounds, and still he made her laugh with his audacity. She pulled her hand from his, eyes cold and uncaring. He gazed up at her; still looked like the sweet youth she'd wanted to preserve forever the night she'd made him into her kind.

Perenelle had once hoped to spend eternity under that gaze. It had never dawned on her how quickly she'd tire of his pretty face and its sick lies, of the syrupy horrors those rosy lips would pour into her ear night after night once he was immortal.

She stood and walked to the bar as she restored her aged face to its true appearance of youth, shook out lustrous black hair, and poured a glass of cognac. Perenelle glared at Adam with the same delicate features he'd seen for the first time almost seventy years ago.

"You go too far, *mon petit*. You'd burn your house to save your family from the flames?" she asked.

"It wouldn't be the first house I've burned."

He needed someone to punish him, someone he feared more than her. That was the reason for the Veil. Despite the troubles between them there had still been a place in her heart, if only a small place, for the boy he'd been, the one she'd once loved and destroyed. That part of her heart had died tonight.

"There's one hope. I never told you our history," said Perenelle. She rose, and led him upstairs. "I taught you to hunt, how to dispose of your victims or call them back, but we parted before I told you what we are, where we came from.

"Vampires are the product of an ancient curse discovered by the Moors, unwittingly brought back to the Vatican with other scientific papers during the Crusades, and unleashed by the Jesuits assigned to study them. The curse spread from Rome through Europe like a plague, by contagion, vampire to victim. As they began to hunt us down, we came to the New World with other immigrants, once it was populated enough to hide us. But the Autochthones have a different origin."

"The Autochthones?"

"Vampires older than all of us combined. No one knows how old. They originated in Mexico under the Olmec Empire, migrated to New York before there was a city, before there was a nation. They live in the underground; move through the city unseen, but everywhere. They see all and know all that happens. If anyone can help us find the child, they can."

"Can you reach them?"

"The one who created and abandoned me, as I abandoned you, is their leader." Perenelle let her memory drift, saw the dark face of the Autochthones' leader, noble and strong. The real Rahman-al-Hazra'ad ibn Aziz, the man she impersonated in her channeling sessions. "He came centuries ago from Europe to find them, to study their ancient knowledge. To fulfill a quest."

"Did he?"

"He found them, if not what he sought. It won't be easy. But he still owes me for what he did. . . ." She faded, lost in memories of the events that parted them.

"We have to see him, Perenelle. We have no other hope."

She sighed. She'd leave him to his fate if it weren't tied to hers. It was the least he deserved. "Come back tomorrow night and we'll go to him."

"But—"

"Tomorrow. Or not at all." Perenelle opened the front door. "Our accounts are settled, Frederic," she said, using his true name. "Wiped clean. It's over between us. The love, the hate, ends here. Come back tomorrow. I'll help seal your breach because the Veil forces me to, but after that, we're done. I'll die before I save you again."

He looked like he didn't believe her, as a joke rose to his lips. Adam stopped when he saw the truth. Perenelle glimpsed the young Frederic Hartwell in his face for a moment, sad, regretful, before he hardened back into the old Adam Caine. He nodded with a smirk, turned, and disappeared into the night.

Perenelle locked the door behind him, wished it were as easy to lock out what lay ahead.

CHAPTER 22

9:06 P.M.
Gramercy Park, 13 November 1914

He was a bad boy. That's why Frederic was here.

It wasn't his first time and wouldn't be his last, awful as it was to be locked in the closet. It smelled of shoes and cedar, filled with woolen clothes that wrapped around him like the enormous leaves of some strange, exotic tree. The closet was warm, but dark, so very dark, like a coffin. The thick clothes muffled any sound, even that of his weeping. Frederic was exhausted, but afraid to close his eyes and sleep, didn't know what might come for him in the darkness.

When in his own bed he always insisted that the door to the closet be tightly shut so nothing could creep out to get him overnight. No matter how well he said his evening prayers, he was still afraid there were things hiding in there that could take him away in the dark, the way they had taken his mother's mother.

He'd heard her shriek one night, a year after she moved in, shout about the things that were coming out of the closet for her. She woke the whole household, hysterical, fled her room before they could get to her. His grandmother ran screaming into the street in her bedclothes, until they caught her and carried her back inside.

Men in white came that night and took her away, as she howled and begged for mercy. Frederic never saw her again. The next day they told him she had gone to a nice home in the country, where they would take good care of her and she could sleep without fear, in a room with no closets.

"A padded room," said his father, looking up from his newspaper.

His mother shushed him.

Months later, they took Frederic to his grandmother's funeral. They said it was her heart, but when he saw her stiff and still in the wooden coffin, her dead face painted white like china, Frederic was sure that the things she'd feared all her life had finally caught up to her. He'd waited for her eyes to snap open, for her to leap up one last time to warn them of evil things in the closet.

He hadn't seen anything in here yet, but the fear was there, every time. . . .

The doorknob rattled as a skeleton key entered the lock. Frederic tensed, until he remembered it could be only one person. His mother never came to let him out of the closet after she'd punished him. She always sent a maid to put him to bed. For the last few months one in particular had taken it on herself to do the job, a sweet girl named Jenny, hired less than six months earlier.

When she first met Frederic, she said he reminded her of her little brother back home. After that she'd treated him like a little brother, when his mother wasn't looking on with disapproval. Olivia often warned him that it didn't do to treat servants as equals. It made it that much harder to manage or dismiss them. Frederic always agreed, nodded his head, but behind his mother's back took cookies warm from the oven, smuggled out in Jenny's apron, or sat and sang songs with her while she did laundry in the basement.

The closet door opened and there was Jenny, smiling down at him.

"How's my boy, then?" she asked softly. She wiped his tear-streaked face, lifted him from the floor of the closet, and carried him across the room. "Ready for bed?"

"Yes'm," mumbled Frederic, already half asleep.

"Poor thing. Bet you'll never do that again, now will you? Whatever it was." She smiled down at him sadly. "No time for a story tonight, love. Yer mum wants a word with you."

Jenny laid him down in bed, sheets already turned down. She pulled them up to his chin, smoothed his hair, and gave him a tender kiss on the forehead.

"Don't forget to say your prayers." She leaned in and whispered, "Maybe one to give someone around here a heart. G'night, my little Freddy. I'll see you in the morning."

"Yes'm. G'night, Mummy Jenny."

Frederic closed his eyes and slept.

Olivia had waited impatiently outside the door to her son's room to say good night. It didn't do any good to teach a six-year-old boy a lesson without reinforcing it afterward. Otherwise the point was lost. Once he was tucked in for the night, she would go in and explain it to him one last time.

She hadn't paid much attention to who was putting Frederic to bed. He was to be dressed in his nightclothes and under the sheets by the time she came to say good night. How that happened was a simple matter of house management, assigned by someone beneath her. Until tonight, it had never been an issue of much importance.

As she listened outside the door to the conversation between her son and the maid, Olivia saw that this had been a serious omission on her part. The girl had formed a dangerously intimate relationship with her son, and was not only negating the effects of her punishment by comforting him; she seemed to be telling him that his mother was wrong to do it. Bad enough he had picked up her gutter speech. Worse, he called her "Mummy Jenny," had formed an emotional attachment to someone who should mean no more to him than a divan or settee.

This had to be nipped in the bud, in a way that would put her son back on the right path and teach him a good lesson as well. Olivia left her son's door before the maid came out and saw her. This had to be handled properly. She didn't want to repeat herself. It would be dealt with once, and only once.

Frederic could tell as soon as he woke up that something was wrong. He couldn't tell how he knew, until he heard his father's bellow boom from downstairs. Frederic tensed. When his father was angry, it wasn't good to be around him. He'd had too many canings for minor infractions to forget that. But if his father was downstairs yelling, it wasn't at him. Frederic felt safe enough to get out of bed and slip on his robe, then went to the stairs to see what was happening.

He crept down until he could see into the hallway.

There was a small gathering outside the servants' quarters, all the help that lived in the house. They huddled, trembling, as Frederic's father continued to rant from the back of the house. There was a cry of rage and triumph, and

Nathaniel Hartwell stormed out the door with a riding crop in one hand and a cloth sack in the other, followed by two police officers who had helped in the search.

Hartwell threw the bag to the floor at the servants' feet. Frederic saw his mother's jewelry and his father's gold watches spill out, a fortune to any of the staff.

"Is this how you repay me for taking you in, giving you fit wages and a roof? This? Take my food, my drink, and this is how you thank me?" His face burned bright red, as the servants quaked before him, not sure whom he addressed. "You! You stupid bitch! From your room!"

He reached in and grabbed Jenny by the wrist, threw her to her knees, and whipped her with the crop, across the back and face as she shrieked in pain.

"No! Sir, I never! I didn't! I couldn't! Frederic! Please! Tell them!" She turned to the boy, held out her arms, begged, eyes wet with tears. His mother pulled him close.

"You leave him alone. He knows you did it. He saw you. Didn't you, Frederic?"

He froze as she spoke the lie, his eyes locked to Jenny's.

Frederic loved the girl, didn't want to condemn her, but he knew she'd be gone one day, while his mother would always be there, ready to repay any betrayal. His father and the police looked to him for confirmation. Jenny shook her head.

Frederic blurted out the words he'd always regret.

"She did! I saw her!"

Jenny screamed and sobbed, continued to plead innocence as Frederic's father whipped her out the door and into the street for all to see. The boy turned away, but his mother grabbed his head and made him watch. He cried out Jenny's name and tried to go to her, determined to recant his accusation. Olivia held him back when he moved forward. He stopped as soon as she touched him, knew it would be worse for the girl if he didn't.

A paddy wagon waited outside. Frederic's father still lashed the girl, who'd given up any resistance. The officers stood by, waited for Hartwell without even the decency to look away. Frederic's father finished his work, snapped fresh blood from his crop to the curb, and stood upright, panted.

"Let that be a lesson to you all!" he shouted to the other servants, neighbors, and passersby. Hartwell didn't specify what the lesson was, but Frederic took it to be that his father was not a man to cross.

The officers picked a broken Jenny off the ground, handcuffed her, and took her away, bloody and weeping. His father came up the steps to the front door, tousled Frederic's hair with a sweaty smile as he passed, anger spent.

"That's the way you handle these things, boy. Never let anyone betray you. Come down hard, come down fast."

Hartwell was true to his word. He made sure the girl got a fast trial, if not the fairest. A judge friend gave her the maximum sentence when convicted, fifteen years of hard labor.

He came to dinner the following night. At the table the judge mentioned in passing that the girl had killed herself after she heard the sentence, hanged in the cell. It was said as if almost overlooked, like some petty detail of a minor business deal. Frederic promptly threw up.

"Good Lord," said his father. "Whatever's wrong with the boy?" His mother glared at him and stood, wiped Frederic's mouth with his napkin and laid it over the puddle around his plate.

"He's been ill lately," said his mother. "I'll see to him." He was sent to his room with a servant, while maids cleaned up and the men retired to the study. Olivia came up to see her son later, before he went to sleep.

"Are you going to punish me?" he asked.

She smiled at him, but with no warmth, no tenderness.

"No, dear. I understand you're upset that your little friend met such a sad end. But you have to understand how common these things are among her kind."

"But she didn't do it. I know she didn't!"

"Do you? What do you know? She's only been here a short time. What could you possibly know of her?"

"I know . . ."

He almost said "I know I loved her," but stopped, knew from the sharp cold glint that appeared in his mother's eye it was the very thing she waited to hear, confirmation of unforgivable treachery. She would snatch the words out of Frederic's throat like a wicked witch in the fairy tales Jenny used to tell him, and use them to cut the girl out of his heart. He lied, tried to at least save his memories of Jenny from his mother, even if he hadn't been able to save her.

"I know she was honest."

"Do you now?" His mother smoothed his sheets, pulled them up around his throat. "You know better than I? She was a thief, Frederic, nothing more. Thieves lie until you trust them, then they rob you. Trust your mother."

She kissed his forehead and walked to the open door.

"Jenny didn't do it," Frederic whispered.

Olivia stopped at the bedroom door and closed it, kept her back to him. "What are you saying, then, Frederic? That someone else stole our belongings? That someone collected all those precious objects from our rooms and planted them in hers? Who are you accusing, Frederic? Who would do that, and why? Just to get rid of her? What kind of person would do that, Frederic? What kind?"

Your kind, he wanted to say, but kept silent as he watched her back shake with rage. If he accused her, if Frederic actually said the words, he'd open Pandora's Box. Jenny had told him that story, too. When you let all the bad things out, there was no way to put them back in. He was afraid that if he freed the truth, his mother would kill him for it, the way she'd killed Jenny, without ever laying a hand on her.

"No one. No one would do that," he said.

Frederic saw her relax as she opened the door and stepped out. Olivia turned back to him one last time before she shut him in, silhouetted against light from the hall.

"*Je t'aime, Frederic. Rappelez-vous que.*"

He looked up at her, curled his lips in a good imitation of a smile. "*Oui. Je t'aime trop, ma mere.*" She smiled back and closed the door. He did love her. She was his mother.

But now he feared her, too. Maybe even more.

CHAPTER 23

2:43 P.M.
East Village, 26 December 1986

Christmas was over, but the sidewalks were still almost empty on St. Mark's Place. Lori sipped hot tea inside Dojo's Café, at a window seat with a view of the cold street and craved a cigarette, just one. Surely there was one somewhere in her bag, tucked away like a lost dollar in a zippered pocket, a ripped lining? She fought down the impulse to search. Even if she wasn't pregnant, she still had to quit. Just in case, one day . . .

"God. This is awful," said Steven. "Even by New York standards." He read the *Post* coverage of Nina's death while Lori looked at the *Daily News*. Both papers had covers about Nina's death: "HOOKER, HONCHO, HACKED!" "MURDER IN MIDTOWN!" It was grim. The girl had been disemboweled, her customer's head bashed in. The fact that she'd been found with a minor city official who'd made headlines a few months ago on charges of seducing an underage babysitter made it front-page news.

"I don't know how we can help her brother," said Lori. "The cops are going to have to solve a case this big. Her letter's not going to tell them anything that helps."

"I know. We'll hear him out, let him have the letter, and wish him luck. Uh-oh . . ."

Steven saw Jim first, as a battered matte-black Harley roared to rest at the curb. He didn't know how he knew that the gaunt teenager who rose from it was Jim, but he was sure. Steven was reminded of *The Rime of the Ancient Mariner*, one of many poems his schoolteacher-mom had read him aloud to expand his horizons when he was a kid:

"*Alone, alone, all, all alone. Alone on a wide wide sea! And never a saint took pity on my soul in agony . . .*"

The kid climbed off the bike, loped inside and looked around, saw them when Steven waved. He walked over and held out a rough hand, manners intact despite the shaggy blond hair, worn jeans, biker jacket and boots.

"Steven and Lori? Jim Miller." Jim took Lori's hand when she extended it, glanced around warily, like a man on the run. "Do we have to talk up here?"

"No," answered Lori, looked to Steven for confirmation. "We can move to the back." Jim seemed relieved, disappeared to a rear table before she could say more.

"Paranoid. Great start," said Steven with a sigh. He stood, picked up his cup, and headed after him. Lori picked up her cup and bag as their waitress panicked, tried to direct them. Jim took a table as far from the front of the restaurant as he could find.

They ordered fresh drinks and paused, awkward.

"We were sorry to hear about your sister," said Steven. He folded the newspapers and tucked them under the table on the seat.

"You don't have to hide those. I seen 'em, all over town. The things they say about her . . ." His eyes were sunken, red, the eyes of someone beyond redemption, beyond hope. "You said you got a letter?"

Lori nodded. "It doesn't say much, just that she met a kid named Marlowe when she got here. And that he introduced her to . . ." She hesitated, and looked at Steven as she pulled out the letter. "Maybe you should read it yourself."

Lori handed the letter to Jim. It was handwritten in hot-pink ink on worn Garfield stationery. Tears welled in his eyes and were crushed back as he unfolded his sister's letter and began to read. Lori knew he'd die before he'd cry in front of them.

Deer sirs or Madam

Im writin in anser to yur ad in the voice. I hav a true story of vampirs for yu, of incent girl driv to prostution & unspeekable horrors by

unhumn monster! Ill not reveel His name until we hav a deel ok? tell
me what yull pay Ill give yu proof. it started at the bus stashun when
His boy Marlow picked me up & took me to Him to help me. He is
surely the Devil Hisself, trapped me & my baby I feer there is no escap.
Im in an awful place, a horrble place & so afraid. He made me a hoor,
made me see things lik ise on drugs, i seen starnge horrible. Im scard
for my son, i just want to sav him. Ill meet yu any time or place yu want.
Im very serious & no my story is wurth big money to us both & i meen
BIG! its all in my diary which was sent away. I had to leeve home cause
a bad times but they still love me & will help yu how they can. If I die
theyl send it to yu so yu can get the VAMPIRE who did it but yu must
giv the $ to my baby. Theres lots more i can tell but not till yu tell me
how much, call or write soon I need to heer fast!

Yurs,
Nina Miller

Jim stared down at the letter in silence for a few moments before he
spoke again. "A vampire?"

Lori and Steven looked embarrassed.

"Yeah, well . . . That's why we wanted you to read it," said Steven. "I
know it sounds crazy. We're doing a fiction book about vampires. We put an
ad in a local paper asking for true stories to inspire us. . . . That's why she sent
us the letter."

"We never got to talk to her, so we don't know anything else. Maybe she
had a breakdown, or was on drugs—"

"No! Not Nina," said Jim.

"You said you had her diary? Maybe it explains why she thought her pimp
was a . . ." Lori couldn't keep saying the word.

Jim pulled a book from his jacket pocket, a little girl's diary with a plastic
cover, pink and pretty, worn and abused, like Nina. He held it in his hands
like a precious relic.

"I didn't read it yet. But I will, and I'll look for someone who knew her,
someone who might know who . . . would do something like this."

Lori reached for the diary.

"May I . . ."

"No!" Jim snatched the book away.

"I understand," said Lori. Jim breathed slower, calmed down. "There's something else. I'm sorry to bring it up, but . . . her letter said something about a son?"

"I think about that innocent every waking hour, knowing the bastard who killed her must have it." He withdrew into himself, clutched the diary like a life preserver.

Lori opened her mouth, realized her throat was almost too dry to speak.

"You can keep the letter if you think it'll help. I wish there was more we could do . . ."

"There is," said Jim.

Lori had already opened her purse to pull out money to pay the bill when he answered. Steven sighed, halfway out of his seat, and sat back down.

"I don't know New York. If I find names in her diary, I need help finding them. If you could just . . ."

"The police can do a better job. You should take her diary to them, tell them what you know," said Steven.

"I can't. I can't go to the police."

He put the diary back in his pocket, sat back, arms folded. Case closed.

"Jim . . ." Lori shook her head. "I'm sorry, but we're not detectives, we're not the people to help you."

"But she wrote you! She asked for your help."

"To tell her story. Not avenge her death," said Steven. "I know that sounds cold, but it's true."

"We can take the diary to the police for you," added Lori.

"No. No police."

"Then there's nothing we can do." Steven stood up again. "Lori?"

Jim looked like he was struggling with a decision. As Lori rose from her seat, he jumped up. "Look, she wanted to sell you her story. It's yours if you want it."

Steven and Lori stopped and stared at each other.

"I'll tell you everything you want to know about her; you can see the diary after me, anything you need for your book. Please. Help me. Help me find her killer. This monster smeared a guy's brains down a wall. My sister was gutted like an animal. Whoever did it must have her baby. I have to find him. Any money can go to her son, like she wanted."

Lori saw a light go on in Steven's eyes.

He remembered yesterday as well as she did, a long day spent without any ideas to get the project done quickly and both of them back to their separate lives. Jim was right, dammit. Nina's story could make a good book, a great book. Lori hated herself for even considering it, she really did. But like it or not, this opportunity could turn the whole thing around.

"We have to talk," Steven said to Jim, and pulled Lori out of his earshot. "Shit. What do you think?"

"It's a good story. With the tabloid coverage it's getting, it could turn into a new Black Dahlia case . . . hell, they're still writing books about that."

Lori's brain was already spinning out the outline. Small-town girl leaves home, comes to big city where she's pimped out by a vampire and brutally murdered—God forgive her, she could see the pitch. A glossy picture book of allegorical paintings based on true stories from Nina's own diary, with family photos and childhood memories from her brother? The movie rights dangled almost in reach.

"We can't help track down a killer!" Steven said in a low voice. "Baby, we just ain't that Scooby-Doo!"

"I know, but we can . . . I don't know," said Lori, "find phone numbers, addresses, ask a few questions. Enough to get him talking and see the diary."

She tried to tell herself it wasn't completely self-serving. If they told Nina's story they could do damage control to restore her reputation. They could keep Jim out of trouble, gather as much evidence as they could and persuade him to let them turn it over to the police investigation. Yeah. That's it. Everybody wins. It's all good.

"It's pretty crazy, still," said Steven. "Okay, say we try, what's the worse that happens? We spend a few weeks following leads. Even if it's a waste of time, we get enough to write the book and put his sister's memory to rest. It gets too weird, we bail."

"What about the kid?"

Steven made sure Jim wasn't listening, talked low. "You really think it's alive? Considering what happened to its mother? The killer probably had it for dessert."

Lori didn't answer, afraid he was right.

They went back to the table.

"Okay, we're in," said Lori. "For now. One thing we have to get straight. We can't be accessories to a vigilante crime. If we help you find Nina's killer, you agree we turn him over to the police."

"And we get exclusive rights to the story," added Steven. Lori glared at him. He shrugged back. "So we can keep anyone else from telling more lies."

"Help me, you can have anything you want," said Jim.

"Great." Lori sighed, the tension broken. "We'll meet again after you read the diary and get some names." She waved for the check. Steven looked as they waited, tried not to meet Jim's empty gaze.

Jim was silent, sure he'd done the right thing.

He needed their help; he knew that. New York was a big city. He didn't know it and didn't know anyone in it but them. He'd say whatever he had to say to get their help. After these people helped him find the man who'd killed his sister, no matter what he said to them now, no matter what he agreed to, when they found him, he'd find out what had happened to the baby, and then kill him for what he'd done, no matter what he said now.

Man or monster, he'd kill him.

Kill him dead.

CHAPTER 24

Central Park South, 26 December 1986

We must be going the wrong way. I'd sense them by now if there are as many as you say," said Adam. Perenelle had been true to her word. His car took them from her town house to the Columbus Circle subway station as soon as he arrived. They'd breezed in unseen by token attendants, walked to the end of the station and down cement stairs to the tracks.

Adam regretted it as he ruined his Boccaccio loafers in the filthy tunnel, dry and dusty as an Egyptian tomb. They stayed in the center of the tracks, away from the third rail, kept an ear out for trains, and dodged stray rats.

"We can't sense them. Autochthones are not the same as us. Don't forget that."

"Are you sure this is the tunnel?"

Then thousands of rats surrounded them, where nothing and no one had been a moment before. Adam choked on his words, froze as a carpet of gray fur flowed around their ankles long enough to stop them, then vanished just as quickly. Mushroom-pale figures appeared from the tunnel the rats had disappeared into. They drew nearer. Some were dressed as vagrants, others nude or nearly so in rags. Their bodies were thin, skins almost transparent. They didn't breathe, didn't speak, just stared at Adam and Perenelle in silence. Perenelle bowed to the one closest to her.

"We seek Rahman. Take us to him."

There was no response. Adam almost laughed.

"Take me to your leader? Is that the best you can—"

Perenelle whirled on him, fangs bared. "We wouldn't be here if not for you. Mock me and I leave you to them."

Adam relented. The things looked flimsy, but they were everywhere. He couldn't see well enough in the dimly lit tunnel to tell how much of a threat they posed.

"Rahman. Take us to Rahman."

They seemed to consider her request, or took a moment to translate it. The closest one waved an arm and led them through the crowd, across the tracks to an iron door in the wall. It opened with a rusty creak and the creature slid inside. Perenelle held the door open for Adam to go first.

"It is your path, after all," she said.

He frowned, afraid to anger her again, and entered the narrow stone passageway on the other side.

Hernando slowed as he passed his reflection in the dark window of a closed Forty-second Street subway shop. He adjusted his black beret, tossed strings of colored beads and gold chains hanging from it to one side. Every bead awarded by the KnightHawks for bravery, every chain given in gratitude by chicks he'd saved from muggers.

Kenny caught up, laughed. "Shit, again? Who you gonna meet down here?"

Hernando smirked, posed.

"You never know, man. When you seen as much as I have . . ."

Kenny headed to the stairs. "Right. You been with Angel a year? Gimme a break!"

"KnightHawks, man! Not Angel. I don't work for that starfucker."

"Don't start that again," Kenny said. Hernando breezed past him down the concrete stairs into darkness, thanks to a broken bulb. Kenny sped up, caught Hernando as they emerged back into the light. "Hey. Don't take off like that. Rules have reasons, man."

"Angel's rules. Angel's reasons."

"Safety, asshole. Safety in numbers. Angel says . . ."

"Fuck Angel!" shouted Hernando.

He shot ahead and around a bend. Hernando heard Kenny's sneakers thump down the stairs behind him, but he was long gone before Kenny could catch up.

"Shit, 'Nando . . . Stop fuckin' around, man!"

A train was just pulling out. Kenny's voice faded as Hernando stepped onto a newly deserted platform. He heard a sound from the far end of the station, moved closer to see what it was. There was a cute girl his age alone on the other side. Hernando grinned as an express train roared through the station and cut off his view. Maybe he'd take a walk upstairs, swing over and offer his protection—

A body threw him to the cold concrete floor and rolled him to the edge of the platform. Hernando pulled back a fist and opened his eyes to see Kenny on his chest.

"Stupid fuck! Don't leave like that," yelled Kenny. Hernando threw him off, rolled on top, and pinned him to the ground.

"Fuck you!"

The girl screamed from the other platform.

"You hear that? Cut this shit out!" cursed Hernando. As the train passed, he shoved Kenny away and stared across the tracks to see if the girl was hurt.

"Where is she?" he asked, almost to himself.

"Get the cops!" gasped Kenny as he fumbled to his feet. "You know the drill!"

"Fuck the drill," said Hernando. He rolled from the platform onto the tracks. Gold chains clinked lightly as he landed on his feet. "No way they get here in time." There was a wail from an empty tunnel ahead, then a sound he'd never heard before and hoped never to hear again—a thin, bloodless howl like a starved beast closing on its prey.

"What the hell was that?" Kenny's face fell. Hernando looked at his fear-filled eyes and laughed.

"You such a damn pussy . . ." Hernando stepped across a puddle on the garbage-strewn tracks and kicked a rat out of the way as he made his way over the electrified third rail. He headed for where he'd last seen the girl.

"Get back here!" Kenny shouted in vain. Hernando yelled for Kenny to get the police, then headed down the tunnel.

Hernando wasn't stupid. He knew better than to go in without backup and knew Kenny would call for help. Hernando turned on his flashlight and entered the tunnel.

"Shit!" He almost dropped it. They were right in front of him, still as the grave. Two ragged bums in baggy pants and torn snorkel coats held the girl between them, hoods pulled down over their faces. One covered her mouth with a pale hand. How could he not have noticed the smell, like rotting meat or something dead?

They were only a few feet away, heads down, faces hidden. Why didn't they move? Sweat broke out over his body. That hadn't happened since he was a kid up against his first gun.

But this was different, wasn't it? Just two winos who thought they'd have a party with some bitch going home alone. They weren't the least bit dangerous, matter of fact they seemed familiar . . . Shit! What's wrong with him? Hernando chuckled. It's Joe and Eulogio, two of his homies, fuckin' around! Some joke. The girl must have been in on it all along.

"Hey, man, you had me goin'!" He laughed and stepped forward, extended a hand to slap palms, and felt a cold dry claw take it, pull him closer as the smell came back and Hernando realized he'd made a mistake.

He snapped out of the hallucination, swung his flashlight at the thin white arm that pulled him under the hood toward a mouth filled with yellowed, ivory fangs. The flashlight was heavy-duty, doubled as a club when he needed it, and it did the job when Hernando swung it. The brittle limb snapped off with a sharp crack as the creature recoiled, shrieked like a bat, and let go of the girl to clutch an oozing stump. The other thing released her and pulled its partner to safety. The girl was still in a daze, but pulled out long enough for her eyes to focus on Hernando as he moved closer.

"It's okay, you're safe now. Come on!" He reached out to the girl, leaned in and shone the light in her face. "You okay?"

The girl looked at him and screamed like she saw something awful, the same way he thought he'd seen his friends before. She lunged and clawed at his face. Hernando was caught by surprise, too late to keep her nails away from his eyes as she attacked, blinded him on the left side with pain and blood.

He swung his fists up, fended her off as he fell back. She scrambled over him and ran away as Hernando clutched his face, tried to decide whether or not to save the torn ball of jelly in his hand.

Before he could move, Hernando felt cold hands grasp him, three, then four, six, eight, twelve, as he was lifted and carried away. His captors' minds touched his, eased his pain and soothed him into twilight sleep as they carried him deep into the tunnel, away from the sound of the girl's screams in the distance behind him.

CHAPTER 25

7:46 P.M.
Central Park South, 26 December 1986

Cracked tile walls passed Hernando as he came to, rolled his head to see that they vanished into gloomy, arched ceilings above. Iron talons held him like Krazy Glue, carried him into a deserted station he'd never seen before. There was no light except for a faint glow of gas lamps high on the walls. It didn't matter. He'd find his way out. Somehow.

He gathered his strength and struggled, kicked his way to the ground, and smashed one of the things to its back with a single punch. Hernando looked around, desperate for a weapon, and wished Angel hadn't been so strict about his damn no-gun policy. He raised his fists and strained to see through the blood and sweat that distorted his vision.

"Fuck off!" He stumbled backward into an abandoned pile of rotted wood and tarnished wire. Hernando groped for something heavy enough to use as a weapon, light enough to lift. His hand found a metal rod, rusted, but right. He gripped it firmly and whipped it out in front of him, took out the side of one of their heads with a dry crunch.

His remaining eye was used to the darkness now, so he could see better as he knocked them down. Pasty shapes shuffled toward him in a mass. More pushed forward to take the place of every one he felled.

A light appeared from a side passage, a sputtering torch that cast a sickly yellow glow over the skeletal forms that swarmed the station like roaches.

Hernando stifled a scream as the sea of colorless flesh parted to admit the torchbearer, then almost gasped with relief.

It was a tall black man in floor-length robes, long white hair grown past his shoulders to his waist. He looked almost albino, with semitransparent skin and large golden eyes, barely more human than the things under his command.

"Help me!" Hernando swung the pipe at a tiny monster that stretched out a claw to tease him. "For God's sake, help me!"

The man raised an ashen eyebrow, smiled without mirth.

"God . . . ?" His voice echoed like a knock on the door of an empty tomb as he reached Hernando's side. "No great love of God here, I'm afraid."

Hernando was unable to use his club, unsure if he should, unsure of anything as he sank into the man's icy eyes, twin bottomless pools. He took Hernando's weapon, as gently as a patient parent takes a toy from a child before putting it to bed.

"No need for this . . ."

The pipe hit the ground with a clatter as the man leaned forward and handed the torch to one of his minions. He lowered his head, tenderly took the boy's throat in his teeth, and broke the skin ever so gently. Saliva flowed into the wound, into his victim's blood and brain, enthralled him body and soul to the ageless thing that suckled softly at his jugular.

Hernando didn't protest as the others lifted him from their leader's embrace, carried him to an ornately carved marble well at the center of the station. They bound his ankles with rope and hoisted him up over its mouth. His arms dangled, blood rushed to an already light head.

Their leader gently spun Hernando around to face him as the others shredded his clothes away with knives, razors, nails, tied his arms tightly behind him.

"We are the last of the ancient B'alam, former shamans to the Olmec, now abhorred by all, known only as Autochthones. Once, this land was ours. Darkness and delight in our mysteries are all that remain." Hernando noticed that a light burned below him in the well, a green glow like those chemical necklaces the girls wore at clubs and street fairs.

He squinted down the well as the things around him wet his skin and shaved his head and body, left him raw and red. One pulled herb-filled earth from a pouch covered with drawings, stuffed a handful of it into Hernando's mouth, and carefully stitched his lips together. They sang in soft whispers and carved symbols into his skin with thin daggers, kept him spinning as they finished one row and began another.

By the time the music stopped, blood blocked Hernando's ears. Every sound boomed, hollow, as if under water. He stared at the distant glow below and watched his blood drip toward it. A smell billowed up and caught him by surprise, sweet, spicy, like cinnamon or nutmeg. He twisted his head to see the source.

Nothing he'd ever feared in childhood prepared him for what crept toward him. The well below was filled with a shambling mass that gleamed with uneven green light as it lurched upward, an enormous white Worm so vast that its bulk filled the farthest reaches of the pit that contained it. Its skin was thick with slime, stank of decay. Bones and skulls, undigested bits of old prey, were visible beneath a cloudy surface.

Hernando saw a tubelike mouth rise, smelled spicy breath as it quivered inches from his face. Long, wet tongues lapped out and slid over Hernando's face with a loud slurp, engulfed his skull, then ripped and retracted with their trophy. Tentacles whipped up and took hold of bare flesh, twisted the rest of the body down into the hole as the Autochthones' god slid back to its lair with a satisfied sucking sound.

The Mass was over.

Perenelle watched the enormous white Worm drop back into the well as they approached the station platform. The throng that led them parted to allow their leader to walk through their midst. Taller than any of them, he was pale, with just enough color in his skin to look almost human. His hair was nearly white, his eyes gold. He held a tall wooden staff wrapped with a carved Worm, extended his other hand to greet her.

"As salaam alaikum, Perenelle de Marivaux! It's been too long." His deep voice rolled like thunder over the sea of colorless bodies that surrounded him, their pale eyes blank, unseeing. The Autochthones had abandoned sight centuries ago for other, sharper, senses.

"Alaikum as salaam, Rahman-al-Hazra'ad ibn Aziz," said Perenelle with a bow. "Indeed, it seems forever, my lord." Perenelle felt her heart leap at the sight of him, no matter how different he was from the lover she'd fled so long ago. She'd never expected to be so affected, thought all feelings for him had faded during their decades apart. They'd only slept and woke now, much to her dismay. She raised a hand to meet his.

"I considered seeking you out, many times. But after so long, I feared any contact would bring you only pain." He brushed his lips against the back of her hand, held it softly in his palm like a precious object he was wary of breaking.

"Some pain," she breathed, "is worth the risk."

Adam bit his tongue. This was worse than he'd imagined, like watching his mother on a date. While Perenelle and Rahman engaged in lengthy mutual compliments like some archaic diplomatic ritual, Adam distracted himself by looking around.

Perenelle had said the Sheep Meadow Station was New York's best-kept secret, a cathedral built to house the Autochthones' worm god. She hadn't told him it was exquisite. Adam had roamed America for most of his twenty-year exile from New York, but visited Versailles during a few years spent in Europe. Even the Sun King's gilded excesses paled by comparison. It was as if the architects had been given free rein to design a station worthy of royalty. Time had only dimmed its turn-of-the-century splendor.

Adam stood beneath a tiled mural of the great white Worm rising from the well beside him to engulf a victim that hung overhead, a mosaic of the grotesque sacrifice that had just ended. He inched away, tried to ignore the soft gurgles from deep within the well while Perenelle pled his case.

Perenelle could tell that Rahman only half listened to her.

They'd maintained casual contact over the last few decades, when the Veil had need of the Autochthones. Perenelle knew she'd been his only real visitor in the last hundred years, and could only imagine living alone with the Autochthones for so long. A part of her wondered if he was thinking instead about some chance of reconciliation. It wasn't until she told him about the vampire baby that he paid any real attention.

"You want us to find the child?"

"There has to be some trace, some trail to follow. It must be retrieved before the council finds out and calls a meeting of the Veil."

"You don't negotiate well, Perenelle. Never admit you're desperate before you set a price."

"I face eternal entombment, Rahman. I've known you too long to play games. I'd hoped you felt the same."

He nodded, turned away to think. She knew Rahman had no particular interest in helping Adam, and he'd paid his debt to her many times over in the last fifty years. She could only hope that he still felt some trace of compassion for her.

Rahman turned back to her.

"I'll find the child for you, if you agree to my price."

"Which is?"

"The child."

There was no way she could let him have the baby, knew it would be only for experimentation and that destroying it would be more of a mercy than putting it into Rahman's hands. With or without Nicolas's Book of Abraham, he would find a way to use it to further his research. It would be more than wrong. It would be sinful, monstrous, and the last thing she would ever do.

If she had a choice.

Perenelle stilled her face to cover her feelings and, faced with eternal entombment, did the only thing she could under the circumstances.

She agreed.

"Frederic . . ."

Perenelle called him over by his real name, instead of the one he'd playfully picked for himself when he returned to New York after exile. He turned to see that Rahman had changed, darkened his skin and hair to look more like the Moorish nobleman Perenelle had once loved. She led him to Adam's side with a smile. Adam casually extended a hand like he was at a downtown party. "Rahman. Heard so much."

He ignored Adam's impertinence and his hand, walked past him to sit on a tall mahogany throne in the center of the station, behind the marble well.

"Perenelle has explained all."

Down to business. Adam was almost relieved.

"Can you help me?"

"You must be patient. I was once like you . . ." began Rahman, and made a dismissive gesture that infuriated Adam. All Old Bloods over a hundred insisted on acting as if they were so profound you could never understand them. It always angered him, especially now. He did his best to hide it and said nothing. Objections were useless. Once the speeches started, it was best to bite your tongue and let them have their say.

"We'll recover the abomination you've unleashed. Meanwhile," Rahman took Perenelle's hand, "curb your appetite for destruction. Follow the counsel of this good lady here."

"Her advice brought me to you. I thank you both."

Adam headed toward the rails. This was over as far as he was concerned. It was their job to find the baby now, before it did any damage.

His little problem was over.

CHAPTER 26

8:23 P.M.
Lower East Side, 26 December 1986

Kirk felt like a fool when he found the baby.

He knew something was up. 'Manda had been too quiet since she got home on Christmas, too willing to do anything he asked, all to throw off suspicion. This explained why she'd been acting funny. The dumb bitch had gone and kidnapped someone's kid!

He'd only found it by accident, 'cause he came all the way back to her room to check her stash and cash, make sure she wasn't holding out on him. He'd dug through a closet and there it was, wrapped in blankets, curled up asleep in a corner.

Kirk almost dashed the thing's brains out then and there to teach 'Manda a lesson, but decided to find out where she got it first. Maybe there was ransom in this, or a sale. It was pale, but looked like a healthy white baby boy. Could be a few bucks in that. The baby stirred, but didn't wake when he picked it up and went to look for 'Manda.

This was going to be fun.

'Manda was on the roof with Glenda and the rest of the tribe, watching the sun set over Alphabet City. She stared into one of the fires they'd set in steel drums while she tried to decide which one to take downstairs to Baby's closet tonight. It would be easy. Baby had fed on them all, except for Kirk. She'd led each of them up with Glenda's help after her visit upstairs, snuck them in and out like they were keeping a secret game from Kirk. 'Manda's little blade had been busy. They all belonged to Baby now. None of them could refuse an invitation back to its nest.

The twins were in a corner, still shooting up even though they'd found a better high. Trick's boom box blasted the harsh industrial shit he always listened to over the block. The steady beat and shadows dancing in the ruby sunset made their desolate roof look like a music video on MTV. Treat nodded out after she shot, dropped off to dreamland. Trick turned up the volume, tenderly slipped the spike from his sister's arm, and started preparing his own fix.

Others who'd already shot up drowsed singly and in pairs, curled in dark piles on the roof, nothing but food to 'Manda now, food for her Baby, her new god. She looked away, stared at the cityscape before her, endless blocks of run-down tenements, beyond them glass and steel skyscrapers whose lights blinked off as the city went to sleep. For a moment, she saw it through Baby's eyes, alive with energy, hot with blood, life ready to be drained. She knew Baby was waking up, slowly connecting to them all as it grew in strength with the night.

Something was wrong.

'Manda heard the others stir, moan, as they felt it, too. Something wasn't right. She knew it even before the rusty roof door swung open and Kirk stepped out with Baby in his arms.

There was a time when 'Manda would have been afraid of the look on his face, the broken grin that meant he was going to hurt her bad. He had that look on his face the night he beat in her belly, killed the child in her womb.

It would be different this time. 'Manda smiled back as she walked away from the fire to meet him. The others watched them, silent, poised like a pack of wild dogs scenting a kill.

"Got somethin' here belongs to you," said Kirk.

"Give it to me." 'Manda spoke quietly.

Kirk's grin died.

"Stupid bitch. Don't tell me what to do."

He lifted the baby, held it up to face her as its eyes slowly opened, gazed placidly around it.

"Where'd you get this?"

'Manda stretched out her arms, stepped forward. Kirk whipped the baby back out of reach.

"It's mine. My Baby." She advanced. "Give it to me."

He tossed the baby under one arm, slapped her fingers away. "You don't get shit till I know what's goin' on!"

"Give it to me."

"Fuck you."

He slapped her in the face, full handed, full strength. Her head swung sharply to the side, so hard that he thought her neck would snap. She should have hit the ground like a sack of rocks, but instead, 'Manda turned back to him still smiling. The mark of his hand burned like a brand on her pale cheek.

"Give me Baby."

Kirk hesitated, unsure what to do. Firelight flickered across the roof like lightning.

"No," he said.

Now what? Kirk felt for the gun that he kept tucked under his shirt behind him. He wasn't entirely alone in this.

"Back off. I'm warning you . . ."

"It's mine. Give it to me."

"I'll give it to you." He pulled out the automatic, pointed it at her forehead. The others leaned forward, as if to strike, but held back.

"You tell me what's goin' on here or you're both meat."

'Manda quivered like she needed a fix. She couldn't take her eyes off the baby. It was fucked. The thing stared at her like a hypnotist he'd seen on *Donahue*. She finally met Kirk's eyes.

"Give it. Or else."

"You shittin' me?" Kirk had to laugh.

He dropped his guard a moment too long.

She rushed him, nails extended to claw at his eyes. Kirk fired impulsively, without even thinking. He didn't mean to, it was reflex. He'd already justified it in his head as he pulled the trigger. There was silence when she fell, like the gunshot had broken life's soundtrack. They all froze like wax figures around the scene of the crime.

"I didn't mean it," Kirk began as they closed in on the body.

"She's dead." Trick said it first, accusing. He moved toward Kirk.

"Don't try it," Kirk warned, pointed the gun.

Then the baby cried, like no baby he'd ever heard.

Kirk held the damn thing away from him as a ragged wail broke from its lungs and out its mouth; the lament of a banshee, screeching brakes of a car out of control, a derailing passenger train, a jet about to hit the ground. A roar of death and destruction that bawled from the big bang at Hiroshima down to the last hiss of gas at Auschwitz, from gasoline sparking to life on flaming crosses to the shrieks of burning witches at the stake. The sound dug into Kirk's brain with visions of flesh crawling from his body in layers to leave bloody muscle and bone exposed, burning dry in harsh winter wind. . . .

"No!" Kirk screamed, hurling the baby at the corpse at his feet. He backed away as the thing sat up unharmed by 'Manda's side. It whimpered and tried to suckle her wound, pawed at her like a kitten, but got no response. It raised yellow eyes and glared at Kirk like an enraged panther. Kirk flashed on a nature show he'd seen as a kid, tried to push away the sight of a big cat that stared at a gazelle just like this before it chased it to the ground and shredded its throat.

The baby's scarlet mouth opened, gore-smeared lips struggled to form a word. Kirk stared, nearly frozen as he tried the knob behind him, but the door had jammed when he fell back against it.

"Ma . . ." The baby growled, spoke in a tiny voice thick with blood. "Ma . . ."

"No . . . Please . . ."

Kirk didn't know what else to say, didn't know what was coming, but knew he wouldn't like it. He wished he'd had the sense to pick another building for them to live in, one with an easy escape from the roof. There had to be a way out. There was always a way out.

"Mama . . ."

The word hung in the air like the stench of decay.

The thing gripped 'Manda's ruined T-shirt, tugged, groaned the word again like a prayer.

"Mama!"

Then she woke.

Kirk wailed, screamed like a scared little girl, unashamed. What he saw was impossible, but was really happening, and he knew all the chickens were coming home to roost tonight.

'Manda moaned and rolled, choked up bile and blood as she rose to her feet reborn, pale, graceful, strangely beautiful in the firelight. She raised her hands, rubbed blood between her fingers, licked at them and giggled, laughed aloud as she snatched up the baby and snuggled it to her freshly whole bosom.

"Baby! My Baby . . ." She nuzzled its nose warmly. "You called me mama!"

That's when Kirk gagged, as his guts churned and tried to fight their way out to escape his fate. 'Manda turned. He knew she'd look for him sooner or later and the time was now, as she approached him with that awful bright face, a face that should be dead, had been dead, but beamed at him instead, like a proud parent.

"His first word!" 'Manda cradled Baby on her hip, smoothed back its thin hair. She glanced back at Kirk. "Ain't you proud?"

"Yeah! Yeah, sure . . ." Kirk played along, hoped there was still some way out, one last hustle, one more con.

"Me too." She played with the child, a child Kirk was sure was as much a monster as she was. He should have let her keep the other one. Too late.

Baby made a noise like a cheetah clearing its throat. Kirk tensed, pressed back against the door.

"Hungry? Oh, dear . . ." She looked around. "Anyone seen his bottle?"

They all went into motion, like a nest of giant roaches, swarmed over the roof looking for Baby's damn bottle. Like it needed one.

"Here! Here it is!" Trick found it, hopped over a flaming trash can to fall with it at 'Manda's feet. He lifted it up to her from the ground, like the Holy Grail. She took it with a grateful smile.

"Thank you, Trick. Oh. But it's empty!"

She held it up for all to see. The bottle was scarred clear plastic with a ruined nipple, the tip chewed off in ragged strips.

They sighed, moaned in unison. The thing growled again. 'Manda shook her head, sauntered toward Kirk.

"Poor Baby. So hungry." She was in Kirk's face now, her icy breath laced with death. "What's a mother to do?" The others chuckled, tittered. He could feel their anticipation building.

"What's a poor mother to do?"

Kirk never saw it coming. With one move she uncapped the bottle, slit his throat with a fingernail, and pressed the bottle to the wound to fill.

He gurgled, paralyzed with pain as she rammed her knee into his crotch and jammed him against the door with her elbow. Rusty metal rammed into the soft flesh of his back. When the bottle overflowed, 'Manda stepped away, let Kirk drop to the ground as she screwed the top on and slipped the nipple into Baby's mouth. It sucked greedily while Kirk gripped his throat, felt warm blood spurt through his fingers as he scrabbled for footing, fumbled for the doorknob.

"No, you don't. Not till he's full."

She brought her foot down on his kneecaps, cracked both clean in half, and walked away as Kirk passed out from the pain.

The others stood in stunned silence, Baby's spell broken when 'Manda turned to face them. Treat shrieked. The adrenaline rush cleared the heroin high from her head in an instant. The others panicked, too; surged in a body with her toward the door, for the gun.

"Stop it! Stop, all of you!"

'Manda scooped up Kirk's gun and fired it into the crowd. They gasped, scattered as Trick stumbled, fell, wounded in the leg. He panted, gaped up at her in fear.

"No, 'Manda, please . . ."

"Shut the fuck up!" She pulled the trigger, twice. His body danced on the tarpaper roof as life twitched from him. 'Manda laughed as the others froze, stared. She looked around, the gun dangled loosely in her fingers. "Oh, get over it. Trick."

She spoke his name, invoked his vampire soul.

"Trick."

Nothing happened. The rest of them shuffled, muttered, afraid. She raised the gun as a warning, snickered at them.

'Manda kicked the corpse.

"Get up, you lazy fuck!"

He snapped upright, howled.

"What a fuckin' rush! Man!"

He was on his feet before any of them saw him move. Trick grabbed the gun from 'Manda. She surrendered it willingly.

"Man! You gotta try this!"

He turned to Treat. She backed away.

"No! Trick, honey, please . . ." The bullet tore through her pleading hands to sever an artery in her neck. The second shot took out a lung. She fell dead at his feet, mouth still open to beg.

"Treat! Yo! Up and at 'em, sugar butt!"

One hand grabbed his ankle, the other his thigh. She pulled herself to her feet and threw herself on him, crushed him in her arms, planted a wet kiss on his lips. Her tongue pulled from his mouth, ran across her own bloody lips as she stared into his eyes, shining orbs that reflected the fire in hers.

"Let's play."

They both sniggered. Treat took the gun as the others scattered in panic. She stopped Glenda with a shot to the leg, ripped open her throat with bare hands to feed.

The music was much clearer now, thought 'Manda, as she rocked Baby in her arms. Much better. She followed the techno now, like steps that led her up from the smoky roof into a sky filled with pretty pictures that made her feel nice.

'Manda lapped spilled blood from Baby's cheeks and swooned with bloodlust as the others churned in a chaotic, fire-lit mass. They emptied the gun, then bumped one another off with whatever they could find and called one another back to life, were fed upon, then fed, until they were all killed and brought back, till all gleamed under the moonlight with the dull glow of the newly undead.

Kirk woke in time to witness the end of their party, managed one last scream as they descended to feast and tear him apart. The last to die, the only one who wouldn't come back.

They danced the night away, rocked to the beat of the boom box and ignored shouts from the few living nearby to turn it off. They would deal with them later, when hunger was on them again. The tribe would visit them in their homes and on the streets, in the subways and in their cars. No one would be safe. Their new god was Baby and their new addiction was to life itself.

The night was theirs.

IV

NIGHT

New York City
Saturday, December 26, 1986

The gates of Hell are open night and day;
Smooth the descent, and easy is the way:
But to return, and view the cheerful skies,
In this the task and mighty labor lies.

Virgil's "Aeneid"
Book VI, line 126

CHAPTER 27

Lori balanced her checkbook at Steven's loft while they waited for Jim to show up. It gave her a deluded sense of control over her life to know exactly how little she had to pay her bills, as if knowing the full measure of the hole could tell her how to fill it. As usual, most of her current pay went to old bills, left her ready to run herself back into debt until the next freelance job. It would be nice if they could make some real money with this book, enough to get ahead for once.

"More tea?" asked Steven.

He slouched toward the stove, hadn't said much since she'd arrived. Lori knew he had doubts about playing detective, especially if Jim kept a tight rein on the diary. Maybe her pregnancy still stood between them, until she could bring herself to be honest about how it had ended. Maybe she should stop obsessing. Steven was always lousy morning company before his third cup of tea. Lori wrote it off to that instead of what might be going through his head, and smiled.

Maybe therapy was working.

Lori handed him her empty cup from the couch as he passed. There was something a little too easy about how they shared each other's space, the casual way each anticipated the other's needs. They fit together too well for Lori to spend much time around him. Sometimes it felt like she'd never left. She was afraid that if she stayed too long, one of these days she'd forget she had.

The intercom buzzed, saved Lori from giving him any more thought. Steven went to answer it.

"Heads up, Nancy Drew."

He buzzed Jim in and their first day on the case began.

"I read the diary," said Jim. He held it in his hands, smoothed the worn pink plastic cover with rough fingers like he was trying to stroke some secret from its surface. "She never says who the baby's father is. I'm thinking the man put her on the streets did that, too. She was a virgin when she left."

"I'm sorry." Lori didn't know why she apologized every time they met. None of his misfortunes was her fault, but she always felt guilty when she heard bad New York stories, as if she were personally responsible. This one was the worst ever. "Did you find anything else?"

"The name of the man who put her on the street, made her do things you can't imagine . . ." He opened the book. "Caine. Adam Caine."

"Adam Caine? Not *the* Adam Caine? You're kidding, right?" said Steven. He left the couch and went to a table in his studio on the other side of the loft, flipped through piles of art magazines. "Hell, that was easy."

"You know him?" shouted Lori.

"I wish! He's a rich patron behind a couple of downtown galleries. Kind of a mystery. Moved here from Europe a couple of years ago, started throwing money around downtown."

"How rich?"

"Fuckin' rich," he called back. "Capital F, capital R. No one knows how. Young guy, old money." He pulled out a stack of magazines and brought them back to the couch. "He's everywhere. Here he is at Pace last month. There's something about an opening this week at Phoebus Gallery. He's an investor." Steven tossed an open magazine onto the coffee table while he flipped through another.

Lori picked the magazine up to see a stylish young redhead posed like an escaping teen idol: head turned away from camera, but not quickly enough, hand up to shield his face.

"I remember this guy," said Lori. "Wasn't there some kind of scandal in SoHo last year?"

"Loosely linked to a murder trial. Young artists lured into a sadomasochistic sex ring, promised gallery shows, total art-world casting couch," said Steven, still flipping through pages. "It came out when one family didn't give up after their daughter disappeared, plastered the city with posters and offered a big reward until someone talked."

"That's right," said Lori. "When they arrested the gallery owner and dealer, they claimed the first death was an accident."

"Yeah, but the next two . . ."

Steven poured himself more tea, started to wake up.

"How was Caine involved?"

"The gallery owner killed himself before trial. His note swore Caine had nothing to do with it, but no one believed that." Steven found a photo of Caine between David Bowie and Andy Warhol and laid the magazine on the table. Jim glanced at it, looked again, then picked it up and stared.

"There's still nothing to convince police he's connected to Nina's death," said Steven.

"We can start by going to the opening at Phoebus," said Lori. "It's tonight. Maybe interview him? Slip in a few leading questions and see how he reacts?"

They talked options while Jim stared at the picture of Caine. He was no help. Since seeing the photo, he'd been lost in thought.

He'd seen this face before. It seemed impossible.

Jim couldn't tell them that this man looked like one who'd first appeared in his life fourteen years ago, again seven years later, and hadn't changed since the first time Jim had seen him. He could barely think the words, much less say them out loud.

It was impossible. Either his memory was wrong or his eyes. It couldn't be the same man, but Jim knew it was. He'd seen this face every night in his dreams since Nina left, in a recurring nightmare of his mother's death. . . .

CHAPTER 28

Night was coming and with it came fire.

Young Jim Jr. could see smoke in the distance as he marched along the snow-packed suburban street, counted out his steps, hup, two, three, four, the way his dad had taught him on nature hikes when he was a kid. But he wasn't a kid no more, he was twelve, two, three, four, and almost a man, two, three, four.

And Dad was dead, two, three, four.

Dad, dead, dead, Dad.

Otherwise, he could never have snuck out and gone to Bobby Merritt's to drink beer and flip through dirty magazines Bobby's dad kept hidden in his bottom dresser drawer. Bobby dug them out 'cause he was home alone with his baby sister and the dog. Soppin' up the beer was great all right, but not as great as the girls in those magazines. Man!

Jimmy skidded along a glass-slick patch of refrozen slush. Mom would be yelling tonight, pissed that he snuck out, but all she'd do is tell him he was bad. She'd never find out how bad he'd really been.

The fire was brighter.

He could tell now it was no backyard barbecue gone bad. Somebody's house was going up for sure. Curiosity quickened his pace. His heart pounded faster with his feet. Jim stopped short at the top of the hill, slipped on ice that glazed the road and nearly fell.

The fire at the end of the street was his home. Flames filled the front picture windows; devoured his unopened Christmas presents, his toys, his comics, his plastic models—and his family.

Jim ran into the yard as a shadow shattered the window and flew out of the inferno, rolled to his feet in front of Jim. The flames behind him roared brighter, fed by the evening air. The tall young man with pale skin and dark red hair smiled as he knelt and laid a smoking afghan in the snow at Jim's feet.

"Take good care of your little sister, okay, Jimmy?" The man raised a hand to rumple Jim's hair. "I'll be back for her later." The bright smile never left his lips. He stroked Jim's cheek with the back of his hand.

Jim stared back, lost in the stranger's eyes, one gray, one blue. There was something familiar, like he knew him. Like he'd seen him before. Jim smiled back, uneasy.

"Trust me," the man said and hugged him. "I'll be back for you, too. Promise." He kissed Jim briefly on the lips, mouth cool and dry. He leaped up and vanished into the woods before Jim could protest.

Suddenly, he remembered the last time he'd seen the man.

The night his father killed himself.

Muted horns and silky crooning poured from the house behind him. Frank Sinatra, "The Last Dance," his folks' favorite. Notes spilled from speakers licked by flames, but still intact, like the burning bush they read about in Bible class.

The afghan in front of him stirred. Jim's ten-year-old sister, Nina, woke, opened her eyes, and sat up to see their mother spin into view from behind burning drapes and broken glass.

She laughed and danced, oblivious to the Hell around her as she sidestepped across the floor in her good dress, the dark blue one with the white trim. The one she'd worn when she married their father at city hall. The same one she'd worn to his funeral.

It smoked as her long brown hair floated on hot air, sparked into a golden halo. She spun and smiled up at an unseen partner as her dress ignited, fanned by the dance. On the mantel, dry flowers flared into ash and dust, framed family photos cracked and blackened, wallpaper rippled into flame.

Jim staggered to the window, helpless, kept back by the heat, forced to watch as his mother danced her way to death. In the wavering light, distorted by smoke, he thought he could see her partner, his long-dead dad, whispering into her ear. Dry bone peeked through cracked skin as he whirled around the floor with his wife.

Music distorted as heat took its toll on transistors and wire, plastic and wood. Jim's father vanished with the song, faded as the last notes ran out. His dying widow raised smoking stumps to a charred face, gasped with seared lungs for enough breath to scream her last.

Jim covered his sister's face and wept. His wails rose to meet the sirens of fire trucks and ambulances filled with firemen and paramedics that told him that everything was all right, when Jim knew it would never be all right again, that the redhaired man who killed their mother, their father, destroyed their home, their lives, would be back someday, for Nina and for him.

He waved at them from the edge of the woods, face lit red as their mother's spilled blood by the dying embers of their home, blew them a last kiss as Jim remembered the man's oath . . .

Take good care of your little sister, okay, Jimmy? I'll be back for her later. I'll be back for you, too.

Promise.

CHAPTER 29

Jim was trapped in his past. Afraid that the young man in the magazine photo really was the redhaired man who had been there the night his mother died, the night his father died, and still the same, no matter how impossible it seemed.

Afraid that his sister was right.

Jim wanted to believe that Caine was only a bad man who had forced his sister into prostitution, butchered her, and kidnapped her child. He tried to convince himself that the resemblance to a man seen dimly through the tears of a twelve-year-old was coincidence. It was easier to believe that than to believe something like Caine could exist, much less single out his family and pick them off one by one every seven years.

He was alone, that was all he could be sure of, his father, mother, and sister all killed by the same man—or something less than a man. Not knowing which wouldn't keep Jim from tracking him down and finding his nephew, no matter what Caine turned out to be. He could still die. Anything can die.

Lori touched his arm. Jim realized she'd been trying to get his attention for a while and flushed, embarrassed to be so lost in his grief.

"I'm sorry," she said. "But I think we have a plan. . . ."

CHAPTER 30

7:27 P.M.
East Village, 27 December 1986

The sidewalk outside the Phoebus Gallery was filled to overflowing, downtown artists and graffiti kids there for the connections, art investors for the next big thing, East Village locals for the free wine.

Jim waited across the street in the snow, watched them all from his motorcycle, close enough to see who came and left, far enough away that the redhaired man wouldn't see and recognize him. He didn't get this city, the way people looked, or what they thought was important. The idea of an art gallery made sense, you had to sell art someplace, but while waiting here he'd watched a lot of people come and go, and none of them seemed to be here for the art. They talked to one another, exchanged numbers, did business, but no one seemed to look at anything on the walls, only at one another and themselves. It didn't make much sense to him, any more than it must have made to Nina. He saw Lori and Steven arrive on foot from the direction of the subway.

They looked like they'd had a fight on the way.

"I could have paid for a cab, that's all I'm sayin'," said Steven. Lori had stayed at the loft after Jim left, worked with Steven all day on notes for a new outline for the book. He'd made her wait before they left while he smoked a joint and she'd been on his case ever since. It was like old times.

"That's not the point. The subway was faster and neither of us can throw cash away," said Lori.

They spotted Jim before they entered the gallery.

"Shit," Steven said. "What's he doing here? That wasn't the plan." They hurried across the street to Jim's side. Lori tried to erase the frown from her face and smiled at him with the same sad, sympathetic look she'd given him since they met. She hated it and knew he probably did, too, but couldn't help herself. She'd never dealt well with death.

"Jim," said Lori when they reached him. "What are you doing here? We told you we were going to check him out alone tonight. He could have seen a picture of you at Nina's, we can't take a chance he might recognize you. . . ."

"I know. If I see him, I'll stay out of sight. I just . . . I had to see Caine for myself."

Lori looked unconvinced.

"Okay. Wait here, we'll fill you in when we come out."

"Great," said Steven, and headed across the street. "Let's play." Lori followed him, hurried to keep up, turned one last time to shout to Jim.

"Stay there!"

Jim nodded, waved.

Adam sipped a glass of Beaujolais while he looked over the art, immersed in a sea of life that soothed him like a warm bath. Backing this little gallery had been a good idea after all. He was almost able to delude himself that all was well, that the issue, Nina's issue, was already resolved now that the Autochthones were on the job.

It was the first night he'd actually relaxed since his ordeal began. He'd even left his limo home and taken a cab downtown. Adam preferred not to have his car seen in the area if he was hunting, and he had a taste for blood tonight. He was determined to enjoy himself. One of the artists on display was a pet project of his. Perhaps this was a good night to move him along a bit. He chatted with the same empty faces he always met at these events, smiled without feeling at their jokes and gossip, put his mind to possibilities for later.

Steven glared at huge spray-painted canvases, colorful graffiti art elevated from the streets to the gallery. He'd taken it personally, felt slighted when the art press sang the praises of subway artists at war with the transit cops, and ignored artists who took years to legitimately work their way into galleries.

Artists like him.

He tried to tell himself that it wasn't envy; that his resentment was only because hip-hop had swallowed black culture instead of becoming part of the larger diaspora. Despite his dreads and brown skin, Steven still had to defend his middle-class roots, argue that speaking "proper" English was not the same as talking white or wanting to be white, that even though his dead father was white he was every bit as black as the B-Boys. White people called him black; why couldn't they?

Steven tried not to be bitter, but still felt betrayed when street thugs were paid big money for contained vandalism. He barely made the rent each month after years of learning to use materials, form, and color from teachers, friends, and paintings in museums, books, and slides instead of learning how to steal spray paint. He stared at the graffiti paintings, tried to see what the buying public saw besides facile airbrush effects and neon-bright colors. Whatever it was escaped him. If this was what it took to succeed, he was doomed to failure.

Steven pulled himself up short, stopped his descent into anger and depression. What made him feel so strongly about a show he would have dismissed a week ago? He looked around, and saw he wasn't the only one who felt this way.

The air was strained, still, like the electric calm before a storm. The mood was dread anticipation, reflected in the faces of the people around him. Steven tried to shake it off, but the feeling held him and everyone else hostage, wrapped the room like a shroud. Without acknowledging it, everyone waited for whatever was coming, as if for the opening curtain to a show.

Something big was about to happen.

There was an explosion at the door, strobe flashes, news camera lights, cheers, applause, and shouted greetings. Steven turned to see that it was K-Pro, the star of tonight's group show, making his grand entrance. *The Times* had described his work in the subways as daring, incendiary. The first graffiti art to make the covers of *The New York Times Magazine* and *Artforum*. The Phoebus Gallery had signed him, determined to make him a media sensation, and they were doing a damn good job.

He entered like Caesar surrounded by generals, in a floor-length fur coat and black leather pants. His fingers glittered with rings and diamond-studded gold ornaments. His name was spelled in platinum Old English letters against a thin, bare brown chest. The music went from late Miles Davis to a recent rap hit that kicked its way through the room, a new CD taking the streets by storm with K-Pro cover art.

Steven winced and saw Lori smile, sympathetic. At least she'd cooled down. He hadn't looked forward to an evening of sniping at each other while they played I Spy.

A pretty Puerto Rican girl handed K-Pro a spray can and he painted his subway tag across the ass of her designer jeans. She slipped her tongue into his ear and her number into his hand, then scampered away giggling, thrilled. The artist worked his way through friends and fans to the bar, slapped hands, punched fists, and turned to survey the room while he waited for his drink. Caine slid up behind him and whispered into his ear, pulled him aside.

Lori nudged Steven, pointed him in their direction. No one else noticed anything out of the ordinary, but Steven didn't like the look of it. Caine spoke quietly while K-Pro nodded, frowned, and shook his head. His eyes glazed for a moment, as if his attention had wandered elsewhere, the way a passing cloud briefly dims a full moon's light. Caine left K-Pro's side as quickly as he'd arrived, so fast it was like he'd never been there at all.

"What was that about?" asked Steven as they watched Caine move to the back of the room. Lori didn't have time to answer before there were loud shouts behind them. K-Pro ripped a bloodred Sold tag off the wall next to a massive canvas.

"I told you I ain't selling *shit* to that damn faggot!"

Black-clad gallery owners clustered around him like nuns and spoke in low voices, placated, pleaded. It didn't work.

"Fuckin' cocksucker!"

K-Pro shook his head and advanced on the canvas. He grabbed two champagne glasses from startled bystanders, smashed the bowls together, and slashed at the painting with the broken stems as cameras went off in a hail of strobe flashes.

"He don't get it!" K-Pro shredded the last intact pieces of canvas in a rage and turned to his dealers, a glass stem still in each hand. "No one gets it! None of you fuckers get any of it!"

The owners watched the heavyset buyer as he edged toward the door behind K-Pro with an entourage of West Village S&M leather men, tried to leave before the artist's wrath was turned on him. It was too late.

K-Pro spun around; his eyes sparked.

"You think you own me, bitch? Think you can buy this nigger like a fuckin' slave?" The kid breathed hard, too hard. K-Pro lunged across the room at the buyer, pulled him from the exit, threw him to the ground, and rolled him face-up. He sat on the fat man's chest, slapped his hands away when he raised them to defend himself.

"I'll kill you before I let you buy me, faggot!"

The boy raised the glass spikes over his head, stabbed the buyer in the shoulder with one and missed him with the other when he rolled to the side in pain. K-Pro reared back to try again, but two of the buyer's leather men dragged him off, immobilized K-Pro with short quick punches to the face and body, and threw him to the floor in front of the destroyed painting.

The buyer nodded to the owners on his way out, held a stack of bloody paper napkins to his shoulder as his leather men supported him on all sides.

"Call the cops! I'm pressing charges against that freak!"

K-Pro struggled to his feet as the men left, a battered boxer who wouldn't settle for anything less than a TKO.

"Get the fuck out of here! I'm sick of making art for you assholes! I'm sick of it all! No more art, no more anything!"

Before anyone could even consider what might come next, his fists flew up to his eyes, holding the sharp ends of the glass stems, and jammed them as deeply into the sockets as he could.

There was a collective intake of breath, a brief silent moment when no one moved. Steven flew forward at the same moment everyone else did, the same moment the screams and blood started to flow.

K-Pro fell to his knees, his wail high and thin. Friends and dealers rushed in and grabbed him, lifted him into the air like a martyred saint, carried him shrieking out to the street and into a cab in a blaze of photo strobes and news camera lights. It was over in less time than it takes to describe. Stunned witnesses whispered in disbelief, as if at a funeral for an unexpected death.

Steven was dazed. He'd seen people go off in public, but this was so surreal he couldn't let it go. The image of the artist on his knees in front of the shredded painting, dressed in gold and fur, shattered eyes bleeding, wouldn't leave his head. Like the whole thing had been a bizarre piece of performance art. He waited for the bows, word that it had all been staged for the cameras.

Lori tugged his arm to point him in their target's direction. Caine seemed oblivious to what had just happened, looked enchanted by a small, framed picture in a corner of the gallery.

CHAPTER 31

A thin black frame held a sketch drawn in red and black marker of a baby devil, *Lil' Hot Stuff*, jabbing a cartoon self-portrait of K-Pro in the ass with a pitchfork, a minor piece compared to most of the art present.

Adam thought the execution tame compared to K-Pro's more daring work, but it had a place in their personal history. It had been drawn on a bar napkin the night Adam met K-Pro and considered taking him on. He would help the boy rise in the art world, succeed in what he wanted, until Adam showed him how little it all really meant. That night was tonight. The piece was complete.

"Mr. Caine . . . do you like what you see?"

He turned to see a young woman beside him, delicate, petite, dark hair parted in the middle and pulled back from a pale round face into a bun at the back. Twin curls framed wide temples. Her perfect ivory skin and somber expression gave her an irresistible resemblance to the central figure in one of his favorite paintings, Caravaggio's *Judith Beheading Holofernes*.

It depicts the actual moment of Holofernes's death, Judith's sword halfway through his neck, his life spurting in a violent scarlet stream to his pillow as the girl grips his hair with one hand, her blade with the other. An old woman stands behind her, holds a sack for the head. A deep ruby curtain hangs behind them all, draped in impossible twists, like a tidal wave of blood rising from pitch-black dark. It was Judith's expression he loved most, her serious devotion to duty despite her youth, much like the expression on the face of the girl beside him.

Adam smiled down at her.

"I like what I see very much."

She actually blushed, beautifully, and nodded at the picture.

"I meant the art."

"So did I. You work for the gallery . . . ?"

"Simone. And of course, I know who you are. You're the reason there is a gallery."

"Yes. I think I will take it. I'll make arrangements with the owners later. Let them know."

"I'll wrap it for you."

She removed the picture from the wall.

"It's an underrated piece, really," said Simone. "Minor, but I think in time it will be considered seminal. It's bound to increase in value." In a low voice she added, "Especially after tonight. Tragic."

She took the picture away to wrap it. Adam stared at the silken nape of her neck as she left and pictured what it would be like to take her here and now, in front of the assembled guests. The success of his work with K-Pro had left him hungry for blood. The girl wasn't worth building a full-blown art project around, but as a quick sketch . . .

It wouldn't be hard to make them all forget what they'd seen after they watched, screaming, while he fed, to have his crew come in and clean up all evidence of the mess. But there would be an investigation of K-Pro's "accident," and he was in enough trouble with the Veil already. No use risking more.

Adam finished the wine, drifted in his fantasy of public carnage until Simone came back with the wrapped picture and her phone number. He took them both, with a kiss to her warm fingers and a promise to call, headed for the door with his prizes.

He paused with longing at the pool of blood on the floor in front of the shredded canvas before he walked outside. While Adam waited for a cab he decided to visit K-Pro in the hospital later, after he'd sobered up enough to understand what he'd done, that his art, his career, his life was over.

He'd paint him a picture. That's it. A portrait of his life jailed for assault, blind and unable to work, no Muse to free him of his demons, his fine young body brutalized and sodomized. Then he would take him. When the boy saw just how bad the rest of his life would be, he would beg for an end to it. Yes. That should tie things up nicely.

Adam savored the boy's death to come, warmed as any lover would be at selecting the perfect gift. He waved again for a cab and toyed with a filigree gold cross dangling from his left ear, the pendant he'd taken from Nina's bedside after her death. It was to have been a memento mori of a successful evening's art. Instead it had become a reminder that he still had work to do to save himself from entombment.

Damn! He'd forgotten all about his troubles and here they were back again. It was this thing's fault. He fingered the cross, frowned. Why keep something that caused him only pain, no matter the outcome? Adam slipped the golden cross from his ear, flung it into the gutter. If only he could be rid of the other souvenir of that evening so easily.

A yellow Checker rolled to a stop at his feet and Adam stepped in. Yes. He felt much better now that he'd discarded his little reminder of the past.

Perhaps he'd even stop for a bite on the way home.

Jim saw a flash of gold when Caine pulled something from his ear and threw it down. He almost followed the cab as soon as it pulled away, but something made him walk across the street first to see what Caine had discarded.

As soon as he saw it, he understood that providence had guided his steps. It was a small gold cross, his mother's, put around Nina's neck one night when she couldn't sleep.

The night their mother died.

It was a sign. The only way he could have it was if he had taken it from Nina's body. There was no question anymore, not for him. Caine had killed Nina. As he picked it up Jim felt the same blind fury that used to hit him in the hospital, the reason they'd kept him heavily sedated—until he'd found a way to fool them. The pills they'd fed him were long gone now, and there was nothing to dull his rage.

He forgot about finding his nephew, forgot everything but vengeance. This was the man who had killed his sister, his mother, his father, the man who'd kill Jim one day if he didn't kill him first.

There was no memory of crossing the street again, of climbing back onto his bike or hitting the road to follow the cab. Jim knew only that he had to catch up to the man who had slaughtered his family and wreak some good vengeance on him. He ignored shouts from Steven and Lori behind him, put all his energy into his single-minded purpose.

To find the man ahead and kill him.

Steven had seen Adam leave, ran from the door of the gallery to the street and splashed through puddles of slush in the gutter, but knew he was too late to stop Jim from following him. Steven dodged cabs and cars back to Lori's side as the motorcycle's taillights disappeared into traffic.

"Great," said Steven. "I knew it, dammit, soon as I saw him here. Fuck!" If they were trying to keep Jim from turning this into a vigilante crime, they'd failed miserably. Anything could happen on the street ahead of them.

"Do we follow him?"

"How? Grab a cab?" Steven was ready to call it a night and try to smoke away the nightmare seared into his mind. "Let them fight it out without us."

Lori stared into the distance, as if there were some slim chance she could still spot them, plot their course, or predict their destination. She didn't want to abandon Jim, but he'd already left them.

"He'll call. If he doesn't, then it's over. Okay?" Steven took her hand. "Let me walk you back to Faith's."

Lori didn't know why she hesitated. She wanted to end this, too, wasn't sure anymore why she'd let herself get involved in the first place. The book wasn't that important. Maybe it was a convenient quest when things started getting too hot and heavy with Steven, a distraction to keep them from talking about themselves. She sighed, turned toward Faith's, and started walking.

"Yeah. Take me back to Faith's."

Neither of them could honestly call it her home. She knew it was only a temporary refuge to keep her from slipping back into Steven's bed and life. Faith's was where she had to be, or she'd spend the night with him, let Steven wipe what they'd seen from her head with gentle massage, followed by vigorous lovemaking and quiet cuddling. Except there'd be no real love or passion, just a simulation of what they'd once had. That was what she couldn't bear, to live a lie to salve her pain, a pain that grew with each reunion. He fell into step at her side as she walked away, as if he'd always been there, as if he'd always be there.

Lori didn't know if she loved or hated him for that.

. . .

The Checker cab barreled up First Avenue, wove and bobbed through traffic like every other cab on the street, leaped from clearing to clearing like a panicked gazelle. Adam rocked back and forth, annoyed, closed his eyes, and focused on getting home, on getting good news about the baby.

He heard the motorcycle but didn't open his eyes to look until he noticed that the sound didn't pass his cab, but kept pace. Adam raised heavy eyelids and saw a familiar face on the bike beside him. Exactly who it was eluded him for a moment, then he saw him pull out a gun and he knew.

Nina's brother. The last of his line.

It hadn't occurred to him that the boy would discover what had happened to Nina so soon and somehow find him. A laugh came to Adam's lips until he remembered the gun.

The first bullet shattered the window and hit Adam's shoulder. The cab swerved, darted back and forth as the driver tried to dodge, screamed a prayer in a language Adam didn't recognize. Adam threw up a hand as another bullet went through his palm and into his chest. They wouldn't kill him, but they hurt, and Adam wasn't used to being hurt.

More bullets tore into him. The cab's frantic movement made it impossible for Adam to keep his balance or defend himself. He regretted not taking his car—his driver would know what to do. Adam reached forward, grabbed the strap above the window, and steadied himself enough to smash his fist through the plastic partition between him and the driver.

Adam grabbed the steering wheel and twisted it to the left. The car careened, smacked the bike and threw it off balance. Adam saw Jim's face for a second. Surprise and fear wiped away hate as Adam twisted the wheel again. The bike fell away and lost its rider, who bounced to the side of the street behind them.

Adam released the wheel. The driver grabbed it and slowed the cab. His passenger leaned forward, hissed.

"Keep driving. No hospital. No police. Take me to the address I gave or die." His voice was enough to convince the driver that he spoke the truth.

The cab sped up, carried Adam home to Fifth Avenue and safety.

Upstairs, in the penthouse, Adam was in his king-size bed, wounds cleaned by his butler, already healing after a quick feeding. He kept a circle of the enslaved on call, available anytime for a late meal if he didn't feel like going out. Usually he fed only enough to nourish himself, but tonight he'd lost control, taken his anger at Jim out on the boy who'd been brought in and torn him to pieces.

In reality, it was his life that was coming apart. If he'd been reduced to calling Perenelle for help after so long on his own, he was lost again, unable to control his passions or their consequences. She'd warned him that his first hundred years would be the hardest, that if he could just stay sane for a century he could handle immortality. After fifty-eight years of night he felt the strain. If he didn't find balance, he'd swing from his current dissolution to monasticism, reduce himself to an eternity of self-sacrificing denial like Perenelle.

He opened the folder beside him, labeled "The Miller Family," pulled from his art files by Marlowe. He knew he'd killed the father, mother, and now Nina, but it had started so long ago that he barely remembered how it had all begun. The cleanly handwritten pages brought it all back to him.

He'd met Jim and Nina's father on his way home to Ohio. They had a drink in the airport bar while waiting for connecting flights. The man had been so proud and happy about his little life, his loving family. He'd been raised as an orphan, so had his wife. That they'd found each other and made their own family, a home of their own, was why he was always so happy, no matter how hard life got, even when he had to be on the road away from them.

Adam had wandered the world in exile for seven years, forced from his home and on the road, alone. He'd decided to teach the man a lesson about life. Adam followed him home unseen and spent a few weeks breaking down the man's business, his faith in his marriage, his family. By the time he was done, the man was on the verge of suicide, and Adam had kindly helped him over the edge.

He went back seven years later for his wife; he'd been listening to *The Flying Dutchman* before he met the man, and made the damned sailor's seven-year cycle the theme for his extermination of the Miller family. Six years later, he made sure that orphaned Nina made it to New York in time to be broken in for her seventh anniversary.

Jim was meant to be the last—the only survivor old enough to remember the others. His end was meant to be the most poignant, the most satisfying. Desolate, abandoned, racked by years of the painful memory of the loss of his family, he'd be desperate for death at Adam's hand, to join them . . . but the boy had spoiled all that by attacking him tonight. He'd have to abandon the piece as planned and kill him now.

Adam fell into a near swoon, floated on blood-induced visions as he healed, searched his past for a way through this madness, something to guide him to safety. He dreamed of his years painting in Baltimore, of Perenelle's visits to him in the sanatorium when he was a boy after he lost his mother.

He drifted deeper until he found himself dreaming of his sainted mother, Olivia. The days when he was still young Frederic Hartwell, long before Adam Caine was born . . .

CHAPTER 32

9:29 A.M.
Gramercy Park, 12 December 1918

Grown-ups always got quiet when something was wrong.

They talked in low voices and looked Frederic's way to see if he could hear what they were saying before they finished sentences, the way they did now. The house was especially quiet, like the day his grandmother died. His father was at work, and after Frederic was served breakfast, no one spoke to him, but that wasn't so odd: The servants had stayed distant after what happened to Jenny. It had been years, but they didn't forget, even if by the age of ten he almost had.

Frederic asked one of the maids if someone had died and she paled, shook her head, and hurried away. He went to look for his mother, sure she'd explain what was going on, but couldn't find her anywhere. She wasn't in the greenhouse, the library, or the parlor, her usual haunts. He asked Roberts, the butler, where he could find her.

"Your mother is away, young master."

"Away?"

"There was an emergency. In Philadelphia. She is expected to return shortly." Roberts turned and walked away as if that settled the affair, but Frederic pursued him.

"That can't be! She would have taken me with her! Or told me herself."

"I can only tell you what I have been told to tell you, master Frederic. You cannot see your mother. She is away and will return shortly."

His tone made it clear that this time the matter was over. Frederic was left on his own. He spent most of the day in his room, reading or playing with his toy soldiers, sure that the butler was lying.

Frederic fell asleep on the Persian rug on the floor under the window. He had a nightmare that he was locked back in the closet, but this time there was definitely something inside it with him, something large and hungry, with sharp teeth and claws, like the big bad wolf, only worse. His grandmother was buried deep in its belly, and he could hear her gurgle, call out to him in a thin scared voice, telling him to run away. . . .

He woke to the sound of her voice; that's what he thought at first. It was late afternoon. Sunlight slanted in thick rays through the windows, illuminated dust motes raised by cleaning. Frederic sat up and listened. He heard the sound again, but this time he could tell it came from upstairs.

All the servants were elsewhere, at their duties or out. Frederic saw no sign of them as he left his room and walked out into the hallway. He could hear the woman's voice, singing in French, singing and coughing.

Frederic followed it upstairs, higher in the house than he usually went. There were upper floors, attic rooms he wasn't allowed to play in. That was where the singing came from. He found the stairs and walked up slowly, heard the voice grow louder and more familiar. At the top of the stairs he found the room and looked inside.

A woman lay on a white bed in a wet nightgown with a spray of bloodstains down the front. She writhed on the bed as if possessed by demons. The song came from her in tortured bursts, between coughs. Frederic recognized it as a song his mother had sung to him when he was young. *Au Clair de la Lune.* The only song his mother had ever sung to him. That was when he realized that the tormented soul on the soiled bed was his mother.

"*Maman!*"

He flew to her side, burst into tears as she screamed and rolled away, stared at him with wild eyes. She burned with fever; her skin was wet with sweat. It took her a moment to focus on his face, but when she saw it was Frederic, she gasped with relief.

"My baby! My Frederic!" She grabbed him and pulled him close. "*Sauve-moi!* They want to take me away from my home, my beautiful home!" A sly look crept into her eyes. "And away from you, my precious boy . . . but you are always here for me, *non?*"

"They told me you were gone."

"They lied, *mon enfant*. You must save me from them. Will you save me, *mon petit soldat?*" The boy nodded, eyes wide with panic. She pulled Frederic's ear to her lips, whispered what to do, and pushed him away.

Frederic ran out and down the stairs, went to his father's study and found the little brass key where his mother had told him it was hidden. He found the cabinet she'd told him about, opened the door with the key, and found his father's pistol. Frederic took it, slipped it under his jacket, and went back to the attic without anyone seeing him. He locked the door to his mother's room from the inside, climbed up on the bed, and sat next to her, gun in hand. His mother pushed herself upright as far as she could, coughed blood as she leaned against the headboard.

"You've done well, Frederic. You must protect me, save your poor mother from them."

"Who, Mother? Who are they?"

The question seemed to puzzle her for a moment.

"Why, the men, of course. Who want to take me away."

There was a sound at the door. The doorknob rattled, and voices muttered on the other side, called out his mother's name. She tensed, looked at Frederic in dread. She mouthed, "Save me," too afraid to speak the words aloud.

"*What do you mean, locked! She's too sick to get out of bed!*" There was a scuffle and footsteps retreated, came back in a few moments. A new key went into the lock, knocked the one on the inside out of the keyhole. Olivia began to howl like a banshee as the new key turned.

"No! They come for me! *Sauve-moi! Sauve-moi!*" She clutched Frederic's arm, shrieked louder as the doorknob turned and the door began to swing open. He raised the gun.

"Stay out! You can't have her! I'll shoot!" He caught a glimpse of faces covered by white surgical masks through the crack in the door.

"*She's got the boy in there!*"

"*Doesn't matter. She has to go. Get her!*"

Frederic panicked as the door opened and closed his eyes, squeezed the trigger. The gun fired, flung Frederic back into the bed as a man screamed out.

"*God damn! He's hit me! The little bastard has a gun!*"

Frederic leaped up, ran to slam the door shut again, and locked it. His mother continued to shriek as they yelled in confusion outside, pounded on the door for him to open up so they could take his mother. The men retreated as Olivia's cries rose, louder and louder. Frederic huddled close to her as she embraced him and wailed; men and women outside shouted for him to open the door.

Then his mother stiffened and stopped in midscream. The pounding stopped at the same instant. There was dead silence as Frederic looked up to see his mother's face frozen, eyes wide in fear, lips dry and cracked, mouth stretched wide in a silent scream. She slid to the mattress. Blood dripped from her lips and nose as she went limp and fell over onto her son. Frederic pushed her off, rolled his mother onto her back and shook her, patted her cheeks as he tried to rouse her.

"Mama? *Réveillez-vous, la mere!* Wake up! Wake up!"

She didn't move, lay there like a doll, eyes wide, face still locked in a mask of fright. Frederic pulled her close, kept his father's pistol in his hand, still warm from firing.

"I'll keep you safe, don't worry, Mother. I'll save you. I will . . ."

Frederic lay alone with her for what seemed hours, until he overheard voices outside again. His father was among them, complaining angrily that he had to come home from work to handle this affair. He called out to Frederic.

"Frederic! Open this door. Immediately."

Ordinarily his father's voice alone would have been enough to make Frederic obey, but his mother's last wish still held sway. He faced down his father from behind the locked door, mother by his side, as he never could in his life.

"No! You can't take her! I'll shoot if you try!"

He heard his father mutter to the other men, heard *"influenza," "miracle if he's not already infected . . ."* The words *pistol* and *wounded one already* came soon after. They conferred at length about how to handle the situation, until he heard his father's last words as he walked away.

"Very well, then. We're agreed. If he wants his mother, we'll let him have her. . . ."

By nightfall, Frederic was barely able to stay awake.

He nodded off and snapped awake as he heard a woman's voice call out to him in French from the hall, the way his mother always spoke to him when they didn't want his father to know what they were saying.

"Cherie? Ouvrir la porte, mon petit . . ."

Frederic looked at his mother's body beside him, still silent and unmoving.

Her eyes were still open. He'd tried to close them, without success. He didn't understand how she could be here beside him and talking to him from the hall at the same time, but was so exhausted from standing guard that he couldn't think.

"*Maman?*"

"*Oui, mon petit. C'est moi.* Come, see . . ."

Frederic went to the door and peered through the bullet hole he'd made in it earlier. The hall wasn't dark, as he'd expected. Instead, it seemed filled with heavenly light, from hundreds of candles. In front of the door was a veiled figure in white, wearing one of his mother's long dresses.

"Mother?"

He looked behind him in confusion.

"Yes, Frederic. I am your mother. What is with you is only my earthly body. It was ill, but now I am free."

"Free? You mean . . . dead?"

There was a hesitation. "*Oui. Je suis mort.* I live with the angels now. In heaven, as I taught you."

Frederic paused. He'd read his Bible and gone to Mass. He knew his church service and his Lord's promise of everlasting life, but he hadn't seen his grandmother or any other dead relatives reappear to reassure him that they'd made it there safely.

But this was his mother. She wasn't just anyone.

"Come, *mon petit*. Let me show you. Come meet the angels, so you will know I am safe in a better place . . ."

Frederic looked behind him again.

The body on the bed looked broken, lifeless, not the powerful mother he'd known all his life. The spirit on the other side of the door seemed more alive, more appealing. As exhausted as he was, it was easier to believe her than not. Frederic unlocked the door and opened it.

The light was more beautiful than he could have imagined. The entire hallway was filled with candles, lit like an offering to his mother's passing. The light was almost blinding after the darkness of his mother's attic sick-room. She stood a slight distance away, draped in white from head to toe, and backed up as he stepped into the hall. His father's gun dangled from one hand, his other was on the doorknob, ready to retreat.

"*Venez à moi . . .*"

She held out a hand. He smelled her perfume as a breeze wafted through the narrow hall, carried it to him like an invitation. Frederic relaxed for a moment, trusted in his heavenly vision long enough to move one step forward.

That was enough.

The men in white surgical masks came from both sides, had been flattened out of sight against the wall until he stepped out of the doorway. They grabbed the arm that held the gun, pulled it away and lifted Frederic up, carried him to the stairs as he screamed for his mother.

He reached out as he passed his mother's ghost, snatched her veils away to reveal that she was only a French-speaking servant girl in his mother's perfume and clothes. He howled as the men carried him off, his mother's dead body lifted and carried out behind him.

Frederic wailed continuously through the night, the next day, and the next. His father was not a patient man, and the house, though large, was not big enough for him to sleep through Frederic's grief. The loss of his wife was disruptive enough to his household. After the third day he made a call to a sanatorium on Long Island, recommended by a friend. There would be peace in his house, one way or another. The boy would heal and come home, or not.

It was up to him.

CHAPTER 33

10:16 P.M.
Upper East Side, 27 December 1986

The blood high was wearing off.

Olivia had taught her son many lessons over the years. He'd learned that not all life has the same value, and to put his above all others'. His mother had done her best before the influenza epidemic took her away, laid the foundation for the man he'd become under Perenelle's tutelage.

Adam rolled over, slipped on a sleep mask. His sealed bedroom was secure, but the lights were never off. There wasn't even a switch. If he had to sleep locked in a room during the day, it was never in the dark.

He missed his mothers, of flesh and of blood, even if he'd never admit it to Perenelle; missed the idyllic days when one or the other was there to help him through his mistakes. But he'd relied on them too much. Tonight had been a warning.

Adam had become careless, sloppy, and stupid, qualities his mothers had never tolerated in anyone, least of all their son. He'd stop relying on Perenelle to save him, as even his real mother would tell him to do if she were still here to guide him. He should never have gone to Perenelle or the Autochthones for help. He'd tried to subcontract his responsibilities, instead of handling them himself. Adam was resourceful, smart. There had to be some way he could find the little bastard on his own.

The breach was spreading. If Jim knew that Adam had killed Nina, he might have told others. Adam would find him, kill the boy and his allies, and start his own search for the baby. As the New Year approached, he made a resolution to be the man his mother had wanted him to be, to stand up and save himself. He'd sleep, heal, stop being a child, and take charge of his life again.

He'd just take care of it.

CHAPTER 34

It was a dark cold night.

Juana Melendez sat alone as always inside her chilly apartment on Avenue C, waited for her only friend to arrive. She knew Benita would be here soon, even if she wasn't sure exactly when. Benita's nightly visit was the only thing in her world that Juana was sure of these days. She thought hard about the other scattered pieces of her life she still recalled, tried to put them into some kind of order, until she heard a tap at the window. When she turned she saw a young girl looking in, even though Juana was on the sixth floor and there was no fire escape out there.

The girl outside the window was pretty, like the girls on TV. They were pretty, too, but not like this one. She was prettier than any Juana had ever seen. She had sparkling blond hair, bright as the sun, and pretty teeth, shiny and white. She hung upside down outside the window, and waved to Juana with a smile.

"Hi," said the girl. "Come here."

Her eyes looked funny, but they made Juana feel happy inside as she stared into them. It made her smile. The girl waved again, but Juana wasn't sure she wanted to go closer. Maybe because she'd never seen anyone hang upside down outside a window before. A boy joined the girl, but he wasn't upside down. He looked like the girl, down to his blond hair, shiny teeth, and sparkly eyes.

"Come closer. We won't hurt you."

"Much."

They both laughed and put hands over their mouths. Juana laughed, too, but she didn't like the sharp teeth she saw before they covered them.

"Let us in," said the girl. "We want to play."

Juana shook her head. The children smiled at each other.

"It doesn't want to play with us, Trick."

"Why not, Treat?" The sparkly-eyed boy pressed a hand to the glass. It cracked slowly, with a funny sound like breaking ice. "Why doesn't it want to play?"

"I can't," said Juana. *"Puedo no . . ."* The truth was that she didn't want to play with them. Even if her memory wasn't what it once had been, she knew this wasn't right, that children shouldn't come to her window at night and ask to be let in. Not like this. "You can't come in."

The girl held out her arms.

"Not even for some of this? A nice big bowl of whatever you like most?" Her arms looked empty to Juana at first, but then she saw that they were filled with a big bowl of ice cream and whipped cream, nuts and fresh fruit, the biggest, best sundae she'd ever seen. Benita used to make them, once a year, but had stopped a long time ago. Even then, she'd never made her one like this. It was upside down, too, but didn't fall out of the bowl, just floated there in the girl's arms.

"All you want," said the boy. "Long as you want."

"Let us in?"

Juana stepped closer. It was like a dream come true. She thought about it, and reached to turn the latch the way she'd seen Benita do.

She raised the window and let her hands drift outside. The air was cold, cold as the bowl of ice cream looked. Juana changed her mind, backed away, but too late. She stood near the window, looked out with fear, afraid to get close enough to lock it again. The girl with the sparkly eyes looked at her and smiled. The boy smiled, too. They smiled too much. Juana backed farther away, but they were in the room and next to her before she could say a word to stop them.

"Shhh," said the girl.

"Shhh," said the boy. They stood on either side of her. The boy wore a T-shirt Juana had seen on TV, big letters with a heart.

"I love New York," said Juana. That's what it meant. "I love New York . . ."

"Me too," said the boy and bit her arm.

"It's delicious," said the girl and bit her throat. Juana didn't scream, just stood between them like a big doll, stared straight ahead, silent. Her face paled as they drank from her neck and arm, but she never made a sound. There was a word for them, but she couldn't remember it. Then it came to her.

Vampiros . . .

The boy and girl looked up at her with happy red mouths as they let her go. Juana stood for a moment as they slid away, fell to the floor as they went to the dresser and looked through her drawers.

Juana's eyes stared up at the ceiling, blank like her TV when the last show was over. She felt something cold run through her body like ice water, something more than the *vampiros* thought they left behind. The boy and girl went out the window, looked back and laughed as they left. A bell rang. It was someone at the door.

"*Juana? Are you there?*" The voice came from outside the door in the other room. "*Juana?*"

Juana didn't hear it.

She'd never hear anything again.

Benita stood in the cold dark hallway. The heat was off, and the bulb outside Juana's door was burned out again. It would be weeks before the super replaced it. He'd complain as usual it wasn't his fault, that the owner didn't spend enough to maintain the building. Always the same story. She should just do them all a favor and bring a fresh bulb of her own next time.

She sighed and pulled out the key it had taken over a year to persuade Juana to give her for emergencies. What did that mean at their age? Anything could be life or death. A trip to the corner could be your end these days.

Benita hesitated.

She knew how private Juana was, but she'd talked to her only an hour ago. Even if she was going out, which she never did, she would have said something on the phone. Benita had been ringing the bell for ten minutes. If Juana was in the bathroom, she'd be at the door by now.

Something was wrong. Benita could feel these things. Better to unlock the door and risk Juana's wrath than to leave her inside alone and in trouble. She turned the key, pushed open the door, and peered inside, cautious. The room on the other side was lit, but still in shadows.

"Juana! *Cómo estás?* Are you all right?"

There was a sound from inside, not a sigh, not a scream, just enough for Benita to know that she was right. Something was wrong, very wrong. She'd lived in this city long enough to smell trouble. She backed away. What if it was something she couldn't handle by herself?

She was being silly, an old woman. Who could be inside but her friend, a sick friend at worst? If she had been robbed, the door would have been forced open. There would be someone on the other side trying to keep her out or get away, not this tomblike silence. Benita stepped inside the apartment.

"Juana?"

The air was cold, like the hall, but more. It was thin, as if drained of life. The kind of air you'd find on a high mountain or distant planet. Benita walked inside slowly, looked around for Juana, expected to see her collapsed in a seat or on the floor.

There was no one in the living room. That left her no choice but to check the bedroom. The lights were off, but Benita could see a crumpled shape on the floor. She walked closer, knew she had to walk deeper into the dark room to find a table lamp. Benita inched around the body, reluctant to examine it for life without light.

There was a lamp next to the bed. Benita switched it on and turned around, smelled something sour in the room, like spoiled meat or bad milk. In the dim yellow glow she saw the body on the floor more clearly. Juana was still, not breathing, but when Benita looked closer, she could see movement under her dress. It rippled, shifted as if something alive crawled underneath. Benita heard a deep gurgle from within. She wanted to call out to her friend, but the way she lay there was so strange that for a moment she didn't dare.

She had to leave and call someone. Benita moved toward the door, but it seemed cowardly when her friend was right here in front of her in need of help. It was better to get her to the bed, lay her down, and then call 911. Benita turned from the door, stepped closer to Juana, and extended a hand.

"Juana, *amiga*. It's okay. *Venga* . . . "

Benita touched the woman's shoulder. It was cold. She snatched her hand away as her friend rolled over and slowly struggled to her feet. Benita backed away. The face she saw was dead, despite the fact that Juana walked toward her. The eyes were glassy, the mouth slack and drooling. The face of the walking dead. Benita had heard of such as a girl, crossed herself as she backed away from the thing.

Benita heard the strange sound again, a low wet burble from inside the creature. The last thing she saw was its eyes explode to release a red wave that poured out of every opening, splashed over Benita's face and into her mouth, eyes, ears, and nose, and silenced her forever. Living blood burned through her body like acid, ate what it could to sustain itself, left just enough intact to keep the corpse mobile, able to carry its tainted contents to other victims.

Benita fell to the floor as Juana's corpse released her and turned to the door, trudged blindly to the front door in the other room. A moment later, Benita's corpse dragged itself to its feet and staggered out to join her dead friend on the night streets, followed as if by instinct to spread the undead plague that had consumed them both.

CHAPTER 35

11:29 P.M.
Central Park South, 27 December 1986

The damn book was gone.

Rahman had spent all night in his laboratory rooms behind the Sheep Meadow Station walls, gone through every shelf of scrolls and ancient manuscripts, opened every box, every casket, and there was no sign of it.

The Book of Abraham was gone.

It had to be Perenelle. She was the only one who knew its value, the only one who'd want to keep it from him. It was essential to the Work, and that work was why they had parted not once but twice in a lifetime.

She'd tracked him down at the beginning of this century, not long after he'd moved the Authochthones from caves in the Catskills to the newly built IRT subway line. She was on fire then, eager to avenge the loss of her husband and her mortal life. They'd battled for years, until the New World wore Perenelle down. In time, she understood that Rahman was her last connection to her old life, the only bond she had with anyone who'd known her when she was human. It hadn't taken long for companionship to warm to a kind of love.

He'd persuaded her to lend him the book, discovered six hundred years earlier by her husband, Nicolas. The book had brought them all together in Paris to translate it, with disastrous results. Despite that, Rahman used it to revive the Work. As in Paris, his experiments in New York had succeeded, but not in any way that could help him.

After his last attempt drove Perenelle away, he'd abandoned the Work again, safely concealed the Book of Abraham. There'd been no reason to refer to it, to remind himself of his folly. It was only now, as hope rose again, that he thought to resume his old experiments.

She'd stopped him cold by taking the book.

Rahman locked his laboratory and returned to his throne in the station to receive the latest reports on the baby. The Autochthones reported to Rahman in a soft whistling language it had taken him decades to decipher.

They moved through the city unseen, saw all, but no trace of the child could be found in Hell's Kitchen or nearby Times Square. He sent them back to expand the search. There had to be some sign of the thing, some clue, something the thousands of eyes he had spread across the city would spot.

He would find the child, but not for Perenelle. Rahman's plans for the infant had become far more important than saving Adam's skin, or Perenelle's. It was his last chance to find true immortality, without the restrictions of vampirism, what he'd come here centuries earlier to find. Rahman sat back, sipped from a goblet of fresh blood warm from the night's hunt, brought to his throne by an attendant. His cheeks flushed with heat as the intoxicant lightened his mood.

Rahman had been spoiled by more than a thousand years of life. It was hard for him to believe he'd considered it such a curse, so long ago, when he first became a vampire. . . .

CHAPTER 36

1:33 P.M.
Mauretania, Ifrikya, 6 September 705 A.D.

The sun seared his vision as Rahman stumbled behind Dahia Al-Kahina's horse, wrists bound in front of him, walked for what seemed miles. The desert was even more desolate than the mountains where they'd been hiding for almost a month. Dahia was the leader of a rebellion in the mountains of Ifrikya, the Berber name for North Africa. For five years competing tribes united under her command had successfully fought off the Arabic spread of Islam.

She was tall, dark brown, her hair a wild mane of black and gray dreadlocks, beautiful in an untamed, savage way. Dahia had captured Rahman in battle a week earlier. He was a Muslim scientist and officer, in an army fighting not for gain but for Allah, to spread his worship across an ever-expanding empire.

There'd been resistance, as expected. His legion and others were sent to reclaim land lost to the Byzantines and cut off any chance for them to still the growing Muslim winds of change. What they found instead of organized resistance were scattered pockets of Berber tribesmen, fiercely independent, tough, used to fighting nature and one another to survive.

Dahia had brought them together against a common enemy. While they could be dismissed individually, united they were winning. They appeared from nowhere like animals to take what they needed, disappeared as quickly back into deserts and mountains. Rahman had warned his superiors of the hazards of war with such an enemy. They knew the land, fought from hiding, picked off his troops, and wore them down like water eroding stone. Rahman was ordered to press forward. Their cause was more than just.

It was holy.

His was the most successful of the regiments dispersed. They massacred hundreds, made the tribes pay dearly for their opposition. The tide turned over time. For every one they killed, two came back, until they were slowly overwhelmed. In the end, Rahman had been forced to surrender, his remaining men weak from hunger and thirst. Dahia rode into their midst like a winged avenger on horseback.

"I only need one," she said, looked them over, and pointed to Rahman. "Take him. Kill the rest."

Rahman protested. He'd surrendered only to save his men's lives, but he was beaten unconscious, heard their dying screams as he was carried into the Aurès Mountains to Dahia's headquarters.

He'd been treated with respect, fed and given shelter. He didn't understand why. Dahia spoke with him often as he healed. They exchanged philosophies, politics. At first he thought she wanted military strategies, his nation's plans to defeat them, but she never asked that. Instead they talked about family, honor, their dreams, what they had wanted their lives to be before they'd arrived here, as soldiers on opposite sides of a great war. She spoke to him as an equal, but it was always clear what they really were.

Captor and captive.

Though he was held hostage, time had passed quickly as Dahia's troops came and went, reported to her how the war fared.

Then today their routine had changed.

She sent her sons out on a secret mission and left soon after they did, took Rahman with her into the desert, his arms bound. They didn't stop until they reached the ancient well she called the *Bir al-Attar,* or the Well of Perfume, dark stone covered with ornate hieroglyphs he couldn't recognize or decipher, in an oasis he'd never seen before.

Dahia prayed for three days, to whom or what Rahman didn't know. At the end, a caldron of herbs she'd mixed and simmered as she chanted was poured into a bowl. She drank half and fed him the rest. Rahman hadn't eaten any more than she had in the last three days and, despite himself, drank it down greedily. As he finished, she spoke.

"Like me, you're more than a soldier. I'm a mother, a teacher. You're a scientist, a man of learning. You've said you always wanted more time, Rahman, to explore, to study. I give you all the time you want, though it will not seem a gift at first." She smiled, stood, and stared down into the well.

"The war's over for me. My sons are arranging the terms of a truce now with your Muslim commander, to save the tribes who followed me. But there must still be a price for your people to pay if they don't honor the peace."

She looked up at Rahman, her face filled with something that looked like a kind of love. "I've enjoyed our time together. You're a man of strength and honor. You've taught me much. I hope I've been your teacher as well. In another world, we might have been comrades, even lovers. But in this world, it ends."

Dahia pulled a sharp dagger from her waistband and tossed it to him so he could cut his bonds. Rahman caught the knife just as Dahia leaned forward and threw herself into the well. He leaped to the edge, looked down into darkness. There was no sound when she hit bottom, however deep the well was, only the sounds of the desert. He'd never felt so alone. It was if he'd always stood there by himself. When it was clear that she was gone for good, Rahman cut himself free, took Dahia's horse, and made his escape.

He didn't know what else to do.

Rahman reached the camp of Hassan ibn al-Nu'man, his Muslim commander, before nightfall. He welcomed Rahman and confirmed that he'd worked out the terms of a peace with Dahia's sons. They rested in a tent nearby. The treaty was already on its way back to the capital.

It seemed the war was over.

Then a horseman rode in with report of a distant battle. Islamic troops had located a rebel encampment, and when they entered, a fight had ensued. The rebels had been killed, all the men, women, and even the children, their encampment burned to the ground as an example. The Muslim commander ordered men back to secure what remained and inform the soldiers to cease further fighting, but the damage was done. On the day of the treaty, the empire had brutally crushed one of Dahia's allies.

Rahman developed a fever that night, one that couldn't be quenched. He felt as if he would die, and did, but felt himself wake again before dawn, ravenous. Rahman smelled food all around him, intoxicating, until he realized it was the scent of living blood in the soldiers. Understanding didn't stop him. He lost control of his rational mind to hunger. Blood was all that could slake his bottomless thirst and he took it, swept through the camp as Dahia's avenger, wiped out the entire battalion on his first feeding as they fought back in vain.

When his blood hunger was satisfied, he instinctively hid from the sun as it rose over the sand and understood at last what she'd done, what he'd become. Her death at the Well of Perfume was no suicide, but a sacrifice; to a god so ancient it had no name. He had become a murderous instrument of Dahia's justice.

Her peacekeeper.

CHAPTER 37

11:54 P.M.
Central Park South, 27 December 1986

It took Rahman decades to uncover the names of the gods Dahia had prayed to the night of her death, and longer to find a way to break free of her control. She had invoked an ancient curse to turn him into a vampire if the Moors went back on their treaty, a secret lost to the ages before she uncovered it. Known only to the ancients of Arabia and Africa, it raised a possessing djinn, a demon spirit that manifested itself as an all-consuming hunger.

It transformed a simple human being into a perfect killing machine that fed on human life and blood to live. The Old World's ultimate weapon, it created a nearly invulnerable juggernaut that could even turn the enemy's own dead against them. The transformed vampire not only devoured the living, its victims could be called back from death to continue the carnage.

Like any ultimate weapon, it had one fail-safe; the vampire's only weakness was that creatures that live on energy can't walk in the sun. The raw solar energy overloads their systems into spontaneous combustion. Rahman learned enough to free himself from Dahia's control and give the secret of the curse to his commanders, who concealed it until the Crusades, but not enough to regain his humanity.

For the first century he'd bemoaned his curse, doomed to walk the night to feed like a parasite. When another hundred years had passed, then another, Rahman changed his mind. He'd been a scientist before he was a soldier. As he spent centuries searching for a cure, he began to appreciate the time he had to watch science grow over the ages like a living thing, to carry firsthand experience of innovations to the sons and daughters of the innovators.

He met his beloved mentor, Jabir ibn Hayyan, father of chemistry and its bastard brother, alchemy, in Iran. It was less than a hundred years after his rebirth as a vampire. Rahman had hoped to find a cure for his curse in the new alchemy, what Jabir reverently called "the Work."

"My friend," Jabir told him when they began. "You've lived many lifetimes already. Your existence alone proves the world contains secrets we cannot conceive of, but we will uncover them together. We'll find a way to cure you and for me to live forever!" He laughed. "Is that not a worthy use of what time we have left in this world?"

Jabir died at ninety-four, unable to save himself no matter how long he'd extended his life. Rahman continued their studies, traveled the world looking for the answer to the mystery of immortality, which Jabir had hoped to solve.

It was hundreds of years later in Spain that Rahman met Perenelle's husband, Nicolas. He carried copies of pages from the Book of Abraham, filled with alchemical symbols. Nicolas had bought the book from a merchant fleeing persecution in 1349, when Jews were accused of spreading the black plague and cast out of France. Nicolas came to Spain to find a Talmudic scholar who might be able to decipher what he thought were cabalistic symbols.

He found Rahman instead.

Nicolas had studied the book for decades, obsessed, unable to crack its code. Rahman immediately recognized esoteric ciphers invented by his old master Jabir and offered to help translate the rest of the book. In Paris, they'd succeeded, even though he'd had to force Nicolas to complete the Work.

The medieval quest to turn base metal to gold was the result of greed and mistranslation of secrets concealed in allegory. More important than turning lead to gold, the Philosopher's Stone was an elixir of life, the cure to all illness, and the key to eternal youth—for mortals, but not for Rahman.

The power to cure any ailment and prolong human life made Nicolas and Perenelle rich beyond their dreams, even if the source of their wealth was monstrous to them. They poured their cursed fortune into good works to make up for their sins, built cathedrals, fed the hungry, gave to the poor. In the end, their secret was more than either could bear. They'd betrayed Rahman, tried to destroy him, and he'd fled to look for an answer in America.

When he found the Autochthones, their decline after millennia showed him that even immortality wasn't forever. In the same way humans did, Rahman saw that his life, too, no matter how long, would one day become enfeebled and meaningless. He saw his future in the Autochthones' fate, reduced to mindless repetition of empty rituals. It wasn't until Perenelle tracked him down in New York that he was able to continue the Work where he'd left off in Paris, when she brought him the Book of Abraham.

Now it was gone.

It didn't matter. Without the infant, the book was useless. Once the Autochthones found the child, he'd find Perenelle and retrieve the book. No matter what she'd agreed to, she wouldn't want to surrender it, knowing his plans. But he knew how to get what he wanted from her.

She dared not refuse him.

CHAPTER 38

It was not a good night.

The door buzzer had dragged Steven out of bed an hour ago, and he'd gone downstairs to find Jim outside, nearly unconscious. After Steven helped him up the stairs and called Lori, he watched over Jim the way an asylum orderly watches a potentially dangerous inmate.

He'd seen people crash and burn before, but Jim was way past that. He rocked in a fetal ball on the couch, so far gone that Steven was surprised he'd managed to find his way across the Manhattan Bridge back to the loft, amazed his smashed bike had gotten him here.

Steven stared at Jim with a grim sense of déjà vu. His late mother had had long periods when she'd sink into terminal depressions that even drugs couldn't rouse her from. He'd find her in the dark, weeping quietly on the couch when he got home from grade school. Steven spent more of his childhood than he cared to remember by her side, trying to get her to eat, listening to a drunken litany of the losses of her life, starting with his father. Reasons that finally piled too high to climb, until she faded away, just let go of life one morning, too afraid to continue.

His legacy.

The buzzer told him Lori was here.

"Come on up," he said to the intercom.

When Lori got upstairs, she wasn't sure what to do either.

"We should call 911."

Jim almost flew off the couch. "No doctors! No . . ." Steven calmed him down.

"Like I didn't think of that?" he said to Lori.

"Did he tell you what happened?"

"I'm not sure he can."

"Faith gave me sleeping pills, Valium, you name it. She has entirely too much of this shit, if you ask me." Lori pulled out bottles, skimmed labels. "I say we get him to sleep and talk to him when he wakes up. Give me some wine or something to wash it down with."

"I thought you weren't supposed to take those with alcohol." He rummaged for a tumbler, filled it halfway with red wine.

"My mom called it more of a serving suggestion."

When the pain pills weren't enough to stop the cancer knives from twisting in her throat. Lori frowned, looked at the bottles in her hand, and remembered how her mom had spent her last days propped up on pillows, skin pale and hair thin from chemotherapy. Music played in the background, old jazz, swing, Dixie, blues. Mom always joked about dumping the law and becoming a cabaret singer. She'd have made a damn good one.

"You all right?"

Steven handed Lori the glass, brought her back to the present. It didn't look any better than the past.

"Yeah. Let's see if we can get him to take these." She popped the top off a container, spilled out pills. "We should probably keep an eye on him."

"I'm going to work in the studio. I'll watch him, and wake you if I crash."

Jim swallowed the pills after some argument, finished off the wine, and let them stretch him out on the couch with a blanket over him. He fell asleep almost immediately. Lori went to Steven's bed while he went to work in his studio, as they had so many nights before.

CHAPTER 39

1:47 A.M.

Fort Greene, 28 December 1986

Steven set a fresh canvas on his easel, flipped through his cassettes, and found a live tape of Thelonious Monk to play while he worked, kept the volume low. The opening notes of "'Round Midnight" filled the studio, lifted Steven's mood as he laid out his palette and paints and selected brushes. This was how he liked to work, late at night, alone and undisturbed while the world was asleep. It invigorated him, as if his work fed off his neighbors' dreams while they slept. Painting was more than his art. It was Steven's best therapy. The only thing that saved him from the same void that had engulfed his mother.

He stroked a stick of graphite across the canvas as the music picked up pace, not sure where he was going with his thoughts or the picture. All Steven knew was that if he could lose himself in a new painting, he could still the sinking feeling in the pit of his stomach, and push down the panic he felt rising from the depths where he kept it buried.

When he'd first expressed an interest in art, his supportive single mom took him to the main branch of the local library in Queens and checked out books of famous paintings to encourage him. It was in one of them that he saw a picture that terrified him, then became his inspiration, made him want to paint.

It was Francis Bacon's study of Pope Innocent X, modeled after the Velázquez portrait. Awful, alien, it scared the hell out of him at first. It was a painting of a man in a throne, dressed in papal robes, surrounded by an electric-yellow fence. His face was obscured in a shriek, features scraped into oblivion. All that was left were pain and fear, as if all the majesty of the Vatican had been torn away to show the agony of the church's birth, or maybe its death.

Steven had almost screamed when he saw it, slapped his young hands over it and made his mother turn the page. But later, after she went to bed with a nightcap, he went back to the book, stared at the picture, returned to it again and again for the next week, until he'd memorized every color, every brush-stroke. He made his mother find him a copy to keep after they returned the book.

She didn't understand how he could love such an ugly thing, but it wasn't ugly to him after he'd gotten over his initial shock. For the first time he'd got-ten a glimpse of how his mother saw the world when she slid into her bad days, understood the desperation, the fear and emptiness. It was all there in color, lines, and paint, and he wanted to do the same, to show people what was inside him in a way words never could.

He was only ten then. His father was in the army. Steven grew up moving from base to base until he was six, when his dad was sent to Vietnam and came back in a coffin. His mom moved to her parents' home in Queens, un-til her mother died and left them the house.

Steven was sheltered from the harsher sides of life in South Jamaica. Where others saw only corner-boy drug dealers and winos, hookers, ruined houses and poverty, his mom kept their home tidy, made sure Steven went to the library and his classes, taught him about the world beyond their block, wonders she wanted her son to see even if she never would.

She'd poured any dreams she had left for the future into him as all hope was drained from her after his father's death. When she was on manic highs she gave him a vision of something beyond himself, took him to museums, concerts, long trips on the subway into Manhattan to show him that he could go anywhere, be anyone.

Seeing Jim collapsed on the couch, unable to speak, brought back the other side of Steven's life with his mother, like the snowstorm that gathered outside, like the despair he fought back every day, terrified he'd end up like her, lost, hopeless, empty.

Drained of all life.

That was what he'd recognized in the painting, the faceless terror that possessed his mother on her bad days, crippling fear that kept her home from work, moaning on the couch while Steven rubbed her feet, brought her soup and tea, played soft music to calm her, even if none of it worked.

He was too young then to know that her pain was nothing he could solve. The problem was deep inside, nothing her son could reach to fix, no matter how hard he tried. Not that it kept him from trying, even years after he understood that nothing he could do would ever make a difference in her.

That was what had made him react the way he had when Lori told him she was pregnant, a childhood caring for his mother instead of her caring for him. The fear that the flaw in her was in him, and would be passed on like a ticking time bomb to his seed. The fear of doing to his child what his mother had done to him, inflicting the same nightmare on a helpless child, with as little control.

The song ended and another began as Steven darted in and out, stroked the canvas with the lead as he watched vague shapes grow in front of him, abstract at first, then taking on a rough form. At some point he put aside the graphite, picked up a brush, and ran a broad stroke of pigment down one side of what he'd drawn, swirled the brush up and down again on the other, started to put in patches of dark color, massaged them into rough shadows.

He'd been with Lori for more than two years, explained as much of his past to her as she'd explained to him. Despite the race difference, their damaged childhoods had been a bond between them, made them think each could handle the other's baggage after years of powerlifting their own. But the details, the nuances of his nightmare and the depth of the damage—he'd kept that covered up with stupid macho bravado.

When he'd tried to explain to Lori that it wasn't her child he didn't want to have, but his, she'd been too burdened by her own baggage to carry any more. They'd fought, stopped listening, and somewhere along the way had just stupidly driven each other away.

Vermillion, Viridian, Gold Ochre, and Burnt Umber . . . poetic names of colors ran through his head like the words of a spell as he dripped his brush into multicolored daubs of paint arranged on his palette. Oxide of Chromium. Cobalt Green. Cadmium Red . . .

It was clear that Lori had ended the pregnancy after their fight. He'd gotten what he wanted, or what he thought he wanted. When he saw on Christmas that she wasn't pregnant, and realized she'd aborted without telling him, it hit harder than he'd expected. Somewhere along the way, despite certainty that fatherhood wasn't in his future, a part of him had opened to the idea and then died with the embryo, some small desire he'd never even known was there.

Steven moved back and forth as he painted, added brighter colors, darker, changed brushes as he fell into a regular rhythm. An old girlfriend once told him he looked like a dancer when he painted, that he moved better in his studio than she'd ever seen him move on a club floor.

It took Lori to see it for what it was—she said he looked like a boxer in the ring, moved in with quick hard jabs and back to a safe distance to see the damage. As soon as she said it he knew she was right, that he was always in combat while he worked, that for him the stakes with every painting were as high as a prizefight.

The bout was only a few hours long this time, carried him through what remained of the night into dawn, to the safety of early sunlight. As gray day crept into the front windows Steven stepped back from what he'd been working on, cleaned his brushes as he tried to see the picture for what it was, what it told him.

It was abstract, a bloody bruise of a painting, but he could see enough form in it to understand what it represented. The layers of paint were laid on thick, scraped down to the canvas in spots with a palette knife to see pigment below. It was a layered, textured, tortured open wound, torn and raw, filled with tumors and pus, nothing that would heal easily or anytime soon. His art had done its job again.

It was exactly how he felt, exactly where they were, for all the world to see.

CHAPTER 40

8:37 A.M.
Fort Greene, 28 December 1986

Dawn came slowly, obscured by heavy clouds.

Jim woke on Steven's couch, under a blanket. It took him a few minutes to remember where he was. Then he remembered the night before and wished he could retreat into the deep, dreamless sleep he'd been buried in, far from his past and his present.

Jim tried to remember his life before Caine. He must have played with friends, gone to school, read comics, watched movies, laughed, cried, and misbehaved, done all the things kids are supposed to do. His parents would have loved him, loved his sister, and no matter what his dad said in his last note, they were happy, dammit.

Jim wanted to play the game he used to play with Nina when they were kids. Just keep his eyes closed and pretend he was only visiting friends. His family would be there soon to pick him up. Everything was really fine and the bad stuff was only a bad dream. He stayed on the couch, eyes closed, pictured what this morning would be if there had never been an Adam Caine.

His family would still be in Ohio. His dad would still be working on the road, selling parts, coming home after weeks away with presents from the places he'd been while he was away. His mom would still be head of the block association, still having "the girls" over for drinks and cards once a week, organizing cake sales and raffles for the church, and working part-time at the mall.

Nina would be in the drama club, or a cheerleader, maybe just starting to date, probably some guy on the basketball team. Jim would have been their star player until he graduated this spring and headed for college in the fall. He might even have come here to New York, met Steven and Lori at some downtown bar some night after class and become friends.

He'd have just ended his first semester, been back at home for the holidays, telling them all about his adventures in the big city, his new life. . . . Except it wasn't any of that. It was all death, blood, and tears.

Because of Caine.

Lori saw that he was up and brought him a cup of tea. When he was awake enough, they had breakfast while he told them what had happened. As he talked, Jim could tell they didn't believe him. When he said he shot Caine point-blank more than once and he didn't even bleed, Steven and Lori gave each other a look that Jim knew well. It was the same look the doctors who had locked him up after Nina disappeared used when he told them about the redhaired man. The look meant they didn't believe him. Worse, that what he knew was true, knew was real, they thought was delusion.

He knew now that the thing that had been stalking his family for over a decade wasn't a man but something that survived bullets, something that knew him, had known him for years, and wanted him dead. The terrors of his youth weren't accidents but deliberate acts of cruelty by the redhaired man of his childhood, who had killed his parents, killed Nina, would kill him and who knew how many more.

Jim tried to make Steven and Lori understand, but there was no comfort here, no belief or help. They couldn't bring themselves to believe what Jim saw any more than he could at first. Jim didn't know what Caine was, but he wasn't human. No ordinary man could survive what he had, but still they argued, tried to break down his story.

It was hopeless.

"You said there was no blood. Maybe he wore a bulletproof vest." Lori tried her best to pull Jim back to a reality they could all agree on, but he stubbornly refused to let go of any part of his story.

"Or you missed him. That's the only other explanation." Steven paced, made more tea, anything to keep himself grounded in the now, so he wouldn't fall under Jim's psychotic spell. It was too seductive, too easy to believe in bogeymen, that the cause of all our ills was out of our hands. Steven was sure that after everything that had happened to him, Jim felt better being stalked by something supernatural than believing his life sucked big-time.

"I didn't miss."

"You know how it sounds," said Lori, laid a hand on Jim's. "You saw something. It just can't be that."

"I know what I saw. We have to stop him."

"You make us accessories to attempted murder, and now you want us to help you finish the job?" Steven jumped in.

"If you don't help me, I'll do it myself."

"How? Wooden stakes?"

Lori glared Steven into silence. "Jim, we understand what you've been through, but you asked us to help find your sister's killer, not avenge her death. We have to call the cops, tell them what we know, and let them handle it."

"They let him get away before. You said so. They don't know what he is."

"Tell us, Jim." Steven leaned in close enough to see that Jim's pupils were wildly dilated, with fear or speed, he couldn't tell which. "What is he?"

"You know what he is." Jim stood when they didn't respond. "Don't help me. I'll get him myself."

"Good idea," Steven said.

"If I'm right, no one's safe," said Jim.

"Do what you need to do."

Jim reached for the gun. Steven pulled it away.

"The gun stays here."

Jim considered it for a moment too long, but walked away as Steven held open the door. Lori didn't know what to say. She let him leave, unsure, as Steven locked the door behind him.

"You think we did the right thing?" she asked as Steven flopped down on the couch next to her.

"There is no right thing here. He's stuck in a hole he's been digging for a while."

"He seemed so sure."

"So were the Son of Sam and the kids at Lourdes. We made a mistake getting involved in the first place. We should call the cops, turn in his gun, and tell them that nut is out there."

"He's not a nut."

"That's right. Romanticize him. He's not a nut. He's a tortured hero on a motorcycle. He's James Dean. Whatever he is, he's dangerous."

"More dangerous than Caine?"

"We're lucky he didn't shoot us."

"At least it's over."

Lori said the words to end the argument, but she knew that whatever they'd gotten into wasn't over. Not yet.

CHAPTER 41

10:52 A.M.
Lower Manhattan, 28 December 1986

The sky was still gray.

Light snow drifted down as Jim made his way across the Brooklyn Bridge on his battered motorcycle, avoided slippery patches of black ice on the frozen asphalt. The bike had taken a beating when Caine ran him off the road, but still ran well enough to get him back to the Bowery and his rented room, where he could figure out what to do next. Now that he was alone again.

He couldn't blame them. If anyone told him what he'd just told them, he'd laugh them out the door. That was before. Jim knew better now, even if he couldn't convince anyone else. As he got to the end of the bridge and downtown Manhattan rushed up to meet him, he saw an angry crowd ahead.

He came off the bridge into a mob of mostly black and Hispanic men and women that filled the street behind City Hall. Chanting demonstrators waved handmade signs, spilled off the sidewalk into traffic coming off the bridge.

Jim slowed down with cars that made their way through the crowd. He saw a chubby black man with a mustache at the head of the crowd, wearing gold chains and a bright jogging suit. The man stood under the soaring pillars and arches of an official building identified by words carved into stone overhead as One Centre Street, shouted into the microphone of a portable PA system like a preacher leading a revival meeting.

He ended his speech with a raised fist as the crowd applauded and broke into a chant, shouted, "No justice, no peace, no justice, no peace . . ."

The man held out a hand to an athletic young Latino in a black T-shirt and beret behind him. "Please join me in welcoming the man who knew Hernando best . . . his friend, his leader, Angel Rivera, founder of the KnightHawks!"

A smiling middle-aged black woman handed Jim a sheet of paper as voices around him chanted "Justice, justice . . ." He read it as the new speaker took the microphone. "WE'RE HERE TO HELP YOU," the flyer said in big black letters, and in smaller print underneath, "BE HERE TO HELP US." It advertised a fund-raiser the next night at a club called Palladium for the KnightHawks, a citizens' subway patrol. He stuffed the sheet into his pocket as Rivera began to speak.

"Thank you, Reverend!" There was a round of cheers and applause as the chubby black man waved to the crowd and stepped down. "First, I want to thank everyone for coming out today. You could all be home safe and warm in your beds this morning, but we're all here because Hernando will never be safe or home again. . . ." There was a roar from the crowd, as much a cry of pain as agreement.

"Hernando disappeared in the subway two days ago, after saving the life of Rosie Perelli. We may never know who dragged her down to the tracks, or why. What we do know is that Hernando never came back."

Sheryl Grace stood discreetly behind Angel, lowered her "don't look at me, I'm a movie star" sunglasses, worn in spite of overcast skies, to get a better look at him as he spoke. Heads and cameras turned in her direction, so she slipped her shades back up and raised the collar of her ankle-length down coat to keep the attention on him.

"Hernando didn't just disappear. He was sacrificed. We all know by who . . ." Angel paused, gave reporters and the huddled crowd of demonstrators time to think. *That's it*, thought Sheryl. *Make them wait. Make them want it.* Angel's dark eyes glared, caught individual faces in the crowd. A row of KnightHawks in matching snorkel coats and black berets stood at attention behind him.

"The mayor! Koch sacrificed him! To profit, to greed!" Angel shouted. His audience roared in agreement, just as Sheryl knew they would. The TV cameras were on him like hungry pit bulls. Angel let the commotion die down. When it was quiet, he spoke again. "This fuckin' administration, the same one that tells us to wait for the system to work, while they give tax breaks to corporations and raise our taxes. Wait for justice while they sell out our homes to developers! Wait!" Spit flew from his lips with the word, delivered like a curse.

"Okay. Hernando didn't follow regulations. He had no business on the tracks. . . ." There were groans, mutters. Angel held up a hand to silence them. "They say rules are to protect us. Right!" They laughed as he raised his middle finger to show them what he thought of the rules. Sheryl sighed and frowned behind her glasses. Another sound bite on the six o'clock news gone.

"The fact is, Hernando disappeared doing his job. The job the city's supposed to do. Protecting the people. But there was no one there to protect Hernando. Rosie Perelli is alive today, because of Hernando! Now he's gone! Who protected him? All we get are excuses about manpower, the size of the subway, how no one has the time to look for one lost hero!" He spread his arms upward, clenched his hands into fists as the people, his people, roared their rage to him.

"Whoever took Hernando knew the cops would do nothing to stop them. Did they wait? How long do we have to wait?" A chant began from the back of the crowd, the same one that had started when Angel first appeared. "Justice, justice, justice . . ." Sheryl smiled. She could never get him to admit that he was behind it. It had become his slogan, his rallying cry, his nickname, ever since she'd suggested the headline to a *New York Magazine* editor at a party in the Hamptons.

Angel Rivera. Angel of Justice.

"How long do we wait? How long?"

He left any threat implied; let his look carry the moment, stared out at his people, cold and shivering in the snow, but still his. Angel jumped off the makeshift platform to stand beside an old woman holding a child.

"This is who we're fighting for," ended Angel, pulled them close as the news cameras closed in, practically dry humped his leg. "This is who Hernando wanted to protect." His speech ended to cheers and applause. Sheryl watched him shake hands with his followers—no . . . his fans. She could tell he was still high from the crowd, the cameras. The power . . .

Yeah. That's right. Power, baby. Sheryl smiled as their eyes met. He knew it now for sure. She slipped up beside him as reporters pressed forward and asked questions about her involvement with the KnightHawks' cause and Angel.

"As a native New Yorker who's watched this city sicken over the years, I welcome any attempt to make the streets and subways safe again. . . ." She pulled off her shades, gave them the sound bite they wanted, what they really came out in this weather to get. The ten-second Star Fuck—Sheryl Grace, Tony, Oscar, and Golden Globe winner, sex symbol, superstar.

The cameras lingered on her flawless features, radiant, natural, thanks to a thousand-dollar hour spent at six this morning with her makeup artist. After evasive answers about their relationship, she herded Angel through the press and paparazzi to a limo.

"Sorry about the car," she whispered to him. "I specifically asked for a sedan." The driver closed the door, pulled out into traffic, while Sheryl, safely behind tinted glass, reached for her purse and dug around inside. Angel slid a hand up her leg.

"Bad boy," she sighed, and pulled a cigarette from her bag. Angel yanked his hand away, pouted like a scolded child. She laughed and pulled his hand back to her thigh. "Not that!" She pulled him close and kissed him, whispered into his ear, "Sound bites, baby. TV can't air 'fuckin' this' and 'fuckin' that' on the fuckin' news, much less the finger."

"You said I should talk natural."

She smiled, a look worth a million, and lit her cigarette. "Say what you want, just watch how you say it. . . . It's not easy being a public figure, baby. That's all I'm trying to teach you."

Angel's hands went back to work under her skirt, his rough fingers still cool and damp from outdoors. She sucked in smoke with pleasure, exhaled slowly. "I can't even smoke in public anymore. It's not hypocrisy, it's image making. Thinking what people might think."

"Like whether or not we're fuckin' each other?" His breath was warm wind in her ear, his fingertips surprisingly gentle.

"Exactly. People believe what they want to believe. But you can shape it, spin it. It doesn't matter if we are or not. All that matters is that we can use their interest to promote your cause without ever giving them an answer. . . ." His hand was warming up, quickly. Very quickly.

"Okay, professor, whatever you say . . . Hey!" He glanced up at the rearview mirror, licked his lips as he looked back down for another glimpse at what she'd lifted her skirt to reveal. "Not in front of the driver."

"You're learning." Sheryl smirked and tapped on the front glass. "Home, please."

Class was over. Time for recess.

CHAPTER 42

12:57 P.M.
Central Park South, 28 December 1986

They wrestled on Sheryl's bed at the Plaza Hotel, bodies wet with sweat, limbs twisted together as they came, shouting each other's name. Angel gasped, panted as she rolled off him, scratched his sweaty belly, and tried not to fall asleep. He had to get home soon or hear another lecture from his girl.

Sheryl smiled as she stood up and pushed damp hair out of her face, wandered naked to the shower singing a song from a Broadway show she'd just ended. There were a lot of people who'd pay plenty for a private concert from her, a hell of a lot more for her performance before the shower. Angel grinned despite himself. He'd just fucked a movie star! It's not like that was why he'd started the KnightHawks, but he wasn't going to fight it.

She wasn't just some rich bitch slumming around, like his girl said. Sheryl understood his cause. Sonia was just mad, jealous. What did she think, that he'd leave her for this lady, because she was rich, beautiful, and famous?

Okay, he could see why she'd worry.

He lit one of Sheryl's cigarettes, cursed. Being up here was stupid. Word would be on the streets before he was, even if it didn't make the papers. His girl would be pissed and he felt bad about that because in his heart he knew that Sheryl really was only in it for the thrill. But she got the KnightHawks noticed, got them press coverage. It didn't mean anything.

His girl would understand.

Sheryl came out of the bathroom in a towel, still damp. She leaned over as she dropped it from her perfect body, gave him a long kiss before she pulled a robe from the back of a chair and slipped it on. She sat at the mirror, brushed long auburn hair.

"What's wrong?" She looked at his reflection. Angel hadn't realized he was frowning, but then saw himself in the mirror.

"The rev. He called me Hernando's friend." He put out the cigarette, reached for his pants, and put them on.

"Yeah?"

"Called me his leader and his friend. Hernando hated me. Thought I was a sellout, a liar, that all I cared about was money and fame. All this . . ." Angel stood, pulled on his shirt.

"You don't believe that."

"Don't I?"

"You wouldn't be here if you did. Success breeds envy, baby. Let it go."

Angel stood behind Sheryl, his hands on her shoulders, still damp, still warm. He wanted to believe her, but things were moving too fast, changing in ways he didn't like.

Maybe he was a sellout.

"I'll see you tomorrow night at the benefit," he said, and headed for the door, shoes and coat in hand.

"You'll see, Angel. You're putting pressure on. They'll find Hernando and even he'll have to admit he was wrong about you." She watched Angel open the door without looking back at her.

"Yeah. Sure." But he knew Sheryl was the one who was wrong.

CHAPTER 43

2:12 P.M.
East Village, 29 December 1986

Lori's friend Duane was a dancer.

Modern, interpretive, jazz. Past tense.

Was a dancer, she thought again in the cab with Faith, hit over and over by the news as she had been since she'd heard it last night. Lori had gotten home to find Faith in tears, and cried too when she heard the news that Duane was gone, that he'd died of pneumonia during his short stay at the hospital.

It was cold and gray, a day to match the occasion. They pulled up to the curb in front of St. Mark's Church on East Tenth Street, joined a crowd of mourners in tearful reunions of current friends and old comrades who'd only kept in touch through Duane. Lori found Steven near the door, talking to a lesbian couple they'd met last year at Duane and Robert's commitment ceremony. They showed off their new baby. Steven looked up from the child and saw Lori, hugged her, and gave her a quick kiss, despite Faith's frown of disapproval. They all went inside to look for seats.

Lori was pleased that Duane's memorial looked more like a celebration than a funeral. He'd have loved it. The church was filled with actors, writers, singers, dancers, musicians, friends, and family paying tribute to his ashes with music, dance, and readings. It was the biggest party he'd ever thrown.

She'd pulled something together that morning to say. By the time it was her turn to speak, Lori wasn't sure she could stop crying long enough to read her notes. She walked to the podium, shook off the feeling that she was back in Catholic school and if she messed up Sister Mary Henry would scold her as soon as she got off stage.

"Last night, I found out Duane died. The first thing in my head that day was that I had to give Duane a call. That's the first thing I thought most mornings since I met him in college. I have to tell Duane about what I wrote last night. I have to tell Duane about the guy I met. I have to ask Duane what he thought about what I wore to the party, the restaurant we ate at last week, the movie we went to see. It was sick and codependent, but we loved it.

"Then the bastard went and fell in love."

She paused for chuckles from the crowd, nodded to Robert, Duane's lover of eight years. He grinned back, eyes still bleary from crying.

"Worse yet, he married someone I loved, too, so I couldn't even have the satisfaction of trying to break them up. It didn't matter. There was enough of Duane for everyone. He gave me food, money, clothes, spare joints . . . purely medicinal, he used to say." There was a low laugh from the crowd. Lori tried to relax. She was among friends.

"But mostly love. I won't just miss Duane. There has to be a bigger word for what I feel. If Duane were here in anything but silent spirit, he'd know exactly what word to use, or he'd invent it. When I think of it, I'll let you know. I'm not saying goodbye, because he'll always have a home in my heart. I will say thank you. There's no way for me . . ."

The tears came up again, one of many reasons she hated death and funerals. She choked out the last words: "For me to thank him enough. Thank you anyway, Duane. Thank you . . ."

She hurried off the altar as another friend stepped up to the microphone. Musicians on the stage behind him played as he sang the opening words of "You'll Never Walk Alone." Lori returned to Steven in the pew where she'd left him. He hugged her and let her bury her face in his sweater, runny nose and all.

"Good job."

She pulled away, dug a Kleenex from her bag, and wiped her face. "I feel like a fucking hypocrite. We hadn't talked for weeks."

"I'm sure he understood."

"Yeah, I'm sure those were his final thoughts. Hope Lori met her deadline . . ." Then she was off again, racked by sobs. She felt like shit, should have been there for him, no matter what was happening with the damn book or Steven.

Death always caught her off guard, in the middle of a crisis. Too busy to process until long after it was over, if then. All she could do was hang on, ride to the end, and remind herself of everyone and everything that was still here. Steven felt warm and alive beside her. She needed that now. At the front of the church, Robert was surrounded by friends but still alone. Would she forget to call him now, distance herself from him in case he died, too? Was that why she hadn't called Duane since Christmas, because she knew he'd be gone soon and subconsciously hoped that the less she saw of him, the less she'd miss him? If so, she was wrong. Lori made a mental note to schedule lunch with Robert before she left.

She wasn't losing anyone else.

After the memorial they all went to Red Bar at First Avenue and Seventh Street, Duane's favorite hangout, walked there with the musicians playing his favorite songs Dixieland style, like a New Orleans funeral. People on the street joined in as they passed, loudly sang and danced along to "I Will Survive."

The bar was long and narrow, with red lacquered walls and a big shiny black bar, barely big enough to contain Duane's wake, much less his loss. Lori leaned against Steven at a tiny table packed with friends. She drank more than she meant to while they told stories about their dead friend that made them all look bad, laughed, drank, and told more. When she ran out of money to buy drinks, they kept coming, bought by others. By the time they all left the bar hours later, Lori literally leaned on Steven for support; leaning on him a little longer didn't seem so bad.

"Can I come back to Brooklyn with you?"

She whispered the question into his ear so that Faith wouldn't hear, while they hugged goodbye at the entrance to the subway station that would take him home.

"Oh, man," he said, and pulled her closer. "You sure? I can't guarantee I won't try something nasty with you in this condition."

"I can't guarantee I'd stop you."

"What would Duane say?"

"Go for it. He always was a slut."

They laughed and hugged hard as tears stung her eyes again. Lori left with Steven, dodged Faith's glare as she watched them run down the stairs. The subway ride to Brooklyn was a long, cold, drunken blur. By the time they arrived, even Steven's chilly loft seemed warm and comforting.

Lori didn't sleep for a long time. Words and memories bubbled up through a drunken haze, kept her from passing out completely. Each time Steven thought she'd finally drifted off she'd start another story. She held a SILENCE=DEATH button given out at the funeral in one hand, in the other a black-and-white photo-booth strip of her and Duane wearing silly hats and making faces. They seemed to keep her in the real world, as much as her rambling stories.

Steven and Lori fell asleep tumbled together, her back against his warm belly, limbs entwined as the sun rose in the front windows, sunlight kept out of the bedroom by a lowered shade and blankets pulled over their heads.

CHAPTER 44

1:18 A.M.
Long Island, 17 December 1918

The moon was full.

Frederic was almost asleep when he heard a strange sound in the night, a sort of strangled cry. He left the safety of his bedroom to see what it was. They always locked the doors at night, but he'd learned to open locks years ago.

The sanatorium was housed in an old mansion. It looked abandoned at night. No one was in the halls or dining room, but the French doors that led to the beach were open. A gentle breeze blew the curtains inside as he walked out onto the sand.

The head of the institute stood on the shore, eyes closed, head back, face lit by the moon, in the arms of a slender woman in a long white gown. His expression was ecstatic, his eyes wide, as if he stared into the face of God himself.

The woman's face was obscured, pressed deeply into the doctor's neck, as if giving him a passionate kiss on the throat. She looked up and saw Frederic, stared as if waiting to see what he would do, run or cry out an alarm. He did neither. Her pale face shone so brightly that he couldn't tell if it was reflected from the moon or was her own natural radiance.

The woman's lips were smeared with the doctor's blood, from a small wound on his neck where her mouth had been. As the boy stared at the woman, her features took on the appearance of his dead mother. He saw the blood on her lips, picked up a seashell from the beach, and used a sharp edge to cut the palm of his hand until it bled. Frederic held it out to her like an offering and she smiled, let the doctor's body fall to the sand.

She stepped closer and knelt by his side.

"Are you my mother now?" he asked. She stared into his eyes.

"Yes," said the bright lady who looked like his mother, after only a moment's hesitation. "Yes, my love. I am your mother now. Now and forever." She took his hand, lifted it over her lips, and let blood drip into her mouth until it stopped. Then she closed his fingers in a fist over his injured palm and kissed it.

"You won't leave me, will you?" he asked.

"I'll always be with you." Her eyes filled with tears, tinted with his blood and that of the dead doctor on the beach. "Even when you don't see me. You have but to call."

She walked him back to his bed and tucked him in; left him with a head of beautiful dreams that carried him to dawn, dreams of a mother who would never die, never leave him again.

They found the doctor's body on the beach the next morning. Perenelle had erased her tracks and Frederic's from the sand. No one knew how he died or that the boy had left his bed in the night. Perenelle kept her promise, and never stayed away for long. She picked up the reins of his education where his mother had left off, filled the void left in his heart by her sudden departure.

During her nocturnal visits she raised Frederic as if he were her own son. Among other lessons, she taught him how to convince the doctors that he was cured, no longer melancholic. A year later he was released from the sanatorium. His father promptly sent him off to boarding school.

Perenelle checked on him regularly like any good parent. When she visited, he entertained her with stories of how he'd set boys against one another, stolen things and blamed others, spread rumors, how he'd learned to manipulate mortal emotions and minds as Perenelle had taught him.

When he graduated he moved to Baltimore and began to paint, a gift he'd discovered in school. Perenelle encouraged him, became his muse, inspiration for an art career despised by a father who wanted him in the family business. She'd protected Frederic, advised him, loved and nurtured him until his twentieth birthday, almost sixty years ago, when she could resist no longer.

Before his maturing beauty could fade, her love consumed him, killed him with a bite, and resurrected him in his cramped artist's garret. After celebrating his rebirth with a neighbor's blood, he'd returned to a new portrait of Perenelle begun before his death.

His tools lay heavily in his hand. His paint strokes were thick and uninspired. Where the brush had once danced lightly across the canvas, shaped thick pigment into delicate shadows and light, now he was unsure, clumsy. Pencils, charcoal, and brush were all the same. He could no more draw or paint than he could walk in the sun.

When Frederic turned to Perenelle for comfort, he found his loss even greater. She'd never told him that while the enthralled are drawn to their masters, vampires repel each other, as if driven apart by some natural instinct to preserve their hunting grounds. Like all of them, Perenelle had hoped it would be different this time; that their love would be the one to last. It didn't. Once he was brought back, Frederic could barely touch his former lover, much less embrace her. She left him alone, immortal, abandoned without even the talent he'd sacrificed his mortal life to pursue forever. It took mad decades of killing to find inspiration again.

Time to reinvent himself.

CHAPTER 45

The bottle was almost empty and Jim still hadn't found any answers by the bottom. Whiskey had been his dead father's drink. He'd always said it made a man of you, but Jim had lost his manhood along with his family. He couldn't help them and he couldn't help himself. As he stared at the four cracked walls of his run-down rented room, they seemed to close in, to crush what was left of his spirit. Now that Steven and Lori had abandoned him, he had no one left, no hope of stopping the monster that had wiped out everyone he knew and loved. He could go back to Ohio, pay the price for stealing the motorcycle, and try to pick up what was left of his life.

Or just end it now.

He sounded like his father in the last weeks of his life. He'd talked about wanting to die, about how unhappy he was with everything he'd thought so perfect until then. Nina was a little kid, Jim was only five. He didn't remember much of his father anymore, except his voice and his smell, pipe tobacco and a whiff of his nightly whiskey. Just one for good luck, he used to say, until it wasn't one drink but a bottle a night, to drown the same pain Jim was drowning in now. The only help either of them could find in their most dire hour of need.

He picked up his jacket, dug through his pockets for money to get another bottle. For the moment, it was that or suicide. He found a crumpled piece of paper, pulled it out, and unfolded the flyer he'd been handed at yesterday's demonstration. "WE'RE HERE TO HELP YOU" said bold black letters, an ad for a KnightHawks fund-raiser. Jim thought about Angel, who'd spoken so passionately on the street, and wondered if maybe, just maybe, there was one last person in New York who might be able to help him find justice.

Jim pulled on his shoes and jacket and headed for the door. He felt drunk and stupid, not sure if what he was about to do made any sense, if there was even a point, but he had no other options left.

CHAPTER 46

11:13 P.M.
East, Village 29 December 1986

Angel walked Sonia out of the Palladium and onto Fourteenth Street, surrounded by KnightHawks that acted like celebrity bodyguards, kept lingering admirers from getting too close as he walked his girl to the line of cabs at the curb outside the nightclub. The big benefit was over. Only the high rollers remained, safe upstairs with the other VIPs in the Mike Todd Room, protected by club security. A long line of kids waited outside to get in as the Palladium reverted to the dance club it really was. The designer space inside was all mirrored surfaces and flashing colored lights, as far from the lives of the people Angel wanted to help as he felt tonight.

"I have to go home alone?" asked Sonia.

She frowned at Angel like he had to be crazy or high. He groaned. Sonia was more beautiful than ever in her new evening gown. She was always a natural beauty, but she'd really shown herself off tonight, worked extra hard to look the best she could. It was like she sensed competition, now that the KnightHawks were getting famous.

"Baby, I'll be home soon," said Angel. "Don't wait up."

"It's her, isn't it? That Sheryl bitch."

She cut her eyes at him, sat down in a cab despite her protests. He knew she wanted to pull him in, drag him away from all this, back downtown to the Lower East Side where the world made sense to her. She was wrong. This time. He couldn't blame her for thinking that Sheryl was why he wanted to stay, but she was wrong.

"Sheryl's got nothing to do with it. I just . . . I need to think. Alone. Nothing to do with you. Or us." He held her hand, looked into her eyes. She'd known him long enough to know when he told the truth. He counted on that, saw her relax and fall back against the seat.

"Get home soon, baby. I miss you when you're gone."

"I'll be there." He kissed her, almost too long to pull apart. Angel watched her cab drive away until it disappeared into late-night traffic. She was everything he'd ever wanted in a woman, funny, sexy, loving . . . Real. He loved her, but wanted to spare Sonia the heat of the spotlight he was smoking under, already regretted getting what he'd always wanted. The night went fine from a PR and fund-raising point of view, but it also showed him the road he was on. He didn't like what he saw.

The KnightHawks had started out as nobly as their name, martial arts warriors fighting crime in the subways and on the streets with the same force that criminals used against the public. They became a popular cause, then a symbol. Now they were turning into a trademark.

Angel remembered the first meeting where licensing the KnightHawks' name to other cities came up. When he punched a hole in the wall with his fist, they backed down. A year later, he was booked across the country for a series of "Start Your Own Neighborhood Watch" lectures. There were T-shirts on sale, talk of logo berets and sneakers, the proceeds to support and promote them as they slowly turned into a franchise.

Angel would have felt better if tonight's support for the KnightHawks had been to make the city safer or even to back a charitable organization. Instead, it had turned into a freak show to let rich donors slum with celebrity subway toughs they'd read about. One woman had openly propositioned him, offered to double and then triple her donation if he would fuck her in a bathroom stall. She was rich and married, one of the high rollers at the VIP party after the main event downstairs for the public. He'd be another story for her friends, like the time she'd done a cabana boy in Cancún. Even one of the club owners had pulled him aside, offered Angel cocaine and a blow job before he stumbled off after a shirtless bartender half his age. They were all lined up for a piece of him, one way or another, at five bucks to a five grand a pop.

It made him sick. Sonia had said he'd forgotten why he formed the KnightHawks, and maybe she was right. He liked the attention of the rich and powerful, the beautiful and famous, but there had to be a way to get the group back on track, to pull them off the path he was taking them down.

Angel walked while he thought, left behind the people who wanted his input on various projects, and found himself at the entrance to a subway that would take him home. Maybe it was a sign. Where better to think about where to go than on a train home? Back where it all started.

In the subway.

Jim watched Angel walk away after he put his girl in a cab, followed Angel as he said goodbye to the KnightHawks who'd kept Jim away outside the club. He hung back at the entrance to the Union Square subway station, waited until he was sure Angel was alone, and then trailed him down the stairs.

He followed at a short distance, just far enough back that Angel couldn't tell him from any other late-night commuter. The cold air outside had sobered him up after he left his room, cleared his brain. Even if this was a long shot, he had to take it for Nina, and her lost child. He slowed, had the sense to take his time, didn't want to blow his last chance of getting help.

His moment would come. He just had to wait for it.

Angel walked down to the subway platform with the heavy tread of a man headed for the gallows. There was a time when his heart beat faster when he headed under ground, excited by the chance to make his hometown a little safer, part of a movement. Tonight his heartbeat was slow as a dirge, mourned the loss of his dreams. His ideals had died tonight. No. They had died over a year ago, when the hype started. Tonight was just the funeral, a year too late.

"Hey, Angel! What up, man!"

The voice was familiar, pulled Angel from his funk back to the platform. It was Manny, one of the original members. He walked toward Angel with a new recruit, elbowed the kid in the ribs as they reached him. "Julio, this is Angel, the big boss. Without him, none of us would be here!"

Angel tried to smile, wanted to live up to the awe he saw in the teen's eyes. He knew the look. The kid had only seen him on the TV news or in the press. To him, Angel was a star. It was another sign of how distant he'd gotten from the cause and its members. He wasn't their leader anymore. He was a front man.

"Yo, Angel, what you done is great, man. Proud to be part of it." The boy raised a fist. Angel raised his just in time to meet him with a quick punch of knuckles. His street reflexes weren't completely shot.

"Thanks, man, but you're who makes it great. You and others like you who still believe in what we're doing." He wished he could take back the "still," knew from the look Manny flashed him that he'd said more about his mood than intended. Manny pulled the boy away with a frown.

"Got to get back to work. Later, Angel."

"Yeah. Later, man."

Manny glanced back at him with suspicion. Angel watched them walk away with regret, wished he could offer more than press releases, but he was drained of everything but empty slogans. What was he doing? Where was he taking them?

A downtown train pulled into the station. He stepped in without looking, sat down, and dropped his face into his hands.

"Hi. Excuse me? Mr. Rivera?"

Angel looked up to see a lanky white kid in front of him, stinking of booze. He was in worn jeans, a T-shirt, and a leather biker jacket. His hair was short and shaggy, his eyes bleary, like someone who'd been drinking all day. Just what he needed.

"I'm sorry to bother you—"

Angel cut him off. "Look, man. I'm off the clock. I'm on my way home."

"I know, I just . . . I need help. I don't know who else to ask."

"We all need help, buddy. I can't do any more for you than anyone else. Call a cop."

"It's not that easy."

"Nothing's easy."

The kid stared at him, swayed as the train rocked down the tracks. Angel looked away as the train pulled into a station. The doors opened and closed. The train pulled out as Angel waited for the kid to leave. Instead, he stood over him like he expected Angel to say something, offer advice, fix his problem, when he couldn't even fix his own.

"Look, man, I got no answers, okay? Give me a break."

"Just let me explain . . ."

"Shit! I said fuck off, okay! I'm trying to be nice, but I can't help you, man! Jesus!" Angel stood, headed for the door to the next car, and left him behind. He flopped down into an empty seat, hoped the kid wouldn't follow.

This car stank of rotten leaves and freshly turned earth, like an open grave. It took him a minute to realize that it came from a hooded wino at the other end of the car, wearing a stained snorkel coat. The homeless wandered the streets all summer, moved underground in fall for the warmth in the tunnels. Even Ed Koch couldn't clear them out completely. No matter how much the city dressed up the streets, cleaned up decaying neighborhoods with luxury condos, the homeless were reminders of the rot at New York's heart. Angel closed his eyes, breathed through his mouth not to smell the stench, and tried to chill.

He never saw the wino rise at the far end of the car and rush him, silent, didn't know he was being attacked until he was snatched from his seat. His first thought was that the kid from the next car had come after him in anger, until he opened his eyes and saw the inhuman face under the hood and a mouth filled with long, yellowed fangs.

Jim didn't know if he should follow Angel or not, so he wandered to the door to the next car as he tried to make up his mind. The "get lost" message had been clear, but he wasn't ready to give up without one more try. Jim looked through the dirty glass of the door and saw that Angel was pinned to a pole as he wrestled a man in rags. Jim forgot his own problems as he rushed to help. He opened the door and ran forward without thinking what he'd do when he reached them.

The train bent around a curve, picked up speed, and Angel's attacker fell to the side, slammed them both to the floor as Jim was thrown in their direction. Jim fell forward, pounded on the man's back with his fists. Angel saw that he had help and fought the derelict from below.

The three of them rolled across the car. Jim pulled free. He stood up and grabbed a pole to keep his balance. A face from Hell glared up at him from under the hood and snarled a warning. Jim stared in shock at the jagged fangs and blank eyes, froze for a moment as Angel shouted for help.

"Fuck, man! Get it off me!"

Jim pulled at the thing and it turned to fend him off with one clawed hand, left Angel free to defend himself with a fist. He punched it in the head, knocked the creature to one side. Jim swung a booted foot, kicked it to the floor. Together, he and Angel grabbed the creature's arms, lifted it up, and twisted its limbs behind its back. Despite its frail look, it was inhumanly strong. A shrill birdlike wail rose from its throat like a call for help as it tried to break free.

"What now?" shouted Jim over the roar of the train.

Angel looked around for a weapon of some kind, any answer.

"The door!"

Jim instantly knew what he meant. So did the thing in their grip. It struggled harder as they dragged it to the end of the car. Driven by fear, they shoved their captive in front of them to the exit. The door slammed back and forth, open, closed, open.

They pushed it through and used the last of their strength to lift the thing up and over the chains that formed a protective railing between the train and the tracks. It flew over and down, under the car's wheels. Jim and Angel stumbled back into the train, collapsed on seats just inside.

"Fuck! Thanks, man. Sorry I was such a dick before." He brushed off his tattered tuxedo, clothes torn and dirty from the fight. "Shit. This is a rental. How am I supposed to explain this?" He pulled out a cigarette, ignored NO SMOKING signs as he lit up and took a deep drag.

"What the fuck was that?" asked Jim, still out of breath.

"You're asking me? Twenty years in the subway, ain't never seen shit like that. Man. Now I think I know what happened to Hernando. You really saved my ass. So . . ." Angel took another deep drag from his cigarette, and turned to Jim.

"You said you needed some help?"

CHAPTER 47

9:57 A.M.
Fort Greene, 30 December 1986

Steven woke up without a hangover.

He was glad that he'd insisted they drink water while they sat up talking last night. Lori was still asleep, short hair twisted around her head, face half mashed into the pillow. Beautiful.

Steven tucked the quilt around her, left her in bed and wandered to the kitchen. He heated water and made tea, rummaged in the fridge for food. A few minutes later Lori stumbled in and gave him a quick squeeze on her way to the table. He brought her a cup and the teapot. "How goes it?"

She filled her cup, groaned.

"I drank a bit."

"Yeah. Want Alka-Seltzer or something?"

"Caffeine's enough." She poured milk into her cup. "A hangover's not the problem."

"Is this about Duane?"

"I should have called. He was in the hospital. We used to talk every day."

"Robert told me he was only awake a few hours a day for the last few months. You would have exhausted him."

"I had his room number on a piece of paper. Carried it around and kept putting it off, always remembered when it was too late to call or I wasn't near a phone."

Her eyes watered. Steven handed her a box of tissues.

"My friends are the only family I have left, Steven."

"I know. But you can't save them any more than . . ."

You could save your parents. He stopped, knew the words would hurt and didn't want to hurt her, just to shake her out of this downward spiral. He'd watched her do this too many times in the past.

"I know this is hard. Especially now."

Lori wiped her nose, looked puzzled. "Now?"

"After the pregnancy. I'm sorry that I wasn't there. When you . . ."

"Please." She realized what he was talking about. "Don't . . ."

"Don't what?"

Steven pulled away from her and glared. She knew this face well. He was hurt, angry, and now it was all about him and his feelings.

"You don't understand," she said.

"What? That you don't want my fucking sympathy? For Christ's sake, I practically begged you to have an abortion when you told me, I feel like shit about it, I just want to . . ."

"What? Apologize?"

"No! That doesn't fix anything. I was wrong, that's all I'm trying to say. I would like to have helped you. If you needed help."

"Steven . . ." Lori didn't know what to say. She knew he meant well, but he was just so wrong in so many ways. "I had a miscarriage. There was no abortion. I didn't even have time to decide if I wanted one."

"Oh, God, Lori . . ."

She watched Steven's face melt as he tried to process what she'd said, continued before he could apologize again.

"That's why I didn't tell you. I didn't want your pity. Or worse."

He nodded, stayed silent, eyes wet.

In the quiet, Lori remembered the exact moment when she knew, seven weeks into the pregnancy, after a day of bad cramps. She'd been working a killer schedule, stressed out of her mind, trying to meet deadlines, barely able to sleep. All night she'd felt a weird electrical tingling shoot down her inner thighs, like twin bolts of body lightning. There was only a little blood, but the next morning when she got to the doctor, he confirmed what she already knew.

She'd lost the baby.

Lori was back at work the next day. Later, tests revealed that her body had rejected the fetus. Her white blood cells had attacked it like it was a disease. The doctor told her she might never be able to carry a pregnancy to full term. While she was reeling from that, her agent called to tell her that the third book of the deal was on and she'd be working with Steven for the next year.

"I wanted to tell you what really happened," said Lori. "But all I could think was that you got what you wanted." Steven opened his mouth to respond and she raised a hand to stop him. "I know that's not how you feel. But back then I was afraid. We had to work together. It was easier to let you think I had an abortion just to end any conversation about it. It was stupid. So I'm sorry. I'm the one who's sorry."

It took Steven a while to respond. He looked like he had a lot to say. But in the end all he said was, "No. I am. You didn't have to be alone."

"I did. For me."

"Yeah." He looked away, went back to making a fresh pot of tea. "I get it. It's okay. I get it." Lori sipped from her cup, perched on a stool at the counter.

Steven picked up the teapot and hurled it at the wall. It exploded into little pieces that showered to the floor in a dry clatter. Lori jumped, spilled her cup.

Steven reached out and grabbed Lori by the shoulders. For an instant she didn't know what to expect, half thought she'd follow the teapot into the wall. Instead he pulled her close, pressed her face into his chest with one hand as if to avert her eyes.

His body shook. It took Lori a moment to realize that he was sobbing. She'd never seen Steven cry in the two years they'd been together. It shocked her, but she pulled him closer, felt tears rise in her eyes as they embraced, wept together, finally mourned their lost child and lost love. They stood quietly in the middle of the kitchen, debris still scattered on the floor around them.

"Goddammit, Lori," Steven whispered into her hair, minutes later. "What the fuck happened? What the fuck happened to us?"

"You know what happened."

"Yeah. I guess I do." He released her and sat down, quiet, looking a little embarrassed as he wiped his eyes. "I still love you, you know that? No past tense. I was wrong. I see that now. But there's nothing I can do to fix it."

"No. Nothing can fix us. Or our baby."

There was a pause long enough for Steven to fill it with the only thing he knew she would say, even before she said it.

"But we can save Nina's?" he said. "Jesus, Lori . . ."

"We said we were done," said Lori. "But if there's any chance Nina's baby is still alive, I want to help Jim find it. I don't expect you to understand, I don't expect you to join me—"

"Stop it. I understand. I don't like Jim, I don't trust him, but I know how you feel," said Steven. He sighed. "You know this won't bring back Duane. Or our baby."

"Or my parents, or us. I know. It's not about that. It's just . . ." Lori stopped. Steven was already punching in Jim's number.

CHAPTER 48

Adam called himself Damon Fox in the 1960s.

It was a playful alias, like all the pseudonyms he'd picked since his rebirth. He was a foxy demon by the middle of the twentieth century, a vampire for well over thirty years, clever enough to survive this long undetected. If he didn't take eternity seriously enough, it wasn't his fault. Perenelle had all but abandoned him after he rose from the dead, left him to fend for himself as his mother had when he was only a boy. Finding his way through immortality alone wasn't easy. A sense of humor, no matter how morbid or heavy-handed, was all that had gotten him this far.

He'd survived his death, but after almost thirty years he wondered if that was a blessing or a curse. Staying alive by draining life from others wasn't as simple or as easy as it had sounded when Perenelle first explained what she was and what he could be. The idea of eternal youth had appealed to him at the age of twenty—he'd felt immortal already; to make it literal was all too easy a decision to make.

The reality was a solitary life, without love or companionship. Most vampires avoided one another. Competing for territory, trying to stay undetected; they either preferred to hunt alone or bonded in exclusive communities for reasons he couldn't share. Damon was alone and would be for life, however long that might be.

As he faced another night of feeding, he felt a rising resistance. The barest idea had been growing that maybe he should end it all now, instead of continuing for interminable decades, even centuries, of blood and death. Damon pushed the thought away, put down that decision until later, as always, but it was harder every night.

The moon was nearly full.

Damon lived on Manhattan's East River. He left his apartment and headed west to Times Square, where hunting was always good. With all the glazed junkies, hustlers, and prostitutes, often in the same, it was easy dining. A little heroin only sweetened the blood high.

As he headed west on Forty-seventh Street, he saw a young woman up ahead. Dead white and speed skinny, she looked out of place among the late-night midtown East Side pedestrians. She was dressed like a hippie in a ragged peasant dress and sandals, dirty blond hair long and stringy. Pale blue eyes were framed in heavy black eyeliner, like an Egyptian raccoon.

She stood on the corner of Forty-seventh and Second with a Polaroid camera. Every now and then she'd snap a picture of someone who walked by, the flash a bright white under the yellow streetlights. She'd hand it to the subject and whisper as she pointed down the street. Most walked away with a shake of the head. Only a few looked back, with regret or confusion.

Damon walked in the young woman's direction. He could have pulled her to him with a look, but instead passed by, waited to see if he met whatever criteria guided her. As he walked by, the camera flashed and a voice came from behind him.

"Hey, mister . . ."

"Yes?" Damon turned as if on cue. The girl pulled a wide strip of film from the camera and tore it off, fanned herself with the developing picture.

"There's a party upstairs. Fifth floor." She nodded to a building behind her. "You should go."

She stopped waving the picture, peeled off the Polaroid backing, and held the photo out to him. Damon's face looked like a beautiful porcelain mask, pale, precise. He smiled as he enjoyed his own perfection. Of course she'd picked him out of the crowd. The girl whispered the address and pointed. Damon nodded and went where he was directed. It was a tall old factory building, run-down, but with an odd air of unexpected potential, like the entrance to an ancient oracle.

The hallway was filled with the dull thud of muffled vocals, drums, and electric guitars from upstairs. Damon pulled open the battered metal accordion door to an old freight elevator and got in. It did its duty with mechanical arthritis, ground to a halt, and opened directly into a vast loft space. The high walls were lined in silver foil and silver paint, glittered dully as he walked in deep enough to find the source of the sound.

A live band dressed in black played in a corner while party guests did drugs, posed, walked around, talked, danced, or otherwise grooved. There was a disheveled pile of semidressed bodies in a corner trying to work up an orgy, boys with girls, boys with boys, girls with girls. Damon sighed. After the excesses of the 1920s, the youthful decadence of the sixties seemed dull. It was the one curse of being a vampire: if you'd lived long enough, you really had seen it all.

He wandered from room to room in semidarkness, watched colorful light projections and listened to music, eavesdropped on conversations about relationships, politics, and art. No one seemed to care what anyone did. As Damon flowed through the space it occurred to him that he might enjoy his night's meal here instead of going all the way across town to Times Square.

He heard shouting from one of the back rooms and followed it. There was a fury in the sound that drew him like a shark to the scent of blood.

Damon turned a corner to see a young couple in the middle of a fight. The boy was eighteen or nineteen, in snug-fitting high-water blue jeans and brown loafers, a tight white A-shirt all that covered his lean muscled torso, wet with sweat. His face twisted with rage as he yelled at a young woman crouched on the floor in front of him, arms over her head. He shook his fist and spit at her, pulled money from the woman's purse, and left with a final word hurled over his shoulder.

"*Faggot!*"

Damon raised an eyebrow as he looked again and saw what his usually acute vampire vision hadn't noticed before. The woman was really a slight young man in his late twenties, bleached blond, as frail as the 1940s' Hollywood movie goddess she dressed like. She pulled herself up on her knees, sobbed in silence as she picked up her purse and collected its scattered contents. Cosmetics, Kleenex, keys, cigarettes, matches, and a straight razor with a silver case; she slipped it back into her bag, glanced up at Damon to see that he'd seen.

"Girl needs protection," she said in a smoky voice. "You never know how a date will go."

"Boys will be boys," agreed Damon. He crouched next to her, handed her a lipstick that lay at his feet. She looked up, eyes full of tears.

"Can't say why I love him so, apart from sex," she said with a tiny laugh. "Once it's over he's got no use for me, except for cash. Usually doesn't matter. But tonight . . ." Damon extended a hand and helped her to her feet. She smoothed her dress, tried to pull herself together as best she could. "Tonight was different."

She pushed around tousled hair, sprayed and coiffed into a forties' style, like her makeup. Damon saw a bruise beneath her pancake base. She noticed his attention, pulled out a compact, and stared into the mirror as she touched up her foundation to cover it better.

"I must look an awful mess. . . ." She freshened her lipstick, peered at him over the edge of the compact mirror. "That's a gentleman's cue to tell me I'm lovely as ever."

"I can only assume." Damon smiled, dazzled her with a tenth of his full glamour, enough to get the best table at any club. He'd made many a meal of young men and women in his time, but this was the first time he'd found both in one. The boy-girl intrigued him. "My name is Damon. May I offer you a drink, miss . . ."

"Erika. No, thanks, got all I need here."

She melted a little, tears still wet, reached under her skirt and pulled a small packet from the top of a stocking. Erika removed a small brown vial of cocaine and small spoon, unscrewed the black plastic cap, and took several strong snorts up each nostril. She extended the works to Damon, more out of courtesy than anything else, seemed relieved when he declined.

They talked for hours about her hustler boyfriend and drug habit while the party went on around them. She'd come to New York to be a window dresser, but wound up performing in downtown drag shows at night. She loved it, as much as she loved her young hustler. His friends had been teasing him about her lately, so he had to go and get all butch tonight in front of everyone to prove he was still a man.

"Like he doesn't get paid to suck dick all night. The bastard. That beautiful bastard . . ." The tears started again. Damon brought her drinks, and when she'd snorted up the rest of her cocaine he got her more, took it from those around them with a word or bought it off passing dealers she pointed out. Somewhere after midnight Erika moved from coke to speed, popped down little white pills with glasses of champagne cocktail.

Damon didn't remember exactly when suicide had come up.

He'd waited patiently for the subject to arise, as he was sure it would, maybe because it was on his mind, and then encouraged her to explore it. There were so many reasons her love would go bad. He was younger, a closet case, violent, and a junkie. It was only a matter of time before he left her or killed her. Erika was doomed to end her life alone or in violence.

Going over past romances brought no consolation. Damon wrung each failure out of her, every drop of heartbreak, pain, and misery, astonished at how much she had to tell, how easily it came. It was as if she'd waited all her life for someone, anyone, to listen.

When she ran out of words she seemed to run out of energy as well. Erika slumped forward, spent, as tears started again.

"I'll never see him again, will I?"

"No."

"I can't live without him," she said, and started sobbing again. Damon sat closer to her. He'd spent all night talking with Erika, heard her entire life story. It was late, but the sun wouldn't be up for hours yet. He still had time.

"I can't go on. Not like this," she whispered.

"Then you have to change. Can you?"

She whimpered, sniffed as she cried.

"Can you change, Erika?"

"No. I can't. I know I can't."

"Then what? What's left?"

He pushed her ever so slightly with his mind, enough to drop her over the edge. Erika slipped a hand into her purse, fumbled until she pulled out the straight razor, and turned it over and over in her hands. Tears hit the shiny silver casing as it glittered under the flashing party lights. She looked up at Damon with a sad smile.

"God. I can't even do this. I'm such a coward. . . . Please?"

She held it out to him with both hands, like an offering. He took it from her hands, leaned closer. "Are you sure?"

"Yes." She lay against him and lifted a wrist into the air. "Please. Please . . . I want it to be you." Damon looked around. There was no one else in the room.

He opened the straight razor and ran it along the soft skin of Erika's inner wrist, gentle as a lover. He traced a light path from her palm to midforearm with the tip of the blade, then went back and slit her wrist ever so slightly, along the vein, just deep enough to start a flow.

Damon pulled the cut to his lips as Erika gasped, first surprised, then with pleasure as he suckled, drank deeply. His saliva ran into her veins, put her under his power, and soothed her down from the screaming edge of panic as he fed.

He felt her life energy flow into him, fill him as his skin warmed with her blood, flushed a soft rose. Erika sighed softly, and then was silent, eyes blank.

Damon laid her wrist down before she died, took the razor and went to work. There was still enough of a heartbeat to pump what remained of her blood out around the body. He slit her other wrist as he had the first, rearranged her body and posed it with the open razor in her right hand, then stepped back to see if it looked convincing.

"Fabulous."

The voice behind him was soft and male.

Damon had been careless. He'd let the blood high distract him. The man in the doorway was slight, wore rumpled slacks, a button-down shirt and baggy jacket. He carried a large calico cat and an instant camera. He stepped into the room and closed the door behind him.

"It's perfection. Except everybody knows Erika's a lefty. That's the kind of thing that always gives you away on TV." His bleached silver hair was long, bangs low as if to hide his face. Tinted glasses obscured his pale blue eyes, as he looked the body over. Despite his shaded lenses he sucked in every detail. "You're an artist," said the man, a statement, not a question.

"I was once."

"You still are. I know art when I see it."

Damon stared, not sure whether or not to kill him. The cat hissed, leaped out of the man's arms, and ran to hide under a canvas in a corner. Damon lifted the razor from Erika's right hand, wiped off his prints with a paper napkin, and moved it to her other hand.

"Maybe your medium's changed and you just don't see it yet." The man walked closer to the body. "Poor Erika. At least she died for love." He lifted his Polaroid camera and snapped a flash photo of the death scene. The man pulled the picture from the camera, waved it idly as he waited for it to develop.

"You listened?"

"It's my party. I throw them to listen."

"But you didn't stop me."

"How? My family's Slovak, from the old country; we still recognize your kind when we see them." He peeled the picture from the Polaroid backing and looked at it critically. He nodded and held out the photo. "Fabulous. Very Catholic. You are an artist, whatever you say."

Damon took the picture from the slender man and stared. The saturated high-contrast color image was raw, stark lit by the naked flashbulb, but beautiful, like a fashion-magazine reenactment of a crime scene photo. Erika's body lay in the center of the frame, head tossed to one side, shoulders squared, arranged on the couch like the forties' movie icon she'd dreamed of being.

The straight razor was draped in one hand, arms at her sides, slashed red wrists turned delicately upward as if in prayer, like a martyred saint. Her eyes stared heavenward, her face a cool mask of inner peace.

"Perhaps you're right," said Damon.

He slipped the photo into his pocket without protest from the photographer. The man suddenly seemed to see his situation and backed away from Damon. "I hope you're enjoying the party."

"I am. I should thank you." Damon was at the man's throat before he could move farther away, and stroked his sweaty cheek. "Surely there's something I could offer in return?"

"Thanks, no." He didn't flinch. "Love to live forever, but what a bore to have to be there for it."

Damon laughed, still high from the blood. The man's answer amused him, so he decided to be generous. "True. Maybe I'll see you later. Maybe not. Say your prayers at night." He slipped away, left the party unseen by all but his host and victim, and neither would tell.

For weeks he thought of Erika and her death.

Not with desire or longing, but satisfaction. Somehow, the hours he'd spent with Erika, listening to her story long enough to understand what would make her want to die, gave him more enjoyment than just killing her for food. Their encounter had become something greater than a hunt, something he couldn't quite define.

Delaying the kill had certainly enhanced his pleasure, but persuading his victim to embrace it first had excited him in a way he didn't understand. Damon was sure he'd reached a turning point that night, but didn't know what it was yet. It reminded him of something he couldn't quite place. Then it came to him.

His mother's smile.

When she heard that the maid Jenny was dead in prison, by her own hand. The smile was there for only a moment. No one else at dinner caught it. A mere flicker across her lips before her brow furrowed into the concern and sadness expected of her, but young Frederic had seen it.

He never got his mother to admit she'd planted the stolen goods in Jenny's room, but her expression when she thought no one saw was enough to confirm it. He hadn't stopped loving her, he could never do that, but he'd seen how far she'd go to get what she wanted.

It was so clear now, how she'd orchestrated the whole thing from beginning to end with a tug of one little thread that unraveled an innocent girl's life. Damon could appreciate it now, divorced by decades from the grief of Jenny's loss. His mother had been a master manipulator, on a par with Machiavelli or Sun Tzu, whose works Perenelle had given him to read in school. Without ever having heard of their books, Olivia had lived *The Prince* and *The Art of War* by instinct.

She had taught him well during the years he spent at her knee, as Olivia bullied servants and crushed tradesmen, put her husband's competitors out of business with a scandal here, ended love affairs with a rumor there. No one dared oppose her. She'd controlled her world and everyone in it, including her son, taught him by example how to mold and twist the lives of others to meet his needs.

Listening to Erika beg him to end her pain had been the sweetest sound he'd heard since his dear mother called him back on the beach after his dog's death. Erika's plea told him that their little talk had made her death preferable to life, no matter what she left behind. He'd shaped her end with his words, like a sculptor. She hadn't just died; she'd died willingly, fed his body and his soul.

Damon liked the feeling.

He'd try again, maybe going slower next time, taking days, even weeks. With all the time in the world to refine his technique, he could do more than consume lives to live. He could paint his victims a picture, show them everything he'd learned: that love and happiness were lies. By the time he was done, they'd betray their dreams and everything they held dear; beg him to end their suffering with the blessing of release, the sweet gift of death.

A bold new vision opened up to Damon, filled his spinning head with a renewed sense of purpose, a real reason to live forever. The man at the party was right. He was still an artist, but now pain was his palette, human life his canvas; with his words, the stranger had given back the gift Perenelle took away with his old life as Frederic.

She'd taught him to survive, but it had taken him this long to find a way to truly live. He'd finally found a place to channel his rage and torment, into a new kind of expression, a living art with an endless supply of ready material. The future was so bright that Damon laughed, swept away by boundless joy as he dressed and left the house to begin a new work of art. His idle thoughts of self-destruction were gone.

He was whole again.

CHAPTER 49

It was feeding time at Café Piranha.

Adam's long white limousine slid to the curb in front of the restaurant. One doorman escorted them from the car to the entrance while another opened tall glass doors for Adam and his guest, Simone, the slender salesgirl from the Phoebus Gallery.

Adam had spent the last few days trying to find Nina's brother, with no luck, and decided to take a night off before resuming the search. He'd called the girl to his penthouse, supped lightly from her throat before they left, careful to take just enough to control her completely. He had more ambitious plans for her last night on Earth.

They breezed past a long line of eager young people outside. All stared with an almost palpable desire to be them. The maître d' didn't even look for a reservation when they entered, just nodded when she saw who it was and snapped her fingers to summon a waitress in a flowered silk sarong to take them inside.

Couples sat at fake cane tables, shaded from synthetic sunlight by plastic palm trees in a vast dining room decorated in cartoon Caribbean colors. Waiters wore calypso outfits. Strolling "native girls" sold cigarettes, Café Piranha T-shirts, bumper stickers, pins, and pens, while Meat Loaf bellowed "Bat Out of Hell" overhead.

The back wall was a neon mural of a gigantic fish about to eat a smaller fish, about to eat a smaller fish, about to eat a smaller fish. Café Piranha's slogan, EAT OR BE EATEN! flashed above the school, projected in turquoise and salmon laser light. The waitress led Adam and his date up a short curved flight of stairs along the back-wall mezzanine to his usual table overlooking the bar.

It was the heart of a mock oasis, lit by twinkling track lights and burning bamboo tiki torches, where horny yuppies frolicked barefoot in soft white sand imported from Tahiti. Shoes in hands, pants rolled up, they swilled exotic frozen drinks, mingled, and singled one another out while waiting an hour or more for a table, willingly stranded Robinson Crusoes looking for Fridays.

It was one of Adam's favorite hunting grounds. He'd decided it would be the perfect place to find a suitable Holofernes for his Judith. Simone's resemblance to the central figure in Caravaggio's masterpiece had inspired him. He would take the couple home and have them reenact the beheading in the painting for him. Adam smiled, ordered an aperitif for himself and a steak for the girl, as rare as possible, to build up her blood for the evening ahead.

He reached across the table to adjust the white silk scarf wrapped tightly around Simone's wounded neck, stroked her soft warm cheek with his fingertips before he pulled away. The girl smiled brightly, enthralled, saw only him. He smiled back, took her hand in his.

"What are you thinking?" he asked.

"How beautiful you are," Simone said, with the trembling voice of first love, eyes wide in surprise, as if she'd only just noticed how bewitching he was. Adoration no longer held any appeal for Adam. He'd heard the same tone in so many entranced voices over the long years that the sound of mindless idolatry had become irritating. It was one of the reasons why he kept Marlowe untouched, saved him for later when he ceased to be of use. He spent too much time around the boy to listen to this worshipping prattle from him.

Adam started to reply when a couple at the door distracted him. The woman was blond, tall, and slender, the man was black with dreadlocks, a distinctive enough pairing that he remembered them from the gallery.

It couldn't be coincidence. He was being followed.

Adam sucked delicately on the girl's pinkie as he watched them talk their way past the maître d' and enter the restaurant. He tasted a trickle of fresh blood, realized he'd nipped the tip of Simone's finger without thinking. She still stared lovingly at Adam as she bled. He wrapped her finger in a napkin and returned her hand to her. The couple separated. The man went to the bar and the woman headed his way. Adam couldn't help but laugh.

He'd spent the last two nights trying to find Jim, without luck, and now his allies were so stupid as to come to him. Either they hadn't believed young Jim's story of the chase, or were foolish enough to think they'd be safe approaching Adam in public. He would have to teach them how wrong they were.

The blonde arrived at the same time as Simone's steak, only lightly braised, as ordered. Adam allowed the waiter to fuss over them while the blonde hovered just out of range, obviously waiting for the help to leave before she approached.

Lori felt like a Christian entering the Colosseum just before they released the lions—a lot of room to run, but no safety in space. Not if Caine was what Jim said he was. She shook off the thought. That was crazy talk.

It had been her idea to follow him here from his home and confront him directly, as if he were just another celebrity interview. It was what she knew, how she'd dealt with famous and feared men like him in the past. She'd ask questions. Even if Caine didn't answer, word would spread that she was asking. Someone would surface to provide answers. Someone always did.

She glanced at Steven, who waited at the bar if she needed him. He lifted a Heineken to her. Lori steeled herself and spoke.

"Adam Caine?"

He didn't respond at first, kept his eyes on the girl seated across from him as she picked up the sharp serrated knife the waiter provided and cut into her steak. Blood bloomed to the surface, spread across the white plate as she sawed a chunk of rare meat free and pushed it past full young lips, painted vivid red in a pale face.

"My name is Lori Martin. I'm a freelance reporter for the *Village Voice*. . . ." It was partly true. She was once, and still had her press pass; hopefully flashed fast enough for him not to notice that it had expired. "I'm doing a piece about the incident at the Phaeton Gallery, and I was wondering if I could ask a few questions?"

"How did you find me here?"

"One thing about the famous, you're easy to find. Anything to say about K-Pro?"

Adam's guest didn't look away from him while she ate. A subtle smirk played around the edges of her lips while she ate, as if they shared some deep, secret joke. The girl stared into Caine's eyes while she chewed, slowly, like she was drugged or hypnotized. A trickle of blood ran down the side of her mouth as she swallowed. She caught it with the tip of her tongue and took another bite. The whole thing looked as staged as a downtown performance piece.

Girl eats meat.

Lori tore her gaze away, stared at Caine instead, and waited for a reaction of any kind. He finally looked up. When she met his eyes, she was sorry he had. It was like staring into the eyes of a predatory beast, even if they were the most beautiful eyes she'd ever seen. One gray, one blue. She stepped away to escape his magnetic charm, but he pulled her back in with a sad smile.

"Such a tragedy," Caine said. "Such talent, such beauty spoiled."

"Did you know him well?" Her journalistic instincts saved her from paralysis, kicked in as she held out her microcassette recorder to better capture his voice. He glanced at it with a fleeting smirk.

"I was a patron of sorts." He sipped his drink. "You were there, last night." It wasn't a question. It made Lori more nervous that he knew.

"Yes. I meant to interview you then."

"I left soon after. It was a busy night for me, but I'm sure young Jim told you all about our close encounter." He stared at his dinner partner, wiped her bloody chin with his napkin. "I'm almost over it."

He casually pulled open the front of his shirt to reveal a delicate dimpling in the white skin of his perfect chest, lifted a lock of shimmering auburn hair to expose a light, round scar at his temple. *Bullet holes*, thought Lori. *Last night those were bullet holes.* She felt her skin crawl. She'd always wondered what it would feel like, and here it was, every bit as awful as it sounded. Caine laughed at her reaction.

"Why pretend? I'm an old friend of the family, but I'm sure he's told you that as well."

"He told us a lot of things."

Lori couldn't believe she was talking to him instead of running and screaming, but something held her glued to the spot, like a witness to a car crash. She glanced around the room to free herself from his gaze, tried not to give away Steven's position, hoped he was somehow still an ace in the hole, an element of surprise that could save them.

"Looking for help? No one sees anything I don't want seen." Caine reached across the table, took the girl's bloody steak knife, and wiped it clean with his napkin. "Let me demonstrate . . ."

He stood and plunged the knife into the girl's chest.

Lori screamed.

"You're so beautiful," the girl said to Caine.

The blank smile never left her lips as blood drained from her face. Waiters still raced back and forth, customers still drank and flirted, flashed Safe-Date cards at the bar as if nothing out of the ordinary was happening.

Everyone around them continued to eat dinner, to live, laugh, and love. Caine gripped the handle of the knife, sawed his way down the girl's chest while she puckered dying lips to blow him a last kiss. Lori backed away as he split the girl's chest open like a lobster; blood sprayed over nearby diners as her body dropped to the floor.

Loudspeakers played the Beatles' "Birthday" overhead as a waitress carried a cake to a nearby table, strolled unseeing through the girl's scattered intestines to get there. She held the candlelit treat out for the birthday boy to extinguish, unaware of the bright spray of blood that decorated his clothes and those of his companions.

He grinned as he blew out the candles to applause with a single breath, one side of his face fouled with gore, the other neatly shaved and groomed, every hair still in place. They cut the cake, served thick white slices on white china plates pooled with blood like raspberry sauce, and happily lifted reddened chunks to their lips. They toasted their friend's health with champagne stained pink with the girl's blood.

Lori snapped, slapped at them and screamed to no avail. None of them felt or heard her, no matter how loudly she shrieked. She looked back at the body and Caine was gone. Lori ran; slipped in the girl's blood as she tried to get away, fell to the floor and crawled sobbing toward the door, to freedom and sanity.

Then she looked back and saw the footprints.

They made themselves as she watched, one wet, red step at a time from the pool of blood that still spread from Caine's table. They stopped at her side. Feet faded into place over them. She saw Caine's boots first, then the pants of his expensive black suit, both drenched in fresh blood. His hands glistened like twin rubies at the ends of wet black sleeves. He gripped the front of her jacket, lifted Lori to her feet, then released her.

"Are you going to kill me?" Lori asked, in a voice so clear it surprised her. She didn't feel clear. Caine chuckled.

"Let's see." He leaned close to her face, breathed death. "I could have your utilities cut off, your lease revoked, freeze your bank accounts and throw you out on the street with no place to go, nowhere to turn. I could watch you die slowly, cold and starving in the streets of New York." He held up a bloody finger. "With one phone call."

"But that's not soon enough, is it?"

"No. It's not. First you, then the nig—"

There was a sharp crack. Caine flew back and hit the floor. Something almost like blood oozed from his chest. Steven had finally come to her rescue. He came up from the stairs behind Lori, Jim's smoking gun held out in front of him with both hands.

"Jesus Christ! I've never . . . Did I really hit him?"

"We have to—"

Caine was up before she could finish, roared and reached out with nails like claws until Steven squeezed off two more shots into his head. Lori saw the lit tiki torches on the wall near her and grabbed one. Steven emptied the gun into Caine, pulled the trigger again and again while she smashed a flaming torch against Caine's shoulders until the can at the top cracked and spilled, covered him with burning lamp oil.

He shrieked, went up in bright yellow flames like the Scarecrow with no Dorothy to save him. Caine burned faster than any human would, as if actually made of straw, and leaped over the railing, still ablaze, down and outside to the white limousine that gleamed at the curb. A waiting chauffeur held the door open and closed it on his smoldering master.

Steven shoved the empty gun into his pocket, grabbed Lori, and together they ran for the stairs. They watched through ceiling-high plate glass windows as the smoking car rolled away into the night.

"Oh my God." Steven felt the gun heavy in his pocket, and looked around at the still calm room, pulled Lori for the exit. "We have to go . . ."

Lori realized what Steven had: the only thing that kept everyone from seeing what really happened was Caine. Now that he was gone, his spell would fade. As soon as she had the thought, the restaurant erupted into chaos.

A waitress slipped in the girl's remains, fell, and dropped a hot dinner over a table of customers. When they saw why, everyone in the room screamed and flooded the exits in a panicked wave. Sirens rose in the distance as Steven and Lori ran, far from the panicked scene behind them, the only two who knew how bad it really was.

CHAPTER 50

Adam felt better, but still hurt.

He sank into the depths of his massive black marble tub, laid there by his servants, then bathed in blood from willing sacrifices hung upside down from an overhead railing. Their throats slit, they bled into the tub to nourish his flesh as their fading lives revived his strength. It had taken almost his entire stock to fill the bath, but he was nearly whole again. He drank deeply from the crimson pool. His burned skin healed, turned baby smooth in gentle waves as he rose back into the light.

He would make their deaths memorable, thought Adam.

"I deserve that much at least," he said.

The words echoed off tile walls, unchallenged. The seeds of their destruction had already been planted in their minds as he fled, ready to blossom as soon as he was healed and ready to finish the job. Adam sank beneath the surface again, closed his eyes, and considered their fates.

Yes. He deserved to have some fun.

It wasn't just humiliation that had him already planning the best way to kill the couple while he recovered. Not even he was vain enough to be driven by embarrassment at being bested in public—or burned, or shot for the second time with the same gun. No.

He'd allowed them to escape, knowing what he truly was, and worse, he'd left behind the remains of his latest victim, lost control over the minds of witnesses before he could call in his staff to clean up all traces of his evening, as they had so often in the past. Now there would be another police investigation, and more publicity. The consequences of his crime were spreading.

The Triumvirate would pay him another visit soon, Adam was sure of that. If he could eliminate Jim and the couple by then, he'd only have to get rid of the baby to seal the breach. How much damage could it have done in the few days it was free? He was sure the Autochthones would report that its lifeless body had been found in a Times Square trash can, seared into ash by the sun. His nightmare would be over soon. For Jim and his friends, it was just beginning.

He'd make sure of that.

CHAPTER 51

9:43 P.M.
Fort Greene, 30 December 1986

Steven hadn't seen what was happening at first.

Lori was talking to Caine. Everything seemed fine. Then he stabbed his date. No one reacted, and neither did Steven. For a while it hadn't seemed at all extraordinary, even though the girl was bleeding to death in front of him. He hadn't felt alarm, or the need to act, not even when he saw Lori scream and back away.

It was as if it were on TV, happening to someone else a long way away, not here and now, not to a woman he loved. Steven had even turned around and ordered another beer, made a joke to the bartender while Caine gutted the girl. He'd finished half his drink before he turned back and saw Lori on her hands and knees, crawling for the door. It wasn't until Caine stood over her, lifted Lori to her feet, that Steven had snapped free and was able to break out of the trance that held him.

Steven didn't know if everyone else had seen it and done nothing, if everything was invisible except to him, forced to watch, unable to act. He knew only that he'd been mind-raped, helpless under Caine's control.

He wanted to run as far from the city as he could, dig a deep hole and hide where no one would ever find him. Instead, he stood at the counter of an allnight bodega in Brooklyn, waited for the counterman to fill his order so he could go home with Lori, lock and bolt the door. Not that locks did any good, or even Jim's empty gun, still warm, tucked away in his pocket. No one was safe from whatever Caine was, anywhere. They knew that now.

There was a bogeyman and it ruled the night.

Steven stared out the window, numb. The sun would rise in a few hours. They could sleep in safety, even if only for a day. Vampires had to stay put during the day, didn't they? While Steven waited for the food he watched Lori shop for soup, milk, canned food, anything that would keep them inside for as long as possible. They would take their supplies and hide. It was the only plan they could think of now.

Steven kept an eye on the door, scoped out their surroundings for a safe exit if necessary. He caught a glimpse of them in the store's grainy black-and-white security monitors and had to laugh. They looked like they were about to hold the place up.

The counterman glanced at him, wary, a Middle Eastern immigrant still suspicious of black men in his store at odd hours, especially bloody and in the company of fearful white women. Steven laughed again. The clerk glared at him in warning, went back to the sandwiches with a grunt.

Lori brought her groceries to the register and asked the clerk for a pack of cigarettes. Steven said nothing. If she was smoking she wouldn't open her mouth when he pulled out the ball of hash he'd been saving for a special occasion. If he'd ever needed oblivion, this was the night. He paid the bill and they left.

Dishes were piled high in the sink upstairs, like the unopened bills on the table next to the door. Steven had neglected both to work on the book. The sink smelled. Lori didn't complain. Dishes and bills could wait tonight.

They went to his bedroom in the back and closed the blinds. Steven tried to put what had happened out of his head as he pulled out his pipe, lit some hash, and inhaled deeply. Lori didn't even stay up for a cigarette. She stripped to her underwear, climbed into his flannel-covered king-size bed, and fell asleep almost immediately. It was her gift. Steven couldn't sleep when stressed, stayed up all night obsessing unless he got stoned, while Lori could barely stay conscious under pressure.

Ordinarily he would have been grateful that the night ended with her almost naked in his bed, but there was no victory in it tonight. Steven put the pipe down when his vision started to blur, climbed into bed beside Lori, and did his best to sleep.

He thought he heard sounds from the sink. Dishes shifted, water bubbled. Steven ignored it and did his best to turn off his brain. He looked at the clock radio before he closed his eyes and almost laughed. It was Wednesday, the thirty-first, New Year's Eve morning. At least, for once, he knew where he'd be at midnight.

In hiding.

CHAPTER 52

10:44 P.M.
Lower East Side, 31 December 1986

"Is it really cool for the baby to be here?"

"Of course, stupid. It's his party."

'Manda grinned a toothy fake smile at the girl who'd asked the question, a bleached-blonde punk in black they'd picked up on St. Mark's Place while they handed out xeroxed invitations for their New Year's Eve party. It was a good turnout. No matter how abandoned it looked from outside, the house was almost full.

Feet in sneakers and boots pounded on worn hardwood floors to loud throbbing music as the guests danced their way to midnight, but there were no neighbors to complain. Everyone living nearby had been wiped out as the nest fed. All that was left were dim shadows of their victims. They wandered the night streets like mindless flesh ghosts, feeding on their leftovers. Zombies, Glenda called them. None of the nest knew why their dead didn't come back to life as vampires like them, but it was better that they didn't.

Less competition that way.

'Manda held Baby cradled in her left arm, adjusted its blanket with her other hand. It slipped her finger into its mouth and sucked on it, hungry. Baby was having a fine time tonight. The party was to celebrate its first New Year's Eve with its new family in its new home. 'Manda was determined to make it the best ever. She wanted Baby to be happy with her forever.

Trick and Treat had a girl pinned between them on the dance floor. The twins slid up and down her front and back as they passed a joint between them. The girl was already stoned on something stronger, the hypnotic mind link the twins were using to drain the life from her before they even shed any blood. 'Manda knew that high well. She'd learned after she came back to life that it wasn't blood that kept them alive but something deeper, something pulled from their victims when they linked minds to cast the illusions that made feeding as much a game as a hunt.

The blood was just a high, made them feel warm and alive again, flushed their bodies with human sensations. The link, the energy drain, was what kept them alive, but the real fun was that they could use it to make their victims see anything or nothing. They could fool them into ignoring danger, into desiring them and their kisses, keep them unaware when kisses turned to bites, in any imagined fantasy.

Or they could take them, invisible to victims even in mirrors, unnoticed by anyone as they drained life and blood in full view on the dance floor, the way the twins did now with the girl who thought she was dancing alone. They nipped their partner's neck as they closed in on her from either side, bit deep and drank while she smiled in solitary ecstasy.

'Manda felt a slight twist at her mind. Even though she wasn't under Baby's control anymore, it could still make its needs felt. It was time to feed. 'Manda drifted around the dance floor, held Baby's hand up as if her infant was her partner, whirled in a circle as she decided which one of the party kids to take.

Not that one. Not her, not him, no . . . Yes. There.

She moved close to a skinny boy in black jeans and a Ramones T-shirt, with long dirty hair. He stood on the edge near the drink table with a half full plastic cup in one hand. The other was jammed into a front jeans pocket, cupped over his small semihard dick as he watched the dancers with hunger and envy. 'Manda liked that. He reminded her of boys she'd teased in high school. The ones who wanted a girl way too much to ever get one. Boys she could get to do anything she wanted with a smile and the slightest promise of reward, just because she had tits.

Depeche Mode kicked out of the speakers "Just Can't Get Enough," upbeat, bouncy. 'Manda bobbed to the beat and moved closer to the boy, willed him not to see Baby on her arm as she slid into place beside him. She moved to the music, slow, seductive, rocked from side to side like a cobra until she drew his attention.

"Havin' a good time?" she asked, shouting to be heard over the music.

"Could be better," he said.

"It could always be better," she answered with a smile.

"I bet you can make anything better."

"Yeah? Want me to make you better?"

He blushed and sipped his scotch, afraid to answer with the truth, afraid she was just teasing him, which she was. Just not the way he thought.

'Manda realized he'd never go any further unless she pushed, so she lifted the cup from his hand and took a long, slow sip. She locked eyes with him while she drank, felt her body reach out to his with invisible tethers that held him fast, started to pull his youth, his vitality into her hungry body. Baby stirred on her arm, felt the life flow, tapped into it through her as 'Manda licked the rim of the cup and handed it back, empty.

She pulled the boy into a wet booze-flavored kiss. He dropped the cup and his hands came up, dropped into place around her waist and slid down to settle on her round hips. 'Manda ground her pelvis against the boy's boner as his tongue slid between her lips, roamed across and under her tongue. She lifted a free hand with her little penknife gripped tightly in it, blade open, and made a small slit on either side of his throat.

Baby's mouth sucked tight to the left side while she took the right. The boy tensed for a moment, as if he understood for an instant what was really happening to him, then relaxed as their saliva filled his wounds and took control. He pulled 'Manda and her baby closer as they fed like leeches, filled his head with dreams of sex and satisfaction as they emptied his body.

CHAPTER 53

The street outside the crumbling Lower East Side social hall that housed The World was packed with the usual crowd—bridge and tunnel trash, downtown club kids, and local celebrities. The cool and wanna-be cool fought to enter the club before the New Year started. A long row of yellow cabs and limos pulled slowly through slush and snow and let passengers out to battle a gauntlet of clubgoers at the door.

The crowd parted as if by command when Perenelle stepped out of her cab. She breezed in with a nod to the doorman, without ticket or payment, as always. He bowed as he lifted the velvet rope to admit her, turned with a big grin to watch her walk inside.

Perenelle had learned to enjoy being an object of desire. She'd been a plain woman in life, barren, past middle age when she died, but in death she could be as young and beautiful as she wished. Her long, dark hair was held up with gold clips. A full-length red leather coat flowed over a short blood-colored velvet dress and thigh-high boots. It was a party, after all.

She loved feeding at clubs while she enjoyed the music and dance. A century in Tibet had been spent learning to control her curse, how to survive by draining life from crowds without killing or taking blood. She'd persuaded others to follow her example, but it was easy when surrounded by so much flesh to see why some couldn't resist gorging on the fresh blood of New York's young.

Partygoers milled around the coat check, greeted friends, pouted, posed, or stampeded upstairs to dance. Perenelle moved through the pandemonium in the peeling deco lobby without effort, through open double doors to a cabaret downstairs.

Dim blue bulbs in the low ceiling illuminated faux cracked marble walls. White candles in glass globes lit round tables draped to the floor with luminous white cloths, patrons seated on worn chairs reupholstered in red glitter plastic. It was a perfect place for Perenelle to watch the death of the old year and the birth of the new. She sat near the stage, where a thin young woman under a spotlight shouted angry poetry into a handheld microphone, accompanied by a sad-faced guitarist.

A waitress wearing cellophane wings and a white tunic appeared as if on cue. Perenelle asked for a cognac and the girl rushed to fill her order, ignored others who tried to wave her down. Perenelle relaxed, amused. She'd been worried about Rahman's plans for the baby, but would abandon those fears for tonight. He hadn't found the child yet. There was time to keep him from doing anything rash. Besides . . . she'd already made sure of that.

Without the Book of Abraham he could do nothing.

The room slowly filled with a typical downtown stew: artists, performers, gay muscle boys, movie actors, and ad execs. Everyone was there, from downtown fashion victims to lean KnightHawks in black T-shirts and berets.

She'd made a good life here. The Triumvirate of the Veil had kept the city safe for her kind for half a century; had let Perenelle enjoy longevity in peace and comfort. She'd be damned if she'd let Adam ruin it.

Perenelle left the table when she finished her drink, drifted upstairs to the grand ballroom. The floor was filled with dancers that bounced and whirled to the music of the Pet Shop Boys. It reminded her of street festivals in Paris when she was young and alive. She swayed to the music, joined the throng, felt her system link to dancers nearby and draw power from their bodies as they moved around her. Even without blood, the connection to so many lives gave her a surge of energy.

As midnight approached, a wave of costumed waiters and waitresses moved through the crowd with trays of plastic champagne glasses. The girls wore the same cherubic wings and white tunics as the waitress downstairs. Waiters wore only tight diapers and big white ribbons across their chests, 1987 written in gold.

Everyone crowded to the edge of the stage and went wild as a downtown drag star stepped into the hot white spotlight. She was a tall, lanky bald man in thick makeup, dressed in a bright red satin cocktail dress and fishnet stockings. She adjusted big foam boobs as the audience settled down, thudded fingers against the mike to see if it was working.

"Testing . . . helloooooo?"

The crowd roared as speakers snapped on, blasted her raspy voice from the walls. "Anybody wanna get laid?" There was a chorus of catcalls from the back of the room. "Gimme time . . ."

She warmed the audience up, joked, teased, and taunted as she strutted back and forth, rolled mascara-heavy eyes under thickly drawn eyebrows, and gnashed nicotine-yellow teeth. Quips whipped back and forth in a frenzy of mutual heckling, as the crowd went wild.

"Okay, quiet down, we're starting for real now. Ladies and gentlemen . . . Oh, why pretend. Look, sluts . . ." The house screamed with laughter. "It's almost time, get ready for midnight!"

A projector threw live TV coverage of Times Square on the back wall of the stage, as the audience counted down with the clock. The music rose louder, Prince's "1999."

"Fifty-nine, fifty-eight . . ."

Perenelle counted with them, caught up in the excitement. As she looked around the room, she spotted Adam on a balcony high above the dance floor, a girl on one arm, a boy on the other, laughed as he prepared to toast the New Year in his own way.

Perenelle felt a flash of fury. She hadn't seen him since she'd introduced him to Rahman, the night she'd saved him yet again. The sight of Adam making merry when he'd brought them all so close to Revelation, brought her to the brink of entombment, enraged her. No matter that he could control what the humans saw. This was the kind of public excess that had gotten him banished for twenty years, two blissful decades of peace.

Now he was back to destroy them all with his careless games. He'd learned nothing. While the vampire changeling he created wreaked who knew what havoc, he was here toying with new prey in front of everyone. Adam might not remember the events that cast Damon Fox out of New York for two decades, but she did.

CHAPTER 54

2:17 A.M.
Midtown East, 1 February 1965

Grand Central Terminal is a dramatic introduction to New York City. The abrupt transition at the end of the trip from the bare bulbs of the long, dusky tunnels to the warm illumination of the expansive concourse announces with a flourish that you've arrived.

The main room is a man-made cavern with the majestic gravitas of a cathedral, establishing the city's dominance as soon as you enter. Perenelle waited with the rest of the Veil's high council under the faint stars of the vaulted ceiling's illustrated constellations, their brightness dimmed by years of smoke residue. A handful of late-night commuters walked past without seeing the hundred men and women standing around the station, all dressed in the traditional black of one official function of the Veil.

Judgment.

Damon's train would arrive from Westport soon. He'd be collecting his bag about now as he reveled in memories of a weekend spent committing atrocities on the unsuspecting Connecticut populace.

That was all about to end.

His last romp had been in all the papers and on TV.

Two hardworking career girls, roommates, slaughtered in their Upper East Side apartment in August 1963, gutted and slashed almost to pieces.

Only the assassination of President Kennedy in November had pushed them from the headlines, until a year later, when a black teenager arrested for another assault confessed to the vicious murders. It all would have been forgotten eventually, except that he had an airtight alibi that emerged during his trial, complete with photographs.

It was the year after Martin Luther King Jr. marched on Washington to make his immortal "I Have a Dream" speech. At the peak of national attention on the civil rights movement, the story of a young black man falsely accused of the murder of two white women inspired a book, a movie, and a TV series. It took months for the Veil to cover up the facts and keep police from finding the real killer: Perenelle's only offspring, her little changeling, Frederic Hartwell, aka Damon Fox.

He'd followed the Veil protocol in finding a fall guy for his crime, but had been careless in not making sure his patsy wasn't drunk and loud on the boardwalk with friends and a camera that night. Perenelle had helped Damon locate a suspect more satisfactory to the Veil's council, a junkie with a violent record and no alibi, who deserved the punishment he'd receive, even if not for this.

After one bite, he confessed to the police when arrested, offered details of the case that could have come only from the real killer. Perenelle had Damon coach him personally, made sure that the city could prove their case. Long after his conviction, the incident remained a scandal that rocked the NYPD for over a decade. Two years after the murders, the breach was finally closed, and Damon was to stand before the Veil for punishment.

Damon breezed out of the gate to the tracks and into the concourse and stopped in the middle of the room. He saw them immediately, even if no one else in the terminal noticed. The Hundred, dressed for his funeral. They closed in from all sides, blocked every exit. He saw Perenelle on the steps to a landing on the right, turned to her for explanation.

"I'm sorry, Frederic."

She used his real name only when it was bad, like a disappointed mother, when something he'd done was coming back to hurt him. If the high council had come in person to welcome him home to the city, it was very bad this time. He dropped his bag to the floor, folded his hands in front of him like a schoolboy called before the headmaster.

"May I ask what this is about?"

"The murders in 1963."

He relaxed. "Oh, that. That's done, right? Got a new confession that sticks, case closed, breach sealed."

"It's not that simple, Damon." Dr. Townsend Burke stepped forward. Damon had always suspected that he was part of the first Triumvirate of the Veil, with Perenelle and Rahman, but had never been able to prove it. Not that it would help him now. "It's taken nearly two years to resolve this. Two years of investigations and the danger of discovery."

"You know the Veil's rules and still you break them," Perenelle said. "The council feels that . . . a penalty would change that." Her face had the same helpless look his must have had when he saw the maid Jenny whipped into the street by his father, before being carted off. He suspected he faced a similar fate.

"The last vampire guilty of a breach approaching this magnitude was Tom O'Bedlam, and his consort, Claire. No other vampires have suffered their punishment since then. None have deserved it."

Damon paled, lost the color and the high he'd gained from his last feeding before getting on the train. He'd been sure that if he kept the humans from further investigation, he was off the hook. He'd promised to be more careful with his art projects in the future, but that didn't seem to be enough. He was being threatened with the thing he feared most. Eternal entombment.

Locked in the dark closet forever.

The lights dimmed as shadows rose. Adam felt a new presence. They were not alone. Vampires couldn't hide themselves from their own kind, with the exception of three.

The Triumvirate of the Veil.

When they were ready to reveal themselves, Adam saw them, two men and a woman, expensively dressed in black as if for a high-level business meeting. Their corporate aspect made them more intimidating. There was mercy in court, none in business. They stood in a row, features unseen, blurred like hummingbirds' wings. No matter how long Damon stared, their faces remained out of the reach of even his enhanced vision.

"Damon Fox. We are here for you."

"Good to meet you," said Damon, and nothing more, afraid to incriminate himself. He tried to keep his voice level, his tone light, even though he was terrified.

"Don't toy with us. We know all you've done."

The voices cut through Damon's head like razors, muddled his thoughts. He suppressed his anger, had to conceal his resentment of their interference in his affairs, or risk greater punishment than he already faced. If worse was even possible.

"Your actions threaten us all with exposure and genocide at the hands of humans. This alone is our greatest crime, and you have violated it."

"I corrected it! I . . ."

It did no good to challenge them. His only chance was to convince them that punishment wasn't their only solution. The room faded around him. In the sudden darkness, all he could see were his shadowy judges. For the first time since Perenelle had killed him and brought him back, he felt a kind of fear.

"As a fledgling less than a hundred years old, you've been forgiven much. This cannot be overlooked. It's the judgment of this court that you be sentenced to eternal entombment."

"God, no!"

Damon fell to his knees, bowed his head to the floor, and started to plead, but knew there would be no mercy, no more than he'd give one of his victims at the sight of a tear. To protect themselves and the rest of their kind, the Triumvirate of the Veil would erase him and all he'd done, even his memory, from their history and the minds of men.

The Triumvirate faded from view, along with what remained of the room. Damon was left sealed inside a narrow coffin of cold stone, confined alive, forgotten by all but those who had trapped him here.

He'd spent countless nights locked in a closet screaming for release, only to wake hours later when his mother sent a servant to unlock the door, carry him to bed, and dry his tears. There would be no escape this time, no comforting sheets at the end of his ordeal.

Eternal entombment. The words had chilled him, but the reality was far worse than imagination. The stone sides of his narrow cell seemed to close in on him as he counted the seconds, minutes, hours, days, years, decades, centuries, and millennia of his confinement.

He felt human lives outside end and new ones begin, as cities rose and fell, empires crumbled into dust. Mankind left Earth for the stars, the planet died around him, the sun went out. Damon alone remained, a living corpse, still conscious, blind and hungry in the dark as he screamed forever, unheard. . . .

Then it was over.

Damon opened his eyes and saw the vast room, almost empty, abandoned by his judges and the high council. He gasped in relief, gripped the floor he lay on to be sure it was real. A voice spoke.

"Frederic . . ."

It was Perenelle.

She crouched beside him, beautiful, even more welcome than the first time he'd seen her. They were alone with the humans, except for armed Veil enforcers nearby, waiting to take him away.

"As one of the founders of the Veil, I've persuaded the council to show mercy. You won't be entombed." He collapsed with relief in her arms. "But you are banished from New York. For twenty years."

"Twenty years!" Damon sat up with a frown to protest, and she slapped him back to the floor, furious.

"Be grateful, fledgling! You could be sealed in stone right now. They've already revised Veil law. Vampires will be bound to their creators for their first hundred years, so after this, anything they do to punish you until then, they do to me."

Damon grasped her hand and kissed it.

"Dear lady, how can I ever repay my undying gratitude for your intervention on my behalf . . ."

She pulled away from him.

"End these games now, Frederic. Find another way to fill forever. I saved you this time, but I won't let you take me down with you. I'll kill you first."

She walked away as the officers of the Veil led him out to the limousine that would take him to the recently renamed Kennedy International Airport. He could go anywhere in the world he could reach before sunrise, as long as he was far from New York and stayed away for the next twenty years.

But two decades passed too quickly.

CHAPTER 55

11:59 P.M.
Alphabet City, 31 December 1986

It was almost midnight at The World.

"Ten, nine . . ."

The birth of the New Year, and Adam was already deflowering it. Perenelle felt her rage rise as she watched him bite into the soft throat of the girl on his arm, drink her blood as he veiled it from the sheep around him.

"Eight, seven . . ."

Adam looked up and his eyes met Perenelle's.

She knew he had to sense her presence. It was only a matter of time before he acknowledged it. Adam smiled as he rolled the girl away and pulled the boy's neck to his lips, all without losing eye contact with her.

"Six, five . . ."

He bit, broke the boy's skin, and sucked hard, greedy. Perenelle watched a trickle of blood escape his lips and roll down into his victim's collar. *Look at you*, she thought. *My beautiful boy . . . look what you've become.*

"Four, three . . ."

Perenelle tensed, felt others around her tense, too, still connected as she fed.

"Two, one . . ."

Adam released the boy, raised his glass of champagne, and drained it as the illuminated ball in Times Square on the video screen descended and the New Year began. The crowd screamed as they threw confetti into the air, bounced balloons that fell from the ceiling, shouted, stamped their feet, and burst into fresh dance as music blared from the speakers. Colored lights and strobes flashed as mirror balls whirled back into action.

Perenelle watched Adam pull his charges close and lead them down to the dance floor. She glared after him, furious despite herself, couldn't help reaching out and touching the minds of those nearest him for a parting word as he headed for the exit.

Adam felt Perenelle before he saw her, but chose to ignore it. He had only one night to relax before hunting down Jim and his allies, and he wasn't about to let her ruin it. He played with two pets he'd found when he came in, and couldn't help flaunting them in her face once she saw him.

After midnight he walked downstairs with his dates to leave. There was no reason to talk to Perenelle. She'd made it clear that she was through with him. Once the baby was found and Jim was dead, he'd have no need for her again.

As Adam pushed through the crowd, a young woman in black leather and thick eye makeup with a ring in her nose turned and spoke to him in an accent he recognized as Perenelle's.

"*Is this the only reason you came back to New York? To finish the job you started?*"

The girl turned away from him, unaware that she'd even spoken. A shirtless young man in worn jeans spoke as he passed Adam.

"*To expose us all?*"

Adam turned back to face Perenelle and shouted over the music.

"Don't judge me!"

He flashed her the finger and whirled away, and a new voice mocked him as another anonymous heckler danced by.

"*I've never judged you, chéri . . .*"

And another face pushed through the crowd.

"*I'm not your mad mother . . .*"

Adam stopped before he reached the door.

The boy and girl on either side of him froze and waited for instruction as Adam turned back.

Perenelle could tell from his face that she'd gone too far. Olivia was sacred to Adam, no matter how insane she'd been. Then, they'd only dared call her strong-willed. Today, they'd call her a malignant narcissist; sadistic, paranoid, pathologically craving power over others, even her own child. But no matter how she'd abused Adam, she was his birth mother. However long he'd been in Perenelle's care, he'd always be Olivia's son first.

A girl next to the last boy to speak raised a hand and slapped him hard in the face. The boy looked at her in shock, as Adam's influence faded and the girl rushed to apologize. Then another boy struck someone else who'd spoken for Perenelle, another struck another, until everyone who had spoken for Perenelle had been punished.

But it didn't stop there.

Others picked up Adam's anger and slaps flew, one after the other, turned to punches as the violence grew and moved in a wave toward Perenelle. As blows cascaded across the room, Perenelle retreated as her mind pulled nearby bodies close for protection. Half the room moved in to shield her. The other half surged forward to attack, driven by Adam. Perenelle saw his face, a mask of rage, as the mob flowed forward, grabbed chairs, bottles, anything as weapons to assault those that kept Adam from her.

Despite having survived the terrors of the French Revolution and the Civil War, Perenelle had forgotten the power of a mob. The press of bodies brought back old memories, painful ones. As she pushed bodies back to keep Adam's pawns away, the room divided into equally matched forces, each determined to defeat the other.

Perenelle knew that turning the room into a riot would bring the risk of exposure she feared most as officials looked for an explanation afterward. She had to stop the battle now, while she could still make them all think it was a drunken fight, make them forget she and Adam were there before police arrived.

But he wouldn't give up.

As Perenelle weighed her options, the host of the show broke through the crowd with a broken chair leg, dress torn half off, and raised the wooden club like a stake. His painted eyes reflected Adam's anger as he leaped at Perenelle.

He missed as she moved aside easily, whipped the stake from his hand. She looked up to see a new wave pour at her as bodies surged through the front door to the dance floor. This had gone too far. Something had to be done.

Red light filled the room, settled down to a pulsing glow from one of the balconies overlooking the stage. At the center of the ruby light were three dark figures, dimly seen but unmistakable.

The Triumvirate of the Veil.

"This will cease."

The mob stopped, relaxed, and dropped their weapons, under the Veil's control now. They stood silent and blank while the Triumvirate spoke.

"Adam Caine. You've been warned, time and again."

He started to speak in his defense, but the light rose until Adam shut his mouth.

"Your fate will be determined soon."

The light began to fade.

"As will Perenelle's . . ."

By the time the red light vanished, music played and the crowd moved about as if nothing had happened. The Veil had made them all forget the last few minutes and their injuries. Adam was nowhere to be seen. Perenelle wasn't surprised or sorry that he hadn't taken the time to say goodbye.

Adam burst out of The World, furious.

He couldn't challenge the Veil, but he would deal with Perenelle. He was running out of time. If he could find the damn baby and seal the breach, he could put all this behind him and leave New York for a while, cleanse his palate.

His body hummed with life, mouth still rusty with the aftertaste of the couple he'd nipped on the balcony before his fight with Perenelle. Adam turned south to head for the Lower East Side, opened his leather jacket to expose glistening gold chains around his neck, pushed back sleeves to expose bracelets that glittered harshly under the streetlamps. Bait for his catch of the night. Adam was hungry, not for life or blood, but for the thrill of the chase that kept him sharp. The air was cold, sharp. He could hunt in peace with few witnesses. Work off some anger and think of ways to tie up loose ends.

Last night had ended badly. Killing Simone hadn't been enough to keep him home. He'd have fun tonight, then find Jim and his friends, kill them all, and wait for the Autochthones to find and destroy the baby. He might even be able to bargain with the Veil, once his crime was undone. He'd be safe again, free to return to his life, his art. He'd just take care of it, take care if it all. He had to smile.

His mother would be proud.

CHAPTER 56

Their dead were coming back to life.

At the stroke of midnight Baby's nest had stopped picking off party guests one by one, had taken the last of them in a riot of blood and killing. They chased them screaming through the locked building, enjoyed their terror as much if not more than the blood and life they got when they caught them. An hour later they fed on remnants, slowly drained the last drops from the survivors. Dance music still bounced off the walls, the only sound left in the building except the muffled whimpers of the dying.

That's when the first victims started to revive, stumbled to their feet in the same dull-witted mechanical way the nest had seen their dead rise before. Glenda was right. They were zombies, mindless, clumsy. All they wanted to do when they got up was spread their infected blood to make more zombies like them.

The first time she saw it happen, 'Manda would have puked if she hadn't already been dead herself. One of the damn things had stumbled up to her and its eyes exploded. Blood poured out of its head through every hole it could find, eyes, nose, mouth, and ears, flowed like a fountain. She moved fast now that she was like Baby, too fast to get caught by crap like that. 'Manda slid out of the way and the blood hit the ground, pulled itself together like the Blob, and tried to get to her before she jumped out a window to get away.

They found out the blood didn't last long on its own, just long enough to get from one body to another. If it didn't infect someone else right away, the zombie blood dried up and blew away like dust. Once they knew how easy they were to beat, the nest started playing with the zombies.

They came out only at night. All you had to do was show up on the right block for them to come for you. It was easy to lure a zombie into an alley and drop a full trash can on it from three stories up. They called that game Splat! Trick invented it one night when he kicked a loose cinder block out of a blocked window and everyone outside watched a zombie explode like a blood-filled balloon when it was hit by accident.

The twins were playing a new game, Duck Season, with Kirk's pistol. Treat roamed the dance floor with her twin brother, shimmied between the bodies scattered across the glossy hardwood. She had the gun, took aim as one of the corpses shook, sat up, and stumbled to its feet, walked toward them. Another stood up behind it.

"Duck Season," yelled Treat and stopped dancing, arms extended. She held the pistol with both hands as she took aim, squeezed the trigger, and sank a bullet into the forehead of the zombie closest to her. It dropped back to the floor as Trick danced past, took the gun from her hands, and pointed it at the next zombie, shuffling up from behind the fresh body.

"Wabbit Season!"

He pulled the trigger twice and blew the top off the zombie's head. It dropped to the floor. Infected blood spurted in his direction, but the body was too far away for it to reach Trick before it dried. Treat took the gun back when she whirled past, as a new zombie rose.

"Duck Season!"

The twins kept playing their game to the music. 'Manda understood. The young ones needed to have their fun. It was hard to keep them united to protect Baby.

When they were alive, they were random strangers bonded by Kirk's drugs and the needle, but grew into a kind of family that protected its members. Since the change they felt one another in a way they never had before. They wanted to stay together for the same security they'd enjoyed when human, but the new feeling was like an itch to get away. It was hard for them to stay in the same building, but they'd been used to withdrawal symptoms and worse when they were alive. A little irritation wasn't enough to keep them apart. Some had even learned to like it.

Something else was bothering Baby tonight.

It was cranky, squirmed in 'Manda's arms like it sensed something wrong outside, something or someone. As 'Manda moved toward the open window and the street below, Baby perked up, raised its head, and sniffed the air, as if something special was out tonight. Something good. 'Manda went back inside to call the other members of the nest to join her outside. Maybe tonight's fun wasn't over yet.

Maybe it was just about to start.

CHAPTER 57

12:33 A.M.
Lower East Side, 1 January 1987

Adam walked down Avenue C.

There was an annoying lack of prey on the street. The neighborhood below the club was littered with empty tenements and new construction. All he would find here would be AIDS-tainted junkies and tubercular tramps. Better to head west and pick off the last of the club kids straggling home after last call.

He saw a flicker of movement when he turned, as if someone had just ducked out of sight behind him. Adam stood still, then sauntered to the center of the street. An attacker from either side would have to cross rows of cars to get to him, slowed long enough for Adam to have the advantage.

He was wrong.

Despite his precaution, he was flung to the ground. Adam hit the asphalt, felt whoever struck him leap off his back and away. Thin, high titters echoed from the shadows around him. Adam rose to his feet in a flash. The block was empty. Whoever had jumped him had decided to toy with him.

Adam brushed off his clothes, scanned his surroundings. Laughter rippled down the street again, seemed to surround him. There was something familiar about the sadistic style of the stalk—like a vampire playing with its dinner.

He was right. Adam felt them now, in the shadows as they drew closer. He walked, wary, listened with senses beyond human. They rushed through the buildings alongside him, followed him like a wolf pack while they sniffed out weakness.

It angered Adam. He knew this Bloodline and had permission to hunt here. He was not the prey. It would do them good to be taught a lesson. Adam isolated a set of footsteps that pattered alongside him, just out of sight behind boarded windows and cinder-block-filled doorways. With a quick leap to the left, he shattered the wooden planks that blocked the window and was inside the building.

Adam yanked out a skinny blond teenager in worn jeans and an I ❤ NY shirt. He squeezed him by the throat and stared into glittering eyes that confirmed that his assailant was one of the undead. The boy hissed and struggled but Adam was stronger.

He lifted the boy, slammed him down on a splintered wooden board left in the window frame. Impaled, the boy squealed, a loud, thin shriek like wet air from a pierced balloon. Adam lifted the body and threw it into the middle of the street, where it fell limp, wooden stake sticking out of the heart on his T-shirt.

"Trick!"

The word shattered the silence, rattled broken glass windows down the abandoned street. Adam stepped out of the window to the sidewalk, stood in the empty street next to his handiwork.

"Trick? Is that his name or his job?" He goaded them to bring his assailants out for the kill.

Adam had only the slightest of warnings. Just enough to step aside as a girl that resembled the boy flew at Adam's back from behind. She hit the ground, rolled to her feet, and howled, rushed at Adam, claws and fangs bared. He downed her with a backhanded slap, reached down, and twisted her head sharply, far enough to snap her neck. The body dropped to the ground, twitched rapidly like a broken mechanical toy winding down. Her end would be agonizing: she'd be unable to control her body or heal before death set in.

"Is that the best you can do?"

Adam raised his arms in victory. It was a challenge, a dare. If he could get them out into the open, he would know how many there were, the scale of the threat. There was no answer. He knew this was the stillness before the storm, as he waited for their next move, the other shoe to drop.

Now.

They swarmed out of the blank buildings almost faster than even his expanded vision could spot them. Almost. His hands slashed, steel-hard nails deadly; his feet swung in arcs like clubs, met his mark every time. The pack ripped his clothes, scratched his skin, but did little damage. They realized that he was no ordinary victim, but neither side was willing to back down. The pack seemed guided from outside, by someone with a vendetta against Adam, determined to make sure he didn't escape, no matter the cost to the army that flew at him.

Adam grew weary, his strength faded as he felt the tide turn. He had to act now, take out whoever would do them the most harm, to give him a distraction so he could get away.

He picked a young woman in a baggy belted T-shirt and acid-washed jeans that acted the most like a leader, reached out and grabbed her by the arm as she swung at him with a makeshift club. Adam pulled her hard in the direction she was moving, carried her with the force of her momentum into other members of the nest and felled them. The sudden force of his retaliation took them by surprise. They froze, awaited new instructions.

Adam didn't give them time. The girl stood, swayed on her feet, and turned. He thrust out a hand and shattered her ribs to rip out her heart. It was one of his trademark moves, most effective when surrounded. It inspired fear and had scattered mobs. It had become almost cliché after overuse in horror films, but was still his favorite.

The key was to let your victim see his heart in your hands, just before the brain died and the body fell. That was the look on the girl's face now, as Adam raised her heart high over his head for all to see. Her eyes widened, her lips formed a word he couldn't quite make out before she dropped.

The others gathered around, moaned, lifted her, and bore her over their heads to a nearby tenement like ants. Adam felt the psychic pain of the cry that rose from the building's depths before he heard it, a banshee scream that told Adam he'd found the nest's commander.

He hadn't anticipated what would rise out of the dark to perch on a second-floor windowsill. His grail. Nina's brat, eyes sunken and skin pale, but still alive and the proud father of this tattered band of junkie bloodsuckers.

"*Mama!*"

The thing keened its hatred of the man who'd killed not one but two mothers, in the same way. Adam would have laughed at the irony if not for the look on its face.

Well, he thought. *This is awkward.* There would be no easy way home tonight. Negotiation would have been his next approach, but it was clear that there were no rational minds here to sway with kind words. To his surprise, rather than fly at him, the baby dropped to the ground and was carried by one of the nest to its mother's side to grieve.

The wail that rose from its tiny throat filled the air like funeral bells. The rest of the nest rolled, wept, and whipped themselves like flagellants as it suddenly occurred to Adam that no one seemed overly concerned with him. He'd actually bought himself the time he needed to escape.

He flew down the street and away from Baby's brood, kept the location fixed in his mind, the key that freed him from bondage to the Autochthones. He would tell Marlowe where to find the baby, have him bring back the head as proof for the Veil that it was dead, and burn out the rest of its nest.

Once he got to the numbered avenues, Adam felt safe taking a cab home without being followed. He rolled uptown, happy at last, as he saw the end of his trials and tribulations. In twenty-four hours there would be no baby, no nest, no trace of any connection to him, no censure from the Veil. His crisis would be over. He just had to tie up loose ends. Adam closed his eyes and pictured himself on a South American beach under a full moon, sucking the life out of a pair of Brazilian twins.

A vacation was definitely in order.

CHAPTER 58

It was almost time for the drill scene.

Marlowe was celebrating New Year's his way, watched a Herschel Gordon double bill in a Times Square theater. *Bloodsucking Freaks* was his favorite, about a crazy theater director who kidnapped beautiful girls for a private torture show in his basement. They were stripped, drugged, and treated like animals, forced to satisfy the director and his loony assistant.

Then the call came in from the boss.

Pain started in his head just as a giggling doctor on the discolored big screen was drooling over a drugged-out girl in a bikini.

"You best get out, girl!" screamed a regular in the audience.

Others laughed and threw popcorn at the screen. Marlowe grabbed his head and almost threw up. Adam's summons was stronger than ever. Marlowe rubbed his temples, tried to make it through the scene before the tug on his brain dragged him out.

The doctor drilled into the top of the girl's skull, slipped a straw into the hole, and started sucking as fans around Marlowe squealed and hooted. The director and assistant killed the doctor when he was done, like they did every time Marlowe saw it. He was too sick even for them.

Marlowe tried to laugh with everyone else, but gave in to the pain and lurched to his feet. He stumbled over protesting patrons to the aisle and out the door, ran through Forty-second Street's late-night mix of hookers and johns, drug dealers and junkies to the corner to grab a taxi.

His head pounded all the way uptown. Marlowe didn't even care if he got back the cab fare. Anything that got him to the boss faster, anything that ended the ripping tear in his head sooner, was worth it.

When Marlowe got upstairs, Adam was pacing the room, a snifter of cognac in his hand, a wicked gleam in his eye. "Dear boy. Remember when I told you Nina's baby was no longer your concern?"

Marlowe groaned inside, tried not to let Adam see his dismay. "I thought you had that covered, Mr. C." He didn't look forward to any more punishments for failure.

"No need. I found it last night. It seems to have made some vicious new friends. I need you to fetch it during the day while they're asleep." Adam wrote down the directions on a creamy sheet of his stationery, folded it, and handed it to Marlowe. "Our original arrangement stands with an amendment. Bring me its head, then burn out the nest."

Marlowe nodded and left. There was no point in questioning Adam. He'd find out what kind of friends the baby had when he got there, even though he could guess. He headed out to the subway to take the train home and catch a few hours' sleep until the sun was up.

CHAPTER 59

He'd been waiting almost an hour for a train.

Marlowe could have walked home by now. He looked around and lit a cigarette when he was sure there were no cops around to search him and find his weed. There was no one on the Lexington Avenue line platform but him. Everyone else in the city was on holiday.

His only company was a few rats on the tracks. He threw his match at them. They darted back behind the rails, seemed to check him out before they disappeared into the tunnels. Marlowe thought about the night that had gotten him into this mess.

The night he'd met Adam Caine.

It was like any other at Danceteria. Marlowe had moved from floor to floor of the three-story club, from hip-hop to techno, mixed his music like he'd mixed his drinks, for maximum effect. He pushed his way past a crowd of people on line at a bathroom door, acted like he worked at the club to get in first, and opened the door to a scene from a Dario Argento movie, pure Italian slasher porn.

A redhaired man was crouched on the tile floor over the body of a girl, her throat all but ripped out, her blood on his face and body, puddles all around them. She must have struggled on her way down. There were wet handprints and streaky finger lines across the walls and mirrors. Marlowe backed up when the man looked up and bared bloody fangs. There were shouts to be let in, as people on line protested.

Marlowe slipped back outside and shut the door behind him.

"Sorry, folks, got to close this up, someone's sick, puke all over. Big chunks, projectile, up and down the walls, across the floors . . ." The crowd dispersed, disgusted, as he continued to describe what he assured them they didn't want to see. Marlowe ducked back inside and locked the door behind him.

When he turned, the room was spotless and the man was immaculate, combing his hair in a mirror. Marlowe stared. The man continued to comb until he seemed satisfied.

"No. You didn't imagine it."

The next moment the room around him was the butcher shop he'd seen before, body back on the floor, walls and tile smeared and splashed with fresh blood. Then it was all gone again.

"I control the vertical. I control the horizontal." The man laughed. "I could have walked out of here sight unseen. Quick thinking, though. I like that in my staff."

Marlowe wasn't sure he'd heard right, felt himself grinning before he even realized he had his hand out to shake on the deal. He froze as it got close to the vampire, but didn't pull it back.

"You're not going to eat me, are you?"

The vampire smiled and moved close to Marlowe in a weird way that was superfast and slow-motion at the same time. He spoke softly, directly into Marlowe's ear.

"Not tonight."

He took Marlowe's hand, gripped it firmly, and they shook, the sweaty palm of the boy pressed against the cool dry skin of the undead. There was a series of coded knocks on the door and he released Marlowe's hand.

"Welcome aboard. Let them in."

Marlowe unlocked the door and six people in black coveralls entered with a body bag, buckets, and tools. His cleanup crew. The vampire dropped his illusion and the room reverted to real. While two of them packed up the body, the others cleaned the room, scrubbed down blood and gore, left things sparkling clean. They all exited unseen with the body, followed by the vampire. He handed Marlowe a card as he left.

The name was Adam Caine.

The address was Fifth Avenue.

Marlowe could smell the money.

"Tomorrow, sunset. Bring the *Times* and the *Journal*."

Marlowe was there the next night and every one after.

He'd done well working for Adam, even though he lived like a pauper and saved his money for the future. His reward was supposed to be what he really wanted, ever since he'd seen Adam crouched bloody on the floor and realized that vampires were real. Realized that something he'd only seen in movies and TV shows was something he could have.

Something Adam wouldn't give.

He'd made the mistake of being too useful. Marlowe was only a skinny black kid from a group home in Jersey, but there were people he knew, places he could go, things he could do that Adam couldn't, even with all his powers. He'd seen Marlowe's potential from the first moment they met, when few others had.

Adam was better off with Marlowe alive and able to move in daylight for him. As long as Marlowe was Adam's day agent, he'd never get to cross over to the dark side. He had to find a way to force Adam's hand, to make him see that he'd be better off with Marlowe working for him as a vampire. . . .

An express train roared through the station and distracted him. Marlowe stepped closer to the edge of the platform to see if a local was coming yet. Something moved below the edge. At first Marlowe thought it was rats again, but it was something bigger. He stepped back, away from the tracks. He'd worked for Adam long enough to know there are things that go bump in the night and that it's best to avoid them. He'd forgotten that there are things that can't be avoided and come for you, no matter how fast you run.

Marlowe backed away from the edge of the platform, but pale things waited behind, surrounded him, closed in, and sent him into a light hypnotic sleep. The Autochthones lifted Marlowe and carried him out of the station, down to the tracks, and into the endless tunnels of the subway system.

CHAPTER 60

3:37 A.M.
Central Park South, 1 January 1987

Rahman could feel the boy's fear and confusion as he arrived. Beneath that was his hunger, his desire. Rahman smiled. The Autochthones had kept Caine under observation since their meeting, knew his every move. When he found the baby it was inevitable that he would try to double-cross them. It was easy to collect Adam's messenger en route.

The Autochthones had brought the boy up from the tracks, carried Marlowe over their heads to Rahman like a sacrifice. They lowered the boy to his feet before Rahman's great chair, unharmed but terrified, despite a brave front. Marlowe brushed off his blue fifties' style thrift-store suit, polished worn patent leather shoes on the calves of his trouser legs, and straightened his skinny tie. Rahman tried not to laugh. The creature was an unlikely ally, but Rahman was not one to turn down a gift, no matter the quality.

"What has Adam told you?" he asked in a voice that rolled through the station. Marlowe fidgeted like a frightened schoolboy before the headmaster's cane, but to his credit held his ground.

"Kill the child, bring him its head, and burn out the nest."

Rahman smiled. It was as he'd suspected.

"That won't be necessary."

He extended a hand and the boy pulled a folded sheet of paper from his jacket, withdrew it slightly as Rahman reached out. "Look. You'd have to fight for the baby at night. I can see your guys are a scrappy bunch. But I can get it for you when it's asleep. Like I was for Adam. Just make me a vampire when I do."

Rahman was beside Marlowe before he could move away, and ran a long fingernail along the boy's bobbing Adam's apple, like a surgeon contemplating his first incision.

"Why not send you as my slave?" asked Rahman.

"Because I ask so little," said Marlowe. "It costs you nothing."

"There's always a cost." Rahman knew he could get the baby with a single bite, but was amused by the boy's presumption. He decided to grant the boy's wish, pulled him close. "Very well. I agree to your terms."

Rahman raised a hand, sliced the flesh of his own thumb with the sharp ebony nail of his forefinger. A thick, colorless plasma dripped as slowly as syrup from his wound. Rahman slipped it into the astonished boy's mouth and made him drink deeply.

Marlowe felt the dry thumb in his mouth, started to object until a honey-thick liquid filled his head with visions. Intoxicated, he swooned as he was made blood brother to the leader of the Autochthones, shared their blood. He saw an unfamiliar life flash before his eyes, Rahman's, one of violence and glory; he rode desert sands on horseback, fought battles, killed men by the sword and with his bare hands. Images of the Autochthones' more ancient past rolled through Marlowe's mind, as millennia of history poured through his head in seconds.

When he woke, Rahman leaned over him.

"You'll rise as soon as you die. No one need call you up. Choose any time you wish, as long as it's after you bring us the infant. If not, we'll have eternity to punish you."

The Autochthones led Marlowe back to the main tunnel and released him. He stumbled down the tracks. His head still spun with dreams; the walls of the subway tunnels seemed covered with ancient mosaics. He was alive and free and he'd finally gotten his wish. Immortality was his. Marlowe could hardly wait to try it out, like a new gun, and he would.

But first he had a baby to deliver.

CHAPTER 61

9:53 A.M.
Lower East Side, 1 January 1987

Marlowe had doubts as soon as he found the house.

It looked like a typical drug squat, a condemned building on an abandoned block, but Marlowe was pretty sure he wasn't going to find a bunch of junkies inside sleeping off their last fix.

What was he doing walking into a vampire hideout? Sure, they were helpless in daylight, but what about hidden from the sun? The Autochthones were still up and around under ground. He'd seen Adam up early indoors as long as he stayed out of direct sunlight. How asleep were the baby's sitters in the cool dark of their own home? Maybe they'd take him out as soon as he walked inside. . . .

Marlowe breathed deeply at the door of the derelict building, calmed down. He couldn't really die anyway, not now. Not if what Rahman had said was true. He'd made his deal with the devil. He pushed the front door. It swung open easily. They were either careless or sure that they were safe. The walls inside seemed solid enough, but Marlowe stepped carefully, unsure of the rotted wood under his feet. There was no one on the first floor. He'd expected that and looked for a door to the downstairs, sure that they'd be hidden away from the sun.

It was easy to find. Marlowe opened a basement door and pulled a flashlight from a knapsack on his back to check out the stairs before he went down. He remembered a Stephen King book where vampires sawed off the steps and lined the floor below with knives. Even if he was coming back to life, he didn't feel like going in that manner.

The staircase looked fine. Marlowe walked down slowly, kept the light as low and close to his feet as he could. At the bottom of the steps the basement was large and open, without any hiding places. Marlowe shone the beam of the flashlight around the room, spotted a dark mound at the far end. He walked toward it, avoided broken bottles on the way. When he got close enough, he could see that the mound was a pile of sleeping bodies.

Vampires.

Instinct told him what he was looking for was underneath. Marlowe almost laughed. What morons. No booby traps, no clever defenses. He guessed this was the baby's idea of protection, nestled under them like he was back in Mommy's womb. Even though they were all full-fledged vampires, Nina's little bastard was still their leader. Pathetic.

It didn't take him long to realize that their defense was still a problem. He'd have to dig his way through them to get to the little monster. This was where he'd find out just how awake they were during the day.

Marlowe picked a small one first, so he'd have a chance of getting away if it woke up and attacked. He pulled it off the pile and rolled it over to see that it was a girl. She stirred, but didn't wake when he dragged her across the dirt floor. Her mouth was smeared with caked blood, but her lips were still soft, full, and appealing. She didn't look that dead. Marlowe could picture her mouth pressed against his, or wrapped around his hard cock, until it opened and he got a glimpse at the sharp fangs inside. He shuddered and dropped her feet, went back to the pile.

Marlowe knew from watching Adam that blood was like a drug to them. The junkies had just traded one high for another, with a new kind of crash. They must be sleeping off a big holiday meal. That made them easier to handle. Marlowe was relieved, but wasn't done. They were out cold, but there were still more than a dozen left. It would take a while to move enough of them to get the damn baby out. Marlowe pulled off his jacket and went to work, for the first time wished that he'd considered exercise at some point in his life.

Rahman sat back in his chair and let his mind drift as he followed the trail of blood he'd released into Marlowe. He could have used the Autochthones' mind tricks to leave his body and follow him in astral form, but had no need. Until the boy was a vampire they were still connected. Rahman could see through his eyes, and watched as Marlowe dragged the unconscious undead off the baby.

He saw the boy free the infant and bundle it in his knapsack to protect it from the sun. Marlowe lifted the bag, carried the baby outside and away without stopping to burn the nest as Adam had ordered. Rahman was amused. The boy had compounded his betrayal of his master. What more was he capable of doing? Rahman would have to keep an eye on this one.

He had ambitions.

CHAPTER 62

•

4:36 P.M.
Fort Greene, 1 January 1987

Steven woke, sweaty, stomach tight, bowels tense.

He rolled out of bed, only half noticed that he was alone as he stumbled to the bathroom and sat on the toilet. He pissed and tried to keep whatever was left in his stomach from erupting into the sink, wished he'd smoked a joint before going to bed. But they'd needed to stay alert in case of attack.

When he left the bathroom, Steven went to the kitchen. A full kettle was already on the stove, along with a note from Lori. He warmed the water while he read her message.

After a day in hiding she'd decided to go the library to research how to kill vampires, and would call him later. Even though their world had been turned upside down, Lori was on top of it. She'd always reminded him when to pay bills, sent in invoices on jobs they'd done together. She'd been the responsible one while he buried himself in the studio, painted all night, slept all day. Steven had always wanted to believe he was here to protect Lori from demons in the dark, but the truth was that, once again, she was out saving them both.

The only thing he could do now was wake up and wait for her call. Steven made a cup of tea when the kettle whistled, reached for his stash box, and pulled out his hash pipe. He started to light it and stopped as he had the night before. No reason to let Caine catch him napping at the end of the day. He smoked too much, anyway.

Steven flopped down on the couch, sipped his tea, and tried to kick-start his exhausted brain. He looked at the clock. It was already after noon, later than he'd thought. If Lori had left as early as her note said, she should have called to say she was on her way back by now.

Steven tried to focus his attention on something else so he wouldn't freak, went through bills and found them filled with disconnect warnings. He didn't have nearly enough of the book advance left to begin paying them. Typical. Almost thirty and he was still living from check to check, none ever big enough to cover his expenses. Just like his mother. He shoved the bills away, decided to wash the dirty dishes. That would be some tangible sign of change, progress he could at least see at the end of the day.

The sink stank. He must have put off washing dishes longer than he'd thought, something else he'd inherited from his mother. Steven always ignored little problems until they were major malfunctions and let messes grow until they seemed insurmountable.

Was it genetic? Had his mother accidentally made a mess of her life, or had she been programmed by her parents to self-destruct? Had her genes programmed him to do the same? Steven ran the water until it warmed, dug under the dirty dishes to open the drain so that rancid water would run out and let fresh water fill the sink.

He tried to clear his head as clean dishes went into the rack, one by one, until he was down to silverware at the bottom. It was still obscured by murky dishwater despite the running tap. At the bottom of the sink, he felt something slimier than the dishes. Steven winced, repulsed. He had to start wearing rubber gloves. He steeled himself and plunged bare hands into the water once more. The job was almost done.

Wet tentacles whipped out of the suds, wrapped around his forearms, and tightened to hold him in place. Steven closed his eyes and shook his head to make sure he was awake. The tentacles were still there when he opened his eyes. He struggled, but they held fast, pulled him closer to the water. There was a face under it, barely visible, eyelids shut. They opened as the features rose to the surface, wrinkled by water, rotted, a face Steven recognized as it broke the surface and glared at him, angry, accusing.

His dead mother.

The last time he'd seen her she was in a coffin, dressed in her Sunday best, face painted like a doll, eyes closed in mock slumber. The eyes that stared up at him now from the dishwater were yellow, stained, the skin moldy and transparent with underwater rot. Instead of the loving smile she always had for him, she scowled, angry, resentful.

"You left me . . ."

The voice bubbled from the depths of the sink, as if freed from a backed-up drain. It scared Steven with its familiarity as much as what it said. He pulled as far away as he could, breathed through his mouth to avoid the smell of decay, but was dragged down by greasy tendrils that held him fast.

"You left me to die!"

Flecks of moldy spit sprayed his face as his dead mother's face rose above the water, sneered as she continued.

"I begged you to stay! I could smell the angel of death, feel its hot breath on my cheek, but you cursed me. Cursed me and abandoned me to death by drowning! They didn't find my body for a week. A week under water, drowned, rotting, because of you!"

Steven knew it wasn't true, but he'd lived with the guilt since her death, like it or not, the tiny shadow of a doubt in the back of his head that it was his fault.

When he graduated from high school he'd been accepted to the Cooper Union School of Art with a full scholarship. Steven found an apartment in the East Village, a part-time job nearby, and told his mother he was moving out. They had their first big fight, one that lasted for months.

He'd moved out anyway, but the phone kept them connected. She'd call three or four times a week to drag him back out to Queens to help with a problem at the house, to take her to the store, to cry on his shoulder about how lonely she was.

Steven hated it, but said nothing, never admitted even to himself how much of a drain their relationship was and had been his entire life. He always thought of the Norman Bates line from *Psycho*, a line that stuck in his head the first time he saw the movie on late-night TV: *"I don't hate her . . . I hate what's she's become."*

Then he signed up for a summer course in Paris.

He wouldn't be just across the river—he'd be across an entire ocean for an entire summer, unavailable, inaccessible. When he told her, she freaked, wept, screamed that he was leaving her alone and unprotected, the way his father had. That had been the real fight, and the last one. He refused to give in, fought down the guilt, and yelled back, let out everything he'd ever held back, and flew away.

She died while he was gone.

Neighbors found her body in the tub after no one saw her on the streets for a week, notified him in Paris through the school. It was an accident, and even though there was nothing he could do to save her, he came back early to take care of things. She'd won again.

"You were drunk! They told me you slipped, hit your head!" Steven strained to get away.

"I died because you wished me dead when I begged you to stay! I needed you and you abandoned me! Left me to go be with the white people and their art! Left me for their women! Left me to knock up that white whore . . ."

Her eyes narrowed, cloudy corneas disappeared behind puffy lids as she frowned. *"Fucked that blond bitch and stuck a black baby in her. Did you think she'd love you for that? Any more than your father loved me after he stuck you in me? He didn't die in Vietnam . . . I told you that all your life, but I lied! He left! Left me with a half-black bastard he was ashamed to call his son! Abandoned you, the way you abandoned me!"*

She spit in his face. It burned like acid, dripped down his cheek as Steven's face was pulled closer to hers.

"No! That's not true," yelled Steven, nose to nose with the apparition, no longer able to avoid the stench. He could see tiny veins pulse under the surface of the decayed skin, pumping bile through her distorted features. "My father was a war hero, you fucking liar. . . ."

"You pathetic half-breed—I should have killed you in my womb . . . like you killed yours . . ."

"I didn't kill it! I didn't!"

"You deny you wished your baby dead? That your hate killed it in your bitch's belly? Killed it like your hate killed me? Like you're killing yourself with your drugs and drinking?"

She changed from his dead mother into the face of a crazed black junkie. Crack smoke poured from his nostrils like dragon's breath. It was Steven's own face, dazed, mad, his worst fear of his future. Not dead, but crazy, addicted, homeless, another one of the broken black men he saw every day in the subway, wandering the streets of the city, lost.

"Spare change, man? Quarter, dime, nickel, penny?" asked the face. "Please, man, jes' need some sleep, some food. So hungry, so damn hungry . . ."

Twin knives slid up from the water, on either side of the head. Corroded blades shimmered from rust to shiny sharpness before his eyes. The face in the water melted back into his mother's, soft now, tender and loving.

"Come to momma, baby. I came back to save you. Come to me. I love you, Steven. I need you. . . ."

Steven summoned up all his will to resist her siren call, fought not to drop down onto the blades, shove them through his eyes and into his brain. He reminded himself that this couldn't be real. His mother was dead, long dead, and she had loved him, encouraged and supported him, no matter how crazy she was. He'd never wished her dead, no matter how angry he'd been. This had to be illusion, a spell cast by the vampire. He'd ridden out worse acid trips. He could fight his way through this.

"*It's so easy.*"

The voice cooed, seductive. The tentacles wrapped around his neck, inched Steven closer to the sharp tips of the knives and sweet release. "*You killed me,*" said the dead voice. "*I never would have drowned if you'd stayed. It's your fault. There's only one way to make it up to me. Come home to momma. Come home to me and your daddy . . .*"

"No! You're not my mother! You're not real! You're a lie, a fucking lie!" Steven screamed, opened his eyes, and came to up to his elbows in sink water, knives clenched in his fists where they'd been all along, blade points a bare inch from his face. Steven dropped them, threw himself back and away from the empty sink.

He'd won.

They'd seen Adam's game with the blinded graffiti artist at the gallery. The only reason Caine hadn't killed them immediately was that he wanted to play with them first. He'd planted this vision in Steven's head like a depth charge, a way to wipe him out by remote control. Who knew what he had planned for Lori? Steven picked up the phone to call the library. Maybe he could get them to find her, deliver a message and warn her in time.

The phone was dead.

Steven cursed, flipped through the stack of bills, and found the final cut-off notice. Lori might have tried to call him hours ago. He grabbed his coat and headed out the door.

Out on the street, he saw that his hallucination had taken longer than he'd thought. The sun was low in the sky, too close to sunset for him to reach Lori before nightfall. Steven started for the subway, then ran back upstairs to dig Jim's gun out of the drawer where he'd put it after he shot Caine. The pistol was still empty. Steven reloaded it, picked up a box of bullets, and left. He stopped at a pay phone around the corner, just long enough to leave a message for Jim at his hotel, then ran to the subway as fast as he could.

There was still time to save her.

CHAPTER 63

Lori went into therapy to find a way out of the hole she'd fallen into after being orphaned at twelve, when her father died a year after her mother.
He'd left Lori in the custody of a Wicked Stepmonster, an uncaring stepmother young enough to be her big sister. It took a decade for her to see life
as anything but a tragedy. The last few years had been a tribute to the work
she'd done. The relationship with Steven, as badly as it ended, had been the
healthiest in her life. Even ending it was a sign of growth.

Now she was back where she'd been at twelve, terrified and alone. Her
stomach was wrenched into a tight knot, bowels churning, knowing it was
only tension and fear that wanted out. Thousands of dollars, years of her life
spent on the analyst's couch, gone in a night. Not even a night. Less than an
hour that sent her running back to Steven's afraid for more than her life.

Afraid for her sanity.

The Forty-second Street library felt solid, built of stone that sheltered her
like a fortress. Though she was still vulnerable, Lori felt safe here, secure,
protected, as she had in her parents' house until death knocked at their
door.

Lori couldn't reach Steven. His phone was disconnected. He hadn't paid
the bill again. When she lived with him she made sure he sent checks out on
time. It didn't matter. She'd leave the library soon, kept making notes from
books as she looked for the way out, a way to kill the undead. Lori recorded

passages in a low voice into her microcassette recorder to save herself writing it all down. Someone shushed her. She whispered lower, annoyed.

Lori finished the last page and rewound to check what she'd recorded. She looked up to find herself alone. The large reading room was empty, silent. She looked at her watch. It was almost six, closing time, but too soon for everyone to have left without her noticing.

Lori slipped in her earphone and pressed Play.

Her dead father's voice filled her head. She ripped the plug from her ear. Impossible. She picked the earphone up and put it back in, played the tape and listened again.

It was still her father's voice.

"*Lori, pumpkin. Where have you been? I've been so alone, so alone . . .*"

Tears filled her eyes. She hadn't heard his voice in so long that it was a shock to recognize it, to hear his pet name for her, a name no one had called her in more than fifteen years.

"*So alone, baby. Why don't you ever come see me? Come on, pumpkin. Join me . . .*"

The voice was familiar, so real, even though she knew it couldn't be his. It hurt, opened the door to memories of the past, to the awful afternoon she'd found him dead. She realized that the voice wasn't coming from her earphone anymore, but from the library shelves behind her.

"*I want us to be together again. You, me, and your mother, one big happy family . . .*"

Lori stood, afraid, but was drawn to the sound. She gathered her things into her backpack and followed the voice, left the books she was reading on the table. The voice moved away as she got closer, led her to a small door against the rear wall, one she hadn't noticed before. She tried the doorknob. It turned. Lori opened the door and stepped through like Alice in Wonderland.

The other side wasn't a room of the public library, but the attic of her old house. Her backpack was now her old schoolbag. She was in a dress she used to wear to school. Lori was a child of twelve again, looking for her father, the way she had the day she came home from school to find the house empty, her stepmother out on one of her shopping expeditions and her father's car alone in the driveway. Sunlight trickled in from a tiny window at the far end, outlined a familiar figure seated on a trunk near the window.

"Daddy . . . is that you?"

She asked the question the way she'd asked it then, knew it was her father, but didn't understand why he didn't get up to greet her, or why his silence scared her.

"Daddy?"

There was no sound except for a persistent buzzing, the sound of summer flies. She could see them whirl lazily around his head. Lori didn't want to cross the narrow room for a better look, past storage boxes and old furniture, framed family pictures and her mother's clothes, artifacts of their past together.

Her Wicked Stepmonster had made him hide them all out of sight when she redecorated the house, unable to get him to throw out the life she hated and tried hard to make him forget. Lori was all she couldn't hide away, the only part of his past he wouldn't bury.

Lori's heart beat faster as she moved ahead, knew what she'd find, didn't want to see it again. Even so, she was pulled forward; her feet moved as if by remote control as she reenacted the moment she'd spent years in therapy to purge from her memory, like some hideous flashback.

Her father sat like a dressmaker's dummy, arms limp at his sides like empty sleeves. She made it to his side and reached out to touch him, screamed as he fell to the floor, pistol in one hand, a wedding picture of him and her mother in the other, his brains and blood splattered across it.

Lori saw a note on the floor by the trunk, as she had then, picked it up, and ran. She tried to escape the attic, but the door was stuck, just like then, kept her locked in the hot little room, the tomb, with her dead father and mementos of her dead mother.

Trapped, she sat and wept, her back to him, finally looked at the note she knew so well. The sun set outside as she read it again and again by the dwindling light. It said: *"I'm sorry, pumpkin. I know I'm a coward. I just can't live without her anymore. You'll be okay. We'll all be together one day. Forgive me. I love you. Daddy."*

When she stopped reading, it was dark in the attic. Lori felt her way to the wall switch, but the light didn't work, the way it hadn't worked that day. She was trapped alone in the dark with her father's dead body and the hungry, noisy flies.

Lori knew the corpse was across the room from her, didn't move, afraid of touching it in the dark. He would be cold by now, clammy. She didn't want to remember him like that. She tried to remember happier times with her father, pleasant memories she could take with her instead of dead staring eyes, the empty shell under the window.

She remembered a day she went to his office with him and was presented to all his coworkers, daddy's little girl. He was so proud of her that day, the way she smiled and spoke so politely to the other partners at his law firm.

Afterward, he took her to lunch at the 21 Club with his secretary, Marcie, the bleached-blond bitch who wheedled him into marriage after Lori's mother died, pretended sympathy while she did her best to erase everything in his life before her.

That day she'd acted the role of the perfect employee, done her best to pretend she had no other plans for him. Marcie told Lori how sorry she was to hear about her mother's illness, offered a willing ear or a shoulder to cry on while she patted Lori's father's knee under the table, talked about how hard all of this was on him, on them all.

Lori saw through Marcie with a child's clear vision, hated her that day and every day to come, long after the funeral where she played hostess at Lori's mother's wake, long after she married Lori's father a barely respectable year later, almost to the day.

"Lori? Pumpkin?"

It was almost his voice, she thought. An amazing impression, but it wasn't her father. It couldn't be.

"Honey? Come to daddy, baby . . ."

The idea that anyone would mimic her dead father scared her more than the voice. The sound didn't scare her, no matter how spooky it was. It was that someone could be so sick, so cruel as to torment her with her dead father's voice in the dark, his body on the floor. That scared her much, much more.

"Why are you doing this?" she said, in tears. "Why?"

"Because I love you," said the dead voice, still pretending to be her father. "Because I want us to be together."

Her father's corpse glowed in the dark then, so she could see it as it stood, dried blood congealed around the gaping head wound. Her dead mother rose from the floor, too, stood smiling by his side, face pale, throat blooming with flowery cancer tumors.

"We're both here. Together. Waiting for you to join us."

"Come here, baby," said her mother. The sound fluttered from her ruined throat in a whistle, even harder to listen to than her father's voice. "We love you, pumpkin. Join us, so we can be one big happy family again."

"No! You're not my parents! You're not!"

They approached, arms outstretched, reached for her. Lori backed away, shook her head, shouted, "No, no, no," over and over. The figures dimmed, distorted as she screamed them away. They thinned and faded as she denied them. One shadow remained behind, between her and the window.

"You renounce them, but you can't renounce me. I was in the shadows then. We're old friends, you and I. My pain was born in an attic, too. . . ."

The voice was still familiar, but not her father's. A young voice that sounded much older.

The voice of Adam Caine.

"I've been with you all your life. Shaped you. Changed you."

"No," Lori said. He was lying.

"I was there when you lost your mother. Your father. I was with you the first time you said yes to a man. I was with you the day you killed the result at an abortion clinic."

"You have no right," she whispered. Tears stung her eyes. He was more of a monster than she'd imagined.

Adam shimmered into view from the dark as he revealed himself. She watched him drift across the room toward her. A cloud passed from the full moon outside. Moonlight shone on his face from the window, made it glow like fine porcelain.

"I was there every time you stumbled, made you feel it a little more than you would have without me. The richness of feeling you pour into your writing is mine. I made you."

"No!" Lori screamed and pounded her fists at him when he reached her. He was behind her before she could turn, pulled her close like a passionate gigolo in a tango embrace. He snarled into her ear.

"You belong to me."

Caine swung her around to face him, held Lori with one hand and opened his shirt with the other.

"Can you imagine even a little of my loneliness?"

His chest was smooth and hairless. Her eyes were drawn to it as he slipped the fingers of one hand inside the shirt and pulled it back to expose his flesh. It was pale, nearly translucent, and beautiful without flaw. He ripped a gold ring out of a pierced nipple. The torn skin released almost colorless plasma, thick as honey. It oozed slowly from a wound that had already started to heal.

"You don't have to die. Join me in the dark . . . forever."

Lori resisted. She'd pieced together a profile of his methods and motives from what little she knew of his crimes. This was a game for him, to bring his victims as low as he could and then pick them off. She was supposed to surrender now, give in to his wish that she join him. Let him drain her life thinking she'll be brought back, when it was just a lure to pull her into his deadly embrace. She willed Caine away, threw him back with her mind, and pushed harder to shatter the spell he'd cast over her.

"No! This isn't real! Stop it! Stop!"

She was a writer, Lori told herself—she knew fact from fiction. As she believed the truth, her words took effect, as they did when her parents' ghosts faded. She watched the world around her melt. Walls, windows, floor, flowed into new forms, turned into Bryant Park behind the library. She'd walked outdoors while under his spell. The library was closed, empty, and dark behind her. How long had she been entranced out here? It was night, not even a glimmer of sunlight to be seen.

Only Caine still stood in front of her, hand extended.

"Join me . . ."

Lori barely had time to answer before Caine was knocked to the ground. It was Steven.

Caine was caught off guard for only a moment. He leaped back to his feet, grabbed Steven's jacket, and lifted him. Steven's toes barely reached the ground. Caine tossed him yards away and turned back to Lori. She was still frozen where he'd left her, no time to move. Caine pulled her back into his arms as she stared over his shoulder in shock.

"Sorry." He gripped her hair, pulled her head to one side to expose her throat. "You should have accepted my offer . . ."

As he leaned forward to bite, something else hit him from behind. There was a satisfying crack. She couldn't tell if it was Caine's bones or what had hit him. It didn't matter, the force made him release her.

"Back off, bastard!"

It was Jim. He'd come prepared, with a sharpened stake the size of a baseball bat. As Lori stumbled away from Caine, Jim kept him away, pounded his makeshift club into the vampire's raised arms and kept swinging until Caine backed off.

Lori saw Steven's body on the ground, still. Not his body, she told herself. He was still alive. He had to be. She ran to Steven's side while Jim forced the vampire to keep his distance. Steven was winded but still breathing when Lori reached him, started to revive when she crouched beside him. She helped him to his feet.

"Careful," Lori said.

"My pocket . . . the gun . . ."

He tried to clear his head as Lori realized what he meant. She hesitated.

Lori had always hated guns, even before her father's suicide. Ordinarily she'd never touch one, but this was no ordinary situation. Before she had time to think, she fished through Steven's pockets and found the pistol. She held it in her hand, metal still warm from his body heat.

Lori could see that Jim had Caine backed against a tree. The vampire scrambled up the massive trunk backward, silhouetted like a huge spider against the bare branches above them. He was far enough from Jim for Lori to use the gun without fear. She clenched her teeth, walked with the pistol held out in front of her with both hands to steady it, took sight along the barrel, aimed up, and fired. Lori hit Caine once, recovered from the recoil, and fired again.

He dropped from the tree to the ground, popped up like a jack-in-the-box, and gave Jim a backhanded slap that felled him. Caine turned to Lori, fangs bared. His eyes gleamed red with blood and fury.

Lori walked forward, terrified, squeezed the trigger over and over as she emptied the barrel into him, close enough that every bullet hit its mark. Maybe they wouldn't kill him, but they had to hurt. If they slowed him down enough, it might give them time to find another way to stop him.

Caine fell with a dull thud as Jim struggled to his feet and picked up his club again, raised it. He drove it down like a stake, jammed the pointed end into Caine's chest hard enough to pin him down.

"No . . . please . . ."

Caine's words bubbled out though bruised lips in a desperate rush. Jim twisted the stick, tried to drive it in. Steven stumbled over to Lori. The two of them stood next to Jim, ready to help. Lori watched him carefully as Steven took the gun, pulled bullets from his pocket, and reloaded it.

"Kill me and you'll never find the child."

It was enough to stop Jim, the one thing that Caine could have said that could. Jim looked at Steven and Lori with despair in his eyes. He wanted to finish off the thing that had destroyed his family, but was suddenly faced with an answer to his last question. He turned back to Caine.

"Is it still alive?" asked Jim.

Caine hesitated. Jim twisted the stick again. They could see bullet holes begin to close as the amber fluid that oozed from them slowed. Lori was sure that if they gave him too much time he'd be healed, able to defend himself again.

"It's a vampire."

Jim jammed the stick forward again. "How could you . . ."

"I didn't," Caine said, too quickly. He grabbed the club with bloody hands. "A nest of downtown junkie vampires. Killed Nina, turned her baby. I'll tell you where it is." He gave them the address and Lori wrote it down. He spoke persuasively, hypnotic, almost won them over. "You can give it peace. Free me. I can help you."

Lori saw Jim's eyes narrow as he decided.

"Fuck you," said Jim and jammed the stake through Adam's chest. The point was dull, moved slowly as Jim shoved it through Caine's rib cage by sheer force, powered by raw hate.

Adam panicked for a moment and then relaxed, felt rough-cut wood miss his heart by millimeters. He used his grip on the stake to shift it more, forced his mind into crystal-sharp focus. It wasn't too late to save himself. Prod the boy. Provoke him. Goad him into carelessness.

Jim's face floated dimly in front of him, red with rage, irrational, blubbered like a baby as he confronted his family's killer, his archenemy. Adam stifled a smile. Poor fool. He still didn't even understand the game.

"Why did you do it? My father, my mother, my sister . . . Why did you kill them?"

"Why?" Adam chuckled, bared his teeth; his own blood rose in his throat as he forced out the words he knew would hurt the most. "Because . . ." He gagged on his own gore, but still managed to choke it out. ". . . I could!"

He laughed. Tears ran down the boy's cheeks as he screamed and rammed the stake deeper into Adam, quickly, careless, dug in with his full weight. Caine gasped, leaned up and grabbed the boy's jacket to pull him down, and hissed two last words.

What was left of Jim's world exploded.

They all stood stunned as they watched the vampire play out the ending they'd seen in a hundred movies and TV shows, aged and withered into a dry mummy before their eyes. Lori saw Jim's eyes widen as he pulled away from the husk on the ground. She touched his arm.

"What did he say?" she asked.

"It was nothing! Nothing!"

He jerked away from her, as sirens rose in the distance. Lori looked at Steven. There were always sirens in New York, but after the gunshots there was no point in waiting to see if these were for them. Only the vampire had kept them from being seen so far, and he was dead. Here they were, about to flee another murder scene. To think she'd once worried that her life was getting too routine, too literary . . .

Jim stood frozen over what was left of Caine's body.

Steven grabbed his arm.

"Come on, we have to get out of here."

Lori got on the other side of him and together they pulled Jim to the street and hailed a cab, got in, and gave the driver directions to Steven's loft. Jim stared ahead, unseeing, silent as the grave. Tears flowed from his eyes in a steady stream. Lori held his hand and squeezed it, but got no response. They'd find out what was wrong with him later. In the meantime, she almost relaxed. If they'd really done what it seemed they had, the worst of their ordeal was over.

They'd slain the dragon.

CHAPTER 64

7:32 P.M.
Chinatown, 1 January 1987

Jim curled in a ball in the back of the cab and wept as they crossed the Manhattan Bridge. He shivered, not from the cold but from Caine's last words. The man was a monster, no doubt now. Only a monster could be cruel enough to put such a thought into his head with its dying breath.

Caine had opened a door to memories best left buried, memories that sent Jim back over a year ago to the last time he'd seen Nina. They were in their room at the Murphys', in the middle of a fight. They'd been fighting more and more lately.

For six years Jim and Nina had lived either in group homes or on the run. The Murphys gave them the first safe place they'd had since their mom died, but it wasn't enough for Nina. She watched too much TV, saw too much of the world outside their little town, and hated Ohio, hated the farm, and wanted out.

Jim had lived all those years with fear, for his sister and himself. His stomach always hurt, his gut churned every morning when he woke up and wondered if this would be the day the redhaired man found them, and came for him or his sister. He'd never had time to think about what his life could be other than that. Because he took on the burden of their survival, Nina had time to dream. The only future he'd ever imagined was a day or two ahead, maybe a week, but Nina saw life passing her by while she stayed by her brother's side, safe or not.

"I can't do this anymore. I can't stay here all my life," she'd said the last night he saw her. "It sucks."

"Give me time, Nina. We can save money, make plans . . ."

"You always want to wait! God, Jim! I'm so tired of this! I want to see a real city, New York, Chicago, anyplace but here. I want to live my life, not keep runnin' from whatever you think killed Mommy and Daddy!"

"But he's still out there. The redhaired man. Whoever he is, he's waiting for us. For you . . ."

"I don't care. You saw him, not me. I can't hide anymore, Jim! I want to live. I want to dream. I want to be something other than what I am, what we both are. Which is nothin'! Nobody!"

Jim had slapped her in anger and fled, ashamed of himself.

He wanted to say that she was ungrateful for all he'd done, but he understood how she felt. God knew he did. Jim wanted a normal life, too, anything but what they had. He'd be eighteen soon. Maybe they could take a trip someplace she wanted to go, check it out, see if they could make a new life someplace far away from everything that haunted them.

Except that he couldn't let go of his fear, couldn't forget what he'd seen when their mom died, what he knew was true. He wanted to believe that Nina was right, that he'd imagined it all in the madness of watching their life go up in flames. Except he hadn't. He wasn't sure of much, but he was sure of what he'd seen that night.

Jim went to the barn to escape, like he always did, got stoned on weed and drank whiskey until he blacked out. The rest of the night was a blur of shattered images and random sounds. He had vague memories of a girl under him in the barn later that night, crying out in what sounded like passion to him. He'd made it back to the bedroom, and the next morning when they all woke up, Nina was gone.

He'd always been sure that he'd gone out and found some local neighbor girl to help him forget his fight with his sister, until Caine made him remember everything. It was a curse that made every nightmare up until now seem tame, would haunt him to his death. The real truth about that last night with Nina, blocked from his mind by the vampire until now.

It wasn't some eager farm girl or stoned cheerleader.

His worst fear had come true. The redhaired man had already located them and bided his time until he found the cruelest way to part them he could. She must have come to the barn looking for him, to apologize for their fight, to continue the conversation. Instead, Jim had raped her, tricked by the vampire into seeing his sister as a stranger, taken her like an animal in a stoned drunken frenzy, heard her screams and pleas to stop as passionate cries to force himself on her more roughly. He'd violated her, driven her out of their safe home and right into the arms of the monster that had made him do it.

Jim always thought Nina had run away because of their fight, which never made sense to him. They'd fought before. Now he knew the real reason, knew she fled because he'd raped her and worse. Because of him, she'd worked her way to New York to give birth to their incestuous child, and then had been lured by a devil into prostitution to support it until he killed her. Caine told him all of that with two words, when he unlocked Jim's worst nightmare. . . .

"Goodbye, Daddy!"

And the truth tumbled out, never to be buried again.

Jim was damned to Hell, as surely as Caine. His only satisfaction was that he'd sent the beast to its master first. Of all the horrors he'd seen in his life and this city, this was truly the worst, the last he could bear. He'd held out this long, for years against all odds, but this broke him. All that was left was to find the child and redeem its soul by ending its unnatural existence.

Then his own.

Jim sobbed, rocked, ignored Lori's concerned hand on his. He could never explain to her, to anyone, what was wrong.

He would take his secret to the grave.

Adam opened his eyes and chuckled, even though it hurt. Like all his prey, they saw only what they wanted to see. It had been easy to make them see him die. Adam focused what was left of his energy and sent out a mental call to his bodyguards to come rescue him.

His limousine arrived moments later. Two muscle boys gently lifted Adam into the back of the car. He'd be taken home to recover, then he'd make his attackers pay for this indignity, and the suit. First he needed to rest and heal, which reminded him of Marlowe, who still hadn't reported back with the baby. He'd failed him. No matter. Adam smiled with ruined lips.

The boy might still be of some use.

CHAPTER 65

If only Adam were dead . . .

The thought drifted through Perenelle's mind as she lay on satin pillows and hand-stitched Indian cotton quilts in her darkened meditation room. She stroked the forehead of the young blond broker she'd held behind after the usual weekly meeting of his channeling group, could never remember his name. He'd had many questions tonight and the answers had kept him here to ask more. Now he was asleep, exhausted, drained. Perenelle had been careless. She'd let herself draw more from him than she needed to as he stared into her eyes, entranced, awed, while "Rahman" spoke to him in private.

Witnessing Adam's excesses had her exceeding her own limits again. Perenelle stared at the broker's pale throat like it contained a rare and expensive vintage she'd waited far too long to drink. She'd avoided blood for over a century, until losing Nicolas in Tibet sent her over the edge. For decades after she was a creature of blood and sadism that delighted in the deaths of her victims, enjoyed every one. Her joy had been lost and she'd been determined to take everyone else's, one life at a time, with an eternity to finish the job. She'd become everything in New York she'd sworn in Paris never to be, a monster, and had turned Adam into one, too.

If he were dead, she could forget that period of her life had ever existed, could remember the joy of mingling with leading spiritualists in the 1930s as she established her house in the Village as a sanctuary for them and herself.

If Adam were dead, she wouldn't be staring at the pulsing jugular on the broker's neck, remembering how easy it was to pierce the skin with a quick bite of sharp teeth, how sweet the nectar beneath tasted . . .

As she thought of all the ways Adam could come to a bad end, the air before her rippled and Rahman stood there, as clearly as if he were in the room. She knew his presence was only an illusion, an astral projection of his mind. Rahman never left his station anymore.

"Perenelle," he said. "I have the child. You have something I need."

"You can't have the book. Not when I know what you'll do with it."

"That's not your concern. Unless I succeed." Rahman scowled. "Bring me the book."

"Never."

Perenelle stayed where she was on the pillows, the broker still unconscious by her side. Rahman shook his head with a grim smile, not the reaction she'd expected.

"You will bring me the book. If not, I'll be forced to reveal your little secret. Or should I say, your three little secrets?"

Perenelle paled, sat up. "You wouldn't."

"I need the Book of Abraham to complete the Work. I'll do anything I must to get it. If you don't bring me the book before dawn, I'll make sure every vampire in New York knows there is no Triumvirate of the Veil—"

"No!"

"That it's all been a clever illusion, crafted by you, with the help of the Autochthones, using powers we taught you. The power to control other vampires the way we control humans. The power to fool them into seeing and hearing what you want them to see."

"You bastard . . ."

"You've kept them in thrall for half a century, controlled like children. Tamed like sheep. What do you think they'll do when they find out that you've been their judge, jury, and executioner all this time? Their puppet master? That they curbed their appetites, restrained their passions, for your vision of order?"

Rahman laughed.

"Before dawn, Perenelle. Bring the book."

He vanished and left her alone with her choice and her sleeping broker. Perenelle saw half a century of hard work erased; a fall back to the decadent times when she'd conceived the Triumvirate. Tom O'Bedlam hadn't been her only reason for creating the Veil. The vampires of New York had become careless, brazen. It was impossible to stop the advance of forensic science that would let humans distinguish vampire crimes from those of ordinary killers.

The Veil made them accountable, forced them to clean up evidence, use good judgment to escape detection. It ended territorial battles between them that drew unwanted attention, kept them from creating unsupervised new vampires.

For decades, no one had listened to Perenelle when she'd said the same things the Triumvirate did. Tom's act of blatant terrorism had given her a way to convince them all that they needed to unite to stay safe. Capturing Tom and Claire, giving credit to an imaginary trinity of powerful vampires working in unison, had been enough to convince them that the Veil was a real force, with real power to defend them, even if it was borrowed from the Autochthones and Rahman.

In the last fifty years the Veil had grown from the benign martial law of an illusory Triumvirate into a real democratic society. Perenelle still faked Triumvirate elections and remained its spokesperson to guide it, but it was a matter of time before "they" announced that it was safe for them to drop their secret identities and the drama. Then the Triumvirate would hold public elections and function like any other government, not a cult of personality.

What did it matter how it began? Like the manipulations that had brought the Temple of Dendur to the Metropolitan, any lies she'd told to protect her people were justified. The vampires of New York lived in peace, if not always in harmony, and if the truth was revealed, she would face worse than their collective vengeance. Once the Triumvirate was exposed as a sham, the Veil would be dissolved and the idyllic world she'd worked so hard to create would end. New York would be an open city. No mortal would be safe. In time, humans would discover the truth about vampires and destroy them all.

If she gave Rahman the book, he'd stay silent. What then?

In her quest to create a secret democratic society and turn its rule over to elected heads of the Bloodlines, she'd lost any ability to control the Veil or the council. Once the high council heard what Adam had done, they'd insist he stand trial. Not even the intervention of the Triumvirate, no matter how persuasive she made them sound, could save them both from certain entombment this time.

She'd done her job too well. Even she was bound by the Veil's rule of law. If Adam was to be judged, there was nothing she could do to stop it, nothing she could do to save him or herself. If they couldn't seal the breach, the best they could hope for was a merciful sentence. When she remembered how most of them felt about Adam, mercy seemed unlikely. They'd be sealed away forever like Tom O'Bedlam, and everything she'd worked for almost a century to achieve would still be over.

Perenelle added Rahman to the growing death list in her head. The only man worth anything in her life was long gone, swallowed by an avalanche in the mountains of Tibet. But in truth, her husband, Nicolas, was responsible for her predicament. If it hadn't been for his obsession with the Book of Abraham, the search for someone to translate it that led him to Rahman, she wouldn't be in this situation.

It was her husband's desire to study the Book of Abraham that led him to Spain, where he'd found Rahman. It was Nicolas's obsession that had led Rahman back to Paris. It was Nicolas's need to know the book's secrets that had made him agree to work with the monster to produce the elixir of life, even after he'd realized the full price they would have to pay.

She thought of that last night in Paris in tears, knowing it was soon to be repeated, and that there was nothing she could do to stop it. . . .

CHAPTER 66

7:19 P.M.
Paris, 12 September 1365

Night was the only relief from daily life in Paris.

The city took hours to settle down after dark, like a great beast slowly descending into deep slumber. The shouts of the vendors, the curses of passersby, the screams of children playing in the street, and neighbors calling out to one another, all slowly quieted as Paris dreamed. It was Perenelle's favorite time, when she could sit in peace, husband by her side as they spoke softly of their great work, the consequences success would have on their future, for them and all mankind.

But not tonight.

She was hard at work in the back room Nicolas used as his laboratory, helping him with the experiment. Here he'd gathered everything they needed for their studies, containers of exotic ingredients imported from foreign lands, piles of books and papers he'd pored over for decades, equipment to process any solutions they mixed. They'd completed all the steps of distilling the elixir except the final stage, and waited for Rahman to return with the last ingredient to complete the process. He'd refused to translate that part of the book until they were ready.

Thunder rumbled in the distance. A brief storm had passed through the streets, pounded down on the city like God's wrath. It lasted only a few minutes, and it was as the rains ceased that Rahman appeared in the back doorway, lit by a flash of lightning, as if in warning. He wore a long cloak wrapped around him and kept one arm concealed beneath it.

"Is it ready?" he asked.

Nicolas stood by the table filled with equipment they used in what Rahman called the Work. He lifted a small wooden case, opened it to show Rahman three vials of bright red fluid that still churned slowly, though cool for hours. Rahman smiled and took it from his hand.

"After centuries of searching for the answer to Jabir's quest, the time has come to see if my old mentor was a genius or a fool." He pushed the cloak back from his hidden arm, and it fell away to reveal a naked sleeping infant.

Perenelle was filled with sudden fear at the sight of the child. "What is that for?"

Rahman paused. "The final distillation requires an innocent body, untouched by impurity, to process the philter. It's the only way. Once it's ingested the elixir, its blood becomes the final solution we seek. We have but to retrieve it."

Perenelle advanced on the vampire. "Retrieve its blood? How, pray tell?"

Rahman smiled, and it wasn't pleasant. "As one would expect. Did you think there'd be no sacrifice, no price to pay for the secret of the ages? I took the child from a foundling home. Is one small life, already lost, worth so much more to you than the answer to all your questions? To eternal life and wealth beyond measure?"

Nicolas snatched the case from the vampire's hand.

"No! We would never have agreed to such a thing!"

Rahman moved quickly, but not to retrieve the vials from Nicolas, who held them poised to smash against the stone wall. The vampire snatched Perenelle instead, who stood dangerously close to him and the infant. Before she could resist, he rolled her close and bit deeply into her exposed throat.

Perenelle felt a moment of pain, then pleasure as the vampire's essence spread through her body from the wound. The sensation lasted only a moment as he drank and she lost consciousness.

Her eyes opened and saw the rough wooden beams in their ceiling, lit by the fireplace and tallow candles on the table. It looked different, brighter. What she saw was sharper, richer than before. She heard voices from above and turned her head. Rahman was standing, infant still cradled in his arm. Nicolas was crouched over her, his face contorted by a grief she'd never seen. She raised a hand to stroke his cheek.

"I'm all right, beloved. Alive and unharmed . . ."

Nicolas shook his head, tears dripped from his eyes to her cheeks. She felt each one hit like summer rain, smelled the salt and something else, something delicious. Perenelle looked at Nicolas' throat and saw a warm vein pulse there, felt drawn to the rhythm of the beat beneath the skin and an urge to take that soft skin between her sharp teeth, to bite and drink . . .

She screamed, realized that she was not unharmed, that the monster had killed her and brought her back to life as a creature like him. Perenelle gripped Nicolas's coat as he sobbed over her, listened to the vampire deliver his ultimatum.

"Now you have no choice. To save your wife you must save me. Give me the vials. Help me complete the Work or she roams the world as one of the undead, feeding on infants and adults alike, as I do. An eternity of torment for her as she watches you fade and die of old age. If she doesn't feed on you first."

Nicolas helped Perenelle to her feet and embraced his wife, despite the danger.

"Beloved. I can't let you suffer like this."

"Then kill me. Kill me before you give in to this unholy thing's wish." She held him close, knew her pleas were in vain. Neither of them knew how, and Rahman would never give them the time to find a way before he forced Nicolas to do his bidding.

In the end, Nicolas' love for Perenelle was too great.

"No. I'll save him. To save you." He looked away from her as he handed the vials to Rahman. Perenelle knew she could have knocked them from his hands at that moment, hurled them to the floor, but Rahman would only force him to start the Work again. She let helplessness mask her real feelings.

If there was a cure, she wanted it.

Rahman uncorked the first vial, lifted it to the baby's lips and poured its contents into the infant's mouth. The child drank as if the red fluid was mother's milk. They watched as it finished the solution and grew still as the formula ran through its system. The infant's skin burned bright, glowed with an inner light as the philter began to affect its chemistry.

Over the next few hours, Rahman gave the infant two more infusions at carefully measured times. After the third, Rahman carried the infant to the worktable, cleared a space and placed a large basin in front of him. He lifted the baby overhead by its ankles and picked up a large knife.

Perenelle looked away.

It had taken only a few years of marriage to convince her and Nicolas that she could never bear children. Perenelle was barren. New life had always been sacred to her and now she stood by silent while the vampire took that of an innocent to save his own and hers. She closed her eyes, but could still hear the baby's blood pour into the white basin.

"Is it done? Do you have what you want?" asked Nicolas. Perenelle turned to see the vampire lay down the dead infant's body. He used a ladle to lift some of the potion from the basin, now a dully-reflective gold liquid. Rahman poured the elixir into a cup and handed it to Nicolas.

"We'll see. Drink."

"What? This was to cure you, not . . ."

"Drink. All science needs a standard by which to judge success. We have to see if the elixir is what we sought before we see if it will cure me. And your wife."

He held the cup out and Nicolas reluctantly took it. He stared into Perenelle's eyes as he prepared to sip.

"For you, my love."

He drank and nothing seemed any different.

"Is something supposed to happen?" he asked Rahman.

"Yes," said the vampire, and plunged the dagger he'd used to sacrifice the child into Nicolas' heart. Perenelle screamed as her husband's body fell to the floor. Rahman knelt over him. The dagger was driven deep into Nicolas' chest, hard to remove as the vampire pulled it out. The blade was covered with Nicolas's blood. He lay on the dirt floor, eyes wide in shock, lifeless. Perenelle fell to the floor beside him and wept.

"Why do you weep, my wife?"

She stopped and raised her head from his bloody chest, saw Nicolas stare at her with a strange look of wonder in his eyes. She stood and helped him to his feet. He was dazed as he felt his chest and pulled open his shirt to reveal whole flesh where his mortal wound had been. Nicolas looked up at Rahman, and despite himself, laughed.

"We did it. God in heaven." He stared at Perenelle as if he saw her for the first time. "We've conquered death itself."

He embraced her for only a moment before the vampire pulled them apart.

"One more test."

Rahman lifted a cup of the elixir to Perenelle's lips, and she drank, eyes locked on her husband's gaze. When she lowered the cup, she felt no different.

"Nothing."

Rahman grabbed her hand and cut her palm with the dagger. In moments the flesh healed, the skin was whole again.

"That proves nothing. My flesh heals instantly since I drank the elixir," said Nicolas.

Rahman gripped Perenelle by the shoulders, turned her to face Nicolas and pushed her close.

"What do you feel? Love? Or hunger? Do you want to embrace him? Or feed?"

Perenelle felt Nicolas near her, the warmth of his body, the scent of his blood beneath the skin, so close, so much of it. She wanted to pull him into her arms, hold him close, but not as a lover . . .

"Please!" She turned her head away, closed her eyes.

Rahman relaxed his grip.

"Then we've failed."

It was the only time in the ages she'd known him since that Perenelle ever saw anything close to remorse in Rahman's eyes. It was as if for a moment he realized that all he'd done, all his atrocities, had been for nothing.

He fled, left Nicolas and Perenelle in the ruins of what remained of their lives.

CHAPTER 67

8:12 P.M.
West Village, 1 January 1987

The past held no answers to Perenelle's present woes.

The elixir had provided immortality at full strength, but they soon discovered that even diluted to the thousandth part, it could cure any disease and extend human life. Perenelle and Nicolas sold their skills to the highest bidders: lords and ladies they'd never consort with otherwise. They concealed their identities to prevent others from stealing their secret or forcing them to reveal its source. In a short time they'd amassed a fortune, used it as well as they could to redeem themselves with good works, starting with the reform and rebuilding of the local foundling home where Rahman had stolen his victim.

In time they faked their deaths and left Paris to conceal their longevity. They traveled the world for centuries in search of help, in the end went east to Tibet. There they found, if not a cure, at least hope that Perenelle could lead a life something less than that of a bloodthirsty killer. It was hope that had died with Nicolas, until Perenelle found a new peace in the West Village.

The scars of that night in Paris stayed with her, not just in her curse but in the conviction that her kind needed to be controlled, kept from pursuing their more violent, selfish natures. Rahman's actions that night, his unfeeling disregard for human life, were her first inspiration for the Triumvirate of the Veil. Now he threatened to destroy it unless she let him go down the same damnable path with the immortal infant. There was no choice.

She knew what she had to do.

CHAPTER 68

Marlowe sat alone in his room in his underwear, a blade from his razor in one hand while he tried to decide if it was the least painful way to end this life so he could begin his next. His eternal life.

The only question in his head was whether or not he trusted the Autochthones enough to die right now. It would be a pretty funny joke, wouldn't it, if they got him to deliver the baby and then kill himself without bringing him back. That would tie up all the loose ends pretty nicely, just the sort of thing he would do in their position.

Suicide was a pretty heavy sin to carry to the next life, however long it was. He could still die one day. Would he go to Hell then for killing himself now? Like he wouldn't go to Hell anyway for living on the lives of others, his punishment worse the longer he lived.

He knew he had to decide soon. Now that he hadn't shown up at Adam's with the baby, the boss was going to be pissed enough to kill him anyway. It was one answer to his problem, except that he knew Adam. It wouldn't be the clean, painless end Marlowe wanted. It would be slow and cruel, something Adam could savor for centuries as he replayed it in his head over and over again, as he did the others. He'd seen some of Adam's files, helped him update them. The vampire's talent for torture was endless.

There was a knock at the door.

"I'm busy!" Marlowe had paid his rent for the rest of the week, even though he didn't expect to be here that long. He couldn't think of anyone but the landlord who'd knock at his door at this hour until it smashed open and three of Adam's goons burst in.

"Get dressed," said the biggest, and threw him a handful of clothes. Marlowe felt his gut twist. The choice was out of his hands. As he climbed into a shirt and pants he wished he'd taken less time to decide. Whatever was ahead would make his years under the iron fist of the Spanking Man seem like summer school.

Marlowe stared out the windows as the limo made its way uptown. He knew it would be the last time he ever saw the city through these eyes. Columbus Circle, the Plaza Hotel, Central Park . . . none would ever look the same.

If he saw them again.

The long white car slid through the building's metal gate into the underground garage. Two of the goons took Marlowe upstairs in Adam's private elevator. It stopped at the penthouse and the door opened into the familiar lobby. Everything had a strange clarity, as if Marlowe were tripping on acid. For the first time he noticed intricate details in the sculptures, the paintings on the wall, the tiles on the floor, the grain in the wood of the furniture, with all the immediacy of a death row convict's last look at the world on his walk to the gas chamber.

He expected to be led to the study, but instead they took him in the other direction, to Adam's private quarters. Marlowe had never been past the big vault door into the boss's bedroom before. No one ever left there in one piece except Adam and his cleaning crew. He started to shiver, not sure if he'd be an exception.

What Marlowe saw when they led him inside gave him a little pleasure. Adam was battered, shot several times, with a huge hole in his chest. He lay on the bed naked and near death, displayed like a damaged Greek statue, skin white as ancient marble.

"Marlowe, my boy," Adam said, in a quiet voice that still chilled with its strength. "I knew you'd come." As if he'd had a choice. "Closer." His boss raised a hand like an old man on his deathbed, vision dimmed.

Marlowe pulled away, but muscle-bound body boys gripped his arms, dragged him within reach. Adam's hand gripped Marlowe's fingers like a steel vise, no matter how frail he looked.

Adam smiled weakly.

"The baby. Did you find it?"

Marlowe considered lying, but Adam would know if he did. Better to tell the truth. His situation couldn't get any worse. The worst he could do was kill him.

No. The worst he could do was kill him even more slowly.

"Yes."

"Good, good. And you recovered it, I trust?"

"Yes."

"Then what did you do with it?"

Marlowe hesitated. "Took it to someone else."

Adam smiled through the ruins of his face. "The Autochthones. You took it to them, didn't you?"

"Yes . . ."

Adam sighed, a disappointed parent. "What did they promise you? Wealth? Eternal life? I'm sure they lied to you, as you lied to me."

Marlowe felt the pressure on his hand increase. Bones compressed and started to give, just a little.

He'd never been as afraid as he was now. Not on the nights he'd curled under the covers hoping the Spanking Man was coming to take another kid to the basement instead of him, not while dragging vampire junkies off the baby, not while he crept through the subway tunnels carrying the child to the Autochthones. This was his end: he knew that. The awful part was not knowing exactly when or how.

"So young. So naïve. A deluded virgin, wandering in a deep wood, unable to see the forest for the trees." Adam released him and Marlowe whipped his hand away, rubbed it, sure that something was broken.

"There's such perfection in virtue, Marlowe, the power to tame unicorns, to appease gods. Virgin sacrifice has a longstanding tradition with good reason. What deity would not welcome an offering of perfect purity? It's an homage worthy of any god, never refused, always answered."

Adam beamed up at him as if he were at peace, as if he forgave Marlowe everything. That only scared him more. Adam was not a thing that knew the meaning of the word *forgiveness*.

"You always said you were here when I needed you," said Adam.

The thralls grabbed Marlowe. One held him while the other tied his ankles, strung the other end of the nylon rope through a ring over Adam's bed, and hoisted him up upside down into the air above him.

"I need you now. . . ."

Marlowe shrieked, knew it would do no good, that no one could hear anything from the soundproofed bedroom and that even if they did, by the time help arrived it would be too late and too little to save him.

He was raised into the air, swung just within reach of Adam's hands. One of the goons pulled Marlowe closer, ripped open the front of his shirt to bare his sweating throat and chest. Adam raised a long silver dagger as Marlowe stopped screaming and prayed.

"O my God, I am heartily sorry for having offended Thee, and I detest all my sins because of Thy just punishment, but most of all, because I have offended Thee . . ."

Adam lifted the dagger and sliced it across Marlowe's throat, cut off his Act of Contrition along with his vocal cords. Another swipe of the knife and the boy was slit from throat to navel, like a butchered pig.

Marlowe felt blood bubble up in his throat instead of the words of his prayer, watched his life shower down as Adam gulped greedily, rubbed blood into his hair, over his naked body, fell into a rejuvenating swoon. Adam's flesh grew, healed, and became whole before Marlowe's eyes as life faded with his sight, as his vision blurred and went black.

CHAPTER 69

It took only a few hours for Adam to revive completely. He'd saved him-self again, so many times over the years he'd lost count. While his staff cleaned his bedroom he took a long steamy shower until he felt whole and refreshed, with a pleasant blood high in the bargain. Adam ran hot water across his neck and considered his next move.

It was probably best to leave the country for a while to avoid the Veil un-til he could find a way to get the baby back from the Autochthones and clean out its nest. Europe. Or South America. Maybe South Africa. He'd always enjoyed himself there in the past. He dried and dressed, left his bedroom in clean clothes and headed for the study. A quick drink, he thought, then maybe a late-night hunt while he planned his trip.

Adam entered his study humming, something from the second act of *La Bohème*, his favorite opera. Everyone so surprised that Mimi would actually die after all they'd done to save her, despite how much they all loved her. Bet-ter than most, Adam knew that love seldom redeemed anyone.

He poured a glass of cognac and stopped. He wasn't alone. Someone stood in the shadows behind him, holding a snifter. It wasn't the Triumvirate. They were all he feared tonight. He relaxed, until his uninvited guest spoke.

"You killed my parents."

Not a question, but a conclusion.

Adam turned, astonished.

Marlowe. Dear dead Marlowe.

He was absolutely the last thing Adam expected to see. This was becoming a bad habit. If his victims kept rising, he'd have to stop killing altogether. The boy stepped into the light, whole, beautiful. No sunglasses. His eyes glittered like stars. Adam scowled. Marlowe was wearing one of his suits. The custom-made Versace. He'd make him pay for that.

"I'm surprised I didn't see it sooner."

He was sipping a snifter of Adam's cognac, insolent pup, a rather full glass. The other hand held a manila folder, with Marlowe's full name on the tab, filled with sheets of paper covered in Adam's tight, precise handwriting, his file on Marlowe's progress over the years. The same kind of file he kept on all his subjects. The boy tossed it onto the table, into the light.

"And Griswold! All those years of torture in that damn foster home. I should have recognized your style. I'm one of your little art projects. No wonder you never let me see all your files."

"You always were a bright boy." Adam finished pouring his drink. He decided to bluff it out. He had a lifetime of experience over this brat. He'd wipe him out as easily as he had Nina.

"Our meeting was no accident," said Marlowe. "It was a reunion. You raised me, made me want the power your curse could give me, made me want to live forever. Made me bargain with the devil for what you could have given me anytime." He stepped out of the dark, scraped fingertips along a windowpane as he passed. Steely nails left long grooves as they screamed across the glass. "How do you think I should repay the Autochthones for their gift? What's a proper price for immortality?"

He grinned and vanished.

"Marlowe?" Adam went to his most charming, charisma on full. Glamour poured off him in waves even he could feel. "Marlowe, dear boy . . ." He couldn't help but seduce him like this. "Don't you see? I planned for you to meet them, a plan that included your harsh childhood. Not as abuse, but as a kiln, a firing oven, to shape and strengthen you! Don't you see?"

He smiled at the dark, invited anything in it to come to him with gestures learned from an old fakir he'd eaten in India. He could have brought a cobra to ground with half the skill.

"You've accomplished everything I dreamed of for you. The Autochthones acted on my instructions from the beginning. I was just on my way to thank Rahman for his . . ."

There was no one there.

Adam looked around, saw and sensed no one, nothing. He must have imagined it. Adam laughed. A silly fantasy! Could it actually be guilt, after all this time? He really had to stop drinking blood, the high was beginning to dull his . . . What was that? That sound. Something was out there, slapped against the walls in the distance.

Still, he sensed nothing, and saw no one.

Was he hallucinating? His blood ran colder than usual. The Autochthones. Or the Triumvirate. They were the only ones who could invade his mind like this, the only ones he couldn't detect. The sound drew closer, closer . . .

Slap! Slap! Slap!

Had the Autochthones learned of his plan to double-cross them by destroying the baby? Had the Veil discovered his failure? Was this their way of settling accounts?

"What do you want? I'll pay, gladly!" A great wind threw his words to the walls. The sound of slapping grew, echoed down the halls of the penthouse as Adam fought to maintain his balance in the gale.

"What do you want?"

The answer came as if from miles away, but loud as thunder, the sound of a giant bending down to grasp his prey.

"You've been a bad, bad boy, Adam . . . Bad, bad, bad, bad . . ."

The Spanking Man.

He knew what that meant, from all the times he'd wound up Allan Griswold and sent him reeling after his young charges in piggy bliss at the thought of another whipping, drawing fine lines of blood to the surface for lapping, another dozen stripes for every "bad" . . .

". . . Bad, bad, bad, bad, bad, bad, bad, bad, bad, bad, bad, bad, bad, bad, bad, bad, bad, bad, bad, bad, bad, bad, bad, bad, bad, bad, bad, bad, bad, bad, bad, bad, bad . . ."

The word repeated like a stuck record, rolled over Adam like thunder. He backed toward the window, hoped for any chance of escape, even into a swift death. . . .

He saw his pursuer emerge from the dark, so much worse than anything he could have envisioned. Obviously Marlowe's work, not the Autochthones'. His resurrection was not a dream. Rahman had the baby, Marlowe had eternal night, and Adam had a date with the Spanking Man.

Marlowe lurked unseen in the dark, laughed as Adam stared up at the scarred, naked gray giant that stepped into a dim pool of light holding a silver-spiked patent leather paddle. It slapped Adam to the floor and stood over him like an angry ogre.

The thing wore a black rubber butcher's apron, squeaky wet with blood. Large yellow teeth, pale and soft like boiled corn, squished together across a broad mouth in an otherwise featureless face as Marlowe's avenger happily grinned and murmured, *"You've been a bad, bad boy . . . Bad, bad, bad,"* on and on as Adam's pain began and spread, endless and unstoppable.

CHAPTER 70

Rahman didn't look surprised to see Perenelle when she arrived at Sheep Meadow Station with a wrapped bundle. He didn't gloat, just extended a hand for the book as she worked her way through a mass of Autochthones surrounding the baby. It lay in a makeshift cradle on the station floor. The elder vampires circled it, bowed as if the infant were a holy object. Rahman sat on his throne and scowled at the proceedings. Perenelle hesitated before she handed the book over to him.

"Is there no way to talk you out of this madness?" said Perenelle.

"What would you have me do instead?" asked Rahman. "Let it live? Destroy it outright? At least this way there is some hope for me. For us." He opened the bundle, sighed in relief as he saw that the Book of Abraham was really there.

"No good can come of this."

Perenelle turned to go.

"Don't judge me, Perenelle. I have no choice," said Rahman.

She whirled back on him. "No choice? You live like a god in your own little world, control faithful hundreds who see all, know all! You run this city! How else could I have created the Veil?"

"Fool! You think I'm here by choice? That they worship me? For centuries they've kept me prisoner, made me their slave while pretending I was the master. Every time I tried to leave, they brought me back. They need me, the sense of purpose I bring them. Before me, they had nothing but mindless repetition of empty rituals. I gave them direction again. They won't go back." He leaned closer, whispered into her ear, "I need power, a new Philosopher's Tincture, true immortality, the ability to travel in daylight. The power to escape."

"But the child . . ." Perenelle felt a pang of pity for it, even though she could clearly see that it was no longer innocent. The infant had seen more of life and death than most humans would in a lifetime. There was no telling what it would become if it lived.

"There's no hope. I've had time to examine it. The child was lost once it drank the blood of the junkies who sheltered it." The Autochthones parted to let them through as Rahman led her to its side. She could see that the baby looked paler than it should, thinner. Living on the lives of others usually left vampires with a look of radiant good health, even if only the illusion of life. Something was wrong.

"The junkies were all infected with the AIDS virus, shared by needle. When the baby fed on them, the virus came into contact with the infant's vampire blood and mutated. The junkies died and came back as flawed vampires. They don't regenerate the way we do. They're dying, slowly, so is the infant.

"But their victims are a further mutation, mindless zombies that carry a vampire HIV-infected blood that brings them back to life only to reproduce itself. A mutant plague is spreading through downtown now, like a fire, leaping from body to body. Turn your attention to that crisis, if you're worried about Revelation. The baby is doomed, no matter what I do."

Perenelle stared at the infant and let her mind consider what Rahman had told her. If he was right, she had to act fast to cleanse the nest, track down its victims, and cover up a plague of unknown proportions. Adam's folly had spread far wider and faster than she could ever have dreamed. She left Rahman to the Work, fled Sheep Meadow Station with far more worries than she had when she'd arrived.

Her worst fears were about to be realized.

CHAPTER 71

11:37 A.M.
Fort Greene, 2 January 1987

The day started late, after a good night's sleep, their first in days. Steven woke up in bed with Lori. She opened her eyes and smiled, actually looked happy to see him for the first time in over a year.

"Hi, you," she said, laughed, then kissed him as she hopped out of bed. It was if the breakup, the last year of fighting, the hell they'd lived through since Jim turned up had never happened.

Jim was gone, left them a note about meeting a friend and that they shouldn't worry, so they didn't. Lori went to the kitchen after the bathroom and dug through Steven's cabinets, found what she needed to make pancakes. Steven made tea while she cooked up two stacks that they drenched in butter and syrup. They ate in silence. The morning's high leveled off as they both started to think about what was still left to do. Lori was the first to finally voice it.

"What do you think Jim wants to do about the baby?"

"You mean does he want to kill it? Or want us to help him kill it?" asked Steven.

The words sounded harsh when finally said out loud, brought back the night they'd fought over whether or not to kill their own child. When you took away the other words said that night, that was all that was left. Here they were back there again, a little older, a little wiser, but still deciding whether or not to end a life.

"God. We signed on to save it, not . . ."

"That was before we knew the truth. It's not just a baby, Lori."

"That doesn't make it any easier."

They left the kitchen and curled up together on the couch, listened to music as they had in the past when making tough decisions.

"I remember when I was trying to decide about the abortion," said Lori, after they had lain there awhile. "All the information was so impersonal. It wasn't even an operation. It was a procedure. I'd be in and out in no time. It was so easy to forget what it really was."

"Yeah. This would be more hands-on. I can't even picture it. A stake through the heart? Cut off its head? Oh, my God . . ."

"So we wait for Jim. Then decide if we can be part of it. I feel like a coward putting it on him, but it's true. It's all up to Jim," said Lori as she pulled closer to Steven. His arm held her tighter while they waited to hear what Jim had to say. She sighed. All the feelings of victory that morning were gone. They were still in a bad place.

At least they knew that things couldn't get any worse.

CHAPTER 72

5:23 P.M.
Lower East Side, 2 January 1987

The street was filled with an angry crowd that threatened to turn into a mob at any moment. The Lower East Side neighborhood was mostly Puerto Rican. Block residents spoke more Spanish than English. Everyone talked at once, so fast that Garcia couldn't translate what they said. His partner looked irritated and worried. Two cops alone in a 'hood on the edge of panic weren't safe.

"Come on, Garcia, you speaka da Spanglish, what's goin' on here?" said Murphy. He let his hand slip over his gun, still holstered, but he wanted to be ready. Just in case.

"Give me a break, Murph. My grandparents spoke Spanish, all us kids learned as little as possible. You always say immigrants should learn English and we did. Happy?"

Murphy scowled, scanned the people packed around him to see if anyone looked like he had weapons. He didn't like the time it was taking backup to get here. He'd called in for it twenty minutes ago.

"*Que? Los Desaparecidos? Que es?*" said Garcia.

"What is it?"

Garcia signaled Murphy to shut up, listened to the rush of words that poured at him from all sides. He shook his head, turned back to his partner.

"You won't like it. They say the Disappeared are in the basement."

"The what?"

"Los Desaparecidos . . . People have been vanishing from the neighborhood all week, then coming back at night to . . ." He paused, knew how crazy it sounded. "They say to take others, then hide during the day. They reported it, but we're the first to check it out. It's bad. They want to burn the building down before the sun sets."

"Lucky us. I'm surprised they left their torches home."

Sirens rose at the far end of the block as backup arrived. People parted to let two patrol cars through. They moved slowly down the street and stopped in front. Officers climbed out to join Murphy and Garcia at the entrance to the building, and got a quick briefing from Garcia. He took the lead when he was done.

"We'll go down and check it out, report back. Keep things up here under control." Garcia led Murphy to concrete steps at the side of the building. They walked down into darkness.

Murphy flipped a light switch and nothing happened. He waved his flashlight around the ceiling until he found a light fixture. The bulbs had been shattered. A quick check of the floor showed fragments of glass from the broken bulb.

"Someone wants to keep things dark."

They walked down a long brick hall to the end of the building and found an unlocked door that opened into the basement. That alone was suspicious. Garcia opened it. The room was pitch black, no light inside at all. There was no sound. If there were people down here, as the crowd said, they'd hear breathing. Wouldn't they?

He took a step inside, shone the light, and almost jumped when he saw that the room was full. There were people all around him, standing as if at attention awaiting orders. Silent.

"Jesus Christ . . ."

"What is it?" Murphy was behind him, just outside the door. He heard a noise inside, like something wet and fast. Garcia made a sound that Murphy couldn't identify. He heard something heavy drop to the ground.

"Garcia!"

Murphy opened the door and looked inside with his light. His partner was on the floor, surrounded by people of different ages and genders who looked like locals, except for a few club kids and yuppies. They said nothing, just stared straight ahead, the ones who had eyes. The others had empty sockets where their eyes had been. Dried blood stained their cheeks, eyelids, and lips. Their arms hung straight at their sides. No one moved.

Murphy dropped to one knee beside his partner, rolled him over to see what was wrong. Garcia was limp, looked dead, eyes open but glazed. He had no pulse. Murphy radioed back upstairs and filled them in, stood to leave when he heard the odd wet noise again. Almost like a clogged pipe clearing. He looked around, but no one else in the room had moved. When he looked back down at his partner's body, the mouth moved.

"Garcia?"

He was wrong, his partner must have been unconscious, not dead. . . . Murphy leaned closer to see why his eyes were still glassy and fixed. He heard the sound again, bubbling up from Garcia's chest as his eyes swelled and exploded. Living blood poured from Garcia's eyes, ears, mouth, and nose in a steady stream, covered Murphy's head, and worked its way inside him, took over his body before he could scream.

The sun set outside as officers called down to Garcia and Murphy and got no response. They called for more backup, and were spared a trip down into the basement when its occupants surfaced for the night, led by Murphy and Garcia. They took out two more cops before they were gunned down. As the cops they'd killed rose and stumbled toward their fellow officers, more backup arrived and called back to headquarters for SWAT. A second call was made from police headquarters to the mayor's office.

The city was officially on alert.

CHAPTER 73

8:22 P.M.
Bowery, 2 January 1987

The bar was on Bowery, near Jim's SRO hotel.

Angel had met him hours ago, and even after drinking steadily since then, Jim still hadn't found the courage to ask what he'd gone there to ask. He was still reeling from the news about Nina's baby, couldn't share that with Angel, but needed his help if he was going to set the child free. He'd already filled him in on the story of what they'd done to Adam Caine last night. After what they'd been through on the subway, Jim knew that Angel wouldn't have any trouble believing him. His only question was whether he had the right to pull anybody else into his mess. Angel brought two fresh beers from the bar, and raised his mug to Jim.

"Once again, congratulations. You found the bastard who murdered your family and did what had to be done. You saved a lot more lives, putting another one of those things into the ground, man."

Jim knocked his mug against Angel's, drank, and turned to him as they sat back in their booth.

"Angel . . . There's still something I need to do."

"Name it, man, I'm here for you. Just tell me what, where, and when." Angel stared at Jim with a smile, a little unsteady from beer, but sincere.

"My sister's baby. It's like Caine. Like that thing on the subway."

Angel almost dropped his beer.

"Shit, man. What you gonna do about it?"

"I don't know. . . ."

"You know. Believe me."

Angel stared him down and Jim knew he did know, even if it broke what was left of his heart. It wasn't bad enough that he hadn't been able to save his sister. Now he had to kill her child. Their child. He told Angel where he thought the baby was, and what little he knew, but nothing more.

"I can't do it alone."

"You don't need to, man." Angel clasped his hand. "What do we need?" His pager went off, beeped until he pulled it from his belt and switched it off. He looked at the number and whistled.

"Shit! Mayor's office. I got to make a call. But we're gonna fix this for you." He stood and pulled on his coat. "Talk to your friends, see who else we got. I'll call you later." Angel walked out into snow, starting to fall again.

The storm was growing.

CHAPTER 74

8:41 P.M.
Central Park South, 2 January 1987

Secured behind locked doors in his laboratory, Rahman mixed the last of the elixir's ingredients as instructed by the Book of Abraham. It all made sense again, processes that had faded in his memory over the last century. Instead of celebrating, he was at a loss, angry and impatient. Rahman finally had the vampire infant, the key to his experiment, but now it wailed continuously outside in the station, made it almost impossible to concentrate. Rahman left his lab to see what was wrong.

The Autochthones rolled around the station floor in agony, unable to placate the infant with worship or bound children laid at its feet. They tore at their skin, ripped their own parched flesh and muscle to appease their new god, all to no avail.

Rahman felt a fool.

He'd sought freedom from the Autochthones for so long that he'd become as irrational in his obsession as Perenelle was in hers. The thing was a vampire baby, no more, an abomination, but no messiah for the Autochthones and no salvation for him. It was already deteriorating, skin dry and leathery like the Autochthones', less baby than gargoyle. How could it save him if it couldn't save itself?

Rahman sighed deeply, as the infant howled on. If the damn thing didn't stop soon he'd have to dash its brains out to get some peace, elixir or no elixir. Then Rahman felt the presence of new and unfamiliar life.

"Mind if I crash the party?"

Marlowe. Back from the dead.

The boy strolled up the tracks with a confidence he would never have exhibited in life. He had a perverse grin on his face, a look of savage satisfaction, and a bundle under his arm.

"I brought a present for the baby," he said and climbed the stairs at the end of the platform, walked over to the ring of worshippers around the noisy infant. He carried an Armani shopping bag, weighed down by a paper-wrapped bundle inside.

The crowd of supplicants parted for Marlowe. Rahman heard the baby's cries subside at the boy's approach, watched it scent the air like a small predatory animal. Its pale face wrinkled into a smile as it gurgled, raised its hands.

Marlowe slowly knelt beside the baby, lifted and unwrapped his bloody bundle with every ounce of drama he could wring from the moment. This was his payback for the Autochthones' gift, a bonus. He wanted it to be good enough to satisfy them that they'd been well paid, enough to keep them off his back forever.

Really forever.

The baby laughed out loud when Marlowe pulled the parcel's paper away to reveal Adam's grimacing face inside. His eyes rolled up to the baby in impotent rage, tongue cut out, teeth pulled, lips sewn shut so he couldn't speak or bite.

It had been a daring risk on Marlowe's part to turn him into this, based on an idea he'd had after years of watching horror movies. If the only way to kill a vampire was to destroy its heart or brain, he'd always wondered how long one could live with only a heart and brain to sustain it.

Quite a while, Marlowe had learned, much to his delight. He'd dismembered Adam while he was still unconscious, lost in his vision of the Spanking Man. Marlowe skinned Adam's torso, cut his head from his body, careful to preserve the heart and spine. He'd tucked them both up inside a pocket of skin he'd sewn under Adam's chin, big enough to hold Adam's pounding heart for as long as it still beat. The severed head with organ pouch was about the size and shape of a basketball.

Marlowe rolled it over to the demon child.

He'd wanted Adam alive and conscious for the presentation, wanted to be sure the full measure of his revenge was understood. It was. Marlowe could see it in his eyes. He was still in shock, dazed, but grasped enough to glare at Marlowe in helpless fury.

The gift calmed Baby. It played with Adam's head, cooed and gurgled peacefully as Rahman smiled and finally spoke.

"Thank you, Marlowe. You found the one thing capable of quieting it. I never did well with children, even in life. You seem to have a way with them."

"I know babies love their toys. I thought it should be something special. It is sort of a birthday."

"Perhaps it is."

Rahman looked down at the contented child, and considered that his lack of faith might have been premature. The baby played with its new toy, rolled Adam's head back and forth and laughed as it slapped him on the face, scratched, then plucked out one of his eyes and suckled it like an overripe grape. Rahman and Marlowe laughed along with the happy infant, enjoyed the momentary delight of a child's simple joy.

There was time for work later.

CHAPTER 75

City Hall was locked down tight when Angel arrived, but busy, despite the late hour. He had to get through three separate checkpoints before he was admitted to a downstairs office where a deputy mayor had set up the task force. Angel knew that he wasn't one of the administration's favorites, so if they were calling him in for advice, the situation was serious.

It was a power room. Angel could tell at a glance as soon as he entered: military, police, politicians, all caught in middiscussion when the door opened.

"We're agreed, then. Our best bet is seal off the affected area, evacuate surviving residents, and go in to clean up what's left." Angel recognized Deputy Mayor Jonathan Richmond as the speaker. They'd had limited contact with each other in the last few years, which worked for both of them.

Richmond stood before white boards illustrated with city blocks and numbers and lists of officers available, troops needed. He saw Angel and pulled papers in front of him together in a rush, as if his mom had caught him with a dirty magazine. Richmond extended a hand, stepped in front of the boards as if to hide them.

"Yes, Angel Rivera, this is who I was telling you about, Colonel. The leader of the KnightHawks. His organization knows the subway system better than the MTA. If there are any points in the affected area that could let any-one in or out, he can tell you."

It was the only good thing he'd ever had to say about Rivera or the KnightHawks. Richmond kept his bland face neutral, masked his anger at having to admit Rivera to the meeting, much less make him a consultant. The administration was still fighting off the aftershock of Rivera's public demonstration behind City Hall a few days ago. Now he was being forced to treat him like a vital part of the Mayor's team—not to mention the ridiculous donation they had to make to the KnightHawks to get Rivera to come down.

"Yeah, no problem. What exactly are you trying to keep where?" asked Angel.

Everyone in the room shut up and looked at Richmond. It gave him a brief thrill that they all knew he was in charge, looked to him for the answer.

"That's on a need to know basis." Richmond faced off against Rivera who was giving him his best street attitude, but Richmond didn't back down. He knew the streets, had peeled himself off them to get scholarships and grants to get out. "We're dealing with a biological outbreak. It's enough for you to know your help is critical." He saw Angel back down, but Richmond knew he wasn't done.

It wasn't over between them.

It was pointless to challenge Richmond now, surrounded by his gang of white power boys in uniform. Instead, Angel looked at the map they laid out, the area the National Guard was to help quarantine.

Angel knew it well. He lived only a few blocks away. Looking over the maps he noticed something else. The address where Caine said vampires held Jim's nephew was smack in the middle of the "affected area." Whatever was going on, Angel was pretty sure it was connected to the nest Jim was looking for.

That also meant something else. It meant that the house Jim was looking for was about to be in the center of a National Guard lockdown. Like his job wasn't hard enough.

Jim wasn't going to like the news.

CHAPTER 76

10:36 P.M.
Upper East Side, 2 January 1987

Being a vampire was much, much better than drugs.

Marlowe wasn't sure about the whole blood-is-the-life thing, but the Sensurround pump in perception alone was worth the price of admission. He was seriously trippin', as his B-boy dope dealer would say. He was young, rich, and eternal. It was like every night was a private party and he had forever to enjoy it.

Marlowe sat back in Adam's long white limo as it slid through the night, swift and silent, like the human-shaped shark that had owned it. The car was his now, along with the penthouse, the bank accounts, the investments, and everything else Adam had owned, everything Marlowe had ever wanted.

It was easier than he'd expected to take over Adam's staff. A quick nip and they were all dancing on Marlowe's strings now. Either the Autochthones' blood in him made his control stronger than Adam's or any vampire could take them over with a new infection. Whichever it was, they were now as devoted to his needs as they had been to Adam's.

Tonight his needs drew him back to his old Times Square haunts. He'd spent his first night as a vampire dealing with Adam and his debt to the Autochthones. Tonight he wanted to visit his Jill. Now that he wasn't afraid of death . . .

Maybe he could do more than look.

He laughed as he walked into the club unseen, unheard by anyone. If anyone looked his way, he willed them not to see him and they didn't, like some kind of Jedi mind-fuck. This was good, he thought. This was very good.

Jill walked into the backstage bathroom that doubled as a dressing room. There were lockers on one wall, a urinal on the other, a toilet stall and shower in the back. The walls were plastered with worn and faded porno magazine pages of girls who'd appeared there.

She stepped into the narrow shower stall and soaped the lube and perspiration from her skin. There wasn't much point, the room was so small and overheated that she broke into a sweat as soon as she was dry, but she needed it. Even if her admirers couldn't reach her she could still smell the booze and pot, the sweat and come. Their stinking sex molecules came at her through the ducts, stained the air like moist smog. That was what touched her, what she washed off, the microscopic airborne feel of their fingers, their tongues, their dripping cocks.

She climbed out cleaner and rubbed the towel, still damp from the last shower, across her skin. When she turned to reach for her robe and a cigarette, she saw the kid in her chair. Cozy, like it was his room.

"Hey, Jill. Remember me?"

"Yeah . . . Marvin, right?"

"Marlowe." He smiled, too toothy.

"Right. You're here a lot."

"You're pretty special."

Jill had learned from years in the business how to handle a creep. Talk long enough to find out if he's dangerous. If he is, grab anything before he gets to you and do your best to bash his brains in while you scream for help. She wasn't sure about this one yet. He'd spent too many nights here to be normal, but it was funny, she got a good vibe from him now, a comfortable buzz, like from an old friend. Something in his eyes . . .

"I always liked you best," he said. "Guess that's why I want you to be my first."

"You're . . ."

"Yeah. A virgin."

She smiled. She'd seen this before, too. Not the worst way to make an extra buck, breaking in some cute young thing. And this one was cute. Out of the question here, but if he was prepared to make an offer they could find someplace to go.

"So, you been wantin' me to be your first all this time, huh? You wouldn't be mine, you know."

"No shit. No problem."

"That's peachy. What did you have in mind?" She lit a cigarette, a little annoyed at his smug approval. Like she needed it. "I don't usually do this, you know." She didn't expect him to believe her. It was a negotiation.

"I didn't think you did. Not for just anyone." He waved a hand, noncommittal. "But I'm not just anyone."

He whispered the last words in her ear, when she hadn't even noticed him get out of his chair. Must be the bump of coke she took before going onstage, she thought. His finger stroked the inside of her bare thigh and made a trail in a spray of water left there. She snickered, pulled her head back to get a better look at him.

"What makes you so special?"

"I'm not like other boys," he said, and laughed. His nose nuzzled her throat. He nipped at her neck. For some reason it scared her. She looked around for blunt objects within reach.

"I think you'd better go," she began.

Then she looked into his eyes and didn't want him to go, thought there was nothing she'd like more than to put this kid's virgin tool in her mouth. She dropped to her knees and opened his pants, slipped his cock into her mouth, and stroked it with one hand while she fondled his balls with the other. The kid loosened his pants, slipped them down while he put a hand on the back of her head, cupped her skull in his palm, and pulled her closer, as her head reeled with pleasure like none she'd ever experienced. . . .

Marlowe watched his Jill with fresh eyes. He'd never appreciated the pulses of life that slid across her skin while she performed as much as he did now. He felt his cock rise as soon as she dropped to her knees. It took only a second in her mouth to realize his cock was wet and warm, but there was no pleasure. No sex.

He grabbed her head with both hands, pushed her down as far as he could before she choked, then threw her on the floor and spread her legs, shoved his cock inside her pussy, her ass, her mouth, pounded away, but nothing provoked passion in him.

Marlowe did everything he'd spent his virgin lifetime watching on tape and in magazines, everything he'd fantasized about, and it was nothing.

Nothing. He threw Jill aside, sat up, and panted like a rabid dog while she whimpered. Idiot! He'd traded his soul for an eternity of incredible unprotected sex, unafraid of diseases that affected mere mortals. Instead, he was dead from the waist down.

"You fuckers!"

He screamed at the Autochthones, at the universe, at God and the Devil, and threw himself back on Jill's naked body, bit hard into her neck in fury, and felt a lock on her soul. Her life oozed into him like cosmic honey, flowed between them as his system fed. An orgasmic charge ran through him as he sucked at her throat, pleasure he could never have imagined possible. Marlowe suddenly got it, the whole deal, how it worked, what turned him on, what his eternity really was.

Jill writhed, deeply entranced, long enough for him to take her life like a thief in the night. Marlowe flushed with Jill's heat as he consumed her. Her blood and life poured into him like the last swirl of dirty water down a bathtub drain.

Marlowe rolled off, spent. His head throbbed with new sensations. His skin was warm again. His body pulsed with life, but more than he'd ever had when he was alive. There was nothing he couldn't do. He stood without effort, wiped what blood he could from his clothes before he remembered he could leave the building unseen by anyone.

He didn't have to worry about what people saw or thought they saw, he could control or kill anyone who got in his way. He was fucking eternal! Marlowe threw the soiled towel down on Jill's body, had already lost interest in her. The night was young. There was still time to make new friends.

He laughed and strutted out whistling, wiped bloody fingers off on his suit. There were plenty more where it came from. A quick trip home for a shower and a change and he could hit the downtown clubs before closing. It was starting out to be a great night, and best of all . . .

He wasn't a virgin anymore.

CHAPTER 77

11:42 P.M.
Fort Greene, 2 January 1987

They downed beers by candlelight at Steven's loft, his power cut off until he got down to Con Edison the next day with a check.

"This is how they're closing down the area." Angel spread a map out on the table. "The only explanation they gave was a localized biological out-break, a pocket of fast-spreading plague. They said they're going in with flamethrowers to clear out any survivors they haven't evacuated already and burn out the infected."

"How do they know the difference?" asked Steven.

"From the little I got, that's not a problem." He looked at Jim. They both remembered the thing they'd fought in the subway. "I think I can get us in. The question is what we do when we get there, and who goes."

When Jim showed up with the leader of the KnightHawks, Steven had taken it in stride. When he saw that Angel had a case of beer, he'd welcomed him. Now that he'd explained why he was there, Steven regretted that he was drunk. He never liked the deals he made when he was drunk. That's what had gotten him the book contract that pulled him into Jim's life in the first place. Lori was across from him, looked like she was thinking the same thing as she opened another beer.

Jim looked down for a long time before he spoke.

"I have to free the child. Whatever that takes. Anybody wants to help, I'm grateful, but I got no right to ask . . ."

"None of us will be free if we don't do something." Lori surprised herself with her cool logic. "If we're the only ones who know the real danger, we're the only ones who can do anything about it."

"That's the problem," said Steven. "When do we call it quits?" He reached for another beer. "Why not just let the National Guard go in and clear out whatever they find?"

"They don't know what they're dealing with. It has to be us. We're the only ones who know what's really going on, the only ones who can find the baby and make sure . . ." Angel paused, glanced at Jim, who stared down at his beer can.

"So what you're saying is that to help Jim find Nina's baby and put it out of its misery, we have to get through the National Guard, whatever they're locking in, and a gang of junkie vampires?"

"Looks like."

Steven groaned, felt sick again. When they'd killed Caine their ordeal was supposed to be over. Now it was clear that it was just beginning.

"We can't do this."

"Look, man, if Jim had told me his story any other time, I'd swear he was high, but after what we saw in the subway, I'm ready to believe anything." Angel rolled up the map, opened another beer. "I don't know what we killed, but I've seen this shit up close and let me tell you, it ain't going away. We're not doing this for Jim. We're doing it for all of us."

Angel was right. Walking away wouldn't keep vampires out of their lives. Steven wanted to turn back the clock to the day, the hour, the second he'd entered this and walk the other way. He saw from Lori's face that she felt the same. She spoke up, her throat dry, despite the beer.

"You said the area's quarantined. How do we get in?"

"Easy. I give you KnightHawks hats and T-shirts, you walk in as my crew. The real question is what to do once we're inside."

Lori finished her bottle and reached for another, looked at Jim, but his eyes were hollow, dark. He seemed barely to know they were in the room. He'd shut down halfway through his last beer and left Angel to persuade Steven and Lori to help them find the nest and the baby.

"There's someone we can call," said Lori, "Faith's seer, Perenelle. If she doesn't think we're crazy, she might be able help us survive this. If we decide to help." Steven almost smiled. She was back. The planning part of her brain was up and running again. Caine's death had given her that much back, at least.

"Make your call, then make up your minds. I'll find out what I can about what we're facing once we're in. For now, I say we sleep," said Angel.

"Yeah. Good idea. I think Jim's beat us to it."

Steven saw that Jim's eyes were closed. He was slumped against the table, unconscious. Lori brought out sheets, pillows, and blankets. Angel and Steven carried Jim to the couch and covered him with a blanket. Steven left Angel on the floor beside Jim, joined Lori, and went to bed before dawn for the first time in what felt like years.

Steven curled tight against Lori, she pressed back into him. Sex was the last thing on their minds. He held her as if she might disappear if he let her go, as if holding on to her kept him from falling. She gripped his hands just as tight, as they both fell asleep, locked to each other for safety.

CHAPTER 78

Blood sucked.

It was the first great disappointment of Marlowe's new life, once he came down from the high of his orgy the night before. He'd never really tasted blood before, except from a cut finger or dripping from a rare steak. That was nothing like biting into a wrist or throat and having it pump into your mouth in a flood, chugging it like beer just to keep it from spraying you.

And it wasn't like the wound healed when you took your mouth away; it pretty much kept going until it made a mess of your clothes, the room, everything. Marlowe was sure that all this was something someone could adjust to over time, but he wasn't sure he was that someone. Then there was the whole taking-life thing.

Man. He was so damned.

Marlowe lay naked on Adam's king-size bed, surrounded by last night's party guests. Three girls and a boy, club kids he'd picked up at The World, all beauties that never would have given him a second look when he was alive. He'd plied them with drugs and booze and then led them back to the penthouse to the same soundproofed bedroom where he'd met his own end at Adam's hands.

They'd tumbled together in the sheets, stroked flesh, kissed lips, tongues entwined, sucked, fucked, hands in constant motion. He'd fed, slowly at first, then faster, as his partners came, one by one. Then he came, in the only way he could, in an orgy of bloodletting as he drained their lives from their perfect bodies.

What was left was sprawled around him on the bed and on the floor, dead meat, throats torn out. Dried blood covered Marlowe's chest and belly like a bib. Tears poured down his cheeks, red with his victims' blood. He wept, not for them but himself.

He'd been so wrong.

The thing he'd begged for, prayed for, wanted more than anything was finally his and life was emptier than ever. Power, immortality, even the license to kill meant nothing. Marlowe rolled to one side of the bed, curled up in a corner away from the big stain on the sheets. He'd thrown up in the night. Drinking the blood, so much of it, so quickly, had made him sick.

The whole thing made him sick.

He wanted to do penance, but didn't know where to begin. "Thou shalt not kill" was right up there at number five. Marlowe knew that his only orgasms from now on would be when his victims died. There was no way around it. He had to kill to come. He'd done an Act of Contrition every time he jerked off . . . what would it take to redeem his soul after each kill, how many rosaries, how many novenas, every night, the rest of his life, however long that might be?

Sure, he could live at the edges, drain enough life from crowds to survive without killing, give up sexual pleasure for other kinds of games, but what did that make him? A parasite. No glamorous life of seduction and sex, just eternity as a tapeworm, feeding on movie audiences and subway crowds.

Marlowe kicked the naked dead boy off the bed so he could be alone to think. He pulled the stained sheets up to his chin and decided he could learn to live with the act, but not the consequences. It was one thing to kill to live. It was another to know that what kept you alive put you deeper into Hell when you finally did die. His Catholic roots wouldn't let him commit the atrocities he must to survive, not when he knew he'd be judged one day, no matter how far away.

Thousands of years of celibacy with eternal damnation at the end just didn't work. Marlowe called in the cleaning crew. When they were done with the room he locked himself inside the vault against the sun, lounged on clean satin sheets and sipped tequila.

As he saw it, he had only two choices.

Curse God and damn the consequences, kill to live, and burn in Hell when he died. Or repent now. End his ordeal after doing penance. It didn't take long to decide.

Once he knew, he felt better. He couldn't save the baby from the Autochthones, but what better penance than to purge the junkie vampires, send their souls to whatever fate they deserved, and then himself? Marlowe had spared them with the idea of taking the nest over himself, but that was out of the question now. They had to die. He would do it to redeem himself and, in some strange way, Adam, too.

Marlowe slept like a guiltless child, a smile on his lips, now that he knew it would be his last day on Earth.

CHAPTER 79

5:02 P.M.
West Village, 3 January 1987

Perenelle woke in a brittle mood, as if she might shatter or explode at the slightest touch. The air was thick with old incense. Instead of reassuring her with memories of past glories as it usually did, the smell seemed stale, like a sealed Egyptian tomb.

She'd wasted her immortality as surely as Adam and Rahman had wasted theirs, buried herself here to create dreams for bored, naïve mortals. Why had she spent so much time on the illusion of the Veil, devoted herself to protecting others from themselves, while she lived like a cloistered nun?

They didn't know or care about her sacrifice. There'd be no gratitude if they found out, no praise, and now all her effort was wasted. The morning newspaper contained a front-page story about a downtown quarantine where Rahman had said the baby had a nest. It was only a matter of time. They'd find the nest and that would explain the crisis. The purge would begin and spread beyond the Lower East Side, across the city, the country, from nation to nation, until they tracked them all down and destroyed every last vampire on Earth.

It was the beginning of the end of her kind.

Perenelle listened with disinterest to her answering machine while she poured another drink. There were the usual desperate pleas from clients seeking counsel and one from a friend of Faith's.

"... My name is Lori. I met you at a channeling session on Christmas with my friend, Faith, and we talked about vampires. As crazy as this sounds, we killed one. But there are more downtown. If there's anything you can tell us that would help, call me. Leave a message if we're out and we'll call you back . . ."

Perenelle wrote down the number and dialed it.

There might be help in making sure that the last trace of Adam's error was erased. If by a blessing of providence the callers were looking for the same nest, she would most certainly help them. Perenelle downed the last of her cognac as the phone was answered, and arranged a meeting that night. She poured herself a fresh glass to celebrate and sat back down, content. These people would find and burn out the nest for her, remove the risk of its spreading or being discovered. The National Guard was certain that it was fighting a biological attack and would wipe out whatever else remained in the area.

When it was over, Perenelle would kill her little helpers and all would be as it had been. No one would be the wiser, and Adam's breach would be sealed.

The Veil and her secret would be safe.

CHAPTER 80

The National Guard troops were only a few blocks away. Angel carried Sonia's bag down the stairs to the street for her, opened the door to the cab waiting outside to take her to the Bronx.

"You stay at your aunt's until I say it's okay to come back. I'll join you tomorrow night."

"Why can't you come with me now?"

The concern in her face was for him. His work in the subway was dangerous enough, but whatever was happening now scared her more than that ever had.

"It's okay. I'll join you soon. I love you."

They kissed, long and hard as if it was their last. He hoped it wasn't, but with everything going down the way it was, he couldn't be sure.

Sonia's cab pulled off. He was sending her away alone again. It was becoming a bad habit. He went back upstairs to finish packing his bag so he could go to Steven's until the job was done. Troops marched down these streets with orders to shoot first and ask questions later. Forget the danger of contagion. If he stayed, he was more likely to get killed by an overeager weekend warrior.

Angel still didn't know what they were fighting. His sources inside City Hall were either out of the loop or keeping quiet for a change. Whatever was happening was bad, really bad, so bad that the mayor's office was sure the public would panic if they found out. Angel had to find out what it was before they walked into the heart of it.

He played back his answering machine while he gathered clothes, weapons, whatever he'd need. Angel hoped there was a message from one of his contacts. Instead he heard apologies and promises to keep digging. The last voice he heard as he closed his duffel bag was Sheryl's.

"Hi, Angel. Miss you. Back from L.A. I'll call you back or you call me. You know where to find me."

Angel had put thoughts of Sheryl out of his head while she was out of town to promote her latest movie. Sonia didn't run a guilt trip on him, even though she was sure he was screwing Sheryl. He'd done her work for her, berated himself each time he gave in and climbed into bed with the movie star.

He'd decided to stop, which was easier when Sheryl was out of town, instead of sitting naked and wet on his hard dick. His relationship with Sonia was more important. In the long run, there was no one better for him. She'd stuck it out since he was a skinny kid trying to organize a neighborhood watch group to take back the streets. The phone rang as he carried his bag to the door. Angel hesitated, let the machine pick up, and listened to the outgoing message.

"You've reached Angel Rivera and the KnightHawks. Leave your name and number after the beep, and I'll get back to you. Peace . . ."

"Angel. Me." Sheryl's world-famous voice vibrated the speaker as it poured out. "I was hoping you'd be home."

Angel winced, dropped his bag, and picked up the phone.

"Yah, I'm here."

"Hey, baby. How goes the good fight?"

"Not so good. They're evacuating downtown. Some bullshit about a plague."

"I didn't hear it on the news, but nothing makes the news in L.A. unless it's about them."

"No one's heard about this. Still trying to get more info."

"Why don't you come over and tell me more?" she purred.

"Yeah, about that. I've been thinking. We should maybe cool out for a while. . . ." She didn't respond. He was sure that she knew what he meant. Angel hated to lose her, but he knew what he had to do.

"It's Sonia, isn't it?"

"Look, this was my idea . . ."

Sheryl laughed. "Men always think that. You may be the only man I know who's ever picked his relationship over me. I respect that, Angel, even if you don't believe me. I even approve."

She was full of surprises. Angel relaxed.

"This doesn't mean we can't still be friends," she said.

"I don't want to lose you, Sheryl, I just can't . . ."

"It's okay. It's not like I don't have a line outside my door for that." She laughed again. It was a magical sound, worth a million bucks. "So what's this about a plague? Sounds medieval."

"The city's brought in the National Guard to block off half the Lower East Side. A plague's the excuse, but where's the CDC? Why bring in troops?"

"Sounds like I picked a great time to come home."

"Yeah. They expect the 'Hawks to help the National Guard navigate the subway, but no one trusts us enough to tell us what's really happening. I've hit everyone and come up dry."

"Maybe I can help."

"You?" Angel chuckled, despite himself.

"Who has the info, the mayor's office? Ed might not tell me, but anyone under him would."

"Right. What are you going to do, wave a magic wand?"

"Honey, you know what I can wave. These boobs can get more out of City Hall than a hundred of your street contacts. You forget I'm a movie star, baby. I may be your friend, but to some minor bureaucrat in City Hall I'm every wet dream come true."

Angel laughed out loud. He'd spent so much time with Sheryl that he'd forgotten the effect she'd had on him the first time they met. He'd stammered and blushed his way through the conversation as all the blood drained from his brain to his pants. He thought fast. It could work. The one man he knew who had what he needed would be in his office for hours.

"Okay. You sold me."

"Pick me up, we'll go on a fishing trip," she said.

CHAPTER 81

Her guests were on their way.

Perenelle brushed her hair in front of the mirror, still lustrous and black, waited until they arrived to take on the gray hair and wrinkled face they expected to see. Perenelle had been glad to find out that most of the myths about her kind were groundless. She enjoyed her mirror and her endless perfection. Vampires had reflections like anyone else. They could simply choose not to be seen by their victims, as they could choose to stay young and beautiful or hide their youth with a mask of age.

Perenelle had to decide what myth to feed her vampire hunters. If she gave them too much information on how to destroy her kind, it could be shared before she had a chance to get rid of them. She would have to proceed carefully. Timing, as always, was everything. She could tell them anything if she was going to kill them once they did her dirty work. There was a gentle knock at the door.

It was Janos, her butler.

"They're here, mistress."

"Take them to the parlor. I'll be up shortly."

The parlor was the center of the first floor. The walls were covered with shelves lined with books on the occult. That would occupy them while she put on her face.

Perenelle entered the parlor a few minutes later with a cane, old and gray. She immediately recognized the slender blonde from an unpleasant evening with her client Faith. The writer. Perenelle had warned her off her pursuit of vampires then. She obviously hadn't heeded the advice.

The young man with her was tall, black, long hair twisted into thin dreads. He studied a book in his hand, scrutinized Perenelle when she entered with equal interest. He reminded her a bit of Rahman when she first met him, the certainty in his eyes, the strength of his gaze. It was a look she'd seen before, usually in vampire hunters. She shook off the feeling. These two meant her no harm.

"Good evening. Your phone message said you want to kill a vampire?"

The young woman shook her head. "We killed one, but he told us about more. I know it sounds crazy . . ."

"I discount nothing. I have heard far stranger, all true."

"Can you help us?"

"I can tell you what you need to know."

Lori visibly relaxed, as if she'd waited to hear exactly that. Perenelle rang a small bell by her side, and Janos reappeared at the door with a full tray.

"*Merci, bien.*" She looked to her guests. "Cognac? Tea?"

"Tea, please. Milk, no sugar," said Lori.

After a brief look at the cognac and a glance at the girl, Steven sighed. "Same for me," he said. Perenelle poured their tea when it arrived, then poured a generous glass of cognac for herself.

"So. Tell me about your vampires."

It didn't take long for Perenelle to confirm that it was the same nest she wanted destroyed. Their story of killing Adam in Bryant Park was alarming, but inevitable. He'd brought it on himself. If Steven and Lori succeeded in wiping out the creatures he left behind, Perenelle could rest easy.

"There are many ways to kill vampires, invincible as they seem," she said. "A stake through the heart, beheading, or burning. With the number you have to dispatch, I would recommend fire. They'll be weakest during the day, but not necessarily helpless, especially if they're shielded from the sun."

"Fire?" Perenelle saw the young woman's face fall. She evidently hadn't considered arson an option.

"How long have you lived here?" Steven's eyes examined the room. He seemed more curious than was safe.

"The property's been in my family for years." She actually owned the block, along with several others in the area, but kept her ownership under many names. Manhattan real estate had proven the one sure way for an immortal to amass wealth.

"What got you into the supernatural?"

"When one encounters what one cannot explain, one develops an interest in explanations. I am sure your experiences will have you exploring areas you would have thought impossible."

"Personally, I'm hoping never to hear more, ever again. Tell me . . ." Steven put down the book on demons he was flipping through and met her eyes. "Do you believe in vampires?"

She held his gaze and lied with ease. "I impart folklore."

"Of course. But you still tell us how to kill them."

She shrugged, hands raised. "If they do exist, to withhold aid would be wrong, no? Now I must leave you. I have a session in an hour. I must prepare." She stood, walked to the door, and turned. "As must you. You have much to do. Go with God."

She sent them to their fate with an insincere blessing on her lips. If she believed in God at all anymore, it was only that He had created the universe for his own amusement and interceded only to increase the ratings. They needed more help than she or an indifferent deity could provide.

She just hoped they would find it.

CHAPTER 82

7:17 P.M.
Lower Manhattan, 3 January 1987

Deputy Mayor Jonathan Richmond was working late, as usual. While his peers were out snorting coke at Studio 54 or picking up horny secretaries from Queens at the Tunnel, he spent his nights going through their work memos so he knew their jobs, too. That was why he was on the inside track, why the mayor had personally selected him for the job as liaison between the mayor's office and the National Guard while they discreetly cleaned up the mess downtown.

He couldn't help but chuckle as he reviewed the menial duties of the rest of the staff. Whoever the next mayor was, as long as it was a Democratic administration, Jonathan could be sure he'd be a key part of the power structure. So what if he hadn't gotten laid in almost a year.

"Jonathan? Hey, bro . . ."

He looked up to see Angel Rivera in his doorway, dressed for a night on the town. Jonathan scowled. He'd been here earlier, trying to get more information than he needed about the mission. All Angel had to do was brief the Guard on the terrain and lead them through the subway tunnels if necessary. This thing was on a need-to-know basis and there was nothing Angel needed to know that he hadn't already been told.

Jonathan opened his mouth to tell him to leave when he saw someone behind Angel, a sultry woman in an evening dress. She stepped past Angel into the room as he introduced her.

"I'm sorry, we just stopped by on our way to dinner. You know Sheryl Grace?"

Jonathan kept cool, stood and held out his hand. Inside, every muscle in his body had turned to rubber. She stepped across the room on stiletto heels, her hand slid into his like velvet, sent a tingle up his arm and down his chest into his belly.

"Who doesn't? I loved your performance on Broadway."

He managed to keep his voice level, hoped she couldn't tell he was in a hot flush from one end of his spine to the other. *Keep your cool, Jonathan. Keep it in your pants.* He tried not to think of all the times he'd jacked off to nude scenes from her last two pictures, his VCR slowed to frame-by-frame so he could enjoy every second to its fullest. Her eyes bored into his, as if she could read every thought in his head, her hand still in his. He knew that no one in the office would believe this tomorrow.

"Angel was just telling me about the project you two have been working on together. You're pretty amazing to coordinate an operation like that almost single-handed, for one so young. And attractive." The last was added as if it were a spontaneous afterthought, with just the lightest flick of her tongue across her lips. It was all Jonathan could do not to come on the spot.

He took a deep breath and forced out a strained laugh. So. This was all a scam. Angel couldn't get what he wanted to know earlier, so he brought out his Mata Hari. Her hand was still in his. Jonathan could feel absolute electricity flow between them, he really could.

"Ah, yes, well, that's all pretty classified, I'm afraid. He really shouldn't even have mentioned it to you." He shot a stern look at Angel, who was still in the doorway. The KnightHawk leader raised his eyebrows, all innocence.

"Sorry, man, I had to tell her why I was late. Didn't think I was giving anything away."

"You'll have to forgive Angel," she said, her voice lower, just enough that he had to lean closer to hear, as if she were sharing a secret. "He knows my concern for the welfare of the city. 'I love New York' isn't just a slogan to me. I feel passionate about this city."

"I'm sure you feel passionate about many things," Jonathan said, before he realized how lame his cheap double entendre sounded. He was holding the hand of *People* magazine's Sexiest Woman in America and dropping cheesy innuendos.

"We were just heading out for a drink. Think you could tear yourself away? I'd love to hear more about the workings of city government. I once had political aspirations myself. I know it sounds silly." She slid dry fingers from his moist palm, smiled at him the way she had at Mel Gibson in her last film, just before they'd fallen into bed, naked.

"Not at all."

Jonathan's smile stiffened. He knew she was going to pump him for info and odds were good that she'd get it. Confidentiality seemed less important than an hour in her company, maybe even two, if he could resist those lips long enough.

The security guards.

They'd see him leave with her, and she must have signed in. That would back him up when he told the story tomorrow. If they walked out the right way, he could even get a shot of them together on the lobby video cameras. Let them all call him numbnuts after they'd seen Jonathan walk out the door with his arm around the waist of Sheryl Grace, laughing like old friends. Oh, yeah.

Even if he told her everything, what did it matter? He could jack off to this for the next year of late nights at work, longer if he got a copy of the security tape.

"I'll tell you what. I'll join you if you do the honor of letting me pay."

She laughed, and suddenly he was Michael Douglas, the private detective in *Dark Desire*, the erotic thriller that had launched her career and made her a star. Jonathan grabbed his jacket and was around the desk in less time than it had taken Douglas to drop his pants in that one. No, he hadn't dropped them. She'd done it for him, dressed only in a towel and a pearly smile, the one she beamed at him now.

"Let's go out the main lobby. I just have to let the guards know I'll be back. . . ."

CHAPTER 83

Rahman had given the infant the first of three infusions and already saw a change in it. Its skin was ruddy and looked healthy again, its flesh filled out into the appearance of vitality, as if the formula had flushed the mutant disease from its system as its first benefit.

It had even started to feed again. Not on blood, but life, drained fresh offerings brought to it by the Autochthones. They'd fed the baby all night. When there were no victims left, it cried, and the infant's army of worshippers fled into the tunnels to seek more lives for their newfound god, dragged them to the Sheep Meadow Station from the subway system and the snowy streets above.

Ordinarily, Rahman allowed the Autochthones to hunt only late at night, from the fringes of society, disappearances that would go unquestioned. This time he gave them their freedom. The stakes were too high to worry about the risk. The baby needed all its strength to process the elixir. Then Rahman would see if it had the strength to give him what he needed.

If true eternity were ever to be found, he would find it here, tonight.

Adam was dying.

That was all he knew. He'd drifted in a sea of pain for so long that he wasn't sure of anything else. Even though his body was gone, he still felt the agony of its passing, skin flayed from flesh and bone while he watched, helpless. He'd been dying since he arrived here, felt the baby drain his life away until the Autochthones started to bring it new, fresh life to feed on.

He'd started to feed, too, without realizing it, long enough for him to wake up, for his mind to understand what had happened to him. Long enough for him to have hope. Adam kept quiet, continued to steal what life he could, waited to get stronger. It didn't matter how long it took. As soon as he was strong enough, he'd call for help, his last and only hope to save himself. Adam was dying. . . .

But he wasn't dead yet.

V

SUNRISE

New York City
Sunday January 4, 1987

When you walk through a storm hold your head up high
And don't be afraid of the dark . . .

—"You'll Never Walk Alone"
Oscar Hammerstein II
(1945)

CHAPTER 84

7:57 P.M.
Times Square, 3 January 1987

You can find anything in New York.

That was what Marlowe loved most about the city. He was in a Times Square army-surplus store despite the snowstorm outside, browsing through an amazing array of weapons from disabled bazooka launchers to fully functional swords and knives. More than you'd think possible. Marlowe had brought Nina here the night he met her, when Adam had sent him to find her a place to live and clothes to wear. Getting her a knife was Marlowe's idea. On these streets a girl needed more protection than a rubber, for all the good it had done her.

It was swords he checked out today, sabers, rapiers, and his favorite—the katana, choice of samurai warriors. It was compact, lethal perfection. A firm, easily gripped handle and a short razor-sharp blade that curved ever so gently, as if in flight. Marlowe picked out the best, waved it a few times to test the balance, and paid for it with cash, no questions asked. He'd buy a sharpening stone and some lighter fluid on his way back to the penthouse.

Then it was time for some serious smiting.

CHAPTER 85

8:32 P.M.
Lower Manhattan, 3 January 1987

Jim double-checked the page he'd torn out of his hotel's phone book, barely awake, headed to Canal Street. He knew it was wrong to vandalize the book, his mom had raised him better than that, but his hands shook too much to write down the addresses.

Lori and Steven had returned to the loft saying that the vampires had to be burned out. Angel told them about an accident that had taken out a downtown building under construction. Two propane tanks dropped while being delivered and fell down a flight of concrete stairs into the basement. A seal cracked, sparks set the tanks off, and the building went up in a ball of fire. If they wanted to take out a house of vampires fast, that was the way to do it. All they needed were propane tanks and a truck to transport them.

Jim had offered to get them, he wouldn't say how, and they were in no position to ask questions. This was his mission. No matter how exhausted he was, Jim had to destroy the monsters that had turned Nina's baby into one of them.

So he was headed downtown on the subway.

When the train stopped at Canal, Jim got out and stumbled upstairs. The snow still fell with menacing quiet. It was like walking through a den of sleeping lions. Jim checked the address of the first store on his list, one with a truck for deliveries.

He'd called them earlier today, pretended to be a customer to make sure the place had everything he needed. He didn't like to lie, but he did it. His mother had always made him tell the truth. Jim knew she wouldn't approve, but he was sure that she'd understand. Sometimes you had to do a little bad to do a greater good. It was for Nina that he was doing this, Nina and her little baby.

His baby.

It still cut through Jim even to think the words. He had to push the idea away, keep thinking of the baby as Nina's until he could find it and give it peace. Maybe then he could finally rest. Sleep offered no comfort. He didn't dream anymore. The nightmares had stopped after Nina died but nothing took their place. He had one last task to perform, to free the child.

Then he could die.

Jim opened the store's door without setting off an alarm. There were things he'd learned over the years he wasn't proud of, things he'd never told Nina about, things he'd had to do for them to survive. Breaking and entering was the least of it. Inside, he looked around with his flashlight, located the tanks, and went to look for transportation.

He found a van in a garage next to the storeroom, opened the door and checked for keys, found them under the seat. Jim heard a sound behind him.

"All right, take it easy now."

Jim froze. Something poked him in the back.

"This is a gun. Turn around real slow and let's have a look at—"

Jim still had the flashlight in his hand, the big heavy-duty kind, didn't even think before he swung it around behind him, slammed its weight into the side of the man's head.

He stepped back and fell, surprised, as Jim hit him again. Jim raised the flashlight, looked down at an old man with a pistol in his hand. He was probably a manager or clerk on his way out after working late. The man blinked up at Jim, dazed, his mouth flapping like a fish out of water. He lifted a hand to his head and looked at the blood on his fingers when he pulled them away like he'd never seen it before.

Jim had never hurt anyone before, not unless he'd had no choice. Once, when they were living on the streets, a junkie had tried to trade his sister for drugs while he was asleep. Jim woke up when she screamed for him, had to beat the guy up to get him to let her go. He'd freaked out and hit the guy again and again, longer and harder than he meant to, but he got Nina away safely.

It had scared him, not just because his sister was in danger but because he'd never known he had that much violence in him, that he was capable of injuring another human being. Now he'd assaulted an innocent man.

Police lights flashed outside, bounced off the walls of the garage through cracks between the door and walls. Had the old guy called them? Had they heard anything? The man's eyes cleared enough to see the light and know what it was. He looked at Jim, opened his mouth to shout, but Jim moved faster, without thought, brought the flashlight down over and over, until he was sure the old man would never speak again.

Jim froze, held the bloody flashlight up for one last blow if needed, and stared at the mess he'd made of the old man's head. There was nothing he could do, the moment was gone, no way to take it back. Tears rose, filled his eyes as lights from the police car faded until he was alone in the garage with a dead man.

A man he'd killed.

Jim dropped the flashlight and wept, pounded the old man's chest as if he could drive life back into it. All the while he knew he had to be quiet, knew he couldn't give himself away after paying so high a price not to be found.

When he could bring himself to move again, Jim got up, wiped his eyes, and started to roll propane tanks to the van. He would keep moving and meet the others. What he'd done was horribly wrong, but there was no turning back now. His life was over. He could at least redeem his child with his last breath.

CHAPTER 86

1:01 A.M.
Lower East Side, 4 January 1987

Marie danced drunk and stoned, tried to forget the cold as Tommy ran his hands over her ass and his tongue down her throat. They'd scored acid at Save the Robots and headed to this private party on the Lower East Side with some freaky Goth kids they'd met at the bar. At least she thought they were Goth. Why else would they look like they did?

The party was in an abandoned tenement, front doors sealed with cinder blocks, most of the windows boarded up. She'd partied in some weird places, but this graffiti-covered ruin was the weirdest.

Tommy's tongue moved from Marie's mouth to her neck as one of his hands wandered from her butt to a breast. Nice. It took her mind off the other guests. Except for others from the club, the kids throwing the party looked like Halloween. Pale, hair dyed jet black, teeth sharp, skin drawn tight over protruding bones, more ghoul than Goth. If she didn't know better, she'd swear these guys were dead. But that was crazy, right?

It was just the acid they'd scored at the club. She was tripping. Tommy excused himself to get more drinks. Marie danced closer to the speakers, closed her eyes to clear her head. Yeah. That's all she needed. To clear her head.

Tommy wasn't back with the drinks yet.

Marie had a funny feeling, the kind that made her wonder why she was here without anyone knowing where she was. Acid or no acid, it was time to go. She looked for Tommy and saw him across the room with a couple of the kids who'd invited them here. They laughed at something he said, but stared at him the way cats study birds before they pounce.

Marie opened her mouth to call him over, but before she could say anything they jumped him. Other Goths attacked kids near them. Marie screamed and backed away. One of the things came at her, eyes glittering as it called her name with a hunger she'd never heard before, arms outstretched, jaws wide, teeth long and sharp.

Before it reached her, the door crashed open. A stranger in black moved between them like an avenging angel, a flaming samurai sword in his hands. The fiery blade swung and sliced the head off Marie's assailant with a single stroke. The stranger took her hand, dragged her to the open door, and pushed her out.

"Go. I'll get the others. Leave north on Avenue C. I told them to let you out."

Marie left Tommy's body and the nightmare of his death as far behind her as fast as she could.

Once she was gone, Marlowe went back to work, grabbed the remaining survivors and shoved them out the door after the girl to safety. Then he turned his attention back to the nest.

The vampires had scattered as soon as Marlowe cut off the first head, scrabbled at doors and windows, all sealed by Marlowe before he entered. They wailed as he circled the room, swung his burning sword, recited a prayer as he dismembered them one by one.

"Saint Michael the Archangel, defend us in battle! Be our protection against the wickedness and snares of the Devil. May God rebuke him, we humbly pray . . ."

Marlowe wiped out the rest of the nest. Their clumsy defenses were no match for his superior speed and strength. He avoided attacks with ease, whirled in to kill again and again. He sprayed fresh lighter fluid on his flaming sword between victims.

"And do thou, O Prince of the heavenly host, by the power of God, thrust into Hell Satan and all evil spirits who wander through the world for the ruin of souls . . . Amen!"

He was an archangel, the right hand of the Lord, an avenger slaying the spawn of Satan. *Surely this will redeem me*, thought Marlowe as he sent Baby's damned to their final judgment, swung his sword again and again in the name of God.

Marlowe could feel the Holy Spirit fill him as blood sprayed and limbs flew. Celestial song rose in his head as he ripped the throats out of those his sword couldn't reach, bathed in their blood, drank it like altar wine as he made sure none of them escaped. This is what it was to be among the holy, this is what it was to be pure. He was blessed, a crusader for Christ, but most of all . . .

He was saved.

CHAPTER 87

The storm had grown into a hungry animal that devoured everything in its path. It buried streets, covered cars, blocked sidewalks, clogged tunnels as if it could sense its place in history and wanted to be sure no one would forget the night that it held the most powerful city in the world in its grasp, brought New York to its knees. It was the blizzard of a millennium and it covered Manhattan like a cloud of frozen locusts.

Sergeant Lopez and her team were cold, bored, and wary.

There'd been a few more shots from the next streets, but things had quieted down. They'd taken out about six or seven of the zombies, but the fresh snow seemed to be slowing down even the walking dead. Lopez got a call on her walkie-talkie.

"Van headed your way, Lopez. Check it out."

"You got it."

She didn't hear or see anything yet, but it would be here. Light rose from the street as the vehicle rumbled up behind them.

"This is it."

Lopez walked to the barricade with two Guardsmen as backup, waved the driver down. The van slid a little on the ice as it stopped. The passenger window opened and Angel Rivera stuck his head out, grinned. Lopez had never met him, but everyone had seen him on TV. She knew he was in charge of the KnightHawks on the task force. It wasn't that strange to see him here. Just unexpected.

Lopez didn't like unexpected.

"Yo! Hey, you want to let us through?"

"*Hola*, Angel. Good to see you, man, but we don't have any orders on this."

"Yeah, I know, last minute, you know? Got word on some possible survivors, mayor wants us to check it out. Like anyone upstairs cares if we get killed, right?"

Lopez shone her flashlight inside. There was a white driver beside Angel and two others, a black man with dreads and a blond woman, all in KnightHawk uniforms.

"They're with me." Angel smiled at her again. They smiled, too. Lopez frowned. There was too much smiling going on here.

"Just get out while I radio back and check this out."

"Uh . . ." Angel looked at the others; they shifted in their seats. Lopez aimed her flashlight behind them. Something was piled under blankets in the back.

"What's that?"

"Nothing, just some tanks. We had to commandeer the truck."

"Come on." Lopez nodded her head toward the street, opened the van door. "This'll just take a minute. You know how it is."

Angel and the two KnightHawks in back hesitated.

Steven wasn't wild about getting out of a vehicle stopped by armed cops and soldiers on a street under martial law when they were on their way to commit arson. As a fully grown black man who'd managed by some miracle to avoid contact with the law all his life, he didn't want to make up for lost time tonight.

"Let's get out," said Steven in a low voice.

"Yeah. Do what she says," added Lori to Angel. He didn't seem to have a better idea, so they all climbed out of the van except for Jim, who stayed at the wheel in a kind of daze.

Jim didn't listen to what they were saying.

He sat at the wheel, felt the engine running, the accelerator pedal under his foot. All he could see was the road ahead of him as he waited for the interruption to end.

They said words that meant nothing to him. Words didn't mean anything anymore; all that mattered was action. He had a job to do, a mission. With all he'd done to get them this far, nothing was going to stop him now.

He knew what he had to do.

"Sir? Could you join your friends? Sir?"

Lopez addressed Jim, but he didn't respond.

"Sir, I'm going to have to ask you to turn off the engine and step out of the vehicle." She stepped back, lifted her rifle.

"Sure, sure . . ."

Jim nodded, reached for the keys in the ignition, and threw his foot on the accelerator. The van shot forward, and the officer fired.

Lopez was taking aim for another shot when Angel grabbed her arm and stopped her.

"Are you crazy? Read the truck!"

Lopez read the words on the back of the van, realized what was under the blankets, and gulped.

"Yeah," said Angel. "One bullet could take out the block if those tanks blow."

Lopez's heart pounded as she realized how close it had come to stopping. The van was already gone. The only trace was a distant roar from the wall of whirling snow. But the feeling of near death remained.

Angel, Steven, and Lori watched Jim disappear, helpless to stop or join him. Whatever the plan was now, it was in his hands unless they could find a way to catch up.

"Shit," said Steven. "Do you think he'll make it?"

"Damned if I know." Angel shrugged, started walking back toward Lopez. "Guess we'll have to go after him to find out."

Steven sighed, shook his head with resignation.

"I knew he'd say that," he said.

CHAPTER 88

1:23 A.M.
West Village, 4 January 1987

Drums played on the stereo, recorded music of a lost tribe found in an isolated jungle of Brazil, sent to Perenelle decades ago by an anthropologist admirer. A song to their love goddess, he'd said, a ceremony that lasted for three days of exquisite pain that ended in blood. He said it reminded him of her. Perenelle had never decided if he meant it as a supreme compliment or the ultimate insult.

She sipped cognac in her meditation room, waited to hear from the humans hunting the baby's nest that they'd finished the job. Perenelle was bothered by something else, as if smelling the faint, overly sweet scent of something beginning to rot, almost unnoticed except for a vague sense of unease. The blizzard wasn't the only storm rising.

Rahman. He and that damn infant.

She had to see his progress, find out what was happening, but knew that confronting Rahman could put her in danger. Perenelle wondered how she could observe him in safety, and then laughed. Rahman himself had answered her question when he taught her to create her illusion of the Triumvirate of the Veil.

Perenelle lit incense, lowered the lights, leaned back on her pillows, and closed her eyes. Rahman had taught her many tricks. It was time to use one now, a gift he'd soon be sorry he'd given her.

CHAPTER 89

1:32 A.M.
Lower East Side, 4 January 1987

Lopez sent Angel to their field headquarters for a phone after some argument. While he was gone, she was the first to see the walking meatbag. Lopez watched it stagger around the corner and down the street toward them. It wore a dark suit, torn and dirty, covered in blood and bile, but once a damn good suit. The zombie must have been fresh. Its eyes were still intact.

"Showtime. Let's party," she said to the troops under her command. They swung spotlights on trucks around to illuminate it. The thing was headed for the thinnest part of the blockade until it saw Lopez, then it turned, fumbled in what was left of its pocket for something as it reached out to her with the other hand, flapped its dangling jaw. She flinched, recoiled from the shuffling pile of rotted flesh headed her way. It pulled something out of its pocket and held it up as it stumbled faster.

"Guys . . . hey . . ."

Lopez glanced to either side for backup, but the guys were all doubled over with laughter.

"Think he likes you, Lopez!"

"Who's your daddy?"

The thing held up a card in its rotting hand and lunged forward as Lopez blew him away in a panic, fired until she'd pumped her gun clean. The body flew backward and apart, the blood bubbled away into dust in the open air.

She walked over to get a closer look at what her fellow officers and the Guardsmen thought was so goddamn funny.

The hand was a few feet from the body, blown off at the elbow. Lopez walked over, kicked it over to see a SafeDate card in the fingers, the slogan "POSITIVE I'M NEGATIVE" faded but still readable. She looked at the smug, overfed yuppie in the ID photo and snorted.

"Not even when you were alive, motherfucker . . ." She stepped back, signaled to a Guardsman with a flamethrower. "Fry it! Extra crispy!"

The soldier stepped forward, lowered the flamethrower, and fired. Liquid flame flowed, turned the corpse into a bonfire as Lopez retreated from the smoke, held her breath, and fumbled for her face mask.

She was going to take a two-hour bath when she got home, and that still wouldn't get the stink off. That wasn't the worst. Not by a long shot. The worst thing was that, no matter how sick the thought of eating made her, the smell of all that cooked meat, rotted or not, was making her hungry.

All she could think about was a flame-broiled Burger King Whopper and fries.

Steven and Lori backed away when the thing staggered into the searchlights the National Guard threw on it. No matter what Angel had told them beforehand, to see one of the things in person was like a front-row seat at a George Romero festival, too in your face to be real. The way the troops dispatched it with guns and fire was almost worse. Lori had to look away, buried her face in Steven's coat, unable to hide from the stench of burnt dead flesh.

"It'll all be over soon," he whispered.

"Promise?"

He didn't answer.

CHAPTER 90

2:01 A.M.
Central Park South, 4 January 1987

In the tunnel outside Sheep Meadow Station, Perenelle heard music as she approached, music she knew well. It was a thin reedy song sung in voices used mostly for worship, accompanied by flutes made from human femurs and drums of well-oiled skin stretched tight across rib-cage frames. She'd seen and heard the Autochthones celebrate before, but never on so grand a scale. The sound filled the tunnel; so vibrant, so loud that she could scarcely understand why no one had come to investigate. As she listened she understood. No human could hear that song without fleeing.

Perenelle slowed and observed as much as she could before she revealed herself. She saw the Autochthones first, as they dragged and carried humans from the tracks and tunnels to the platform and added them to a throne of human flesh, a pyramid of more than a hundred bodies piled high, gathered from the streets and subways by the Autochthones to feed their new god.

It was a living sculpture, massive, grotesque but strangely beautiful, stirred a deep passion in her to join them, to fall to her knees in worship. Perenelle could see chests rise and fall, heard the slow wheeze of collective breaths in unison, as if synchronized. The baby was perched on top, a wreath woven of flowering herbs around its brow. She saw a misshapen object next to it, held close by a tiny hand.

Rahman was on his throne, watched her arrival and grinned, a nasty gleam in his golden eyes. She didn't understand his amusement until she got

close enough to see that what the infant played with was the mangled head of
Adam Caine. Her once beautiful boy had been savaged, dismembered,
turned into some monstrous plaything for the demon child he'd created.

Though she'd said goodbye for the last time, she could hardly bear to see
him reduced to this. One eye gone, lips sealed, there was no way to tell if
what was left of him was still alive. She hoped not, for his sake. Perenelle
turned on Rahman in a rage, but he silenced her with a raised hand.

"Not my work. His boy, Marlowe. Fair payment for what was done to him."

"Other means could have been taken."

"What? Call in the Triumvirate to decide Adam's fate? That would have
been fair and impartial. . . ." Rahman smirked as he stepped down from his seat.

The child's face was radiant, glowed with energy stolen from its growing
heap of victims. Perenelle could see the surface dead weigh down the living
below as they were consumed. Still the thing fed. Its skin took on a phosphorescent gleam as it drained more life in minutes than Perenelle could have
absorbed in a month.

Rahman strode up to the meat pyramid, his golden eyes brighter than the
infant's. The baby laughed and clapped its hands as another train pulled into
the station, filled with fresh food. Perenelle glared.

"Are you mad?" she asked. "Do you seriously think this many victims will
go unnoticed?"

Rahman laughed.

"By the time the humans know, I'll be gone. Immortal. Untouchable." He
waved an arm at the baby, a ringmaster introducing the biggest and best part
of his show, saved for last. "Do you see? We would have been overcome by
the life he's taken so far, yet he keeps feeding! If the elixir lets it absorb this much
life, the sun itself cannot challenge us. We could live on its energy, beings of
daylight instead of darkness. Would you deny me the chance to find out?"

Perenelle watched as more victims were drained, saw the look of finality
in Rahman's eyes, and said nothing. If this was another dead end, another failure, it would be the end of him. If he couldn't have the eternity he sought, she
knew he'd have none at all. She shook her head, for what Rahman had once
been to her.

"Then let me be," he said. "By dawn I'll know if I've succeeded."

Adam heard a familiar voice. Perenelle, close enough that he would be able to
see her if he could turn his head to face the sound. He felt stronger, but not

strong enough yet. The baby had been given so many victims, so many human lives, that it had stopped feeding on him. Adam had been slowly regaining his strength, was almost ready to make his one and only bid for escape.

But not yet. He knew he had one chance and one chance only. Soon, he'd be strong enough to send out a call to every mind he'd ever touched, to tell each where he was and summon his slaves to rescue him. That thought was all that kept him alive and sane. Freedom, freedom and revenge on all who'd reduced him to this, starting with Marlowe. Soon. He'd be strong enough soon.

CHAPTER 91

Jim could have found the house even without Angel's map. The building in front of him radiated death, the way an eclipse glows with the sun's corona, a thin ring of energy at the edge of oblivion. The windows were darker than they should have been, like something inside had sucked all light into its shadows.

He wasn't afraid. Fear was a thing of the past, from back when he still had feelings. Jim wasn't sure how much of him was left after all he'd been through, but he hoped it was enough to get him through tonight.

The snowfall silenced all sound except the van's engine as it strained to pull forward on failing snow tires. Jim made it to the side of the building, climbed out into a drift and plowed through snow to the sidewalk, looked for a cellar door. He'd take the building out from the ground up, once he made sure they were all inside. It was good that the others were gone. He'd told them he'd find a way to trigger the blast.

He hadn't told them that he was the detonator.

Jim jumped on the sidewalk until a hollow section gave and bounced back. He grabbed a shovel and salt from the van, went to work until he'd cleared worn metal doors. A padlock kept them shut, old and rusted. Jim snapped it off with a single swing of the shovel.

The doors opened with a rusty whine and a dull clatter. Jim looked down the steep stone steps into darkness. A tremor went through him, a feeling of dread so intense that he almost turned back, took the van, and fled as far as he could.

But it was too late now. Whatever end was coming was here and there was no escape. No matter what happened next, he was sure of only one thing.

He wouldn't leave this building alive.

Marlowe heard the noise from above, but paid no mind. He didn't care for matters of this world anymore. His kingdom was death and he would join his subjects soon.

He'd gathered their parts after he exhausted his sword arm, brought them downstairs, where they'd slept by day, as close as he could get them to the underworld. They lay in a row behind him, bodies reassembled like jigsaw puzzles as they waited for final deliverance. Marlowe could feel it coming. Judgment Day. The trapdoors to the sidewalk grated open with protest, and dim light flowed down with the snow.

The end was near.

CHAPTER 92

3:11 A.M.
Lower East Side, 4 January 1987

The snow seemed to be letting up.

It would be dawn in a few hours, and if the clouds cleared they might actually see it. Steven knew they didn't have a choice about doing this tonight, but he would have felt better plunging into the depths of doom at high noon.

Steven and Lori waited for Angel to finish negotiations with the officer in charge. Considering that their comrade had crashed the roadblock, it was going to be a neat trick to talk him into giving them permission to follow. If anyone could pull it off, it would be Angel.

Steven wrapped his arms around Lori from behind, pulled her close despite their disguises as KnightHawks. No one seemed to object. The troops stood in the snow waiting to shoot zombies and roast the remains. What Steven and Lori did or didn't do just wasn't that important right now.

As long as they didn't try to cross the perimeter.

"How long do you think he'll take?" asked Lori. She pulled a battered, nearly empty pack of cigarettes from her pocket and put one in her mouth. Steven didn't say anything.

"Depends on whether Angel is convincing them we're supposed to go in, or if they're beating the truth out of him."

"Thanks. You always know what to say to make me feel better." They both laughed as she lit her cigarette, disposable lighter almost giving out before she got it lit on the third try. "Cheap shit. You get five lights and they're empty."

"I'll buy you one of those for your birthday." He pointed at a patrolling soldier wearing a flamethrower. It was a stupid joke, the sort of thing she'd usually never even smile at, but he could feel her shake in his arms as she tried to keep a straight face. It was like laughing in church.

They saw Angel come back from the makeshift headquarters the Guard had set up in a nearby bodega. The corner store was the only thing lit up on the frozen street. Lines ran to phone poles outside, armored trucks parked in front. Angel brought them cups of coffee. Lori and Steven pulled off their gloves to enjoy the heat of the hot cardboard cups in their bare hands, sipped while Angel talked.

"I made a few phone calls and got us in. We have an hour, then we get treated like anything else coming out of there."

"Great. If the zombies don't get us, the National Guard will," said Steven.

"Don't forget the vampires."

Lori winked at him over the edge of her cup. He could see her eyes twinkle, could tell that she was as wired as he was. It was as if being here and doing something, anything, gave them the sense that they had some kind of power over this insanity. They weren't victims anymore. They were full-fledged vampire hunters.

It was hard not to laugh.

CHAPTER 93

3:17 A.M.
Lower East Side, 4 January 1987

Jim tossed another tank down the stairs and heard the low hiss of a leak. No matter. It would save him the trouble of opening the valve later. Exploding one tank would be enough to detonate the others. He climbed down the concrete stairs and turned his flashlight off to make sure he didn't ignite the gas before he was sure the baby was here.

He felt a dull impact and sharp pain in his left leg and fell forward. It was only after he hit the ground that he realized that his leg had been sliced off just below the knee. Blood spurted as Jim clutched the stump, then thought to pull off his belt and make a hasty tourniquet.

Someone stepped out of the dark into soft light that fell from above, a black teenager in a stylish suit holding a samurai sword. He held the severed limb in his other hand like a trophy, walked forward as he tossed it at Jim's right leg.

"Welcome to Hell."

Jim pulled the belt tight above his knee. The blood flow slowed, but pain started, a dull ache that grew and spread up his thigh. He glared at the boy and wished him dead, but somehow sensed that he already was. The kid's eyes gleamed like a cat's in the near darkness. He smiled at Jim like an old friend.

"I know you. I saw the pictures in your file. You're one of Adam's art projects . . . Nina's brother, right? Jim."

Jim nodded, pained almost beyond speech. He pulled his lighter from his pocket, as slow and easy as possible, hoped the boy wouldn't realize what he was doing until it was too late.

No good. The boy looked down and grinned, flipped it from Jim's hand with the tip of his sword.

"Not yet. We'll get to that. Don't worry."

He crouched beside Jim.

"I understand, you know. The pain you've been through? I've been there. So have they."

He waved the sword blade behind him. Jim saw shadows. As his eyes adjusted to the low light, he could that tell the shadows were dead bodies, over a dozen, laid out in a row. They'd been chopped up and put back together like broken dolls, really dead now, finally at rest.

The way he hoped to be soon.

CHAPTER 94

3:21 A.M.
Lower East Side, 4 January 1987

"They couldn't spare us a truck?"

Steven struggled against snow drifted across the middle of the street, un-plowed since the area was quarantined, held on to Lori for as much support as he gave her.

"We're lucky they didn't arrest us! Damn, man! You're one tough bastard to please!"

"Tell me about it," said Lori. She and Steven laughed so hard they almost fell. Angel chuckled and shook his head. It made him miss Sonia. All he had to do was make sure that whatever else happened, he got his ass home to her in one piece. He shifted the fuel pack for the flamethrower on his back, checked the safety on the trigger to make sure he could flip it off in a hurry.

"How did you get that out of them?"

"Hey. Maybe I can't get us a truck, but I still got some connections." He winked at her.

Lori laughed again. They were all light-headed, almost giddy with the in-sanity of it all. It was so quiet now, so still, even the blizzard seemed to be let-ting up. Then she realized what it was. It wasn't over. They were in the eye of the storm. The worst was yet to come.

She shivered, hoped that they didn't see the sudden fear on her face. They had to stay strong and stay together to get through this alive. They could do it. She repeated it to herself like one of Faith's mantras. They could do it.

Lori saw Angel's finger twitch at the trigger, his face taut and attentive as his eyes searched the horizon for any movement, any excuse to fire. She almost giggled, despite the situation. He was like a kid with a squirt gun playing war with friends. On some level, the little boy in him loved this.

They heard the thing before they saw it. A dry wail, a breathless wheeze that got louder. Something that used to be a woman staggered out of an alley, slowed but not stopped by the thick snow. It fell, twisted its way back to its feet, then plowed forward, moaned from a slack mouth under open pits where its eyes should have been. It sensed them, whether by heat or smell Lori couldn't tell, but it knew where they were, moved closer with each faltering step.

"Jesus . . ." Angel raised the flamethrower.

"What happened to its eyes?" asked Steven, repulsed.

It wore a dress suit and the running shoes women wear on their way to and from the office, work shoes still in a bag on one shoulder. The thing gurgled as it stopped, turned its head in their direction. The sound from its throat was like backed-up sewage about to explode.

"What's it doing?" asked Lori as the creature's jaw snapped open wider. Blood welled up in its mouth, dark and shiny, poured out in a flood like a single organism.

Lori grabbed Steven as fire erupted beside her, caught the infected stream of blood in midair and covered it in flames, dropped it and the dead body to the ground. Angel played the stream over them, made sure everything was incinerated before he stopped.

"Fucking shit, you see that? Jesus Christ!" He cut off the flames and turned to them, eyes shiny with tears. Fresh sweat dripped down his forehead. "Did you see that fucking thing?"

He crossed himself and made the sign of the cross over the remains as well. Lori and Steven followed suit. Catholic or not, it couldn't hurt, thought Lori as they followed Angel back into the street.

"It's only another two blocks," he said. "We can make it. All we have to do is—"

"Angel!" Steven shouted, pointed behind them. "Company." Lori and Angel turned and saw the last thing they wanted to see. Almost a dozen zombies staggered after them. The cold didn't affect them the way it did their human prey.

"You have enough to take them all out?" Steven looked back to Angel, prayed for a yes.

"I don't want to use it up getting in. We still have to get out. Come on, we're faster than they are. Keep going."

They pushed forward, kept an eye out behind them.

"Look . . ."

Lori looked. More of the things approached in front of them and from the sides.

"Shit. We must be attracting them from all over." Angel swung the flamethrower. He sprayed zombies in front of him, set them on fire to distract the others, shot a swath of flame at the ground and melted a shallow path. Steven, Angel, and Lori ran past burning bodies in the snow.

"Make a right at the corner!"

He fired. Steven and Lori followed him down the narrow canyon he carved, flames still licking the snow as they ran. Zombies followed in a horseshoe loop; Angel, Steven, and Lori turned the corner before the gap closed and met a wall of undead, arms outstretched.

"No . . ."

Lori lost heart for a moment. There was no way out, she thought. They'd failed, failed Jim, failed the baby, and failed to save themselves. What were they thinking? The gamble had been outrageous, the odds of survival nonexistent. They would die here for nothing.

She was shaken from her fear by fire, as Angel started burning a path. It would take them into the center of the crowd in front of them, but there was no other way out. She saw Angel burn down as many zombies as he could, watched those that remained back off. They had some survival instinct, after all.

Steven and Lori moved forward, as Angel took out any that looked about to infect them. Burning the zombies cleared enough snow for them to make faster progress. As they made their way through the mob, Lori started to believe again, until the flamethrower sputtered.

"Fuck! Fuck, fuck, fuck!" Angel looked at the fuel meter. He didn't look like a man with good news. "Move it! Fast!"

The storm started up again. Snow whirled down from the sky, obscured the scene as the zombies sensed a change, moved in on them again. Angel hit a few with what fuel remained, but the flames sputtered out. They ran for their lives. The zombies closed in. One reared back to loose its contagious contents when it burst into flame, fired from another direction. Angel turned to see a military truck, an armored Humvee with a flamethrower on top that made theirs look like a toy.

"Fuck yeah!" Angel raised a fist in the air and cheered. "Cleanup crew!"

The way they ran at top speed toward the Humvee proved they were alive and not targets. A soldier who looked in charge waved them in, as others on foot cleaned up the remaining zombies with their flamethrowers.

"They radioed you were on your way, sent us for backup. Don't know who you are, but you've got some pretty damn big friends upstairs. I've got orders to get you in and out." The soldier jerked a thumb at the back of the vehicle.

Angel gave a silent prayer of thanks that Sheryl Grace had gotten his phone message from the bodega. He'd asked her to call their friend Richmond in the mayor's office and offer him a date in public with paparazzi if he made sure that Angel got what he needed. He'd told her that it was over between them in bed, but man, he sure felt like he owed Sheryl something special if she got him out of here alive . . . then Angel thought of Sonia and decided to send flowers.

The Humvee took off and they followed it.

CHAPTER 95

3:47 A.M.
Lower East Side, 4 January 1987

There was a pool of blood on the concrete floor under his severed leg. Jim tightened the belt around his calf, prayed for the strength to live long enough to finish this. He still had to find what he'd come here for, even if he didn't have the strength to do anything about it.

"The baby?"

Jim croaked the words from a dry throat and winced as his leg throbbed. He loosened his tourniquet, retightened it.

"Nina's baby? Gone," said Marlowe. "Long gone. Is that why you're here? To save your nephew? Too late."

"Is he . . ."

Jim couldn't get the word out.

"Dead? Not entirely. But I guess you knew that, or you wouldn't be looking here."

"You killed them?" Jim rolled his eyes to the bodies behind the kid.

"Yes. To make up for what Adam did, to Nina, to the baby, to them, to me. Even to you, I guess. You should thank me."

"Sure." Jim chuckled, faint. "Thanks."

Marlowe smiled back.

"You don't believe me. I wish . . ." He paused. "I wish I could make you understand my loss, the way I understand yours. You had everything and lost it. A home and a family. I never had anything, and when I finally got the world it turned to shit."

Jim felt his head swim, whether from the loss of blood or something the boy was doing to him, he couldn't tell. The room looked brighter, red and fiery, like the inside of a furnace. It was an illusion. He felt no warmth, but it was still as real to him as the pain. Cold fire licked the walls, consumed nothing. Demonic shadows danced across the floor.

"Have you ever thought about Hell? Really thought about it?" The boy paced along the row of bodies as he talked, as if beginning a lecture. "I have. In detail. I fear it. You should, too."

He knelt beside Jim, put a hand on his left knee. It hurt.

"I'm dying. Did you know that? I was supposed to have life everlasting. Eternal youth. But they poisoned me." He waved to the bodies. "They started the plague out there, them and the baby. I should have known, but I was so eager to do the Lord's work I got careless. I drank diseased blood and now I'm going to die, from the thing I feared most. Funny, isn't it?"

Steven's voice called out from the steps to the street.

"Jim? Jim, are you down there?"

Marlowe's vision of Hell faded with the sound. He held the tip of the sword to Jim's throat, nodded for him to answer.

"I'm here," Jim shouted. The others had found him, but now that they had, he wasn't sure he wanted them here. Footsteps came down the short flight of stairs. Steven and Lori appeared, stopped when they saw Marlowe and the bodies lined up behind him.

"Jim . . ." Lori stepped forward, but Steven pulled her back.

"Welcome to the party. We were just getting acquainted." Marlowe smiled at them, sword still at Jim's throat. Lori and Steven looked at Jim's severed leg on the floor, then at each other, unsure if they should run or stay. The smell of propane gas filled the air.

"Jim, you have to come with us. Now," said Lori.

"It's too late." He winced. Blood still dripped from his stump, despite the tourniquet. "I can't. You go."

"Is the baby here?" Lori asked the question of Jim and Marlowe, not sure who could answer it.

"It's safe and sound in midtown." Marlowe raised the sword. "Safer than any of us."

"Let them go," said Jim. "They're not responsible for any of this." He couldn't let anyone else pay for his sins.

"No, they're not," said Marlowe. He lowered his sword. "Leave now and I'll let you live."

Steven started to pull Lori away, but she reached out to Jim.

"Come with us." She looked at the tanks on the floor. "Please. No matter what you think, it's not too late."

"It was too late a long time ago. There's nothing left for me. Go finish the job. Find the baby."

"But where? How can we . . ."

Marlowe picked up Jim's lighter from the floor, began to toy with it. Jim leaned forward with the last of his strength.

"Get out now!"

"No!" Lori wept. "God, Jim . . ."

Steven pulled her away.

"I'm sorry, Jim," he said. "I'm so sorry."

Jim wasn't sure what Steven was apologizing for, not being able to get him out, not finding the baby, or for Jim's life, none of which was his fault. All the pain, all the death, all the suffering . . . none of it mattered. Nothing mattered anymore. Jim saw his life laid out behind him like a fairy tale, two children lost in the woods, eaten by an ogre.

When he was a kid, he'd laughed at the gruesome stories his mother read to his little sister about ghosts and goblins. He'd tease his sister afterward, chase her around the room in a sheet until she ran howling to their mother. Now he knew that fairy tales were true, and not all of them had happy endings.

Lori and Steven backed up the stairs to the street. Once they were gone, Marlowe turned to Jim.

"That was the right thing to do: salvation of the innocent. Do you believe in salvation, Jim? Can we still be saved?"

Marlowe clutched the lighter, no longer Jim's captor but a child pleading for forgiveness. Bloody tears welled in his eyes.

"Do you know your prayers?" Marlowe asked. "Do you believe if we make a perfect Act of Contrition and mean it, really mean it, that there's still hope for us? That's what the priests said when I was in foster care. No matter how bad we were, no matter how bad it got, we could still be forgiven, even without confession, last rites, or any of the frills. Just say you're sorry and really mean it and it's all wiped clean."

He played with Jim's lighter as he talked. "I just want it to end. I think we both do. Suicide would be a sin. But we can play a game. Let's make a bet, say, that this lighter won't work the first time we try it. Whatever happens won't be our fault then, will it?"

Jim's strength faded. He knew he couldn't stay conscious much longer. He'd never make it out of here and maybe that's just the way things had to be. He'd done all he could. He still had friends outside to make things right. Jim just wished he'd used his last chance to tell them he considered them friends, to tell them he was grateful for all they'd done.

The boy leaned closer with the lighter.

Jim could see the ravages of disease in him already. No matter how long it took to kill him, the boy was right. He had the mark of death on him, and Jim thought that the boy probably saw the same in his face. They were both at an end.

"Say it with me. O my God . . ."

Jim pulled himself to consciousness long enough to repeat the boy's prayer, which brought him a kind of comfort.

"My God . . ."

"I am heartily sorry . . ."

"Sorry . . ."

"For having offended thee. I detest all my sins," said the boy, head bowed, eyes closed. He took Jim's hand. "Because of thy just punishments, but most of all because they offend thee, my God, who are all good and deserving of all my love . . ."

Jim sighed. Marlowe continued.

"I firmly resolve, with the help of thy grace, to sin no more and to avoid the occasions of sin. Amen. Okay?"

Jim nodded. The prayer said it all. He was sorry. Sorry for what he'd done to Nina, even without knowing it, sorry for killing the guy at the propane store. Sorry for dragging Lori, Steven, and Angel into this. He was sorry for everything. Marlowe raised his head, opened his eyes in a perfect state of grace, and smiled at Jim like the altar boy he'd once been, his face filled with the love of God.

"So," he said, "does this work, anyway?" Marlowe lifted Jim's lighter. "Bet it won't. This cheap shit never does. . . ."

But it did.

As they both knew it would, the lighter sparked as soon as Marlowe flipped the flint wheel. Jim watched the flame leap from the lighter in slow motion, watched it grow bigger as the fire grew, floated through propane-tainted air like the finger of God.

It curled down to flick at the broken nozzle of the leaking propane tank and ignited it. The casing tore open like a burst balloon as metal shredded, unleashed the explosive force inside it and the other tanks. Jim watched flames fill the room as they had the night his mother died. White heat took his flesh as the light flared up and brightened, expanded into infinity.

His pain stopped.

Jim stood, healed, and looked down a tunnel of light to see figures approach. The one in front was Nina, his dead sister. She smiled, whole and happy, and stopped halfway down the tunnel of light with her hand outstretched. Nina beckoned for him to join her, as he'd always known she would, all sins forgiven.

Jim's mother and father waited behind her, their faces filled with joy. Jim was filled with a sense of completion. He shed his life like a burden he'd carried too long and stepped forward.

A faint movement from behind caught Jim's attention. He turned to see Marlowe crouched, hands over his mouth, wide eyes filled with bloodless tears. Jim reached down and took his hand, nothing but forgiveness in his heart. There was no room for anger or vengeance anymore.

"Is it all right?" Marlowe asked, like a child who fears the worst. "Is it over?"

"It's all right," said Jim. "It's over."

He pulled Marlowe to his feet, held him close as a brother, took his arm and led him down the tunnel toward his family. Whatever judgment awaited them for what they'd done in life, they were home.

They walked together into the light and beyond.

CHAPTER 96

3:52 A.M.
Lower East Side, 4 January 1987

This can't be good.

Angel was by the side of the Humvee, watching Steven and Lori run out of the building waving him away.

"Get back! Get back!" shouted Steven. "It's gonna—"

And it did, before the words could clear his lips. The street shook as the sound of an underground explosion shattered the silence. A fireball crested the top of the condemned brick building as it shuddered and split. Fire filled the windows, gutted the inside of the tenement. They watched the whole thing collapse into itself as it burned, the basement buried in smoking brick and flaming timbers.

Angel said a silent prayer for the dead.

Steven and Lori made it to his side, turned to see what they'd escaped. The ruins glowed like a blast furnace. Anything inside was ash by now. The nest was gone.

Lori sighed, pulled out her cigarettes, and put one in her mouth. She tried her lighter without success, cursed, and threw it away. "Got a light?"

Steven looked at her like she was crazy and shook his head. Angel had to laugh.

"Help yourself," he said, waved at the fire.

"Yeah. Maybe it's time to quit." Lori frowned and pulled the cigarette from her mouth. She slipped it back into the pack and threw the whole thing at the blaze.

"The baby wasn't there." Steven turned to Angel. "They didn't tell us where it is, but as long as it's loose, this zombie plague will keep spreading. We have to find it."

"How do we do that?" asked Angel.

Steven started to say something and then doubled over, grabbed his head in pain. Angel caught him as he started to fall, and saw that the same thing was happening to Lori.

She screamed as she hit the snow.

Adam had made contact, he could tell.

He always knew when he'd successfully summoned someone. He'd finally been strong enough to try, and sent out a call to every mind he'd ever touched, enslaved or not. He told them all where he was, what was happening, and ordered them to get him out. Adam was weaker now than ever, felt the baby start to feed on him again as its hunger for life increased. He had to hold out. It was just a matter of time before help arrived.

He just hoped it wouldn't be too late.

"Shit! You okay?"

Angel helped Lori up, leaned her and Steven against the Humvee's front bumper.

"Yeah. Fuck . . ." Steven took a few deep breaths, and sat up. "I know where the baby is. I'll bet Lori does, too."

"Oh, yeah. We're invited to its new home." She rubbed her temples. "By an old friend."

"Great," said Angel. "Let's talk to the troops."

"You think they'll believe us?" asked Lori.

"You think they believed in zombies before tonight?"

There was gunfire in the distance, the smell of burned flesh in the air. They could hear the sounds of muffled traffic drift in from outside the perimeter. The real world was still out there, waited for them to get back to it. The Humvee started its engine as the cleanup crew assembled to escort them out.

"Let's go." Angel threw an arm around each of them. "The sooner we're done, the sooner you can buy me a drink!"

CHAPTER 97

4:21 A.M.
Central Park South, 4 January 1987

It was a nightmare.

Perenelle stood by the Autochthones' well, beneath the tiled mural of their great white Worm rising to claim a victim. The last of the incoming passengers were led in a trance to the child's sacrificial altar, laid to rest at its feet to feed on. Flickering gaslight illuminated the eerie scene like a shadow play as skeletal Autochthones played their parts, silhouetted against the baby's increasing glow.

The infant turned Adam's head around to face it and looked at him with suspicion. There was no sign of life. Chubby little fingers rolled Adam's head away, sent it bouncing down the mound of bodies to land at Perenelle's feet. She stepped back just in time to keep it from touching her.

Rahman returned from his laboratory with the Book of Abraham and a second vial, read aloud from the book in an ancient tongue as he approached the pyramid. He sent the vial up with one of the Autochthones who fed the elixir to the child as it had the first. Rahman kept reading in a deep monotone that rose above the Autochthones' song, rolled off the walls.

Perenelle shuddered, knew what would follow the third and final infusion. Rahman would bring the child down from its seat of honor and cut it open, drain its blood to release the purified elixir from its body. Once again, she would have been party to infanticide to prolong Rahman's life. She tried to think of a way to stop him, one last trick she could pull out to save the day.

Then all hell broke loose, as the station flooded with people, not brought by the Autochthones but arriving on their own in street wear and nightclothes. They carried makeshift weapons, clubs, stakes, knives, anything they seemed to find close at hand as they headed out the door. They attacked the Autochthones, who fought back to keep them from the pyramid and the child. Perenelle and Rahman stared around, baffled, until Perenelle heard a voice that explained it all.

"Adam!" A young bleached blonde roamed the base of the pyramid in distress, a large canvas bag on her shoulder. "Where are you? Master?" They had to be Adam's slaves, come to save him. He must have found enough strength to summon them before he died. If he was dead.

The girl wept, screamed Adam's name as she pushed bodies aside, searched until she found his motionless head on the station floor. Before anyone could stop her she lifted it, kissed his pale, dry lips with passion, then tucked the head into her bag and ran. Perenelle watched her vanish into the crowd, then moved back, watched Rahman disappear into his laboratory to avoid the battle that raged around them.

If she ever had any chance of stopping him, it was now.

CHAPTER 98

Central Park South, 4 January 1987

A commandeered yellow work train moved down the subway tunnel past Fifty-ninth Street and Columbus Circle, and shifted to the track that Steven and Lori had said would lead it to the Sheep Meadow Station they'd seen in their heads. It hadn't been easy to get the National Guard commander to move a full squad from the downtown quarantine miles away to Central Park, under Angel's authority. The deputy mayor managed to persuade him, after Angel convinced Richmond that if he didn't, he'd be responsible for the plague spreading through the city.

Steven and Lori watched track lights slide by as they crept down the tunnel. He still had his arms around her, held on as if for dear life. The buddy system. Like they were on a field trip from Hell, and as long as they kept track of their buddy, they'd both get home okay. There were lights ahead. As predicted, there was the secret station.

The squad stood at the ready with rifles and flamethrowers as they pulled in. Angel was up front, on the locomotive with the squadron leader. Steven and Lori were on their own in a car at the back end; soldiers filled in the cars in between. They all stared at the chaos in the station through dirty glass and graffiti. They'd worried about how to get in unnoticed, but it was clear that wouldn't be a problem.

It looked like a war was in progress. Humans and vampires filled a subway station that looked like a pagan temple from an old silent movie, fought around a huge pile of bodies and spilled onto the tracks from the platform.

"Oh, my God . . ."

Lori pointed at the top of the pile.

It was the baby. It had to be. Its skin glowed brightly, as if the child was filled with unnatural energy. Other than that it looked healthy, laughed, arms up, waved in delight as if it was conducting the conflict around it.

Steven saw something that looked like a rotted derelict slam against their window and hold on, pound at the glass to get in. A vampire. Older than any they'd seen, but just as deadly. Steven tried to shield Lori with his body as others flooded the tracks to get to their side of the work train. Bony fingers squeezed through the rubber between the sliding double doors of the subway car, parted them slowly. Steven and Lori heard shots in front of them as Angel and the troops started fighting.

"Come on," said Steven.

He pulled Lori away, headed for the back of the train. There was no sense heading toward the firefight ahead of them. The door opened before they could reach it. One of the things climbed up to meet them, dry, decayed, and dressed in rags, more like a mummy than a vampire. It raced toward them with sharp claws, and bared jagged yellow fangs as it drew near.

Steven pulled out Jim's gun as it closed in, fired when it was close enough not to miss. The first bullet hit it in the chest, threw it back. Steven advanced, fired another shot into the head, punched it, and knocked it all the way to the ground. He put one foot on its chest and kicked at the head with his other boot, again and again, until it snapped off the body and rolled down the length of the car.

The limbs flailed like a dying roach, then stilled. Steven suppressed the urge to keep kicking.

"Let's go," he said to Lori. "We can get back to the last station, tell the Guard what's going on."

They went through the door and climbed down to the tracks. Lori followed Steven as he led her over to an empty stretch of tracks, careful to avoid the third rail. There was a distant whisper of movement ahead of them, a wave of distortion in the shape of the shadows.

"What's that?" asked Lori.

Steven's eyes widened. "Shit . . ."

He started to run back to the train. Lori took a few steps after him, but looked back, frozen like Lot's wife, stared until she saw what he'd seen. A shimmering sea of tiny lights matched in pairs, pinpoints of light that rose and fell like rippling reflections on a black lake at night. Subway lights reflected in tiny red eyes in a sea of dirty gray fur that flowed in their direction.

Rats. The vampires' watchdogs.

"Lori!"

She snapped into action, ran after Steven as fast as she could. He'd waited for her, could barely keep up when she raced past him. Long legs carried her down the center of the tracks. Being hit by a train suddenly didn't seem as bad as what was behind them. They hit the station stairs at the same time, bounded up to the platform and kept going. Lori twisted her head to see how close their pursuers were and almost screamed.

The rats poured up over the concrete behind them like a polluted gray wave. They stopped when they covered the edge of the platform and formed a wall of matted fur between the station's prisoners and freedom on the tracks.

"End of the line," said Steven.

CHAPTER 99

Rahman was astounded.

The pyramid of bodies was drained and still the child hungered. Rahman watched it from the doorway of his laboratory, could feel the infant extend its reach, pull energy from the combatants around it. Rahman handed the third and final vial to one of the Autochthones, and sent it through the fighting to administer the last stage of the elixir to the child. He watched the baby gobble it down, greedy for more. Soon it would be time to claim the final product. The petty war that filled the station wouldn't stop him from doing that. Nothing would, not the fighting, not Perenelle, nothing short of the hand of Allah himself.

Autochthones approached from the far end of the station, dragged a black man and a white woman with them to the edge of the child's altar. They were about to carry them up when Perenelle stepped from the shadows and interrupted.

"Wait! Bring them to me!"

Rahman turned to her, mystified. "What are they to you?"

She didn't answer. The Autochthones that held the couple froze, looked to Rahman for instructions. He was glad to see that he still had that much hold over them. Rahman turned back to Perenelle.

"Again I ask: What are they to you?"

She twisted the edge of her cloak, but answered. "I sent them to destroy the baby's nest. I need to know what happened."

Rahman laughed, long and hard. "I love you so, Perenelle. For a moment I thought you were demonstrating pity."

He waved. The Autochthones brought the couple to Perenelle, released them, and retreated into the fight.

"Perenelle?" Steven stared at her face with the studied eye of an artist. Perenelle could see him adding wrinkles and years in his head, as the truth dawned. "It is you."

"Can you get us out of here?" asked Lori.

"What happened to the nest?"

Steven stopped Lori from answering.

"Get us out, we'll talk about it."

"I can make you answer, easily enough. . . ."

Perenelle stepped closer. Her eyes made it clear that she could.

"Please." Lori raised a hand to stop her. "It's gone. We lost a friend, but he ended it first."

Perenelle wanted to clasp their hands, to thank them, but couldn't. The Veil and its secret weren't safe yet. These two had brought in the National Guard. If they lived, she could wipe out all memory of what had happened, but if the squadron was wiped out, the search for their killers would begin here, where the Autochthones had more than a hundred victims piled high. Once the bodies were discovered, the city would hunt their killers down.

"What now?"

Lori looked to her for help.

Perenelle was torn. She'd planned to kill them both. Rahman would do that for her, but she still needed a way to stop him from killing the child, and they might be of use there . . . she tried to make up her mind quickly.

Then the baby made the decision for her.

The sound the child made was a new one.

It tore through Rahman's head like lightning. Singers and musicians stopped, shrieked in agony as all fighting stopped and fighters fell to the ground in torment. The baby stopped and then keened again, a long, shrill sound answered this time by a deeper familiar tone that issued from the depths of the well.

The Worm.

Rahman was amazed. It usually took two days of chanting to rouse the Worm and the baby had done it with a single cry. The ground beneath their feet rumbled as the thing beneath them woke, stirred like an aftershock, and rose through subterranean tunnels that led to the mouth of the well. Something new and exciting was happening, but before Rahman could understand what it was, the Worm rose into the room, higher than ever, and out toward the child.

Instead of showing fear, the baby laughed, lifted tiny pink hands to the great white Worm. The behemoth rose over it, dripped phosphorescent slime, and swayed as the baby cooed and glowed brighter. The Worm leaned down to feed on the child, but as it felt its own life flow into the baby, it recoiled.

Too late.

The infant rose into the air to follow.

Steven and Lori watched it float up from the pile of bodies, light as smoke, arms outstretched toward the Worm. Before the thing could retreat under ground, the child gripped its thick translucent skin with both hands. The Worm wailed but couldn't free itself from the infant's grasp.

It shrank as the child fed, and dropped toward the well. Before it could escape, the Worm slumped to the ground, spent, as the infant drained the last of its energy, over a thousand years of stored life. Rahman stared in disbelief as the Book of Abraham dropped from his hands. The baby floated higher, beautiful, radiant, its body fully restored, throbbing with abundant energy. Its eyes had changed to orbs of pure light.

"What have you done?" screamed Perenelle. "You've doomed us all!"

The wreath of herbs the Autochthones had placed on the infant's head burst into fresh flower, buds grew and bloomed as they watched. Each blossom ignited into searing white light as it opened, bright rays cut through the gloom of the station as the flaming flowers burned unconsumed. The baby drifted over the crowd of Autochthones, Adam's slaves, and the National Guardsmen. They all stared up, the fight below forgotten.

The child rolled in midair to face downward and lifted a hand. Life flowed from the crowd in delicate threads of light, up through the air and into the baby. The humans screamed and fought their way through the Autochthones to escape, Adam's commands forgotten as they fled the platform and down tracks in both directions to survive.

Drained bodies fell and the remaining Autochthones rushed forward for their turn, climbed over the fallen to get closer to their god, who consumed them as they approached. Perenelle turned to Steven and Lori. She waved toward the shadowy doorway they'd seen earlier and walked toward it.

"Hurry. There's a way out."

They didn't move. She turned back and glared.

"Now, while they're distracted!"

Steven and Lori took less than a second to decide to trust her. They followed Perenelle as the last of the Autochthones flung themselves onto the altar of their god.

Rahman gave up any illusion of control, abandoned his pride and his tribe, and ran for the tracks, fled for his life with the humans. As the tunnel brightened behind him, he realized he'd waited too long, his attention held by scientific curiosity. Rahman turned to see the child already upon him, had just enough time to scream before its light engulfed him.

CHAPTER 100

6:36 A.M.
Central Park South, 4 January 1987

Sheep Meadow was covered in deep virgin snow, a frozen field of dazzling white bordered by the twinkling towers of the city. Lights flickered off and on as residents went to bed or rose for work; the endless pulse of the city beat on through the night, no matter what happened beneath Central Park.

Steam rose from a round grate hidden in bushes south of the meadow, snow melted by an open steam pipe to keep the Autochthones' secret escape route clear. The metal cover was lifted and slid aside. Steven climbed up and out with difficulty and reached back to help Lori up the ladder to the surface.

The eye of the storm had moved uptown to hover over Central Park, as if it had followed them from the Lower East Side. Steven leaned down to offer Perenelle help, but she refused, made it up the ladder and outside without effort. She looked around the empty, desolate meadow.

There was a time when sheep had really grazed here, a time when the only buildings were farmhouses and squatters' shanties. The city had been a simpler place to live then, an easier place to feed. For a moment she wished she could go back to that world before electricity, before cars and planes, before television and pop stars. Before any of this madness had begun. She sighed. This was no time for fantasies. It was still a long way out of the park to safety.

"Quickly," said Perenelle. "It may already be too late."

She ran across the snow, then stopped when she realized they weren't following her.

"What's wrong?"

Perenelle turned to the ground behind her and saw what disturbed them. Though she'd moved several yards away, she'd left no footprints in the unbroken snow.

CHAPTER 101

6:39 A.M.
Central Park South, 4 January 1987

At first he thought he was dead.

Rahman-al-Hazra'ad ibn Aziz had felt his life end as he shed his flesh like a worn glove. Light had carried him out, but not up and away through a bright tunnel to an unknown eternity. Instead he was drawn to the baby and pulled into it. Rahman waited for his soul to be consumed, but instead felt renewed. Rahman opened his eyes, eyes that saw with astonishing clarity even by vampire standards.

He floated over the subway tracks, looked down to see his former body a crumpled pile of dry bones and skin on the tracks. Rahman raised a hand before his face and laughed as he saw a child's fingers wriggle. His laughter was joined by a chorus of familiar voices in his head, the ancient language of the Autochthones mixed with the terrified wails of humans. Somehow, perhaps because of the elixir, they'd all been absorbed into the child intact instead of being consumed. Rahman could sense their thoughts as they floated in confusion, wondered if over time he'd be able to read their memories, combine knowledge they'd learned over the ages with his own.

His mind took control of the body, the only one aware of what had happened. Even the consciousness of the child had been pushed down into silence. It was a miracle. Though Rahman had been deprived of draining the elixir from the child's body and drinking it, the final formula was still his.

Even in the body of an infant, he felt stronger than ever before. He'd done more than distill a new elixir of life with the vampire infant. . . .

He was the elixir.

Rahman lifted his new body upward and decided to explore his potential. There was a score to settle with Perenelle. He could feel lives in the park above him, moving slowly through the snow. It had to be Perenelle and her friends. Dealing with them seemed a perfect test.

With the wave of Rahman's tiny hand the ceiling of the subway tunnel above him parted like the Red Sea, stone and concrete rose to let him pass. Rahman wanted to laugh. How could he have lost faith in the Work?

It had made him a god.

CHAPTER 102

7:13 A.M.
Central Park South, 4 January 1987

Lori and Steven hesitated when they saw that Perenelle's feet rested lightly on the surface of the snow, but barely touched it. As if this night weren't creepy enough, thought Lori.

"No time to explain," Perenelle said. "Follow me . . ."

Steven and Lori fought their way through the snow after her, dug through heavy drifts like lost Arctic explorers. Perenelle looked behind them, and her face fell.

"Too late . . ."

Lori and Steven turned to follow her gaze.

"He's here."

The seamless white plain of snow in the middle of Sheep Meadow glowed from beneath, bubbled, and rose in a massive dome, its surface covered in cracks like a network of light-filled veins. The shape rose, rounded, and burst, collapsed as dirt, snow, and stone hailed down around the edges of a newly formed crater, buried the collapsed station below. Above the center of the crater was a small sun, a blinding ball of light that floated up from the depths of the hole to hover above them like a newborn star.

The snow reflected the brilliance around them, lit up the park like noon. Lori pulled her coat tighter around her, colder in the artificial light than she'd been in the dark.

"Perenelle. Beloved . . ."

Rahman's voice boomed through the air from the glowing baby boy, resounded in their heads instead of their ears. The infant's lips didn't move. Lori and Steven saw tears rise in Perenelle's eyes as she stared up at the child.

"Rahman. What have you done?"

"You wanted to keep me from killing the child. You got your wish."

"I never wished this on you."

"It was my wish, beloved, granted in a way I could never have imagined. I've become the Work, the purest example of the elixir ever created. It courses through my veins like living fire."

He rolled in the air and laughed, seemed drunk with the power that had changed him.

"You're irrational, Rahman. You have to rest, consider the consequences of this transformation . . ."

"Consequences?" He spun to face her. *"We are a god. Is that not enough? Join me . . ."* Rahman held out a hand, gestured as trails of energy rose from her body. Perenelle lowered her head, raised the hood of her cloak.

"I'm sorry, Rahman. Sorry you cannot see the truth, and sorry I cannot oblige. . . ." She faded, as the light wisps of energy between them scattered, blew away. Rahman raged, but she was gone, out of his reach.

"Astral projection! Witch! We should have known she'd turn Our own tricks against Us! No matter. We'll find her where she sleeps." He turned to Lori and Steven. *"When We're done with you . . ."*

Rahman floated toward them and they backed away. Steven pulled out Jim's gun, pointed it at the baby.

"Steven!" Lori grabbed his arm. "You can't . . ."

He looked at her in anguish, knew it was true. He couldn't, not even to save their lives.

"No need for that . . ."

Rahman spoke aloud. With a wave of the baby's fingers the gun flew from Steven's hand and across the meadow into a snowbank. Steven and Lori backed away, too late to escape.

The child drew closer.

Clouds on the horizon brightened as it approached them.

"Dawn?" Rahman turned toward the pale light on the horizon as to a mother. *"Can We now face even the sun, after so long?"*

. . .

The storm died down around them, its anger spent.

The park was still, silent, sound muffled by the blanket of snow that covered the great lawn. Clouds thinned, admitted a few fading stars into view in the sky. A pale moon peered out as if to see if it was safe to return.

Rahman forgot about Lori and Steven for a moment, drifted toward the sky as it changed color. Even in the gray light of winter, daybreak brings the world back to colorful life from the monochrome of night. The approaching sun tinted the sky pink and turquoise. Rahman felt the warmth of the approaching day, but faced it without fear. It was a millennium since he'd seen the sun, and the urge to feel it again was irresistible. Surely his new power could make even that possible.

Rahman reached out and lifted his hand to meet a ray of sunlight as it broke through the clouds. He smiled as his fingers played in the beam, watched it grow as it warmed him.

"You see? Even the sun . . ."

Rahman felt something go wrong. The warmth in his hand spread too fast, moved across his skin as the energy inside him changed. Rahman spun away, fled the coming dawn as it powered a new reaction inside him. He tried to retreat beneath the earth, but lost control of the body as the energy inside him took on life of its own. As the solar power built up, souls were cast off and flung out to pursue their own destinies. The sun's energy more than made up for their loss. Rahman felt the body grow stronger.

The elixir was changing again. He'd known that infusing a vampire baby would produce different results than if he used a human child, but there was no way to anticipate that sunlight would trigger a further distillation. Rahman found himself marveling at the simple logic of it, even as he felt himself being torn from the infant's body.

Sunlight streamed through his system as he opened the baby's mouth to scream, but bright light poured out instead, filled his eyes. The city faded from view as Rahman felt himself transformed one last time. . . .

As Steven and Lori stared up, the baby was lost to view in a silent explosion of light and life that filled the morning air over Central Park. It exceeded the brightness of the new day, released a massive burst of vital energy that melted snow, rejuvenated sleeping plants, brought flowers to full bloom in seconds. Grass grew, filled Sheep Meadow with a lush lawn that stopped just inside the circle melted around them.

They held each other as the light blazed brighter, pulled their coats over their faces for cover. When the brilliance died down they uncovered their eyes and saw that they stood at the lush center of an impossible paradise, in a ring of green grass and flowers in full bloom, the air fresh and warm. Steven and Lori watched nearby trees burst into full leaf along the southern side of the great lawn. They were safe, alive, and unharmed at the epicenter of an explosion of new life, bordered by ice.

The baby was nowhere to be seen.

CHAPTER 103

7:21 A.M.
West Village, 4 January 1987

Perenelle opened her eyes, safe at home.

She stood and rang the bell for Janos. When she turned, Rahman was behind her. She took a defensive posture, ready to fight until she looked into his eyes. This was not a vengeful wraith here to do her harm. Perenelle could tell from the calm he exuded and his expression that this was a man she'd never met. The real Rahman, before he became the monster that had made her a vampire.

"Perenelle. I'm sorry for all I've done to you." Rahman bowed his head. She could see candles flicker through his transparent body and wished there were some way to console him. *"There was a time when there was love between us. In my madness I thought I had a way to get you back, but instead, I've lost you forever."*

"Not forever, Rahman. Remember your science. This conversation alone is proof of life after death. Do you have any reason to believe we won't meet again someday? Is another thousand years so long to wait?"

Rahman twinkled with laughter.

"You best me, once again. As you say. Perhaps we will meet again." He reached out, gestured as if to draw her close. *"But before I go, there is much I must tell you. . . ."*

Perenelle leaned closer to hear the ghost's last words.

CHAPTER 104

Steven and Lori stared in disbelief at the faux spring, sure that it would fade like a mirage if they moved to touch anything. They were snapped out of their trance by loud crying. Not the shriek they'd heard in the station, but the healthy howl of a hungry child, tired and a little cranky.

"The baby!" Lori turned to look for it.

Steven grabbed her arm.

"Are you serious?"

"Listen. It's different." She walked toward the sound. "Look . . ." Lori pointed under a flowering bush.

Steven was sure that it was only waiting for them to get close enough to take out both at the same time, but they moved closer to see a healthy baby boy nestled in a patch of overgrown green grass, like Moses in the rushes.

The naked child lay cushioned on a thick bed of flowers, the garland around his forehead still in bloom. He smiled up and gurgled, raised plump arms and stretched tiny pink fingers out to them. Lori reached down to pick him up, but Steven pulled her back. Perenelle's voice came from behind them.

"You need not fear him. The child is alive and well. Human. His body's been purged, all memory of his misadventure wiped away with his vampire soul."

They turned to see her astral form float forward, all pretense abandoned.

"How? What happened?"

"The power of alchemy. The sun was catalyst to an ancient experiment that went awry, with unexpected results for Rahman. And a cure for the child."

She looked down at the human infant restored to full humanity. His body was healed, his soul purged. Lori lifted him as Steven took off his coat and wrapped him up. The baby grabbed Lori's finger as she adjusted his makeshift blanket. She flinched when he pulled her finger into his mouth, relaxed as he suckled harmlessly and laughed up at her. His cheeks blushed a soft rose in the morning sunlight, eyes blue as the dawn sky.

The baby looked so healthy, so happy, that it was hard for Lori to believe that just minutes ago he'd been poised overhead, ready to consume them. For all their fears, for all the pain, it was just a new life, open to anything, good or bad. That's all any baby was. You just did the best you could. Maybe one day she'd still get a chance to find out for herself, with one of her own. Lori rocked the baby while Steven looked at Perenelle, still wary.

"You wanted us dead back there, didn't you? When Rahman was going to kill us, you wouldn't have stopped him if we hadn't been able to tell you what happened to the nest."

"I can't deny we have secrets I prefer kept. The dead tell no tales, but I've seen enough death tonight. I'll trust in your discretion. . . ." She gestured at the baby. *"Many lives were lost to save this infant. For all this to have any meaning, this child must survive. He's in your care now."*

"Our care?" said Steven, and looked at Lori. Even if one day they were ready to raise a child together, they were both sure it wouldn't be this one. "Until we get it to social services, right?"

Perenelle shrugged.

"Keep the child safe, by whatever means. Do what I cannot and you have nothing to fear." She began to fade, until only her eyes and smile remained, like the Cheshire cat. *"If I were you, I'd keep an eye on his progress. I know I will. . . ."*

Then she was completely gone and Steven and Lori were left alone with the baby. It didn't cry, content for the moment just to be held. They exited Central Park, abandoned the ruins of Sheep Meadow and their temporary paradise, walked into the early morning to look for a police officer, and more.

The start of a new life for Nina's baby boy.

VI

DAY

New York City
Saturday, August 15, 1987

There is a light and it never goes out . . .

—The Smiths
(1986)

EPILOGUE

It was a typically steamy New York summer night, so humid you could swim down the street. Despite that, the gallery looked full to overflowing when Lori's cab pulled up in front. She paid the driver, and spotted Steven inside surrounded by friends. His new show looked like a hit. He saw her as she climbed out of the car, and ran a gauntlet of artist friends drunk on free wine to meet her at the door. Lori worked her way through the crowd on the sidewalk, flashed a grin and waved. Steven waved back, got through the mob just as she entered, and hugged her as if he hadn't seen her in years instead of days.

Lori was glad to see him, too, no matter how things had ended between them. They'd stayed together only a month after they faced down Rahman in Central Park. Once the adrenaline rush wore off, they weren't sure if they'd been reunited by love or fear. There was still love, but more to resolve before they could live together again.

Lori moved out while they finished the book, rewrote the outline with Steven to keep their promise to Jim to tell Nina's story. They pitched it to the publisher as something more upscale than a generic picture book of vampires. An illustrated study of modern evil, it wouldn't say if her mysterious benefactor was a real vampire, just that his rich, fast-paced downtown world of drugs and sex had drained the life from her and kids like her.

The publishers loved it; called it *Dracula* meets *In Cold Blood*, with a touch of *The Orton Diaries*. In the end, it became the book Jim would have wanted it to be, the story of an orphaned brother and sister who grew up lost, until found by an ageless evil.

"I've got a copy of the cover," Lori said after Steven's embrace ended. She carried her big bag through guests to the back of the gallery and opened the door to a storeroom. Empty frames leaned against walls, paintings and prints filled open bins, other pictures were stacked on counters for shipment or repair.

Lori pulled a big color proof print from her bag, laid it on an empty worktable, and noticed Steven shudder when he looked down. The cover was his painting of the dim subway station under Sheep Meadow. Deep red eyes peered out of pools of darkness, bared fangs and pale claws could be seen in the shadows, painted from his memory of their time under ground.

A new title ran across the top in bloodred—"*Bite Marks.*" When the book was done, that seemed to be more what it was about. Less about the monster, more about the scars it left behind. Steven and Lori's names were barely visible over a wave of dirty rats that flowed across the bottom of the cover.

"Could our names be any smaller?" asked Steven.

He handed Lori one of the plastic glasses of champagne he'd grabbed on their way back. She laughed, a sound he missed every time he heard it.

"You think? At least they're not asking for another."

"No. Guess we're done."

"Not us, though. Right?" She squeezed his hand. "We're still . . ." He knew she didn't want to say friends, didn't want to belittle what they had between them.

"Whatever. Don't forget to write," Steven said with a laugh. Lori pulled him close, laid her head on his chest. When she looked up, there were tears in her eyes.

"I'm just glad we're alive. And I'm glad you were there. I couldn't have made it without you."

"Same here."

They hugged tighter. She let go, eyes still wet.

"I went to see the baby today," said Lori. "They think they have a home for him."

"How is he?"

"As fine as he can be. Do you think he'll grow up and really forget what he was? What he did?"

"Time will tell."

Lori wiped her face, looked around the storeroom, and realized where they were. She smiled. It hadn't changed since the first time she saw it, over two years ago. The night she met Steven at the opening party for his first solo show, lust at first sight that had turned to love. They'd talked for only half an hour before they slipped out of sight, back here to the storeroom. Lori rubbed the tabletop next to her, caught Steven's eye, and saw that he remembered their first night there, too.

"Wasn't this where we . . ."

"Uh-huh," he said with a naughty grin.

"Happier times . . ."

She was cut off, as Steven's lips covered hers in a kiss.

He lifted her onto the worktable like a fragile work of art, raised her skirt while she fumbled at his pants, until each pulled the other free. He buried himself in her as they made love, real love, one last time, ended where they began. She squeezed him tight as they clung to each other, groaned and gasped what they'd never had time to say, whispered the apologies and for-giveness they both needed.

Their confessions ended as they both climaxed, exhausted, but satisfied. They held on, knew when they parted this time it was for good, that when they left this room they left someplace they could never find their way back to again. Steven and Lori let go gently, until he pulled her back for one last hug.

"I'll always love you," he said.

"Sucker," said Lori, and slapped him on the ass.

They laughed as hard as they had in the days when love was new. Steven and Lori dressed and left the storeroom arm in arm; walked back to the gallery party, back to their friends, back into the light and the rest of their lives.

The sun was finally setting.

Luna X flowed around her run-down East Village studio apartment, fad-ing daylight kept out by sheets hung like heavy curtains over the windows.

Her long black lace dress blew around her like dark smoke as she adjusted the drapes to be sure they were secure. She sang to herself as she drifted around the room, lit candles and arranged cushions on the rocking chair. It was almost time for dinner, and she wanted everything to be just right. She burned incense, put low music on the stereo.

La Bohème. His favorite.

He'd wake soon, hungry. She'd feed him the only way she knew how until he regained his strength. It would take a long, long time, but she was prepared to care for him no matter how long it took. She went to her bed and lifted a small cloth bundle from the crib next to it. It stirred as she soothed it.

"Shhh . . ." she said, and pulled open the baby blanket.

Adam's head was nestled in it, face contorted in rage. Luna X smiled down at him, ever patient. Her precious had such a temper when he was hungry. His teeth and tongue were whole again, but his vocal cords hadn't grown back yet. He tried to mouth words, dry lips still healing from the stitches she'd removed when she rescued him. "Save your strength. Wait till after dinner."

She sat down in the rocking chair with her bundle, loosened buttons on the front of her dress, and pulled it open to reveal pale breasts scarred by deep bite marks. Luna X hummed along with an aria on the stereo as she delicately lifted Adam's cool lips to a nipple. She let his fangs fasten onto her flesh as he bit deep and sucked, fed on her blood and her life, just enough to survive, enough to heal.

The sack sewn beneath his chin to hold his beating heart had grown. There were signs that a new body developed inside, small, fetal, but there. She could feel it under his skin through the blanket when she lifted him, changing shape every day. In time she would bring him other lives to feed on, victims he could drain completely as he regained his strength and grew back his body.

He bit down harder. Luna X gasped and recoiled, despite her adoration. Adam relaxed his grip and she pulled him closer. As blood began to flood his brain, the high soothed his anger, filled him with sensations. She could feel his lips warm against her breast as blood flowed through them. Adam relaxed as he drew on the life beneath her skin. His eyes rolled up like a newborn's, his lids dropped down as he nuzzled closer to Luna X, grew sleepy.

Adam smiled, eyes closed, looked lost in dreams. A little blood trickled down her breast from his cracked lips as he sucked. He was mutilated, weak.

It might take him years, maybe even decades to recover, but when he did, they would pay a visit to each of the enemies who had done this to him, starting with Perenelle. Luna X made herself a promise, a sacred vow, no matter what it took, no matter how long . . .

He would live long enough to see them all dead.

ACKNOWLEDGMENTS

There are a lot of reasons a first novel gets done.

For me, most are thanks to the people in my personal and professional life. I'm grateful for the opportunity to publicly thank the many who kept me going through the birth of this book, in reverse chronological order.

Thanks to my editor at St. Martin's, the delightful Monique Patterson, who felt more like a co-conspirator in helping me complete the Grand Guignol epic I set out to write. Her keen eye and light touch made my work a pleasure. Thanks to my agent, Victoria Sanders, and her associate, Benée Knauer, for seeing a diamond in the rough and believing in it enough to persuade me to keep digging into my personal heart of darkness. To their assistant, Glendaliz, whose fresh enthusiasm over the result rekindled their fire to read the new manuscript.

Thank you, Tananarive Due, for being the incredibly generous and talented writer you are, my friend, soul sister, and for setting a standard I strive to meet. To her husband, Steven Barnes, for reminding me to never, ever forget what scares me, especially when standing in the light. Thanks to Brandon Massey for including me in his trilogy of *Dark Dreams* anthologies, and introducing me to a community of black fantasy writers it took me a lifetime to find, encouragement that kept me going. Thanks to Halcyon Liew, friend and employer, for work that paid my bills and freed me to write while she pushed me to finish the novel. Thanks to Bill Prady for getting me home.

Thanks for all the lengthy conversations about creative crises, local and

ACKNOWLEDGMENTS

long distance, that helped shape the book. Specifically, to my spiritual twin brother, Fred Wilson III, for showing me over the years how context conveys meaning, and how recontextualizing reality can reveal deeper hidden truths. To Joan Griffiths-Vega for her wealth of mythological studies, always accessible by phone or over brunch. To Alyce Myatt, who reminded me that it's mothers who shape their sons, not fathers, which led me to Olivia. To Victoria Cummings, for sharing the mutual pain and bliss of writing in daily chats. And I mustn't forget Frank Rocco, one of my best sparring partners in the creative ring, who ended more than one hour-long rehashing of what I was going through with the book by laughing, "After all this, I'd *better* make the Acknowledgments!" Here you are. A flat-rate national calling plan was my smartest move.

Thank you to all the friends and family who read early versions of *Bite Marks* and kept me believing it was worth finishing—Aimée, Carol, Erick, Kelly, Kurt, Mark, Micki . . . I know I've left people out and apologize— you know who you are by your scars. Thanks to all the other good friends who loved and supported me throughout, some of the smartest and funniest people in New York, who could no more read my novels than drive rusty spikes into their eyes, but cheered me on anyway.

More than I can ever say in words, thank you to my house partner and friend, Linda Lutes, for her endless patience with me through late mortgage and maintenance payments through the many years I was a starving artist. You've been my biggest patron. Without your gentle wit, lefty politics, and support, both financial and emotional, I wouldn't have the clean, well-lighted physical and spiritual space I have to do this work.

Last, but far from least, thank you, God, whoever or whatever you may be, for this amazing game of Life, with a universe of infinite possibilities as a board and all the pieces I've been given to play it. I'm lucky enough to see my life as the blessing it is and always has been, in both good times and bad. I finally understand why it took the life I've lived to live the life I lead. I give in. You do know what you're doing.

Pleasant dreams,

—Terence Taylor
Brooklyn, 2008